Clare Connelly was rai[...] among a family of avid [...] of her childhood up a tr[...] hand. Clare is married to her own real-life hero and they live in a bungalow near the sea with their two children. She is frequently found staring into space—a surefire sign that she's in the world of her characters. She has a penchant for French food and ice-cold champagne, and Mills & Boon novels continue to be her favourite ever books. Writing for Modern Romance is a long-held dream. Clare can be contacted via clareconnelly.com or at her Facebook page.

USA TODAY bestselling and RITA® Award–nominated author **Caitlin Crews** loves writing romance. She teaches her favourite romance novels in creative writing classes at places like UCLA Extension's prestigious Writers' Programme, where she finally gets to utilise the MA and PhD in English Literature that she received from the University of York in England. She currently lives in the Pacific Northwest, with her very own hero and too many pets. Visit her at caitlincrews.com.

SHOCK HEIR FOR THE KING

CLARE CONNELLY

UNTAMED BILLIONAIRE'S INNOCENT BRIDE

CAITLIN CREWS

MILLS & BOON

First Published in Great Britain 2019
by Mills & Boon, an imprint of HarperCollins*Publishers*
1 London Bridge Street, London, SE1 9GF

Shock Heir for the King © 2019 by Clare Connelly

Untamed Billionaire's Innocent Bride © 2019 by Caitlin Crews

ISBN: 978-0-263-27345-8

MIX
Paper from
responsible sources
FSC C007454

Printed and bound in Spain
by CPI, Barcelona

SHOCK HEIR
FOR THE KING

CLARE CONNELLY

For romance readers everywhere, and especially my Advance readers, who are some of the best champions and friends a writer could hope for.

PROLOGUE

THERE WERE THREE things Matthias Vasilliás loved in life. The glow of the sky as the sun dipped into the horizon, bathing the world in streaks of gold and peach; the country he was one week away from ruling; and women—but never the same woman for long, and never with any expectation of more than this: sex.

The wind blew in across the hotel room, draping the gauzy fabric of the curtain towards him, and for a moment he looked at it, his mind caught by the beauty, the brevity, of such a fragile material—the brevity of this moment.

In the morning he'd be gone, she'd be a memory—a ghost of this life. In the morning he would fly back to Tolmirós and step into his future.

He hadn't come to New York for this. He hadn't intended to meet her. He hadn't intended to seduce a virgin—that wasn't his usual *modus operandi*. Not when he couldn't offer any degree of permanence in exchange for such a gift.

No, Matthias preferred experienced women.

Lovers who were *au fait* with the ways of the world, who understood that a man like Matthias had no heart to offer, no future he could provide.

One day he would marry, but his bride would be a political choice, a queen to equal him as King, a ruler to sit beside him and oversee his kingdom.

Until then, though, there was this: there was Frankie, and this night.

She ran her fingertips over his back, her nails digging into him, and he lost himself to her completely, plunging inside her, taking the sweetness she offered as she cried out into the balmy New York evening.

'Matt.' She used the shortened version of his name—it had been such a novelty to meet a woman who didn't know who he was, didn't know he was the heir to the throne of a powerful European country, that he was richer than Croesus and about to be King. Matt was simple, Matt was easy, and soon this would be over.

For ruling Tolmirós meant he would have to abandon his love of women, his love of sex and all that he was, outside the requirements of being King. His life would change completely in seven days' time.

Seven days and he would be King.

In seven days he would be back in Tolmirós, the country before him. But for now he was here, with a woman who knew nothing of his life, his people, his duties.

'This is perfect,' she groaned, arching her back so two pert breasts pushed skyward and he shoved his guilt at this deception aside, his guilt at having taken an innocent young woman to bed for his own pleasure, to slake his own needs, knowing it could never be more than this.

She didn't want complications either. They'd been clear on that score. It was this weekend and nothing more. But he was using her, of that he had no doubt. He was using her to rebel, one last time. Using her to avoid the inevitable truth of his life, for one night longer. Using her because right here, in this moment, sleeping with Frankie made him feel human—only human—and not even an inch royal.

He took one of her breasts in his mouth and rolled his tongue over the tight nipple. It budded in his mouth, desperate for his touch, his possession, and he thrust into her depths, wondering if any woman had ever been so perfectly made for a man?

His fingers fisted in her long, silky blonde hair and he pushed her head up to meet his, claiming her lips, kissing her until she whimpered beneath him and the whole of her body was at his command.

Power surged through him at the way this felt, but it was nothing to the power that awaited him, the duty that would soon be at his feet.

For his country and his people, he would turn his back on pleasures such as this, on women such as Frankie, and he would be King.

But not quite yet.

For a few more hours he would simply be Matt, and Frankie would be his…

CHAPTER ONE

Three years later

NEW YORK SPARKLED like a beautiful diorama, all high-rises, bright lights and muted subway noise. He stared down at the glittering city from the balcony of his Manhattan penthouse, breathing in the activity and forcing himself not to remember the last time he'd been in this exact position.

Forcing his eyes to stay trained in the opposite direction of the School of Art, and definitely not allowing himself to remember the woman who had bewitched him and charmed him.

The woman who had given him her innocence, given him her body, and imprinted something of herself in his mind.

Inwardly he groaned, her name just a whisper in his body, a curse too, because he had no business so much as thinking of her, let alone remembering everything about her.

Not when his engagement would be made formal within a month. Not when his future awaited—and duty to his country called to him as loudly as ever. Then, he'd been one week away from assuming the throne, and now he was weeks away from making a marriage commitment.

All of Tolmirós was waiting for its King to finally wed and beget an heir. An heir that would promise stability and the safekeeping of the prosperous nation: all of that was on Matthias's shoulders, as much now as it had been then. He'd run from this fate for as long as he could. His family had died when he was only a teenager and the idea of marrying, having his own children, as though you could so easily recreate what had been lost, pressed against his chest like a weight of stone.

But it was needed; it was necessary. His country required its King to beget an heir, and he needed a wife. A suitable wife, like one of the women his assistant had vetted for him. A woman who would be cultured, polished and appropriate.

His eyes shut and there she was: Frankie. Frankie as she'd been that afternoon they'd met, her clothes paint-splattered, her hair scraped back into a ponytail, her smile contagious. His gut clenched.

His wife—his Queen—would be nothing like Frankie.

What they'd shared went beyond logic and reason—it had been an affair that had rocked him to his core because, after only a matter of hours, he'd known he was in danger of forgetting everything he owed to his people if it meant more time with the woman—she had been like some kind of siren, rising out of the sea, drawing him towards danger unknowingly.

And so he'd done what he was best at: he'd drawn his heart closed, he'd pushed his emotions deep inside, and he'd walked out on her without a backwards glance.

But now, back in New York, he found himself thinking of her in a way he'd trained himself not to. His dreams he could not control, but his waking mind was as disciplined as the man himself, and he saw no point in dwelling on the past, and particularly not on such a brief event.

Only she was everywhere he looked in this city—the lights that sparkled like the depths of her eyes, the elegance of the high-rises that were tall where she had been short, the nimble alertness, the vivid brightness—and he wondered what it would be like to see her once more. Call it idle curiosity, or simply scratching an itch.

He was a king now, not the man he'd been when they'd first slept together. But his needs were the same. His desires. He stared out at the city and the idea grew.

What harm could come from dipping into the past, just for a night?

'The lighting is beyond perfect,' Frankie enthused, glancing her trained artist's eye over the walls of the midtown gallery. The showing was scheduled for the following day; this was her last chance to make sure everything was absolutely as she wanted it to be.

A *frisson* of excitement ran down her spine.

For years she'd been struggling. Establishing oneself as an artist was no mean feat, and every spare penny she made was funnelled into trying to keep a roof over their heads. It was one thing to be a starving artist when you were footloose and fancy-free—there was even a degree of romance to the notion.

The reality was a lot less enjoyable, particularly with a rapidly growing two-and-a-half-year-old to care for and a mountain of bills that seemed to go on for ever.

But this show…

It could be the game-changer she'd been waiting for.

Two broadsheet newspapers had already sent reviewers to have a pre-show viewing, and the opening night had been advertised across the city. Her fingers, her toes and the hairs on her head remained crossed that she might finally catch her big break into the competitive New York art scene.

'I did think of using small spotlights here.' Charles nodded towards some of her favourite landscapes—sun rising over oceans, but all in abstract oils—gashes of colour scratched over the paper to create the impression of day's dawn. Each picture would be interpreted differently by the spectator, and Frankie liked that. It was her take on each day being what you made of it.

'I like the overheads you've chosen,' she demurred, another shiver running down her spine. Her whole body was a tangle of nerves—and she told herself it was because of the exposure. Not the media exposure—the exposure of herself. Every thought, lost dream, wish, fear, feeling had been captured on these canvases. Even the paintings of Leo, with his stunning crop of black curls, intense grey eyes, so shimmery they were almost silver, lashes that curled precociously and wild. He was her little love, her heart and soul, and his image now hung on the walls of this gallery, waiting to be seen by thousands, she hoped, of viewers.

'The door,' Charles murmured apologetically, in response to a sound that Frankie hadn't even noticed. She was moving closer to the painting she'd done of Leo last fall.

He'd been laughing, collecting dropped leaves from the sidewalk and tossing them into the air with all the enthusiasm a two-year-old boy could muster, and as they'd fallen back to earth he'd watched their progress before crouching down and crunching a new selection into his chubby grip.

His joy had been so euphoric she'd had to capture it. So she'd snapped hundreds of photos from different angles, committing the light to her memory, and then she'd worked late into the night.

And she'd done what she did best: she'd taken a mood, a slice of one of life's moments, and locked it onto a canvas. She'd created a visual secret for the viewer to share in, but only for as long as they looked at her work. It was a moment in time, a moment of her life, and now it was art.

'The opening is tomorrow night, sir, but if you'd like to take a brief look at the collection...'

'I would.'

Two words, so deep, and from a voice so instantly familiar.

A shiver ran down Frankie's spine of a different nature now. It wasn't a shiver of anxiety, nor joyous anticipation, it was one of instant recognition, a tremble of remembrance and a dull thudding ache of loss.

She turned slowly, as if that could somehow unstitch the reality she knew she'd found herself in. But when she looked at Charles, and then the man beside him, all her worlds came crashing down at once.

Matt.

It was him.

And everything came rushing back to her—the way she'd awoken to find him gone, no evidence he'd even slept in the same bed as her, no note, nothing. No way of contacting him, nothing to remember him by except the strange sensation of her body having been made love to, and a desire to feel that sensation again and again.

'Hello, Frances,' he said, his eyes just exactly as she remembered, just exactly like Leo's. How many dreams had she spent painting those eyes? Mixing exactly the right shades of silver, grey and flecks of white to flick, close to the iris? The lashes, with their luxuriant black curls, had occupied much of her artist's mind. How to transpose them onto canvas without looking heavy-handed? They were so thick and glossy that no one would actually believe they really existed.

It had been three years since Frankie had seen this man but, courtesy of her dreams, she remembered him as vividly as if they'd met only the day before.

Oh, how she wanted to drag her eyes down his body, to luxuriate in every inch of him, to remember the strength in his frame, the contradictory gentleness he'd shown when he'd taken possession of her body that first time, when he'd held her in his arms and removed the vestiges of her innocence. How she wanted to give into the temptation to hungrily devour him with her gaze.

With the greatest of efforts, she crossed her arms over her chest and maintained her attention on his face. A face that was watching her with just as much intensity as she was him.

'Matt,' she murmured, proud beyond description when her voice came out steady and cool. 'Are you looking for a piece of art?'

Something seemed to throb between them. A power source that was all its own, that Frankie pushed aside. It wasn't welcome.

'Would you show me your work?' he responded, and it wasn't an answer. It was an invitation, one that was fraught with danger. Belatedly, she recollected that the wall of paintings behind her was of their son and if he looked a little to the left or right he'd see clearly for himself the proof of their weekend together.

'Fine,' she agreed, a little rushed, moving deeper into the gallery, towards another annex. 'But I only have a few minutes.'

At this, she saw Charles frown in her peripheral vision. No wonder he was confused. Without knowing anything about Matt, it was clear that he had enough money to buy everything in the place, probably a million times over. From the fit of his suit to the gleam of his shoes, this was a man who obviously lived very, very comfortably. In normal circumstances, she wouldn't dream of rejecting a potential investor in her work.

But Matt?

Matt who'd crashed into her world, seduced her effortlessly, triumphed over her and gone away again, just as quickly? He was danger, and not for anything would she spend more time with him than she had to.

He's your son's father. Her conscience flared to life and she almost stopped walking, so intense was the realisation, the moral impetus that stabbed into her sides.

'I will take over when Miss Preston leaves.' Charles's offer came from just behind them.

Matt stopped walking, turning to face the other man. 'Miss Preston's company will be sufficient.'

Frankie saw pink bloom in the gallery owner's face and sympathy swelled in her. Charles La Nough's gallery was renowned in New York, and he was used to being met with respect, if not a degree of awe.

To be dismissed in such a way was obviously a new experience.

'I'll call if we need you,' Frankie offered, to soften the blow.

'Very well.' Charles sniffed, turning and disappearing in the direction of the rooms that would eventually lead to the front door.

'You didn't have to be so rude,' she responded, only this time the words were breathy and her pulse was rushing inside her. They were close—just a few feet apart—and she could smell him, she could feel his warmth and her skin was pricking with goosebumps.

Responses she had long since thought dead were stirring to life and demanding indulgence. But she ignored them—such feelings had no place here, or anywhere any more. She tilted her chin defiantly and stared at him. 'And now that he's gone you can tell me exactly what you're doing here. Because I know it's not to buy one of my paintings.'

He regarded her through shuttered eyes. Memory was a funny thing. He'd recollected her in intimate detail over the years, but there were a thousand minute differences now that he stood toe to toe with Frankie Preston. Things his mind hadn't properly written into his memory banks, so that he wanted to hold her still and just *look*.

She remained the most distractingly intriguing woman he'd ever seen, and yet there was no one thing in particular he could ascribe that to. It was *everything* about her—from eyes that were feline in shape and just as green as he remembered, to a nose that had a tiny ski jump at its end and a flurry of pale freckles rushing over its bridge, and lips—*Dio*, those lips.

Pink and pillowy, soft, so that when he'd crushed his mouth to them three years earlier they'd parted on a husky sigh, surrendering to him, welcoming him. His body tightened at the recollection.

Then, she'd been coming home from an art class, carrying a rolled-up canvas in a bag, wearing a pair of paint-splattered jeans and a simple white singlet top, also marked with the signs of her artistic labour. And she'd been so distracted in her own thoughts that she'd walked right into him, smearing a healthy dose of what he'd later discovered to be Cerulean Blue on his suit.

He'd liked her in those clothes—so casual and relaxed.

Now, she wore a dress, black with puffy sleeves that just covered her shoulders and a neckline that dipped frustratingly close to her cleavage without revealing even a hint of the generous curves beneath. It fell to her ankles, and she'd teamed it with leather sandals and a bright yellow necklace. It was a more elegant ensemble, but still so very Frankie.

As she was in his mind, anyway.

But wasn't it more than likely that the woman he'd slept with three years earlier was more a creation of his than a real-life, flesh-and-blood woman? Wasn't it more than likely he'd created a fantasy? How well could he have really known her, given that they'd spent so little time together?

'How do you know,' he drawled, considering her question, 'that I am not here to make a purchase?'

She blotted her lips together; they were painted the most fascinating shade of dark pink—as if she'd been feasting on sun-warmed cherries and the natural pigments had stained her mouth.

'Because you're not interested in my art.'

He thought of the piece in his office, the piece he'd bought through a dealer to keep his acquisition at arm's length—the painting Frankie had been working on the day they'd met—and frowned slightly. 'Why would you say that?'

A hint of pink bloomed in her cheeks. 'Well, I remember clearly how well you played me. Pretending interest in my work is how you fooled me then. I won't be so stupid this time around. So what is it that brings you to the gallery, Matt?'

Her use of that name filled him with a confusing rush of emotions. Shame at having given her only the diminutive of his full name, because surely it proved that he'd set out to deceive her, even from that first moment? Pleasure at the memories it invoked—no other woman had called him that; it was *their* name, it belonged to that weekend, and he would hear it on her lips for ever, calling out to him at the height of her passion.

He wanted her.

Even now, after three years, after walking away from her, he congratulated himself on doing the right thing. He'd been strong in the face of incomprehensible temptation, and he'd done it for his kingdom.

But…

Oh, yes. He wanted her.

Moving slightly closer, just enough to be able to catch a hint of her vanilla perfume, he spoke, his eyes intent when they met hers.

'I am to marry. Soon.'

* * *

His words seemed to come to her from a long way away, as though he were shouting from atop a high-rise, and the floor of the gallery lifted in one corner like a rug being shaken, threatening to tip her off the sides of the earth.

I am to marry.

Her stomach rolled with what she told herself must be relief. Because his impending marriage meant she was safe—safe from the flashes of desire that were warming her insides, safe from an insane need to revisit the past even though it was so obviously better left there. How dare she feel like that, when he'd walked out on her without having the decency to leave so much as a note?

'That's nice,' she said, the words not quite as clear and calm as she'd have liked. 'So perhaps you are after a painting after all? A wedding present for your wife?' She spun on her heel, moving deeper into the gallery. 'I have some lovely landscapes I painted out in Massachusetts. Very pretty. Romantic. Floaty.' She was babbling but she couldn't help it.

I am to marry. Soon. His words were running around and around in her mind, ricocheting off the edges of her consciousness.

'Perhaps this piece.' She gestured to a painting of a lake, surrounded by trees on the cusp of losing their leaves, orange and bright, against a beautiful blue sky. Her heart panged as she remembered the day, that slice of life, when she'd taken Leo on their first vacation and they'd toured Paxton and its surroundings.

'Frankie…' His voice was deep and, though he spoke softly, it was with a natural command, a low, throbbing urgency that had her spinning to face him and—damn him— remembering too much of their time together, the way he'd groaned her name as he'd buried his lips at her neck, then lower, teasing her nipples with his tongue.

Only he was so much closer than she'd realised, his large frame right behind her, so when she turned their bodies brushed and it was as though a thousand volts of electricity were being dumped into her system.

She swallowed hard then took a step backwards, but not far enough. It gave her only an inch or so of breathing space and when she inhaled he was there, filling her senses. *He's getting married!*

'What are you doing here?' She didn't bother to hide the emotion in the question. He was a part of her past that hadn't been good. Oh, the weekend itself, sure, but waking up to discover he'd literally walked out on her? To find herself pregnant and have no way of contacting him? The embarrassment of having to hire a detective who even then could discover no trace of this man?

'I…' The word trailed off as he echoed her movement, taking a step forward, closing the distance between them. His expression was tense; his face wore a mask of discontent. Frustration and impatience radiated off him in waves. 'I wished to see you again. Before my wedding.'

She took a moment, letting his statement settle into her mind, and she examined it from all angles. But it made no sense. 'Why?'

His nostrils flared, his eyes narrowed with intent. 'Do you ever think about our time together?'

And the penny dropped and fury lashed at her spine, powerful and fierce, so she jerked her head away from him and bit back a curse her adoptive mother certainly wouldn't have approved of.

'Are you kidding me with this, Matt? You're getting *married* and you're here to walk down memory lane?' She moved away from him, further into the room, her pulse hammering, her heart rushing.

He was watching her with an intensity that almost

robbed her of breath. Only she was angry too, angry that he thought he could show up after all this time and ask about that damned weekend…

'Or did you want to do more than walk down memory lane? Tell me you didn't come here for another roll in the hay?' she demanded, crossing her arms over her chest, then wishing she hadn't when his eyes dropped to the swell of her cleavage. Indignation made her go on the attack. 'You can't be so hard up for sex that you're resorting to trawling through lovers from years ago?'

A muscle throbbed low in his jaw as her insult hit its mark. Matt Whatever-his-last-name-was was clearly all macho alpha pride. Her suggestion had riled him. Well, so what? She couldn't care less.

'And no, I *don't* think about that weekend!' she snapped before he could interject. 'So far as I'm concerned, you're just some blip in my rear-view mirror—and if I could take what happened between us back, I would,' she lied, her stomach rolling at the betrayal of their son.

'Oh, really?' he asked softly, words that were dangerous and seductive all at once, his husky accent as spicy and tempting as it had been three years earlier.

'Yes, really.' She glared at him to underscore her point.

'So you don't think about the way it felt when I kissed you here?' She was completely unprepared for his touch— the feather-light caress of a single finger against her jaw, the pulse-point there moving into frantic overdrive as butterflies stormed through her chest.

'No.' The word was slightly uneven.

'Or the way you liked me to touch you here?' and he drew his finger lower, to her décolletage, and then lower still, to the gentle curve of her breast.

Heaven help her, memories were threatening to pull her

under, to drown her with their perfection, even when the truth of their situation was disastrous.

Just for a second, she wanted to surrender to those recollections. She wanted to pretend they didn't have a son together and that they were back in time, in that hotel room, just him and her, no consciousness of the outside world.

But it would be an exercise in futility.

'Don't.' She batted his hand away and stepped away from him, anger almost a match for her desire. She rammed her hands against her hips, breathing in hard, wishing there was even the slightest hint of his having been as affected by those needs as she had been. 'It was three years ago,' she whispered. 'You can't just show up after all this time, after disappearing into thin air…'

He watched her from a face that was carefully blanked of emotion, his expression mask-like. 'I had to see you.'

Her heart twisted at those words, at the sense that perhaps he'd found it impossible to forget their night together. Except he'd done exactly that. He'd walked away without a backwards glance. He could have called her at any time in the past three years, but he hadn't. Nothing. Not a blip.

'Well, you've *seen* me,' she said firmly. 'And now I think you should go.'

'You're angry with me.'

'Yes.' She held his gaze, her eyes showing hurt and betrayal. 'I woke up and you were *gone*! You don't think I have a right to be angry?'

A muscle twisted at the base of his firm, square jaw. 'We agreed we would just spend the weekend together.'

'Yes, but that wasn't tacit approval for you to slink out in the middle of the night.'

His eyes narrowed. 'I did *not* slink.' And then, as if bringing himself back to the point, he was calm again, his arrogant face blanked of any emotion once more. 'And it was best for both of us that I left when I did.'

It was strange, really, how she'd been pulling her temper back into place, easing it into the box in which it lived, only to have it explode out of her, writhing free of her grip with a blinding intensity. 'How? How was you disappearing into thin air *best* for me?' she demanded, her voice raised, her face pale.

He sighed as though she were a recalcitrant toddler and his impatience at fraying point. 'My life is complicated.' He spoke without apology, words that were cool and firm and offered no hint of what had truly motivated his departure. 'That weekend was an aberration. In retrospect, I shouldn't have let it happen. I had no business getting involved with someone like you.'

'Someone like me?' she repeated, the words deceptively soft when inside her cells were screeching with indignation. 'But it was fine to sleep with someone like me?'

'You misunderstand my meaning,' he said with a shake of his head. 'And that is my fault.'

'So what is your meaning?'

He spoke slowly, carefully, as though she might not comprehend. 'I wanted you the minute I saw you, Frankie, but I knew it could *never* be more than that weekend. I believe I was upfront about that; I apologise if you expected more from me.' He went to move closer but she bristled, and he stilled. 'There are expectations upon me, expectations as to who I will marry, and you are not the kind of bride I would ever be able to choose.'

She spluttered her interruption. 'I didn't want to *marry* you! I just wanted the courtesy of a goodbye from the man I lost my virginity to. When you crept out of that hotel suite, did you stop to think about what I would think?'

She had the very slight satisfaction of seeing something

like remorse briefly glance across his stony features. 'I had to leave. I'm sorry if that hurt you—'

'Hurt me?' She glared at him and shook her head. It had damned near killed her, but she wasn't going to tell him that. 'What *hurts* is your stupidity! Your lack of decency and moral fibre.'

He jerked his face as though she'd slapped him, but she didn't stop.

'You were my first lover.' She lowered her voice. 'Sleeping with you *meant* something to me! And you just left.'

'What would you have had me do, Frankie? Stay and cook you breakfast? Break it to you over scrambled eggs and salmon that I was going to go back to Tolmirós to forget all about you?'

Her stare was withering. 'Only you haven't forgotten me, have you?'

She held her breath, waiting for him to answer, her lips parted.

'No,' he agreed finally. 'But I left because I knew I needed to. I left because I knew what was expected of me.' He expelled a harsh breath, then another, slowly regaining control of himself. 'I didn't come here to upset you, Frankie. I'll go away again.'

And at that, true, dark anger beat in her breast because it simply underscored their power imbalance. He'd come to her and so she was seeing him again, and he'd touched her as though desire was still a current in the room—it was all on his terms. All his timeline, his power, his control. He thought he could leave when it suited him and have that be the end of it.

Well, damn him, he had no right! 'Did you even think about the consequences of that night, Matt? Did you so much as give even a second thought to whether or not I would be able to walk away from what we shared as easily as you did?'

CHAPTER TWO

FOR THE BRIEFEST of moments he misunderstood. Surely, he'd misunderstood.

As the heir to the throne of Tolmirós, Matthias had *never* taken any risks with sex. That weekend had been no different. He'd employed protective measures. He'd been careful, as always.

'I knew there would be no consequences,' he said, shrugging, as though his heart hadn't skidded to a dramatic halt seconds earlier. 'And I truly believed a clean break would be better for you.'

And for himself. He hadn't trusted his willpower to so much as call her, to explain who he was and his reasons for needing to disappear from her life.

'*How* did you know that?'

His frown was infinitesimal. 'Are you saying there was a consequence?'

'A consequence?' she repeated with an arched brow. But her fingers were shaking, a small gesture but one he noted with growing attention. 'Why are we speaking in euphemisms? Ask what you really mean.'

She spoke to him in a way no one in his life had ever dared, and it was thrilling and dangerous and his whole body resonated with a need to argue with her, just like this. Passions were stirring inside him but he shoved them aside, focusing everything on whatever the hell she was trying to say.

'You are the one who is insinuating there was a complication from our night together.'

'I'm *telling* you your arrogant presumption that you took sufficient measures to protect me from the ramifications of our sleeping together is wrong.'

He narrowed his eyes and her words sprayed around them like fine blades, slicing through the artwork on the walls.

'Are you saying you fell pregnant?' he demanded, his ears screeching with the sound of frantically racing blood. The world stood still; time stopped.

For a moment he imagined that—his child, growing in her belly—and his chest swelled with pride and his heart soared, but pain was right behind, because surely it wasn't possible. His forehead broke out in perspiration at the very idea of his baby. He knew it was inevitable and necessary, but he still needed time to brace himself for that reality—for the idea of another person who shared his blood, a person who could be taken from him at any time.

Rejection was in every line of his body. 'We were careful. *I* was careful. I took precautions, as I always do.'

'Charming!' She crossed her arms over her chest. 'Tell me more about the other women you've had sex with, please.'

He ground his teeth together. He hadn't meant that, and yet it was true. Sexual responsibility was ingrained in Matthias. Anyone in his position would take that seriously.

'What the hell are you saying?' he demanded, all the command his position conferred upon him in those words.

She sucked in a deep breath as though she was steadying herself. 'Fine. Yes. I fell pregnant.' Her words hit him right in the solar plexus, each with the speed and strength of a thousand bullets.

'What?' For the first time in his life, Matthias was utterly lost for words.

When his family had died and a nation in mourning had looked to him, a fifteen-year-old who'd lost his parents and brother, who'd been trapped in a car with them as life had left their bodies, he had known what was expected of him. He'd received the news and wrapped his grief into a small compartment for indulgence at a later date, and he'd shown himself to be strong and reliable: a perfect king-in-waiting.

She lifted her fingertips to the side of her head, rubbing her temples, and fixed him with her ocean-green stare. Her anguish was unmistakable.

'I found out about a month after you left.'

His world was a place that made no sense. There were sharp edges everywhere, and nothing fitted together. 'You were pregnant?'

She pulled a face. 'I just said that.'

His eyes swept shut, his blood raced. 'You should have told me.'

'I *tried*! You were literally impossible to find.'

'No one is impossible to find.'

'Believe me, *you* are. "Matt". That's all I had to go on. The hotel wouldn't give me any information about who'd booked the suite. I had your name and the fact you're from Tolmirós. That's it. I *wanted* to tell you. But trying to find you was like looking for a needle in an enormous haystack.'

And hadn't he planned for it to be this way? A night without complications—that was what they'd shared. Only everything about Frankie had been complicated, including the way she'd cleaved her way into his soul.

'So you made a decision like this on your own?' he fired back, the pain of what he'd lost, what his kingdom had lost, the most important thing in the conversation.

'Decision?' She paled. 'It was hardly a decision.'

'You had an abortion and took from me any chance to even know my child,' he said thickly, his chest tight, his organs squeezing inside him.

She sucked in a loud breath. 'What makes you think I had an abortion?'

He stared at her, the question hanging between them, everything sharp and uncertain now. When he was nine years old he'd run the entire way around the palace, without pausing for even a moment. Up steps, along narrow precipices with frightening glimpses of the city far beneath him, he'd run and he'd run, and when he'd finished he'd collapsed onto the grass and stared at the clouds. His lungs had burned and he'd been conscious of the sting of every cell in his body, as though he was somehow supersonic. He felt that now.

'You're saying…' He stared at her, trying to make sense of this, looking for an explanation and arriving at only one. 'You didn't have an abortion?'

'Of course I didn't.'

Matthias had a rapier-sharp mind, yet he struggled to process her words, to make sense of what she was saying. 'You did not have an abortion?'

'No.'

And something fired inside his mind, a memory, a small recollection that had been unimportant at the time. He spun away from her and stalked through the gallery, through the smaller display spaces that curved towards a larger central room. And he stared at the wall that had framed Frankie when he'd first walked in. He'd been so blindsided by the vision of her initially that he hadn't properly understood the significance of what he was seeing. But now he looked at the paintings—ten of them in total, all of the same little boy—and his blood turned into lava in his veins.

He stared at the paintings and a primal sense of pride and

possession firmed inside him. Something else too. Something that made his chest scream and his brow heat—something that made acid coat his insides, as he stared at the boy who was so familiar to him.

Spiro.

He was looking at a version not only of his younger self, but also of his brother. Eyes that had held his, pain and anguish filling them, as life ebbed from him. Eyes that had begged him to help. Eyes that had eventually clouded and died as Matthias watched, helpless, powerless.

For a moment he looked towards the ground, his chest heaving, his pulse like an avalanche, and he breathed in, waiting for the familiar panic to subside.

'This is my son.' More than his son—this was his kin, his blood, his.

He didn't have to turn around to know she was right behind him.

'He's two and a half,' Frankie murmured, the words husky. She cleared her throat audibly. 'His name is Leo.'

Matthias's eyes swept shut as he absorbed this information. Leo. Two and a half. Spiro had been nine when he'd died, the vestiges of his boyish face still in evidence. Cheeks that were rounded like this, and dimpled when he smiled, eyes that sparkled with all his secrets and amusements.

He pushed the memories away, refusing to give into them like this. Only in the middle of the night, when time seemed to slip past the veil of living, when ancient stars with their wisdom and experience whispered that they would listen, did he let his mind remember, did he let his heart hurt.

He turned his attention to the paintings, giving each one in turn the full power of his inspection. Several of the artworks depicted Leo—his son—in a state of play. Laughing as he tossed leaves overhead, his sense of joy and vitality communicated through the paint by Frankie's talented hand. Other paintings were a study of portraiture.

It was the final picture that held him utterly in its thrall.

Leo was staring out of the canvas, his expression frozen in time, arresting a moment of query. One brow was lifted, his lips were turned into a half-smile. His eyes were grey, like Matthias's—in fact, much of his face was a carbon copy of Matthias's own bearing. But the freckles that ran haphazardly across the bridge of his nose were all Frankie's, as was the defiant amusement that stirred in the boy's features.

Emotions welled inside Matthias, for his own face was only borrowed—first from his father, King Stavros, and it had now been passed onto his own son. What other features and qualities were held by this boy, this small human who was of his own flesh and blood?

His own flesh and blood! An heir! An heir his country was desperate for, an heir he had been poised to marry in order to beget—an heir, already living! An heir, two years old, who he knew nothing about!

'Where is he?' The question was gravelled.

He felt her stiffen—he felt everything in that moment, as though the universe was a series of strings and fibres connected through his body to hers. He turned around, pinning her with a gaze that shimmered like liquid metal.

'Where.' The word was a slowly flying bullet. 'Is.' He took a step closer to her. 'He?'

All the myths upon which he'd been raised, the beliefs of his people as to the power and strength that ran through his veins, a power that was now in his son's veins, propelled him forward. But it was not purely a question of royal lineage and the discovery of an heir. This was an ancient, soul-deep need to meet his son—as a man, as a father.

Alarm resonated from Frankie and until that moment he'd never understood what the term 'mother bear' had been coined for. She was tiny and slight but she looked more than capable of murdering him with her bare hands if he did anything to threaten their child.

'He's outside the city,' she said evasively, her eyes shifting towards the door. Through it was the foyer, and somewhere there the man who ran this gallery. Her fear was evident, and it served little purpose. He was no threat to her, nor their son.

With the discipline he was famed for, Matthias brought his emotions tightly under control. They didn't serve him in that moment. Just like his grief had needed to be contained when his family had been killed, so too did his feelings need to be now.

His whole world had shifted off its axis, and he had to find a way to fix that. To redefine the parameters of his being. An heir was driving his need for marriage and here, it turned out, an heir already existed! There was no option for Matthias but to bring that child home to Tolmirós.

His future shifted before his eyes, and this woman was in it, and their son. All the reasons he'd had for walking away from her still stood, except for this heir. It changed everything.

'I had no idea you were pregnant.'

'Of course you didn't. How could you? You probably walked out as soon as I fell asleep.'

No, he'd waited longer than that. He'd watched her sleep for a while, and thought of his kingdom, the expectations that he would return to Tolmirós and take up his title and all the responsibilities that went with that. Frankie had been a diversion—a distraction. She'd been an indulgence when he'd known he was on the cusp of the life he'd been destined to lead.

Only she'd also been quicksand, and a fast escape had seemed the only solution. The longer he'd lingered, the deeper he'd risked sinking, until escape had no longer been guaranteed.

Besides, he'd comforted himself at the time, he'd made her no promises. He'd told her he was only in the States for the weekend. There were no expectations beyond that. He hadn't broken his word.

'If you'd left your number, I would have called. But you just vanished into thin air. Not even the detective I hired could find you.'

'You hired a detective?' The admission sent sparks through him—sparks of relief and gratitude. Because she hadn't intentionally kept their son a secret. She'd wanted him to be a part of the boy's life. And if he'd known of the child back then? If he'd discovered Frankie's pregnancy?

He would have married her. Her lack of suitability as a royal bride would have been beside the point: his people cared most for the delivery of an heir.

And now he had one.

Every possibility and desire narrowed into one finite re-alisation. There was only one way forward and the sooner he could convince Frankie of that, the better.

'Yes.' She looked away from him and swallowed visibly, her throat chording before his eyes and his gut clenched as he remembered kissing her there, feeling the fluttering of her racing pulse beneath her fine, soft skin. 'I felt you should know.'

'Indeed.' He dipped his head forward and then, appeal-ing to the sense of justice he knew ran through her passion-ate veins, 'Will you come for dinner with me?'

Her refusal was imminent but he shook his head to fore-stall her. 'To discuss our son. You must see how impor-tant that is?'

She was tense, her face rigid, her eyes untrusting. But finally she nodded. A tight shift of her head and an even tighter grimace of those cherry-stained lips. 'Fine. But just a quick meal. I told Becky I'd be home by nine.'

'Becky?'

'My downstairs neighbour. She helps out with Leo when I'm working.'

He filed this detail away, and the image it created, of the mother of his child, the mother of the heir to the throne of Tolmirós, a child worth billions of euros, being minded by some random woman in the suburbs of New York.

'A quick meal, then,' he said, giving no indication he was second-guessing her child-minding arrangements.

'Well?' The owner of the gallery appeared from behind the desk, his eyes travelling from Frankie to Matthias. 'Isn't she talented?'

'Exceptionally,' Matthias agreed, and he'd always known that to be the case. 'I will take all of the artworks against that wall.' He gestured through the doorway, to the display that housed the portraits of his son.

'You'll what?' Frankie startled as she looked up at him, though he couldn't tell if she was surprised or annoyed.

He removed a card from his wallet. 'If you call the number on this card, my valet will arrange payment and delivery.' He nodded curtly and then put a hand in the small of Frankie's back, guiding her towards the front door.

Shock, apparently, held her quiet. But once they emerged onto the Manhattan street, a sultry summer breeze warming the evening, she stopped walking, jerking out of his reach and spinning to face him.

'Why did you do that?'

'You think it strange that I should want paintings of my son?'

She bristled and he understood—she had yet to come to terms with the fact that he was also the boy's parent, that she now had to share their son.

Not only that—he couldn't have paintings of his child, the heir to his throne, for sale in some gallery in New York. It wasn't how things were done.

'No,' she admitted grudgingly, and the emotion of this situation was taking its toll on her. The strength and defiance she carried in her eyes were draining from her. Wariness took their place.

'Come on.' He gestured towards the jet-black SUV that was parked in front of the gallery. Darkly tinted windows concealed his driver and security detail from sight but, as they approached, Zeno stepped out, opening the rear doors with a low bow.

Frankie caught it, her eyes narrowing at the gesture of deference. It was so much a part of Matthias's day that he barely noticed the respect with which he was treated. Seeing it through Frankie's eyes though, he understood. It was confronting and unusual.

'You know, I never even had your surname,' she murmured as she slid into the white leather interior of the car—her skin was so pale now it matched the seats.

There was so much he wanted to ask about that. Would she have given their child his name if she'd known it? The idea of his son being raised as anything other than a Vasilliás filled him with a dark frustration.

He wanted to ask her this, and so much more, but not even in front of his most trusted servants would he yet broach the subject of his heir.

With a single finger lifted to his mouth, he signalled silence and then settled back into the car himself, brooding over this turn of events and what they would mean for the marriage he had intended to make.

'I presumed you meant dinner at a restaurant,' she said as the car pulled up to a steel monolith on United Nations

Plaza. The drive had been conducted in absolute silence, except for when the car drew to a stop and he'd spoken to his driver in that language of his, all husky and deep, so her pulse had fired up and her stomach had churned and feelings that deserved to stay buried deep in the past flashed in her gut, making her nerve-endings quiver and her pulse fire chaotically against the fine walls of her veins.

'Restaurants are not private enough.'

'You can't speak quietly in a restaurant?'

'Believe me, Frankie, this is better.' His look was loaded with intensity and there was a plea in the depth of his gaze as well, begging her to simply agree with him on this occasion. There was a part of her, a childish, silly part, that wanted to refuse—to tell him it didn't suit her. He'd disappeared into thin air and she'd tried so hard to find him, to tell him he was a father. And now? Everything was on his terms. She wanted to rebel against that, but loyalty to their son kept her quiet. All along, she'd wanted what was best for Leo. She'd spent all her life feeling rejected and unwanted by her biological parents, and she had wept for any idea that Leo might feel the same! That Leo might grow up believing his father hadn't wanted him.

'Fine,' she agreed heavily. 'But I really can't stay long.'

'This is not a conversation to be rushed.' He stepped out of the car and she followed. He placed a hand on her elbow, guiding her through the building's sliding glass doors. The lifts were waiting, a security guard to one side.

She hadn't noticed this degree of staff with him back then. There hadn't been anyone except a driver, and she'd never really questioned that. It was obvious that he had money—but this was a whole new degree of wealth.

'Have you had some kind of death threat or something?' she muttered as the doors of the lift snapped closed behind them.

The look he sent her was half-rueful, half-impatient; he said nothing. But when the lift doors opened into the foyer of what could only be described as a sky palace, he urged her into the space and then held a hand up to still the guard.

More words, spoken in his own tongue, and then the guard bowed low and slipped back into the lift, leaving them alone.

She swallowed at that thought—being alone with him—distracting herself by studying the over-the-top luxury of this penthouse. It wasn't just the polished timber floors, double height ceilings, expensive designer furnishings and crystal chandeliers that created the impression of total glamour. It was the views of the Manhattan skyline—the Chrysler Building, the Empire State, Central Park—it all spread before her like a pop-up book of New York city.

Large sliding glass doors opened out onto a deck, beyond which there was a pool, set against a glass rail. She imagined swimming in it would feel a little like floating, high above the city.

The contrasts between her own modest apartment in Queens and this insanely beautiful penthouse were too ridiculous to enumerate.

'Matt,' she sighed, turning to face him, not even sure what she wanted to say. He was watching her with a look of dark concentration.

'My name,' he said quietly, 'is Matthias Vasilliás.'

It was perfect for this man—as soon as he gave her the full version of his name it resonated inside her, like the banging of a drum. *Matt* was too pedestrian for someone like him. He was exotic and unusual.

'Fine.' She nodded curtly, pleased when the word sounded vaguely dismissive. 'Matthias.'

At this, his eyes flashed with something she couldn't comprehend. 'You have not heard of me?'

Something like an alarm bell began to ring inside Frankie's mind. 'Should I have?'

His lips twisted in a sardonic smile. 'No.'

But it sounded like judgement rather than offence, and she bristled. 'So? What gives?' Her frown deepened. 'What's with all the security?'

He sighed heavily. 'This is a light protection detail.' He shrugged. 'At home, there are many more guards.'

'Why? I don't get it. Are you some kind of celebrity or something?'

'You could say that.'

He moved into the kitchen and pulled out a bottle of wine. Her stomach rolled at the memories of the wine they'd shared that night—only a few sips, but it had been the nicest she'd ever tasted. He poured her a glass and walked around to her; she took it on autopilot.

'What's going on, Matt—Matthias?'

His eyes narrowed and she wondered if the sound of his full name on her lips was as strange for him as it was for her. Matt had suited him, but Matthias suited him better. She liked the taste of those exotic syllables on the tip of her tongue.

'My family was killed in an accident many years ago. When I was a boy of fifteen.' He spoke matter-of-factly, so it was impossible for Frankie to know how those deaths had affected him. She could imagine, though.

'I'm sorry,' she murmured crisply, wishing she didn't feel sympathy for him. Wishing she didn't feel *anything* for him.

His lips twisted in acknowledgement. 'It was a long time ago.'

'I'm sure it still hurts.'

'I have become used to being alone.' He brushed her concern aside. 'My father's brother took on many of the responsibilities of my father. At fifteen, I was too young.'

'What responsibilities?' she asked.

'Shortly after their deaths, it was decided that on my thirtieth birthday I would assume my role.' He pinpointed her with his gaze, but he was obviously back in time, reflecting on the past. 'One week before I turned thirty, I met you. I was only in New York for the weekend. One of my last chances to travel as myself, without this degree of… company.' His expression shifted.

'What did your parents do?'

But this wasn't a conversation with questions and answers. It was a monologue. An unburdening of himself, and it was an explanation she'd wanted for such a long time that she didn't even particularly mind.

'I shouldn't have got involved with you, but you were so… I cannot explain it. I saw you, and I wanted you.' He stared at her, his eyes glinting like steel, and her heart was ice in her chest. It had been that simple for him. He'd seen her. He'd wanted her. And so he'd had her.

'I knew it would only ever be a brief affair.'

Her throat constricted with those words, damning what they'd been to such a cynical seduction. 'Yet you did it anyway?'

He was quiet.

'Did you think about how I'd feel?'

'No.' He swept his eyes shut. 'I told myself you were just like me—looking for a weekend of pleasure. Casual, easy sex.'

'I think the term "casual sex" is oxymoronic,' she said stiffly, turning away from him so she didn't see the way his expression shifted, the way a fierce blade of possession pressed into him.

'If I had known you were a virgin…'

'I didn't lie to you intentionally,' she muttered. 'I just got caught up in how I felt. It was all so overwhelming.'

He dipped his head forward in silent concession. 'It is in the past,' he said. 'What I'm interested in dealing with is our future.'

And here it was. The custody discussion she'd been dreading. And as the days had turned into months and her status as a single mother had been firmly established, she'd come to accept that it was a conversation she'd never need to have. Now, though, faced with the father of her baby, she had no interest in denying him his right to see their child. To be a part of his life. Even when his admission that he'd gone into their affair expecting it to be 'casual sex' had cut her deep inside.

'After I left you, I went back to Tolmirós and took up the position that was my birthright.'

She frowned. 'Just what kind of family business are you in?'

His smile was more like a grimace. 'It is not a business, Frankie. My name is Matthias Vasilliás and I am the King of Tolmirós.'

CHAPTER THREE

'I'M SORRY.' SHE blinked slowly. 'I thought you just said you were…' She laughed, a brittle sound of disbelief. 'I mean, is this some kind of joke?'

But she looked around the penthouse with new eyes, seeing the degree of luxury and wealth as if for the first time, understanding how uniquely positioned a person would have to be to enjoy this kind of residence. And it wasn't just this ludicrously expensive apartment—how much would something like this even cost? More than she could imagine, that was for sure. And she saw *everything* through the veil of his words and her stomach dropped and her knees shook. Because it was *so* obvious now.

Even then, staying at a hotel, he'd been so *different* to anyone she'd ever known. He'd spoken to her of ancient myths and he'd weaved magic into her being.

He'd been totally unique. A king.

'It's no joke. That weekend with you was my way of trying to ignore the reality of how my life was about to change, of pretending I wasn't about to take the throne and the mantle of King. But I do not believe in hiding, Frankie. And so I left you in order to return to my country, my people, and my role as ruler.'

His words came to her from very far away.

He was a king.

Which meant… Oh, God. She reached behind her for

the sofa, dropping down into it with a thud and drinking her wine as though it were a lifeline.

'Yes,' he agreed, moving closer to her, the word drawn from deep in his throat. 'Our son is my heir. He is a prince, Frankie.'

'But…he's not… We weren't married.' She clutched at straws desperately. 'So doesn't that mean he can't be your heir?'

His expression darkened and he took a moment to answer. 'It complicates matters,' he agreed eventually, with a shrug. 'But nothing changes the fact he is the future of my people.'

She swallowed, his certainty formidable.

'Do you remember the Myth of Elektus?'

She swayed a little, the words he'd spoken that night burned into her memories. 'No,' she lied huskily, staring out at New York.

'My family has ruled Tolmirós for over a millennium. Our line remains unbroken. Wars and famines consumed neighbouring countries but, within the borders of Tolmirós, life has been prosperous and stable. The myth of our First Ruler is one my people hold in their hearts, even now. It is believed that my family's lineage is at the root of Tolmirós's wealth and happiness. Leo is *not* simply a boy—he is the fulfilment of a myth and ruling Tolmirós is his destiny, as much as it was mine.'

The magic he'd wound around her heart was weaving into her soul once more, and her beautiful child, who *was* so kingly, even as a child, began to pull away from her as she saw him as a figure of the fabric of this faraway country.

But he wasn't only the heir to Tolmirós's throne: he was her son. A child she had grown in her belly and nursed through fevers and helped to take his first step. He was a child she'd read to every night of his life, played ball with, lain beside when night terrors had caused him to cry out.

'My people need him to come home, Frankie. He is part of that myth—he is our future.'

Her eyes swept shut on a wave of desolation. 'You speak of your people, and you speak of his destiny. These are the words of a king, not a father.' She turned to face him. 'How can you not care about him as your son? He is a little boy and for two and a half years he has existed and all you care about is his destiny to rule a country he hasn't even heard of. You haven't asked me a single thing about him!'

His eyes glittered at the truth of her accusation. 'You think I am not burning to know *every single detail* about my son? You think I am not desperate to meet him and hold him to me, and look into his face and understand him? Of course I am. But first I must secure your understanding for what will happen next. We must move quickly if we are to control this.'

'Control what?'

He expelled an impatient breath and his nostrils flared. 'Our marriage.'

'Marriage?' She paled visibly. 'I'm not marrying *you*!'

'With respect, Frankie, that decision was taken out of our hands the minute you conceived Leo.'

'That's not how I see it.'

'Then let me be clear: there is no reality where I will not be raising my son as my son and heir.'

'Fine. Be his father. Even let him be the heir to your damned country—'

Matthias's expression darkened.

'But don't think you can show up after three years and try to take over our lives. Whatever we shared that night, it was fleeting. Meaningless. Just like you said. And it's over. You're just some guy I frankly wish I'd never met.'

His cheekbones were slashed a dark red. 'That may be the case, but we *did* meet. We slept together and now we have a son. And I cannot ignore that. We must marry, Frankie. Surely you can see it's the only way?'

She drew in a shaking breath at the finality of that, and fear trembled inside her breast.

'No.'

'No?' he repeated, and then laughed, a harsh sound of disbelief. 'You cannot simply say "no" to me.'

'Because you're a king?'

His eyes narrowed watchfully. 'Because I am his father, and I will fight you with every breath in my body to bring him home.'

'He *is* home!'

'He is the heir of Tolmirós and he belongs in the palace.'

'With you?'

'And you. You'll be my wife, the Queen of a prosperous, happy country. It's not like I'm asking you to give him up. Nor to move somewhere unpleasant. You wouldn't even have to live with me—I have many palaces; you could choose which you wanted to reside in. Your life will be significantly improved.'

'How can you say that? I'd be married to you.'

'And?'

'I hardly even know you!' The words flew from her mouth and her body immediately contradicted them. Her body knew his well. So well. Even now, dressed as he was, she saw him naked. She saw his broad, muscular chest, his swarthy tan, his wide shoulders, and her insides slicked with moist heat as—out of nowhere—she remembered the way he'd possessed her utterly and completely.

'We will get to know each other enough.' He shrugged. 'Enough to raise a family together, enough to be a good King and Queen.'

He spoke dispassionately, calmly, but the words he spoke, the images they made, filled her with a warm, tingling sense in her gut. 'It's that easy for you?'

'I've never expected any differently.'

'Wait a second. You told me tonight that you're engaged. So what's your fiancée going to say about this?'

'There is no such person. I haven't yet selected a bride.'

Frankie felt as if her head was about to explode. '"Selected" a bride?' She rolled her eyes. 'You make it sound like shuffling a deck of cards and drawing one at random.'

'It is far from a random process,' he said with a shake of his head. 'Each of the women have been shortlisted because of their suitability to be my wife.'

'So go back to your damned country and marry one of them.'

He swept his heated gaze over her body, and goosebumps spread where his eyes moved.

'Think it through,' he said finally. 'What happens if I do as you say—if I return to Tolmirós and marry another woman. She becomes my Queen, and Leo is still my son. *Our* son, mine and my wife's. I will fight for custody of him and, Frankie, I will win.' A shiver ran down her spine at his certainty, because she knew he was right. She knew the danger here, for her. 'I will win, and I will raise him. Wouldn't you prefer to avoid an ugly custody dispute, a public battle that you would surely lose? Wouldn't you prefer to accept this and simply agree to marry me?'

'Simply?' There was nothing simple about it. 'I would *prefer* you to go right away again.'

He made a small sound—it might have been a laugh, but there was absolutely no humour in it. 'No matter what we might wish, this is the reality we find ourselves in. I have a son. An heir. And I must bring him home. Surely you can see that?'

The city twinkled like a thousand gems against black velvet. She swallowed, her eyes running frantically over the vista as her brain tried to fumble its way to an alternative. 'But marriage is so…'

'Yes?'

'It's so much. Too much.' She spun back to face him, and her heart thudded in her chest. Marriage to this man? Impossible. He had embodied so many fantasies in her mind but, over time, the lust which might have become love, given the proper treatment, had instead turned to resentment.

He'd disappeared into thin air, and she'd made her peace with that.

Now? To expect her just to marry him?

'Why? People do it all the time,' he said simply, moving across the room and pouring a generous amount of Scotch into two tumblers. He carried one over to her and, despite the fact she didn't drink often and the wine had already made her brain fuzzy, she took it as if on autopilot.

'Do what all the time?' Her mind was still fumbling for something to offer that might appease him.

'Get married because it makes sense.'

Now it was Frankie's turn to make a strangled sound. Not a laugh, not a sob—just a noise driven by emotions emanating from deep in her throat. 'People get married because they are in love,' she contradicted forcefully. 'Because they can't bear to spend their lives apart. People get married because they are full of optimism and hope, because they have met the one person on earth whom they can't live without.'

She spoke the words with passion, from deep within her soul; they were words that meant the world to her. Words by which she lived. But each word seemed to have the effect of making Matthias withdraw from her. His handsome face tightened until his features were stern and his eyes flinted like coal.

'A fantasist's notion,' he said at length. 'And not what I'm offering.'

It was such an insult that she let out a sigh of impatience. 'It's not what I'm asking for—not from you, anyway.' She ignored the strange thumping in the region of her heart. 'I'm explaining that marriage *means* something.'

'Why?' He took a step closer to her, his eyes so focused on her they were like a force, holding her to the spot.

She frowned. 'What do you mean?'

'Why can it not just be that it makes sense?'

'Making sense,' Frankie said with a shake of her head, trying to break free of the power his gaze had over her ability to think straight, 'would be us working out how we're going to do this.' It hurt to think of sharing Leo, but she pushed those feelings aside. This was about Leo, not her. 'You *are* his father, and it was always my wish that you'd be involved in his life. I can bring him to Tolmirós for a visit, to start with, and we can allow him to gradually adjust to the idea of being the heir to your throne. Over time, he might even choose to spend more time over there, with you. And of course you can see him when you're in New York.' Yes. That all made perfect sense. She nodded somewhat stiffly, as though she'd ordered a box neatly into shape. 'There's definitely no need for us to get married.'

'I say there is a need,' he contradicted almost instantly. His voice was calm but there was an intensity in his gaze. 'And within the month.'

'A month?' Her jaw dropped, her stomach swooped and spun.

'Or sooner, if possible. We must act swiftly. There is much you need to learn on the ways of my people. Much Leo will have to learn too.'

'Hang on.' She lifted her hand, pressing it into the air between them as though it might put an end to this ridiculous conversation. 'You can't talk like it's a foregone conclusion that I'll marry you! You've suggested it and I've said, "Absolutely not". You can't just ride roughshod over me.'

His eyes narrowed almost imperceptibly. 'Do you think not?'

'*Definitely* not. Unless you think I'm not a sentient person, capable of making my own decisions?'

'On the contrary. I think you are very capable of that—which is why I'll expect you to make the right one. But be assured, Frankie, regardless of what you think and feel, I have no intention of leaving this country without my son. It is obviously better for everyone if you come with him as my fiancée.'

She sucked in a breath as the truth of what he was saying settled around her. 'You're actually threatening to take him away from me?'

'I'm asking you to marry me.'

Her eyes swept shut. 'Telling me, more like.' When she blinked her eyes open he was closer, so close her palm was almost touching his chest.

'I'm asking you,' he insisted, almost gentle, almost as though he understood her fear and wanted to ease it. 'I'm asking you to see sense. I'm asking you not to put me in a position where I have to fight you for our child.'

Fear lanced her breast because she didn't doubt the sincerity of his words, nor that he had the ability to follow through. She had some savings, but not a lot. Her adoptive parents were comfortable but by no means wealthy. Not in a million years would she be able to afford a lawyer of the calibre necessary to stave off this man's determination. Would he even need a lawyer? Or would he have some kind of diplomatic privilege, given he was King?

'You're such a bastard,' she said, stepping backwards. It was a mistake; the window was behind her. Ice-cold against her back, and rather like a vice clamping her to the spot.

'I am the father to a two-year-old. A little boy I didn't know about even three hours ago. Do you think wanting to raise him is truly unreasonable?'

'Raise him, no. Marry me? Yes.'

'I want this as little as you do, Frankie.' He expelled a sigh and shook his head. 'That is not completely true, in fact. I still want you. I came here tonight because I was thinking of our weekend together and I wished to take you to bed once more.'

She bit down on her tongue to stop a curse from flying from her lips. 'How dare you?' The words were numbed by shock. 'After all these years? After the way you slept with me and then disappeared into thin air? You thought you could just turn up and have me fall at your feet?'

'You did once before,' he pointed out with insufferable arrogance.

Her fingertips itched with a violent impulse to slap him. 'I didn't know you then!'

'And you don't know me now,' he continued, moving closer, speaking with a softness that was imbued with reasonable, rational intent. It was like a magic spell being cast. His proximity was enough to make her pulse thready and her cheeks glow pink.

But she hated him for the ease with which he could affect her and she did her best to hide any sign that she so much as noticed his proximity.

'You don't know that I am a man who has won almost every battle he's fought. You don't know, perhaps, that I am a man accustomed to getting everything I want, when I want it. You do not know that I have the might of ten armies at my back, the wealth of a nation at my feet, and the heart of a warrior in my body.'

Another step closer and his fingertips lifted to press lightly against her cheek. His eyes held hers, like granite locking her to the window.

'You think I don't know you get what you want?' she returned, pleased when the words came out cool and almost derisive. 'You wanted me that weekend and look how that turned out.'

It was the wrong thing to say. Memories of their sensual, delicious time together punctuated the present, and she was falling into the past. With his body so close, so hard and broad, a random impulse to push onto her tiptoes and find his earlobe with her lips, to wobble it between her teeth before moving to his stubbled jaw and finally those wide, curving lips, made breathing almost impossible.

They were perfect lips, she thought distractedly, her artist's mind working overtime as they studied the sculptured feature.

'You are not seeing anyone else.' It was a statement rather than a question, and his certainty was an insult.

'Why do you say that?' she asked, a little less steadily now.

There was something enigmatic and dangerous in his gaze, something that spoke of promises and need. Something that stilled her heart and warmed her skin. 'You do not react to me like a woman who's in love with another man.'

She sucked in a breath; it didn't reach her lungs. 'What's that supposed to mean?'

His smile was sardonic. 'You look at me with eyes that are hungry for what we shared. You tremble now because I am close to you.' He dropped his fingertips to the pulse point at the base of her neck and she cursed her body's traitorous reaction. 'You do not wish to marry me, Frankie, but you want to be with me again, almost more than you want your next breath.'

Oh, God, it was true, but it was wrong! And there was a difference between animal instincts and intelligent consideration—there was no way she'd be stupid enough to fall prey to his virile, sensual pull. Not again. Only she was already falling, wasn't she? Being drawn into his seductive, tantalising web…

'No,' she denied flatly, moving sideways, proud of herself for putting distance between them, for dismissing him with such apparent ease. If only her knees weren't weak and her nipples weren't throbbing against the lace of her bra. 'And the fact I'm single doesn't mean I'm up for this stupid idea. I'm not marrying you.'

He turned his back on her. His spine was rigid, his shoulders tight in his muscular frame. He paced across the room, reminding her of a prowling animal, some kind of Saharan beast, all lean and strong.

She watched him, her body shivering, her mind struggling to make sense of anything.

'What choice do we have?' He kept his back to her and thrust his hands into his pockets. He was looking out at the city, staring at the view, and his voice had a bleakness to it that reached inside her and filled Frankie with despair.

She followed his gaze; nothing seemed to shine now.

'What choice do I have?' he repeated. 'I have a son. He is a prince, and the fate of my country is on his shoulders. I must bring him home. I owe it… I owe it to my people,' he said firmly. He moved one hand from his pocket to his head, driving his fingers through his dark hair, then turning to face her again. 'And you owe it to Leo, Frankie.' His eyes held hers and there was earnestness and honesty in his expression. 'You want to raise him with me, don't you?'

Her chest tightened because he was right. 'I want to

raise a son who is happy and well-adjusted,' she said finally. 'Who has two parents who love him. That doesn't mean we have to marry…'

'When we were together, back then, you told me of your upbringing,' he said with a soft strength in his voice. 'You told me of weekends spent hiking in the summer and playing board games in the winter, reading around the fire, cooking together. You told me how you'd longed for a sister or brother because you wanted a bigger family—lots of noise and happiness. You told me your family meant everything to you. Would you deprive our son of that?'

She stared at him, aghast and hurting, because, damn him, he was right. Everything he'd repeated was exactly as she felt, as she'd always felt, ever since she'd known the first sting of rejection. Since she'd understood that adoption often went hand in hand with abandonment—for the two parents who had chosen to raise her, there were two who had chosen to lose her, to give her away.

She'd seen everything through a prism of that abandonment, never taking family time for granted, seeing it with gratitude because she had feared her adoptive parents' love, once given, might also be taken away again.

Her eyes swept shut and, instead of speaking, she made a strangled noise, deep in her throat.

His eyes swept over her beautiful face and, seeing her surrender, he pushed home his advantage. 'Marry me because our son deserves that of us. You and I slept together, we made a baby together. From the moment of his conception, this stopped being about you and me, and what we both want. We have an obligation to act in his best interests.'

More sense. More words that she agreed with, and suddenly the pull towards marriage was an inevitable force. She knew she would agree—she had to—but she wasn't ready to show him that just yet.

'It's too much,' she whispered, lifting her eyelids and staring at him with confusion and uncertainty. 'Marrying you, even if you were just a normal man, would be… ridiculous. But you're a king and I'm the last person on earth who wants to be…who's suitable to be… I wouldn't be any good at it.'

'First and foremost, you will be my wife, and the mother to my children. Your duties as Queen will not need to be onerous.' He softened his expression. 'In any event, I think you are underselling yourself.'

But she heard nothing after one simple word. 'Children? As in, plural?'

'Of course. One is not enough.' The words were staccato, like little nails being slammed into her sides. Something deep rumbled in his features, a worry that seemed to arrest him deep inside.

But she shook her head, unable to imagine having more children with this man. 'I don't want more children.'

'You do not like being a mother?' he prompted.

'Of course I do. I love Leo. And if I could lay an egg and have four more children, then I would. But, unfortunately, to give you more precious *heirs* I'd need to…we'd need to…'

'Yes?' he drawled, and she had the distinct impression he was enjoying her discomfort.

'Oh, shut up,' she snapped, lifting her fingertips to her temples and massaging them.

'We are getting married,' he said, and apparently her acquiescence was now a point of fact. 'Do you think the question of sex is one we won't need to address?'

His ability to be so calm in the face of such an intimate conversation infuriated her.

'*If* I were to marry you,' she snapped, resenting his confidence as to her agreement, 'sex wouldn't be a part of our arrangement.'

He laughed. 'Oh, really?'

'Yes, really. And it's not funny! Sex should *mean* something, just like marriage should *mean* something. You're laughing like I'm saying something stupid and I'm not—the way I feel is perfectly normal.'

'You are naïve,' he said with a shake of his head. 'Like the innocent virgin you were three years ago. Sex is a biological function—two bodies enjoying one another: pleasure for pleasure's sake. Marriage is an alliance—a mutually beneficial arrangement. Even those who dress it up as "soulmates" and "love" know it for what it really is, deep down.'

'And what's that?' she demanded.

'Convenience. Companionship. Sex.'

Her cheeks flamed pink. 'How in the hell did you get to be so cynical?' she demanded.

'I am more realist than cynic.' He shrugged insouciantly. 'You will grow up and see things as they really are one day, Frankie.'

'I hope not.'

'Don't be so glum,' he cautioned and, without her realising it, he'd crossed the room and was standing right in front of her. His eyes bored into hers and everything in the room seemed to slow down, to stammer to a stop. She stared up at him, her heart racing, her mouth dry, her eyes roaming his face hungrily. 'You will enjoy certain aspects of being my wife.'

She swallowed in an attempt to bring moisture back to her mouth. 'You're wrong.'

He laughed, a dry sound, and swooped his head down, to claim her mouth with his. 'When it comes to women and sex, Frankie, I'm never wrong.'

Her pulse hammered in her ears and her body went into overdrive, her nerve-endings tingling, her heart throbbing.

She wanted to resist him. God, she wanted to make a point. She wanted to push him away. But with her dying breath, with every fibre of her being, she wanted this more. She lifted her hands, burying them in his shirt, her senses noting everything about him—his warmth, his strength, his masculine fragrance, his closeness, his hardness, his very *him*-ness. Memories of how it had been before flashed through her and she whimpered, low in her throat, when one of his hands moved behind her, cupping her bottom and pulling her forward, pressing her to his arousal until she made a groaning sound, tilting her head back to give him better access to her mouth.

And he dominated her with his kiss, his mouth making a mockery of her objections, his lips showing her how completely he could force her surrender, how quickly he could crumble all her reserves, how quickly he could turn her into trembling putty in his arms.

How little, in that moment, she minded.

He lifted his head, pulling away from her, his breathing roughened by passion, as her own was. 'I have no intention of making your life difficult or unpleasant, Frankie. Through the days, you'll barely know I exist.'

Her pulse was still hammering inside her and her body was weak with desire. When she spoke, the words were faint, breathy. 'And at night?'

'At night,' he promised, lifting his hand and stroking his thumb across her cheek, 'you won't be able to exist without me.'

Matthias stared at his child and inside him it felt as if an anvil were colliding with his ribcage.

The little boy was the spitting image of Spiro, just as the painting had made him appear.

'Hello.' He crouched down so he could look into Leo's face. 'You must be Leo.'

Leo nodded thoughtfully. 'Yes. I am Leo.'

Matthias couldn't smile. He felt only pain, like acid gushing through his veins. How much of this boy's life had he missed? How much was there about him he didn't know?

'We are going to go on an adventure,' he said, standing, glaring at Frankie with all the rage he felt in that moment. The night before, he'd wanted to make love to her until she was incoherent, crying his name at the top of her voice. Now? He felt nothing but rage. Rage at what she'd denied him. Rage at what she'd enjoyed while he'd been none the wiser.

'Come, Leo,' he said, the words carefully muted of harsh inflection even when his eyes conveyed his mood just fine. 'We are going on an adventure together.'

CHAPTER FOUR

HER STOMACH SWOOPED as the plane came in low over the Mediterranean, but Frankie knew it had less to do with the private jet's descent and more to do with the man sitting opposite her. In the incredible luxury of this plane, surrounded by white leather furniture, chandeliers, servants dressed in white and gold uniforms, Matthias still stood out. He was imposing.

Regal.

Grand.

Intimidating.

And he was to be her husband.

Thoughts of their kiss, with her back pressed against a wall literally and metaphorically, flooded her mind and her temperature spiked as remembered pleasures deepened inside her.

The ocean glistened beneath them like a beautiful mirage, dark blue from up here, and dozens of little islands dotted in the middle of it. Each was surrounded by a ring of turquoise water and an edge of crisp white sand.

'That is Tolmirós,' he said conversationally, and it was the first he'd spoken to her all flight. The silence had been deafening, but Frankie had been preoccupied enough wondering just how the hell she'd found herself being spirited away to this man's kingdom—having agreed, at last, to be his wife!

'Which one?'

He eyed her thoughtfully for a moment and her heart rate notched up a gear. 'All of them. Tolmirós is made up of forty-two islands. Some are small, some are large. Like Epikanas,' he said, reaching across and pointing to an island in the distance.

She looked in the direction he was indicating, trying to ignore the fact that he was so close to her now, so close she could breathe in his woody masculine fragrance. When he'd kissed her, it had been as though nothing else mattered. Not the past, not the future—nothing.

'Epikanas,' she repeated.

'Good.' He nodded his approval and the smile that spread across his face warmed her from the inside out. 'You pronounced that perfectly. You will have a language tutor to help you learn how to speak our language.' He sat back in his seat and she told herself she was glad. The plane moved lower, bumping a little as it pushed through some turbulence. 'Epikanas is the main island—my palace is there, my government centre, the main business hub, our largest city. It is where we will live, most of the time.'

She nodded distractedly, turning in her seat to face him, then wishing she hadn't when she found him watching her intently. She skidded her eyes away again, to the seat across the aisle. It had been put into full recline, forming a bed, and Leo was fast asleep, sprawled lengthways.

She watched him sleep and her heart clenched because she knew, risky though this was for her, she was doing the right thing for Leo. If there was any way she could give her son the security of a family, she was going to do it. Her eyes swept shut for a moment as the single memory she possessed of her birth mother filtered to the top of her mind. It was vague. An impression of a faded yellow armchair, sunlight streaming in through a window, curtains blowing in the slight breeze, and the sound of tapping. Her mother had lifted her, hugged her, smelling like lemons and soap.

Then the memory was gone again, like the parents who hadn't wanted her. No matter how hard she tried to catch it, to unpick it and see more of her early childhood, there was nothing.

Determination fired through her spine.

Leo would never feel like she had; he'd never know that sting of rejection. He'd never know the burden of that loss. Unknowingly, she tilted her chin in a gesture of defiance, her eyes glinting with determination. For her son, she would make this work.

'This,' he said, as if following the direction of her thoughts, 'that we are flying over now is Port Kalamathi,' he said. 'The island used to be an important stronghold in our naval operations. Now, it is home to the best school in Tolmirós. It is here that Leo will go, when he is old enough.'

She looked out of her window at the island that was just a swirling mix of green and turquoise. In the centre there were buildings—ancient-looking, with lots of gardens and lawns. She supposed that, so far as schools went, the location was excellent. But wasn't it too far from the palace?

She gnawed on her lower lip and pushed that question aside. Their son was two years old: they could cross that bridge when they came to it. It would be years away. She had more immediate concerns to address.

'What happens next?' she asked, sitting back in her seat, clasping her hands in her lap in a gesture that she hoped made her look calm and confident.

He nodded, apparently relieved she was prepared to discuss things rationally. 'My security has kept the press away from the airport. Usually there are photographers on hand when my plane comes in,' he said.

'But not now?'

'No, not now.' He stared into her eyes and her mouth was drier than the Arizona desert. 'Now, there will be just my drivers and security personnel.'

'Do you have security personnel with you often?'

'Always,' he agreed.

'You didn't that weekend.'

'That weekend, I was still a prince.' His look was one of self-derision. 'I was still a boy, running from my destiny.'

She regarded him thoughtfully. 'You said your uncle was King until you turned thirty?'

'Not King, no.' He shook his head. 'Ancient rules govern the line of succession. My uncle was a *prosorinós*. A sort of caretaker for the throne.'

'What if you'd died too?' she asked, and then heat flushed her face as she realised how insensitive the question sounded.

He didn't seem to mind though. He considered it carefully. 'Then, yes, my uncle would have been King.'

She tilted her head to the side. 'I'm sure I heard once that the legal guardian of an heir couldn't assume that heir's title—lest self-interest lead them to murderous deeds.'

He arched a brow. 'True. And it is the same in Tolmirós. My uncle was not my legal guardian. In fact, I was prevented from seeing him more than once or twice a year during that time.'

She absorbed these words, turning them over in her mind before saying with a small frown, 'But he was your only surviving family? No cousins? Aunt?'

'No. He never married.' His expression shifted.

'And you didn't get to see him?'

He shrugged, as though it barely mattered. 'It is the way it had to be.'

She was inwardly appalled. 'Then who raised you?'

'I was fifteen when my family died,' he said dismissively. 'I had already been "raised".'

'You think you were a grown man at that age?' Her heart hurt for the teenager he'd been.

'I was in school, at Port Kalamathi,' he said, his eyes shifting to the window. 'I went back to school and stayed there until I was eighteen.'

'Boarding school?'

He nodded.

'And then what?' She wished she didn't feel this curiosity, but how could she not wish to understand?

'I joined the military.'

This didn't surprise her. From the first moment she'd seen him, she'd felt he was some kind of real-life warrior. A Trojan, brought back to life.

'And did you enjoy it?'

He paused, apparently analysing that question before answering. 'Yes.'

'Why?'

His smile was tight. 'Tolmirós is a peaceful country. We do not fight wars. Our military training is the best in the world, yet we rarely have cause to require our soldiers.' He shrugged. 'I learned discipline and self-reliance.'

'I can't help thinking these are qualities you already had in spades.'

He shrugged. 'Perhaps.'

There was silence, except for the whirr of the engines as the pilot brought the plane lower and lower, over the dozens of small islands, including the one they were to land on.

'How do you get from one island to the next?' she asked.

'We have a huge ferry network. Look.' He pointed and now she saw dozens of boats moving in the water. 'See the way the islands seem to shimmer?' he asked rhetorically. 'Tolmirós is referred to as the Diamond Kingdom. Each island is like a gem in the midst of the sea.'

She nodded, the magic of that description settling against her chest. The plane dropped lower and lower and it almost felt as though it might land in the ocean. But then land emerged from the depths of the sea and, beyond it, a runway, pale grey, lined with bright red flowers. The plane touched down with a soft thud and instinctively she looked to Leo. He lay where he was, fast asleep, and her heart gave a little tug.

Matthias was watching her; she could feel his gaze and it dragged on her like a tangible force. Slowly, of their own volition, her eyes raised to his.

Her breath locked in her throat; her body was frozen. Her very soul was arrested by the sight of this man she'd lost her head to three years earlier, a man who was so much more than that. He was a king, a ruler of a country, and all that implied.

Hadn't she detected that latent power in him, even when they'd been together back then? Hadn't she known he was someone to whom command came easily?

There was an intensity in his expression, a look of hungry determination, and her pulse raced hard and fast, her heart struggling to keep up with her blood's demands. When he spoke, it was with a contained sense of strength.

'Did you really attempt to find me?'

The question was so quiet she almost didn't hear it, like catching a swirling ribbon on a hazy night.

'It was impossible,' she murmured.

'I intended it to be so.'

The words were sharp in her sides. 'You had an easier job of forgetting me than I did you,' she said simply.

He looked as though he was about to say something, his

expression taut, but then he turned away from her, his eyes roaming towards Leo.

The little boy was waking now, twisting his chubby, robust body against the flat chair, starfishing his legs out so that Frankie smiled unknowingly.

'Mama?' The plane was still moving forward but they'd landed, and Frankie unbuckled her belt and stood, crossing the aisle and undoing his seat belt. He wriggled into a sitting position, from which she plucked him onto her hip. 'Where we?'

'In an aeroplane. Do you remember?' He'd been half asleep when they'd boarded the flight. He still wore his little emoji-themed pyjamas, a gift from her parents at Christmas.

'No.' He shook his head and she smiled softly. 'Who's that?' Leo pointed a finger at Matthias.

'A friend of Mummy's,' she said quickly, earning a swift look of rebuke from Matthias.

'I'm your father, Leo,' he said over the top of her, and now it was Frankie's turn to volley back an expression of outright rage. Her lips compressed and her eyes held a warning.

'Father?' Leo blinked from Frankie to Matthias.

'Your daddy.' The words were said softly but when Matthias looked at Frankie she felt a sharp dagger of judgement. Of anger. She held his gaze, determined to show him she wasn't going to back down from this fight—or any.

'Daddy?' Leo's eyes went huge. 'You say Daddy so kind!' Leo enthused, and Frankie's heart clenched in her chest. She had told Leo that, and many other things. She'd invented a father for Leo that he could be proud of, needing her son to believe a wonderful man had been a part of his creation, even when he couldn't be a part of his life.

'We're going to stay with Daddy for a while,' Frankie

said gently, ignoring the way Matthias's eyes were resting on her with startling intensity. 'Would you like that?'

Leo's lower lip stuck out and he shook his head stubbornly. Frankie dipped her head forward and hid a smile in her son's curls. Let King Matthias, who 'always got what he wanted' suck on that!

'Are you sure?' he asked teasingly, as though he wasn't remotely bothered by Leo's rejection. 'Because I happen to have a swimming pool right outside my bedroom,' he said. 'And you may use it any time.'

'A pool?' Leo tilted his head to one side in a gesture that was so reminiscent of Matthias that Frankie's chest throbbed. 'What a "pool"?'

'What's a pool?' Matthias's gaze lifted to Frankie's, subtle accusation in his eyes. 'How can you not know this? It's like the biggest bath tub you can imagine,' he said, not looking away from Frankie. 'The water is warm and salty, and you can kick and splash to your heart's content.'

'Mummy says no splashing in the bath!' Leo was dubious.

Matthias's eyes held Frankie's for a moment longer and she fought an instinct to defend herself, to defend her parenting, before dropping her gaze to Leo's. She breathed out, not having realised she'd been holding her breath until then. 'In a pool you may splash.'

Leo jumped up and down on Frankie's lap, his excitement at this relaxation in the usual rules apparent.

'Do you know what else?' Matthias leaned forward, smiling in a way that caused Frankie's breath to catch once more. 'We are very near the beach. You can go swimming whenever you like.'

Leo gleefully clapped his little hands together.

'What else do you like to do?'

That was it. Leo began to speak as best he was able, and

Matthias listened and nodded along, even when Frankie was certain he couldn't understand half of what the toddler was offering.

The plane drew to a stop and the cabin crew opened the door—sultry heat immediately blew in, replacing the climate-controlled cool of the aircraft. There was sunshine on the breeze and Frankie sucked it in, deep inside her lungs, pressing her head back against the seat for a moment, letting the air stir through her body, praying it would bring a sense of calm and acceptance to her.

She had no choice but to marry him. She could even see the sense of what he'd suggested. He wasn't just a mere man—a mortal amongst mortals. He was a king, and she'd been foolish enough to sleep with a stranger—she hadn't cared who he was; she hadn't wanted or needed to know anything about him, besides the fact that she'd wanted him with an intensity that had refused to be quelled. And so they'd found themselves in bed—he'd been so experienced and charming that what little instinct she might have had to pause, to wait, had completely evaporated.

She let out a small sigh of impatience. Why bother analysing the past? It had happened, and she couldn't even say with any honesty that she wished it hadn't. Sleeping with Matthias had given her Leo, and not for all the gold in the world would she wish him away.

Nor, if she were completely honest, would she wish she hadn't slept with Matthias. He hadn't deserved her, he sure as heck hadn't deserved her innocence, but he remained, to this day, one of the best experiences of her life.

An experience she wanted to repeat?

For a second she allowed herself to imagine that future, to imagine Matthias making love to her, the nights long with passion, rent with the noise of her pleasure and delirious need, her insides slicked with moist heat.

Foreign voices filled the plane and she looked up to find Matthias watching her, even as Leo chattered to him. Heat burned her cheeks, the direction of her thoughts warming her, and she was sure he knew, and understood; she was sure he was watching her with the same sense of heated arousal.

Frankie forced herself to look past him, to the cabin crew who were making their way into the plane. A woman was at the front and she held a garment bag in her hands. No, several, Frankie noted with disinterest.

Matthias stood and spoke to his servants in his native tongue. Their deference was fascinating to observe. All bowed low and, though they spoke in their own language, she could hear the awe with which they held him.

'This is Marina.' Matthias turned to Frankie, his expression unreadable. 'She's going to help you get ready.'

'Ready for what?'

'Arriving at the palace.'

'But... I am ready.'

He looked at her long and hard, his dark gaze moving from her hair to her face and then to her clothes and, though she was wearing one of her favourite dresses, the way he looked at her made her feel as though she were dressed in a potato sack.

'What?' she asked defiantly, tilting her chin and glaring at him as though his scrutiny hadn't affected her in the slightest degree.

'You are my fiancée,' he reminded her. 'The future Queen of Tolmirós. You will feel more comfortable dressed for that role.'

She bit down on her lip and if they'd been alone she might have had a few choice phrases to utter. Instead, she stood up, keeping Leo pinned to her hip.

'I'm sorry if I don't meet your high standards, Your Majesty,' she said jerkily, panic rising inside her at the enormity of what she was going to do.

'My standards are beside the point,' he said quietly, with all the reasonableness she had failed to muster. 'This is about what will be expected of you. And Leo.' As though their child was an afterthought, he gestured to an old woman in the huddle of staff.

Her smile was kind, her face lined in a way Frankie found instantly appealing. She looked like a woman who laughed a lot.

'This is Liana,' Matthias said, his expression unchanging as he nodded at the older woman. Emotion stirred in Liana's green eyes though, feelings Frankie couldn't begin to comprehend. The older woman's smile dropped—just for a fraction of a second. Then her attention homed in on Leo and it was as though a firework had been set off beneath her.

'Liana was my nanny, as a boy,' Matthias explained, watching as Liana moved between them and began making clacking noises at Leo. He grinned in response and then clapped his hands together. Liana did likewise and laughed, rocking back on her heels so her slender frame arched.

'May I?' she asked, a cackled question, presumably directed at Frankie, though Liana didn't take her eyes off Leo.

'I...' Frankie didn't want to hand Leo over, though. On some instinctive level, she ached to hold him close, to keep him near her.

She stared at Matthias and perhaps a hint of her panic showed itself in her eyes because his expression tightened and a pulse jerked at the base of his jaw. 'Liana will help Leo change into more suitable clothes,' Matthias reassured her, everything about him kind, as if he were trying to calm a horse on the brink of bolting. 'While you are doing likewise.'

It was a simple suggestion, and one that made sense, but the more he made sense, the more Frankie wanted to rebel.

'I really don't see the point in changing,' she said. 'You told me there wouldn't be any photographers...'

'True—' he shrugged '—but there will be staff. Hundreds of them, all looking to see the woman who will become their Queen. Would you not feel happier wearing clothes made for a princess?'

'I'm fine,' she said curtly, dismissively. Then, for Liana's benefit, 'I'd rather stay with Leo.'

He looked as if he wanted to argue with her, as if he wanted to insist. His eyes locked onto hers, he watched her thoughtfully and then he shrugged. 'It is your decision, of course.'

As soon as they arrived at the palace, she wished she hadn't been so stubborn and short-sighted. She was wearing a nice enough dress—but it was nothing compared to the grandeur of this place.

From the outside, it looked ancient. A huge, imposing castle, with the city on one side and the ocean on the other. It formed a square, and his limousine had driven under a large archway and into a central courtyard. The walls ran on all sides and when the car stopped there was a vibrant blue carpet rolled out, leading to glass double doors that had been thrown open. Servants stood on either side. The men were in suits and the women wore dresses. Most also wore white gloves to their elbows. Many had white aprons around their waists.

All looked somehow more formally attired than Frankie. Even little Leo was a resplendent king-in-waiting. A pair of grey shorts had been teamed with knee-high blue socks, shiny black shoes and a crisp white shirt with short sleeves and round buttons that glowed like pearls. His unruly hair had been combed and tamed, parted on one side, and was sitting neatly on his head with the exception of one disobedient curl that flopped into the middle of his forehead.

The three of them sat in the back of the car—a family, yet not. Matthias regarded her carefully. When he'd held his body above hers and entered her and, upon discovering for himself that she was a virgin, he'd looked into her eyes and murmured words in his language that had taken away any pain and replaced it instead with pleasure and need, so that she'd called his name over and over, an incantation, as surely as if she were a witch.

He looked at her with the desire that had rushed his bloodstream anew two nights earlier—desire that had made him want to shelve any conversation of marriage, bloodlines and their future and simply give in to his hunger for this woman. An insatiable hunger, he suspected, even when he had every intention of spending quite some time trying to satiate it.

'Well, Frankie.' He rolled her name around his mouth, tasting it, imagining kissing it against her throat, the sensitive flesh of her décolletage, down to breasts that he longed to lavish with attention. He was hard for her, ready for her already, hungry for her always. He cleared his throat, focusing on her face, forcing himself to be patient. 'Are you ready?'

Her smile lacked warmth. 'If I say "no", will it make a difference?'

His lips twisted in a grimace of sorts and he understood then what he'd failed to see on the plane. She was nervous. She was fighting with him because she was about to step off a cliff, and she had no idea what would catch her. He leaned forward so that his face was close to hers and saw the way her breath hitched in her throat, saw the way she looked at him with a quick flash of desire that she fought to cover with a tightening of her features.

'We have to do this,' he said, wishing in that moment that it wasn't the case. That Frankie didn't have to endure a marriage she clearly hated the idea of. Wishing she was free to live her life. Wishing she was free to marry a man who loved her, just as she'd insisted marriage should be.

'Then why ask the question?' Her words were snapped out but he understood now, and he frowned, wanting to relieve her tension and knowing only one way to do so.

Leo looked from one to the other and Frankie dredged up a smile for his benefit but it was weak, watery.

'Okay?' Leo asked, his little hand curving on top of Frankie's. Matthias watched the gesture with a heart that was strangely heavy.

'Fine,' she said, her smile for their child's benefit.

The door was pulled open and Matthias sat for another beat of time, looking at the woman who would be his wife, and his child. She was nervous, but there was nothing for it. They had to do this. 'Let's go then.'

Three simple words but oh, how much they meant! Because it wasn't as simple as stepping out of a car—this was like crossing an invisible border, one which she could never cross back. When she stepped out of the car, she'd cease to be a private individual. She would no longer be an up-and-coming artist on the New York scene. She'd be a royal fiancée, Matthias's bride, the up-and-coming Queen, the mother of the royal heir. She would belong to this life, to Matthias, and so would Leo.

There was nothing for it though. He'd described himself as a realist, and Frankie had a degree of realism deep in her as well. Or perhaps it was better described as fatalism, she thought, watching as Matthias stepped from the car. His staff stood still, none looking at him. He reached into the car, his arms extended, and she understood what he wanted.

Leo.

Her mouth was dry, her throat parched, her pulse racing. There was no sense in refusing him—it would be easier for her to step out of the car if she weren't holding a heavy toddler in her arms. Besides, with Matthias holding their baby, no one would be looking at her, would they?

'Go with Matthias—Daddy,' she said stiffly, kissing Leo's curls before passing him towards the door. Matthias's hands curved around Leo's midsection and then Frankie shuffled closer. Curious glances slid sideways. The servants were, perhaps, not supposed to look, and yet how could they resist?

This was their future King, arriving home as a two-year-old boy. Curiosity was only natural.

'Mama?'

'I'm coming. I'm right behind you,' she promised. And she was—she had to be. There was no way on earth Matthias would ever let Leo go. She could see that as clearly as she could the brilliant blue of the sky overhead. If she wanted to be a part of her son's life, she had to accept Matthias as a part of hers.

With nerves that were jangling in her body, schooling her features into a mask of what she hoped would pass as calm, she stepped from the vehicle.

Eyes that had been resolutely focused ahead all turned now, and it was like being in the glare of a thousand spotlights. Everyone looked at her, everyone saw her, and she knew what they must be thinking.

Why her?

With a sinking heart and regret that she'd refused to allow herself to be restyled as some sort of queen-in-waiting, she brazened it out. Shoulders squared, smile on her face, as though this was a happy day for her. As though she wasn't absolutely terrified.

His arm around her waist caught her off guard and for a second—a brief second—her smile dropped. Her gaze flew to his face and she saw a warning there. A warning, and a look of triumph. 'Welcome home, *deliciae.*'

Home.

She had only a second to process the word. A second to wonder what the lovely-sounding *deliciae* might mean. And then his head dropped and his lips pressed to hers, and she was dropping out of that present moment and crashing into the past, when she had—briefly—lived for this exact feeling. When his kisses alone had been her reason for breathing.

It was too much—her nerves were already stretched to breaking point and his kiss was a torture and a relief, an agony and an ecstasy.

Her body, of its own accord, swayed towards him as though drunk, demanding more contact, more closeness, more everything. It was a brief kiss—chaste in comparison to how they had kissed in the past, and yet it was enough. *More* than enough to rekindle everything. Flames that she had hoped extinguished flared to life and she had no idea how to put them out again this time.

Damn him all to heck.

He lifted his head, his eyes mocking when they met hers. Embarrassment warmed her cheeks.

'Why did you do that?' she demanded, lifting shaking fingertips to her lips, feeling the strength of his passion even now, seconds after he'd ended it.

His laugh was soft and sent electric shocks down her spine.

'Because you were nervous,' he said quietly. 'And I could think of only one way to calm you down.'

Her stomach swooped with his insightfulness, but the ease with which he could turn her blood to lava spiked her pride. With a hint of insurgency, she murmured quietly, so only he could hear, 'And what if I don't want you to kiss me?'

He laughed softly.

'Why is that funny?'

'You shouldn't issue challenges you don't wish to lose.'

'What does that even mean?'

'It means—' he leaned forward once more, his intent obvious, and yet she still didn't step back, even when she had ample opportunity to put some space between them '—I'm going to enjoy making you eat those words.' And he crushed his mouth to hers once again, his kiss a possession and a promise. A promise she knew she should fight and somehow, frustratingly, wasn't sure she wanted to…

CHAPTER FIVE

'AND THIS IS the private residence, madam.' A middle-aged man dipped his head deferentially, allowing Frankie to walk past. Her mind was already spinning, and she'd only been in the palace an hour. Exhaustion had begun to sink into her skin, making thought and attention almost impossible. Where Leo had slept on the plane, she hadn't—not a jot— and she couldn't even do the maths in that moment to work out what time it was in New York.

Late, though. Or early in the morning. No wonder she felt so wrecked.

The Private Residence was, in fact, more like a penthouse apartment. Where the rest of the palace was steeped in a sense of ancient tradition, with historic balustrades, paintings, old tapestries and glorious wallpaper giving it a sense of living history, this apartment felt completely modern.

'It was redecorated at the turn of the century,' the servant said. 'All of the wiring was renewed in this suite.' He moved deeper into the apartment. 'Would you like a tour, madam?'

'Oh, no, thank you.' What Frankie wanted more than anything was a strong coffee and to be left alone. To soften her refusal, she smiled. 'I'll find my way around just fine, I'm sure.'

'Certainly. There has not been time to properly complete Master Leo's rooms, but a start has been made,' the servant offered, gesturing down the hallway. Frankie moved in that direction as if being pulled by magic, her trained artist's eye making note of small details as she went. Here the walls were crisp white, but not perfect white—there was a warmth to them, almost as though they'd been mixed with gold or pearl. Flower arrangements were modern and fragrant, pictures were simple black and white, portraits and photographs. Artistic and interesting.

Undoubtedly the work of some palace designer or other, she thought with a twist of her lips.

'The blue door, madam,' the servant offered.

With a frown, Frankie curved her fingers around the brass door knob and turned it, pushing the door inwards. The room opened up before her and her heart sank.

How could she have contemplated turning Matthias down for even a moment? This room was every little boy's fantasy, she thought, stepping inside and turning a full circle. Leo followed behind her and he was as struck dumb at the scene as she was.

'Mine?'

Frankie couldn't form a response. She looked at him then back to the room, doubt and certainty warring inside her. 'Yes,' she acknowledged finally, moving to the small bed. Like something out of a movie, it was a pale cream, glossy, with sumptuous blue bedding, big European pillows—almost the size of Leo—and toy-soldier cushions, as if brought to life from *The Nutcracker*. A bay window overlooked a beautiful garden—'The chef's *potager*,' the servant advised with more than a touch of pride in his tone.

Though the room was filled with toys and books, they were all good quality: wooden, old-fashioned, simple. Frankie surveyed them, begrudgingly approving of their selection, their appropriateness for Leo's age and stage indisputable.

'Mine?' he asked again, lifting a set of blocks off the shelf.

'Yes,' she agreed once more.

'There you are.'

The heavily accented voice had Frankie turning and when she saw Liana smiling as she approached, it was natural for Frankie to return the gesture. She liked this woman, though she knew so little about her. There was a warmth and openness that Frankie needed—an ally in the midst of all that was new and frightening. Not to mention the fact she'd kicked off her shoes at some stage and now wore bright pink socks beneath sensible trousers—high recommendation indeed.

''Ello, Frankie.' Liana nodded, and Frankie liked her even more for using her name rather than any silly title or 'madam'. 'You like his room?'

'Oh, yes, it's perfect,' she said. 'I don't know how but someone's managed to fill it with all of the things Leo would have chosen himself, if given half a chance.'

'Ah, it is not so long since Matthias and Spiro were boys. I remember.' She tapped a knobbly finger to the side of her head and nodded sagely.

Frankie's curiosity was stirred to life. 'Spiro?'

Liana's eyes narrowed but she didn't answer. 'You go, you go,' she said. 'I get to know.' She pointed to Leo and when he looked at her she clapped her hands together and held them out to him.

To Frankie's surprise, rather than ignoring Liana and staying with the shelves of new toys and distractions, Leo pushed to his sturdy little legs and padded over to Liana. He smiled up at the older woman, dimples dug deep in both cheeks.

'He likes you,' Frankie said, the words punctuated with the heaviness of her heart.

'And I like him.' She grinned. 'We are going to be great friends, little master Leo. No?'

'Yeah.' He nodded enthusiastically.

Liana turned back to Frankie. 'You go, relax. I keep him happy.'

Frankie was torn between a desire never to let Leo out of her sight again and a need to be alone, to have a bath, to get to grips with all that had happened. In the end, it was seeing Liana and Leo playing happily together, walking around the room and exploring it, holding hands, that made Frankie's decision for her. She turned to leave, but at the door spun back.

'Liana?' The nanny looked up, her face patient. 'Thank you. For this.' She nodded towards Leo. 'And for this,' and she gestured around the room.

'It is my pleasure,' Liana promised after a beat of silence had passed. 'It is good to have a child in the palace again, *vasillisa*.'

The servant who'd brought her to the apartment had left, so Frankie was free to explore on her own. She did so quickly, perfunctorily, looking upon the rooms as she might appraise a new subject she was painting. It helped her not to focus on the disparity in her own private situation and this degree of wealth and privilege if she saw it as an outsider rather than as one who'd been suddenly and unceremoniously sucked into these lofty ranks.

There was the small anteroom, into which they'd entered. The corridor that came this way branched off into Leo's bedroom, and another room beside it, with sofas, a small dining table and glass doors that led to a small balcony. A children's sitting room, she surmised, the décor clearly childlike yet lovely.

Another door showed a lovely bathroom—white tiles, deep tub, a separate shower and two toilets: one regular size and one lower to the ground. The last door revealed a separate bedroom and at first she thought it would be just perfect for her—and to hell with whatever form Matthias thought their marriage would take! But a longer look showed Liana's shoes tucked neatly under the bed and her jacket hung on a hook near the door.

So this was to be the nanny's accommodation?

At least that meant they wouldn't be alone in this residence! Feeling ridiculously smug, given Matthias had no doubt approved the arrangements himself, Frankie moved down the corridor and into another sitting room, this one incredibly grand. Burgundy and gold damask sofas and armchairs formed a set for six, with a marble coffee table between them, and the dining table could easily accommodate ten. It was walnut, polished, imposing, and dark. There was a bar in the corner, beside heavy oak bookshelves, and glass doors led to yet another balcony.

She moved through the room quickly, feeling out of place, like an interloper. It was impossible to imagine she'd ever feel 'at home' here.

The next room offered some improvement. A study, with modern computers, paperback books and an armchair that at least looked as if it had been made this century.

The following room was another improvement! A kitchen and an adjoining sitting room, this was far more homely, despite the large glass doors that showed an exquisite pool beyond. She imagined Matthias swimming in it, his body on display as he powerfully pulled through the water, and her throat was dry.

She swallowed, trying to push away the image, and moved into the kitchen. She almost cheered when she saw a familiar coffee machine. She searched drawers and doors until she located coffee grinds, loaded them into the basket and pressed the button. The aroma filled the room at once and she stood very still, allowing the fragrance to permeate her soul, to reassure her and relax her as only coffee could.

The pretty cup filled, she wrapped both palms around it and continued her tour. Early afternoon sunlight filtered in through the windows as she moved to the next room, and the light was so dazzling, so perfectly a mix of milk and Naples Yellow, translucent and fragile. She stood in the light for a moment, her eyes sweeping shut, before a jolt of recognition had her opening them anew.

The bed was enormous, and it sat right in the middle of the far wall. Where the wall itself was white, the bed-linen was steel-grey, with fluffy pillows and bedside tables that were devoid of anything personal. No photographs, no books, not even a newspaper.

Her heart in her throat, she moved around the bed, giving it a wide berth, heading for another door. Hoping it might lead to a bedroom, she pushed the door inwards and saw only a bathroom—this one more palatial than Leo's, with an enormous spa pressed against windows that seemed to overlook a fruit grove. No doubt if her friendly servant was nearby, he'd be able to tell her what fruit was growing there—she couldn't see from a distance.

The shower was one of those large walk-in scenarios, with two shower heads overhead and several on the walls. The controls looked like something out of a spaceship.

She backed out of the bathroom as though she'd been stung, slamming her shoulder on the way and wincing from the pain. The last remaining door showed a wardrobe—as big as her bedroom back in Queens, but only half-filled. Suits, dozens of them, all undoubtedly hand-stitched to measure, hung neatly, arranged one by one. Then shirts, crisply ironed, many still with tags attached. There were casual clothes too, and they made her stomach clench because she could imagine Matthias as he'd been *then*. Before. In New York, when he'd been simply Matt.

She sighed, propping her hips against the piece of furniture in the middle of the room. What even was it? Square-shaped, with drawer upon drawer. She pressed one out of curiosity and it sprung open. Watches! At least ten, and all very expensive-looking. She shook her head in disbelief and pushed it closed once more.

The hint of a smile danced on her lips as she imagined for a moment the ludicrousness of her clothing in this imposing space, the look of her costume jewellery next to his couture, and a laugh at that absurdity bubbled from deep inside. And if she'd been about to wonder how the heck she was even going to get her clothes, the answer presented itself in the form of a rather stylish-looking woman who introduced herself as Mathilde.

'I take your measurements,' she said, her accent French. 'And organise your wardrobe.'

'My wardrobe?'

'You will need things very quickly, but this is not your worry. I know people.'

Frankie thought longingly of the coffee she'd placed down in the immaculate bedroom next door, and the quiet time she'd been fantasising about disappeared. For, not long after Mathilde's arrival, came Angelique and Sienna, hairdresser and beautician, who set up a beauty salon in the palatial bathroom. One worked on taming Frankie's 'mom' hair, removing all traces of playdough and neglect while still managing to keep the length and natural blonde colour in place. The other waxed Frankie's brows and did her nails—fingers and toes—both tasks Frankie had neglected for far too long.

'I'm an artist,' she found herself explaining apologetically as Sienna tried her hardest to buff a splash of oil paint from Frankie's big toe nail. 'And I like to paint barefoot,' she added for good measure.

Sienna's smile was dubious and Frankie understood. How could she ever live up to this country's expectations of its Queen?

It took hours but when Frankie was at last alone once more she had to admit that the three women had worked some kind of miracle. She stared at herself in the reflection, unable to believe how…regal…she looked. Still dressed in the same clothes as New York, it no longer mattered. Her hair sat like a blonde cloud around her shoulders and she glistened all over.

Exhaustion was a tidal wave coming towards her. She showered in an attempt to stave it off and was just in the process of pulling the same dress back in place when there was a knock at the bathroom door. With a little gasp, she grabbed the dress and simply held it across her front.

'Don't come in!' she cautioned, her heart already racing into overdrive at the very idea that Matthias might stride in and pull her naked, shower-wet body into his arms.

'Of course not, madam.' Mathilde's soft accent came through with a hint of indignation. 'Only I tell you there are some things in your wardrobe now. Not a lot, but enough to start.'

'Oh.' Disappointment fired inside her; how she resented it! 'Thank you.'

'You're welcome, madam.'

Frankie reached for one of the sumptuous robes and wrapped it around herself, luxuriating for a moment in its glamorous softness before moving out of the bathroom. This side of the apartment was empty but still she moved quickly, lest another interruption came to pass and she gave into temptation, pressing her body to Matthias's and begging him to… She pushed the thought out of her mind determinedly, slipping into the wardrobe.

One side was filled with his clothes. She cast a guilty look towards the door before moving to his clothes and running her hand over them, feeling their fabric, imagining them on his body, remembering the warmth and strength of his physique. A deep need opened up inside her gut—she feared there was only one solution.

When she emerged a few moments later, Matthias was in the kitchen, the living invocation of her fantasies. Awareness jerked inside her, desire heavy, the pulse between her legs running riot at the sight of him like this. It was strange, but it was the first moment it truly hit Frankie that this was *their* home. That they would live here, side by side. For how long?

Her pulse ratcheted up a notch.

'You've toured the residence?' he prompted, lifting his head and pinning her with those intelligent grey eyes of his.

'Yeah.' It was croaky and faint; she cleared her throat. 'Yes.' Balling up her courage, she walked towards him, pleased with herself for at least remembering how to walk calmly. 'There only seems to be one bedroom spare,' she murmured.

He looked at her, a smile playing about his lips. 'Was that a question?'

Damn him! 'You can't expect me to…'

'Share your husband's bedroom?'

She fidgeted with her fingers, and then stopped when she realised what a betraying gesture it was. 'Yes.' She forced her eyes to hold his.

'Are we back to pretending you don't feel the same desire I do?'

She opened her mouth and closed it again. How could

she deny her desire, after the kiss they'd shared earlier? Surely he'd tasted her response, felt her need.

'No,' she said softly, her eyes locked onto his with a defiance that gave her some kind of courage. 'But feeling something and acting on it are two different concepts.'

His eyes flared, perhaps showing his surprise at her admission. 'So they are.' He leaned a little closer and her stomach swirled. 'You do not need to worry, Frankie. When we sleep together it will be because you beg me to make love to you, not because I cannot control myself while we happen to be sharing a mattress. *Bene?*'

'I…'

'It is just a bed,' he said, making her feel naïve and childish. 'And I am away often.'

'I…'

He lifted a finger, placing it softly against her lips. 'If you do not adjust to me in your life, then I will have a new room made for you,' he said, and though the offer should have pleased her, it didn't. If she'd felt childish before, she felt babyish now—and like a complainer too. 'Just try it my way.'

It was so reasonable. So measured. 'I just presumed we'd have separate rooms,' she explained, forcing a smile to her lips.

He nodded once, his eyes latched to hers. 'Gossip spreads like wildfire. I don't need servants talking about our marriage before there's even been a marriage. Nor do I want it splashed over the tabloids that my convenient wife and heir are all for show.'

'But we are,' she said with a tilt of her head, relieved to say the words, to remind herself as much as anything.

'He is my heir,' Matthias murmured. 'And you will be my wife. There is nothing dishonest in that.'

She bit back whatever she'd been about to say, nodding

instead. He was right. She'd agreed to this, and she'd known what his terms were. There was no sense demeaning herself by arguing over such a trivial point.

'You'll meet your valet tomorrow,' he said, changing the subject. 'She'll help you with anything you require.'

'Valet?'

'Your point-of-contact servant. The head of your house.'

'I… I don't need that.'

He sent her a look of sardonic amusement. 'You will receive over a thousand invitations every year to social events. Then there's the dozens and dozens of requests for you to serve as a spokesperson for charities, to fundraise on their behalf and raise their profile. Each of these will require a response, and it will be impossible for you—on your own—to know which are worthy of your consideration and which are not.'

Frankie was struck dumb momentarily. 'But why would so many people want…? I mean…'

'You will be Queen—and people will presume you have the ear of the King. There is power in your position, and it is natural that many will want to use that to their advantage.'

'But I won't have the ear of the King,' she said, shaking her head and walking towards the enormous windows that looked over the mysterious fruit grove.

'Nobody will be aware of that. To the outside, our marriage will appear to be a love match—it's natural people will presume I listen to your counsel.'

Bitterness twisted inside her, and loss too—a deep and profound sense of grief at the picture he'd so easily painted. The kind of marriage she'd always dreamed she might one day be a part of. The true sense of belonging she'd sought all her life. The thoughts were dark, depressing. She stamped them out, focusing on the business at hand. 'And my valet will manage all that for me?'

'Your secretary will.'

She frowned, not taking her eyes off the trees below. 'We were talking about a valet.'

'I said the valet is the head of your house. There will be around ten members of staff—not including your security detail—who report to your valet.'

At that she turned to face him, but wished she hadn't. The sight of him, one hip propped against the kitchen counter, watching her thoughtfully, jolted her heart painfully, as though she'd been shocked with electricity. 'Matt—' she used the diminutive form of his name without thinking '—I don't want this.'

His eyes narrowed thoughtfully. 'Why not?'

'It's just strange. I can't see that I'll need that many people working for me.'

'You wish to fire someone then?'

She opened her mouth to say something and then slammed it shut; he had her jammed into a tight corner there and undoubtedly knew it. She shook her head. 'No, I just…'

'Relax, Frankie. You will adapt to all this, I promise.'

'That's easy for you to say. You grew up with this; it's normal for you.'

He shrugged. 'And it will become normal for you.' He stood up straighter and walked towards her, opening the large glass doors. Warmth billowed in from the sunny afternoon beyond. He gestured for her to precede him onto the balcony and, curious, she did. The terracotta tiles were warm beneath her feet. Out here, the fruit trees had a delightful fragrance. She breathed in deeply, letting the smell roll all the way down to her toes.

She was in a foreign country with a man she hadn't seen

in years, a man she'd slept with and then lost all contact with, a man who had fathered her son, and yet, ridiculously, standing beneath that milky sun with the citrusy fragrance like a cloud around her, the colours all green and blue with splashes of bold red where geraniums were growing, she felt completely and utterly at ease.

'My valet will coordinate with yours with regard to the wedding plans. The date has been set for two weeks' time.'

The sense of relaxation evaporated. 'Two weeks?' She jerked her head towards his. He was watching her, those eyes imprinted on her brain like ghosts.

He appeared to misunderstand her. 'This is the soonest it can be. No sooner,' he explained. 'It is necessary to give people time to travel—foreign dignitaries, royals, diplomats.'

'But…what's the rush?'

His lips were a tight line in his face. 'I have a two-year-old who, at this moment, is illegitimate and has no claim on my throne. If I were to die tomorrow, the country would not have an heir. Yet here he is, a living, breathing child of mine—you cannot see that there is a rush to marry and legally make him mine?'

Frankie bit down on her lower lip, nodding even as she tried to make sense of that. 'But you're his father—there's no doubt of that. Surely you could adopt him or—'

'Adopt *my own son*?' There was a look of cold rejection on his face, as though adopting Leo would be the worst thing in the world.

Frankie's stomach swooped and for a moment the wounds of her childhood were flayed open. 'I only meant there must be another way to legally empower him as your heir,' she said, so softly the words were almost swallowed on the breeze.

'If there was, do you think I would have been so insistent on marrying you?'

* * *

He'd gone too far. He could see it in the way all the colour had drained from her face. No, from her whole body! She was as white as the sand of Makalini Beach, her eyes green and awash with hurt.

Damn it!

But he was in shock, still trying to make sense of this, trying to see the best way forward for both of them. The last thing he wanted was to argue with Frankie. None of this was her fault, and he admired her courage and strength in taking her place beside him.

He exhaled softly, turning the words over in his heart before speaking them to her. 'I hate knowing that he was out there for two and a half years and I knew nothing of him.'

She made a strangled noise; he took it to be one of understanding.

'The laws of succession are archaic and unchangeable. Even the fact he is born out of wedlock will require a DNA test to satisfy my country's parliament. They must ratify his legitimacy and—'

'Wait—just a second,' she interrupted urgently. 'You're actually going to get our child paternity tested?'

He turned to her, confused now by the anger that had surged into her face. Relieved too, as it made her cheeks glow pink once more. 'It is necessary,' he said.

'No way.'

Her refusal intrigued him and alarmed him in equal measure. 'Why not?' He bit the words out from teeth that were suddenly clenched tight. Was it possible she'd lied about Leo's paternity?

But why would she?

'Because he's your son! He can't be anyone else's, unless it was an immaculate conception,' she said with quiet insistence. 'And because I don't want him to think he had to have a blood test to prove to his own father what's blatantly obvious when you look at the two of you together.'

He relaxed once more—because, of course, she was right. Leo was a carbon copy of not only himself, but of Spiro too. As quickly as his brain absorbed that fact, it moved onto another she'd revealed. 'You're saying you haven't slept with anyone since me?'

'I...' She swept her eyes shut and shook her head. When she looked at him again a moment later she was calm—cool and somehow dismissive. She was excellent at doing that—at submerging whatever she was feeling beneath a mask of unconcern. He'd seen her do it numerous times and on each occasion he felt overwhelmed by a desire to work out exactly how he could shake that mask loose. He knew one way, of course. One very tempting, very distracting way...

'I'm saying you're the only person who could be his father.'

'Is that not the same thing?'

'No.'

His gut clenched and a dark sensation speared through him. It wasn't jealousy exactly—it was...possession. Primal, ancient, animalistic possession. He didn't want to think of her sleeping with any other man—ever.

'Have there been other men?' he asked, the question direct, and he had the satisfaction of seeing her mask slip for a second.

'Why do you care?'

'Because I like thinking I'm the only man who's known the pleasure of your body,' he said simply, unapologetically.

Heat stained her cheeks and he could resist no longer. He moved to where she stood on the balcony, bracing a hand on either side of her. 'That's kind of chauvinistic.'

His lips twisted in a smile. 'Yes.'

And then, to his surprise, she smiled, a genuine smile

that made the corners of her eyes crinkle and it felt as if the sun was forcing its way into his chest. He stared at her, his own face unknowingly tense, rigid, frozen by the radiance of her expression. 'At least you admit it.'

He continued to stare, drinking in her beauty, but the smile dropped almost immediately and an air of seriousness surrounded them.

'You told him about me?'

She swallowed, her eyes half-closed, shielding herself from him. 'Yes.'

'You told him I was kind?' he prompted, remembering the remark their son had made on the flight over.

She was defensive. 'I wanted him to believe his father was a good man. I wanted him to be proud of you.'

Matthias's breathing was shallow. 'Why?'

She toyed with her fingers in front of her, weaving them together. 'One day, he'll be old enough to ask about you. I didn't want him to fill in the gaps in the meantime. I didn't want him to think...'

Her words trailed into nothingness.

'Go on,' he urged desperately.

'I didn't want him to think he wasn't wanted.' She cleared her throat. 'I told him you were good and kind and funny but that you live far away from us, but that...'

'Yes?' The word was quick to escape from him, an impatient hiss.

'That you think of us often. That you look into the stars and think about the stars above us.' There was defiance in her tone now. 'It's for him, not you.'

His chest felt heavy. She'd created a myth for their son, a myth of him as a good, kind, decent man—she'd done the opposite of what he might have imagined a woman in her shoes doing: she'd praised him and spoken of him in a way that would make their son want to know his father.

It was impossible not to look at her with growing respect, with appreciation. He wasn't sure he'd deserved any of that.

'I don't want him to have a paternity test,' she said quietly, but with a strength that called to him. 'I don't want him to think…'

'To think what, Frankie?' he pushed when her words trailed off into the air.

'To think he wasn't wanted.' She lifted her gaze to his and there was a haunted quality to her expression, a hurt he couldn't comprehend. 'I don't want him to think he had to have a blood test before you'd let him into your life.'

He expelled a breath, his nostrils flaring as he instinctively rejected her take on the situation. 'It is merely a formality.'

'It's unnecessary.' Again, he felt her tender insistence deep in his gut and a protective instinct surged inside him—though what he was wanting to protect her from, he couldn't have said.

'He's your son,' she continued quietly, lifting one hand to his chest and pressing it just above his heart.

And emotions flooded him—paternal pride, completeness, rightness—relief that it was this woman who'd borne him a son and heir. His words were thick with all his feelings when he dredged them from deep within his soul. 'And soon the whole world will know it.'

CHAPTER SIX

MATTHIAS COULDN'T REMEMBER when he'd last slept for longer than an hour or two. He was bone-weary, exhausted to the depths of his soul, but the sight of Frankie fast asleep in his bed arrested him and energised him all at once and he found his feet reluctant to move.

The way she'd smiled at him earlier that day had stayed with him all afternoon, replaying in his mind, so that he had rushed through his commitments, hoping to see her again, to see if he could make her smile once more. Not that he could say what he'd done to change her mood—it wasn't like in New York, three years earlier, when they'd both smiled often and freely.

He'd wanted to see her again, but events had conspired to keep him from dining with her—a problem at the embassy in Rome—and so now she was fast asleep.

Her long blonde hair was drawn around her shoulder like a skein of gold and her breathing was slow and rhythmic. Her lips, parted and pink, were so perfect, and he remembered instantly how they'd felt when she'd kissed him in New York, years earlier.

Tentatively at first, and then with the madness that had overtaken them. He remembered how she'd felt in his arms downstairs earlier today, when he'd taken her by surprise and kissed her, and he remembered the moment when she'd become pliant in his arms. He could identify the exact moment when she'd lost a part of herself to this madness. He'd known he could have deepened the kiss, that he could have taunted her with their desire and turned her into a jumble of nerves and responses in his arms, but he hadn't.

He'd stemmed his own needs, respecting her boundaries, knowing deep down how overwhelmed she must be. Not just by his position as King, and her son's place in the country's order of succession, not even by her future as Queen. But by this, them, whatever they felt. He was a man of far greater experience, of greater years, and yet he still found their chemistry explosive and somehow awe-inspiring.

Even as he stood by the bed, watching her gentle exhalations, desire flooded his system and he wondered how she'd respond if he reached for her. If he strode to the bed, put a hand on her shoulder and stirred her to wakefulness, if he pressed his lips to the soft flesh at the base of her throat that had always driven her wild…

And as though his thoughts had pushed into hers, she moved in her sleep, her eyes blinking open and landing straight on him. Breath that had been slow suddenly stopped altogether as she stared at him.

It was just after midnight, and magic was thick in the air—magic with the power to bring the past into the present.

'Matt?' She blinked, frowning, pushing up so that the sheet dropped to reveal the soft swell of her cleavage. There was nothing sexy about the singlet she was wearing or at least it shouldn't have been. But somehow it was, and he was groaning with side-splitting need.

He swallowed—hard—and he was hard all over, his body wound tighter than a spring.

'I was… You were just…' In the soft milky moonlight he saw her cheeks flush pink and he took a step deeper into the room despite every bone in his body telling him it was wrong.

'Yes?' The word came out thick and gravelled. He cleared his throat, watching her intently.

'I thought I was dreaming.'

His body fired. Desires he'd already been battling surged inside him. 'Was it a good dream?' he asked, taking the rest of the steps necessary to bring him level with the bed. His own side yawned empty and cold. Duty and responsibility were on his side of the bed, but temptation lay here, and he was oh, so tempted.

'I...' She frowned and lifted a hand to the strap of her top. His eyes followed the action and at the sight of the outline of her nipples, straining hard against the fabric of her shirt, he suppressed a groan.

There was the right thing to do, and there was what they both wanted and needed.

Ignoring common sense, he caught her hand on her shoulder, holding it low, and then, his eyes locked onto hers, loaded with challenge, he oh-so-slowly traced his fingertips over her flesh, easing the strap lower, not higher. Her skin lifted with fine goosebumps and her breath stalled in her throat. Her eyes were pleading and he watched her, challenge in every line of his face.

'What did you dream?' he asked, his other hand reaching for the strap that still sat on her shoulder. He didn't push it downwards though. He simply looped his fingers beneath it, his eyes on her face, waiting, still, frozen in time, impatient to know what she was going to say.

'I dreamed... I was... It was years ago,' she said huskily, her beautiful face clouded with uncertainty.

'And do you dream of me often?'

Her slender throat moved visibly as she swallowed and her eyes swept shut, perhaps in an attempt to block him from seeing her thoughts in that expressive face of hers. 'No,' she whispered.

'Liar.' His laugh was without humour. 'I think you dream of me frequently. Perhaps every night, even.'

At her harsh intake of breath he bent lower and, knowing he should stop this madness, he crushed his lips to hers, swallowing the little moan she made, tasting her sweetness, and memories and feelings rushed back at him because she tasted, she *felt* exactly as she had done then and his whole body rejoiced at that familiarity and rightness.

Her mouth was parted and he slipped his tongue inside, duelling with hers, reminding her of this need, and she whimpered into the kiss before her hands lifted and her fingers tangled in the hair at the nape of his neck, just as she had then. Her body lifted, her breasts crushed to his chest and he swore in his own language as impatience threatened to burst him wide open.

'Tell me you dreamed of this,' he demanded, his fingers pushing the straps down now, so her breasts were free of the flimsy garment, and he cupped them greedily in his palms, feeling their weight, their generous roundness tightening his body so his arousal strained against his pants and his whole body ached for her in a way that defied sense and reason.

She had! Oh, she'd dreamed of this again and again and in the groggy half-awake state she was in it was almost impossible to believe this wasn't just a dream. But his hands on her were real—everything about this was real. She arched her back hungrily and pulled him with her hands, pulling him down on top of her, ignoring the voice in her head that was shouting at her to see reason and make this stop.

It was the witching hour and she was bewitched. He was strong, and big, and though she pulled him he came at his own pace, slowly easing his body weight on top of hers then rolling his hips so his arousal pressed to her womanhood.

A sharp dagger of need perforated her senses. It was achingly, perfectly familiar. She needed him.

'Please,' she whimpered, knowing she was stranded on this wave of desire, that she was stranded on an island of sexual craving from which there was no other relief.

He rolled his hips again and his body, so hard and heavy, pressed to her feminine core, stoking her pulse, her needs, her wants. Pleasure was a cloud carrying her away, but reality was gravity, dragging her back to earth.

It had all been so easy for him that weekend three years ago. He'd looked at her and wanted her and she'd fallen into bed with him, despite having intended to save her virginity for the man she was going to marry. She'd had no defences for someone like him, no experience with men at all, really.

And now? She was falling for it again, letting desire make a mockery of all her good intentions.

Was she really going to be this woman? A woman who let passion control her actions and dictate her life. Was she really going to fall into the habit of sleeping with someone she desired even when love wasn't a part of the equation?

'We can't do this.' She shook her head, pulling away from his kiss, and now his body on hers felt like a crushing weight from which she needed to be free. She pressed her palms to his chest and felt the brief impression of his fast-racing heart before she shoved him bodily off herself and rolled out of bed.

'I can't,' she repeated, though he hadn't said a single word. He was simply watching her with the same intensity with which he'd been kissing her a moment earlier.

'I'm not going to do that.' She pulled her straps back into place, her fingers shaking so much she had to curve them into fists and hold them by her side.

He was still watching her, saying nothing, just staring,

and though she was now fully dressed she felt more naked and exposed than ever before. She'd put a stop to whatever had been about to happen—but the inevitably of their coming together was still heavy in the room.

He watched her for a long time, as if seeing all the pieces of her soul. 'How come you were still a virgin, Frankie?'

The question pricked something in the region of her heart. She knew her expectations were out of step with most people's reality, but they were her feelings, her resolves. 'I…just was.'

'No.' He propped up on one elbow, apparently completely relaxed. 'I don't believe it was a matter of you having simply not slept with anyone.'

'Why not?' She challenged, her eyes sparking with his.

'Because you're a flesh and blood woman,' he murmured throatily. 'And I know for myself how sensual you are. How hungry your appetite…'

Her pulse sped up and with his eyes digging into hers she found she didn't want to lie to him. What was the point? 'I wanted to save myself for my husband.' She slid her gaze sideways, aware of how juvenile the assertion must have sounded. She focused her eyes on the wall and didn't see the look of intense concentration that overtook his features.

'Why?' A single word, rough and husky.

'I've told you: sex should mean something.' She frowned. 'I *thought* it should mean something. I was… I think sex and love should go hand in hand and when I eventually fell in love, and someone loved me, I wanted it to be something I shared with them.' When had she first started to align sex with love? She wasn't sure she'd ever know. When had she inextricably bound the two, sentiment and act, together? 'And then I met you.'

There was a self-mocking tilt to his beautiful lips. 'A man who thinks sex is for fun and love is a construct.'

Her heart stammered at the coldness of that assessment. 'A man I couldn't resist.' She shook her head, clearing the vestiges of the past from her mind. 'But that was years ago and I'm not the same person any more.' Certainty strengthened inside her. 'I guess you could say I learned my lesson.'

'We have already discussed this. I need another child, another heir...'

She ignored the cold, callous conclusion to that sentence—*in case anything happens to Leo*. 'That's an entirely separate proposition to what we were just about to do. Sleeping together because we aren't strong enough to listen to common sense, to do the right thing, is simply a matter of poor judgement.'

'You are cutting off your nose to spite your face,' he observed dryly.

His comment was utterly accurate. In putting a halt to their sensual pull she was only hurting herself because she wanted him with all of herself. She needed him. And yet she was resisting him because her pride demanded it of her. Not just her pride—her heart. Her heart, that could have so easily been his; her heart that had been hurt and ignored too many times to easily trust. 'I'm not. I'm just... I'm someone who always wanted the fairy tale,' she said quietly.

But often the most quietly voiced sentiments carried the most resonance.

'There's no such thing as fairy tales,' he said after several beats of silence had passed, and he stared at her for a long moment, his expression a mask of intensity. 'And even if there were, I could not give it to you.'

She sucked in an unsteady breath, lost for words.

'You can get back in bed, Frankie. Relax. I won't touch

you unless you ask me to.' And he turned onto his side, his back to her.

Silence fell. She stood there, watching him for a moment, and when his breathing was rhythmic and steady she climbed into bed, turning her own back on him and hugging the edge of the mattress.

It was a recurrent nightmare but that didn't change the fact that it flooded Matthias with adrenalin as if it was all happening for the first time. He was back in the limousine. The smell of petrol and burning flesh filling his nostrils, his body trapped, his eyes open. His parents were dead but Spiro, beside him, was still alive.

His cries were like nothing Matthias could put into words.

'I'm coming,' he promised, pushing at the metal that was heavy on his chest. 'Just keep your eyes open.'

The driver was dead too. He couldn't see the security agent who had been travelling in the same car as them.

'I can't, Matt,' Spiro groaned, and his dark eyes were covered with tears.

'You must.' Matthias, a teenager, swore darkly into the limousine and Spiro winced. He had to get free. He had to save them.

'I'll be there in a second. Hold my hand.' He reached out and the pain was like nothing he'd ever known before. His arm was broken. He grunted, extending it as best he was able. It was just far enough. Spiro put his smaller hand in Matthias's, and Matthias looked at them; their flesh was the same colour, their hands the same shape. But Spiro's was cold. Ice-cold, like nothing Matthias had ever known.

'Listen to me.' Matthias spoke urgently. 'I can hear sirens in the distance. Can you?' There was a bleating—from far away. 'They're coming to help you, Spiro. They're going to cut you out of this car and take you to hospital. I'll be beating you again in basketball in weeks.'

Spiro smiled—his teeth were covered in blood. Matthias's chest ached. His younger brother's eyes were heavy.

'Damn it—stay awake,' Matthias commanded, pushing at the metal once more. It budged, but only by a tiny amount. 'Damn it!' he shouted again.

'Matt...' Spiro dropped his hand and Matthias jerked his head towards his brother. Stars danced in his eyes and for a second he blacked out. When he came to the sirens were louder, and Spiro was sleeping. At least he looked like he was sleeping.

'Spiro!' Matthias pushed at the metal—it must have weighed a ton. Nothing moved. His own body was broken. Hysteria groaned inside him. 'Spiro!'

He turned towards the front of the car and wished he hadn't, when the sight of his parents' mangled bodies filled his vision. He closed his eyes and prayed, then swore, then reached for Spiro with an arm that didn't seem to want to obey his brain's commands.

He needed to get free so he could save his brother. There was no water—the car had swerved to avoid a boulder in the middle of the road. It had flipped over into a valley and landed on its roof. But in Matthias's dream they were always on the edge of water, and slowly it seeped into the car. Not transparent like the water that surrounded his palace, but a sludgy black, then burgundy, like blood.

Spiro died and Matthias could do little more than reach for his hand.

At fifteen, he lost everyone he'd ever loved.

It would be two hours before the rescue teams could free him. Two hours in which he stared at his brother and tried not to look towards his parents. Two hours in which his heart, though still beating, ceased to feel.

* * *

'Matt?' She pushed at his shoulder; it was damp with perspiration. 'Matthias? Wake up.'

He made a noise and then sat bolt upright, so his head came close to banging hers. His eyes were wide open and when they swung to face hers they were huge and dark. The sun was not yet up but the sky had taken on a dawn tinge—gold and pink warred with silver-grey, bathing the room in a warm glow.

His breathing was rushed, but not in a good way. Not in the way hers had been the night before. He stared at her as though he was drowning and she could save him; he stared at her as though he expected her to say or do something, but she couldn't fathom what.

'Are you okay?' she asked, as slowly his face assumed its normal handsome appearance. His lips closed, his eyes shuttered, his colour returned to normal.

'I'm fine.' He swung his powerful legs off the side of the bed and cradled his head in his hands for a moment. His back was turned to her yet again, but this time she resented that.

'You had a bad dream.'

He made a guttural sound.

'Want to talk about it?'

Another grunt, then he pushed to standing and strolled towards the French windows that led to the balcony.

'I'll take that as a no,' she murmured, more to herself than him.

He heard though and turned back to face her. He was wearing boxer shorts, but it still took a monumental effort for Frankie to keep her attention trained on his face. 'It's nothing.' He pushed the window open and stepped outside. The pale curtain billowed in after him.

Not understanding why, she followed him, knowing he

was seeking privacy and that she should let him have that, knowing she had no reason to go after him. Understanding he wouldn't welcome the intrusion but going anyway. She padded across the room, swallowing a yawn as she went, and emerging on the balcony.

He was staring at the ocean. She followed the direction of his gaze, unable to ignore the appreciative gasp that was a natural response to the sheer beauty before her. In the early morning light the sea shimmered silver and flashes of pre-dawn sunlight made the ripples appear to glisten like diamonds and topaz. The sky itself was a work of art she could never replicate—colours that didn't appear in any manmade palette, and the combination of which, if she'd pushed them into service, would be almost garish.

'He was only nine years old.' Matthias surprised her by speaking. She drew her attention back to his face and something in her chest skidded to a halt. His expression was the most sombre she'd ever seen—not just on Matthias, but on any human being.

'Who?'

He looked at her then, but as though he didn't really see her. His expression didn't shift. 'My brother. Spiro.'

Liana had mentioned Spiro, and now it made sense. Her heart broke for him.

'He was nine when he died.'

Grief clutched at Frankie's chest. 'How?'

'A car accident.'

'I'm so sorry.'

It was the wrong thing to say. He withdrew from her visibly, shrinking into his hard-edged shell.

'It is what it is.'

'Don't do that,' she murmured, shaking her head. An early morning breeze came from the ocean, carrying with it the tang of sea salt and ruffling Frankie's hair. She caught it with her fingertips and held it over one shoulder. 'Don't act like it doesn't matter. You're talking about your brother's death. It's okay to say you're upset.'

If anything, his features tightened. 'What good can come from being upset?' he asked, the words flat, turning away from her, showing he didn't expect an answer.

'Plenty.' She gave one anyway. 'Being upset, talking about how you feel, helps you move on. Helps you process…'

He shook his head. 'Why should I get to move on when Spiro has died?' He gripped the railing and leaned over it a little, staring at the ground beneath. 'Sometimes I think that if I can just reach for him in my dream, it won't have happened. That I will wake up and he will be here. Sometimes I think the accident was the nightmare, only I don't know how to rouse myself from it.'

Frankie made a small sound of sympathy.

'There is no processing this.' His eyes were hollow when he turned to her. 'There is no moving on from it. And I don't *want* to move on. Spiro is a part of me—his life, and his death. I live for both of us.'

Her fingertips ached to touch him, to comfort him, only the memory of how incendiary contact with this man could be was still alive in her gut, fresh in her mind, and so with great determination she kept her hands at her sides.

'Your parents died in the accident as well?' she murmured gently.

His response was a curt nod but the pain in his eyes was palpable, his emotions strong and fierce.

'Oh, Matt,' she murmured, and determination gave way to sympathy and an innate need to comfort him, to ease his suffering. She lifted her fingertips to his shoulder and gently traced his flesh. He was still so warm. A kaleidoscope of butterflies launched in her belly. The sun rose higher; gold slanted across her face. 'I can't imagine what that was like for you.'

'An adjustment,' he grunted, his nostrils flaring, his eyes pinning her to the spot.

She looked at him with obvious disbelief. 'Stop acting like you're too tough to care. No one can go through something like that and not have it change them. You must have been…'

'It changed me,' he stated, interrupting her with a voice that was weighted down by his feelings. 'It changed me a great deal. At fifteen I still believed my parents were infallible, that my sovereignty was guaranteed and that Spiro would spend his life driving me crazy with annoying questions and demands for attention. At fifteen I believed that I was the future King and would one day have the power to do and fix and make just about anything. I truly thought I was omnipotent.'

She nodded slowly, unconsciously bringing her body closer to his. 'I think most teenagers feel that—royal or not.'

'Maybe so.' He didn't smile but his eyes dropped to her lips, tracing their soft roundness with visible distraction. 'By the time I turned sixteen I saw the world for what it is.'

Silence throbbed around them, emotional and weary.

'And what's that?' she prompted after a moment.

'Transient. Untrustworthy.'

She shook her head and the hand that had been tentatively stroking his shoulder curved around it now, so only her thumb swept across his warm flesh. When he still didn't look at her, she lifted the other hand to his shoulder, needing more contact, as though through her touch alone she could reassure him and somehow fix this.

'What happened to you is a terrible tragedy,' she said quietly. 'But you can't let it rob you of your own happiness. Your parents wouldn't want that. Your brother wouldn't either. You say you're living for Spiro, but how can you be when you take such a dim view of all there is out there?'

'I am a realist, remember?' he said, breathing in deep, so his chest moved forward and brushed against her front. Her nipples tingled at the unintentional contact.

'A realist? I don't know, Matt. Sometimes I think you're nudging into pessimist territory.'

His eyes held hers and the air between them was thick, like the clouds before a storm. 'Is that so bad?'

'I…' Her mind was finding it hard to keep up. She looked at him, shaking her head, but why?

'Maybe, over time, you'll change me,' he said and then his smile was cynical and the air returned to normal. She blinked, like waking up from her own dream.

'I'm not sure people really change so easily.'

He stepped out of her reach and nodded curtly. 'Nor am I.'

CHAPTER SEVEN

'JUST A LITTLE this way, please, madam,' the photographer urged, holding a slender tanned arm in the air.

Frankie followed his instructions, but the smile she had pinned to her face earlier was starting to feel as if it was held in place via glue.

'Perfect. Just a few more—over near the balcony.'

The afternoon sun was streaming in like arrows of gold, no less dazzling than it had been earlier that day, when they'd stood on a different balcony and watched the dawn crest over the ocean. But then he'd been wearing only boxer shorts and the trauma of his dream had clung to him like a dark cloak she'd needed to break him free of. Now, Matthias looked every inch the handsome King. A dark suit with a cream tie, his eyes glinted in his tanned face. Black hair had been styled back from his brow, and it was all she could do not to simply stare at him.

Mathilde had presented Frankie with a cream dress for the formal engagement announcement photo session—it was long and had a ruffle across one shoulder that fell to her waist before swishing out into a narrow skirt, all the way to her ankles. Teamed with a pair of heels, she at least had a small advantage on her usual height, so she didn't feel so small when standing beside Matthias.

'It has been forty minutes,' Matthias bit out, lifting his gold wristwatch and staring at the time. 'Surely you have enough?'

The photographer, busy looking at the digital screen on the back of the camera, glanced up and blinked, then nodded. 'Almost, Your Majesty,' he promised. 'Just five more minutes.'

Frankie risked a glance at Matthias's face; it was forbidding and oh, so regal. These engagement portraits were going to make them look as if they were on their way to a funeral rather than a wedding.

'Do you need a break, *deliciae*?' Matthias looked directly at her and her heart thumped in her chest.

She shook her head. 'I'm fine. You?'

He grimaced in response. 'Hardly my preferred way to spend time.'

'Just against the railing, please, sir. Madam.'

Matthias assumed a nonchalant, bored pose and Frankie stood beside him. The photographer shook his head. 'Lean into him a bit more. Like this—' The photographer tilted his head and smiled.

Frankie compressed her lips and looked up at Matthias before moving. He was watching her, his expression sardonic.

With a small sigh, Frankie did as the photographer had suggested, but it was like being exposed to flames. Her head rested on his pectoral muscle; she could hear his heart, feel his warmth. Her smile was barely there, a whisper on her face—how could she smile when standing upright was such an effort? Matthias's hand curved around her back and his fingers splayed wide, moving ever so slightly up and down, up and down, so heat and warmth radiated from where he touched her.

'Smile!' the photographer reminded her. Frankie tried, but all of her was tied up in that moment in simply feeling. Sensations were overriding anything else. The desire she was trying to fight with all her being surged inside her, making her nerve-endings quiver, making her want to burst from the room and drag Matthias to bed, to reclaim what she knew they could mean to one another.

Matthias dipped his head forward and said *sotto voce*, 'You are trembling like a little leaf, *mikró.*'

She looked up at him, for a moment forgetting they weren't alone. Their eyes latched and nothing—no one—existed. They were alone on the balcony, the ancient ocean rolling in the background as it had for millennia. Grey eyes held green, and she lost herself in their depths. She lost herself in the ocean of his eyes, she fell to the bottom, she drowned on the seafloor, wrapped in sand and shells, and she cared not—she forgot everything.

His head dropped slowly, as if on a time lapse, though of course it hadn't really been so slow. To Frankie, though, it was the work of minutes: long, agonising, tense moments when her lips were tingling and her eyes were holding his and she could think of nothing else but a need to sink into his kiss. It was just a brush of his lips to hers, the lightest, most frustrating contact.

He kissed her, the photographer clicked, and her body snapped to life. The moan that escaped her lips was involuntary, just a small husky sound, and then Matthias lifted his head, his eyes not leaving Frankie's passion-ravaged face. 'It is enough,' he said and his words had a cool tone.

'Yes, sir, definitely. That's plenty. Thank you, sir.'

Matthias turned to Frankie and extended a hand, and ridiculously she almost didn't take it. Fear dogged her every move. Fear of this—what she was fighting, the certainty that this passion could subsume her every good intention and intellectual certainty that Matthias was not someone she could trust with her heart, her life, her love.

How absurd. She was overthinking it!

She took his hand, purely because the photographer was there and to refuse would have seemed churlish and strange, and walked with him through the gallery they'd been posing in earlier. At the door she let go, pulling her hand back softly and rubbing her palms together.

'So the engagement will be announced when?'

'Tomorrow.'

They continued to walk down a wide beautiful corridor, lined with enormous floral arrangements. They were fragrant and stunning.

'I need to tell my parents. They're going to be…blindsided.'

Matthias tilted a look at her. 'Why?'

Frankie pulled a face. 'Well, I'm getting married, to a man they've never even heard of. A king, no less!'

'You're marrying your son's father,' he said laconically.

'A man they don't know from Adam.'

'Who's Adam?'

She shook her head. 'It's an expression. I mean, you're just some guy who…'

'Yes?'

She flicked her gaze to him and then looked away again. Ridiculously, she felt uncomfortable addressing the truth of what had happened between them. 'Who got me pregnant and disappeared into thin air.'

She wasn't looking at him, so didn't see the way his features tightened as though he'd been slapped. She didn't see the way a muscle jerked in his jaw and his eyes focused more intently on her face. 'I presume they think the worst of me.'

She shrugged. 'Can you blame them?'

'No.' The forcefulness of his word had her looking at him once more. 'If we had a daughter and this was her fate—'

'My fate wasn't so bad,' she said with a small grimace. 'I got Leo, remember?'

Matthias didn't acknowledge her comment. 'If I had known there was even the slightest chance of you having conceived that night, things would have been very different.'

'Different how?'

'I wouldn't have missed a moment of his life,' he said, the words rich with emotion. Foolish hurt dipped in Frankie's gut—hurt that it was Leo alone he would have wished to see and support. Hurt that a desire to spend more time with her didn't enter into it, when she had pined for his touch, for his smile, for months.

'We can't change the past,' she said softly.

'Nor can we secure the future. But here, in this moment, I promise you, Frankie, this is not how I would have wanted things to be. You shouldn't have had to do this alone. If I could miraculously turn time backwards and change this, I would. With all of myself, I would…'

She swallowed, looking up at him, and she could feel the truth of his regret, his remorse, his desire to have been a part of this from the beginning.

'I know.'

He stared at her, long and hard, and though he didn't speak it was as though his gaze was asking a question of her: did she really understand that? Did she really believe that he was not the kind of man to abandon a young, pregnant woman? Did she know how deeply abhorrent that was to him?

And then, as though he saw her answer, he saw her acceptance of his innocence, he nodded. As though a switch had been flicked, he became a man of action. A king. A ruler. A man without doubt and self-recriminations. 'I will call your parents and explain.'

Frankie let out a laugh. 'You've never even met my parents!'

His eyes glowed with intent. 'I am the man you're going to marry, the man who fathered their grandson, even if I haven't been any kind of a father to him. I owe it to them to explain my absence, and how I intend to remedy that.'

'Hang on.' She laughed again and was surprised to find true amusement spinning through her. His eyes clung to her smile and her heart turned over, sobering her. 'You're not…this isn't…you're not a character in a Jane Austen novel. Nor am I, for that matter. I don't need you to go to my dad and ask for permission.'

His eyes narrowed imperceptibly. 'It is a mark of respect.'

'Respect *me*,' she said, 'and my wishes, and my parents will be okay.'

'I owe them an explanation…'

'You owe *me* an explanation, not them, and you've given me one. I understand. I forgive you. They're nothing to do with this.'

'It is important to me that your parents understand I had no idea you were pregnant.'

'They know that,' she said quietly. 'What do you think I said to them?'

At this, he was very still, as though it hadn't occurred to him that she might have painted a picture of him to her family at all. 'I have no idea.'

'I told them you were an amazing man, who I couldn't contact. I told them we didn't plan to see each other again, and that it wasn't your fault I couldn't find you. I told them I'd tried—they knew about the investigator—but, ultimately, they just feel sorry for you. For what you've missed. My parents are…' She swept her eyes shut for a moment, her childhood and reality hitting her hard in that moment.

'Being parents meant everything to them. The fact you were deprived of that privilege through life's circumstances is something they were saddened by. Not angry about.'

His expression showed scepticism, but she barely registered it.

She forced a smile to her face. 'Besides, they got to be grandparents to Leo, and believe me when I tell you: no child has ever been more spoiled nor adored. No baby has ever been so hugged and kissed.'

His frown deepened. 'Yet they left you living in poverty?'

'Poverty?' She rolled her eyes now and gestured down the corridor. 'My apartment might not have been a palace, but it was hardly a slum either, Matthias. Don't be such a snob.'

His laugh was involuntary—no one had called Matthias a snob in his life.

'Mum and Dad aren't wealthy,' she said softly, a warm smile touching her lips. 'They helped when they could, but my dad has needed a heap of operations for his back and that didn't come cheap.'

Matthias's brow wrinkled.

'Insurance wouldn't cover it.' She recalled the way her father had delayed the necessary procedures, insisting he could manage, when his body gradually betrayed him. 'The last thing I wanted was for them to worry about Leo and me.'

'But you have found it difficult?'

'Financially?'

He nodded.

'Yes. But that was my choice, my business. I knew being an artist would be hard. I have had to do things I didn't particularly like, just to get by, to support Leo. It's why I need the art show to be a success. I wanted my career to be able to support us, but in reality, who knows if that would ever have been possible.'

'What things?' he prompted, homing in on the detail she'd revealed.

'Oh, nothing terrible. I just mean I've worked at school fairs doing sketch portraits, or markets, I've waitressed and bussed tables, doing whatever I can to earn money, so that I can keep doing what I really love.'

'Which is painting.'

She nodded slowly. 'But I've always known I'd probably have to grow up and get a real job some day.'

'Your talent is rare. You shouldn't abandon your art.' The praise, so casually given, made her stomach roll.

'Thank you. But, talented or not, it's not an easy world to break into.'

He seemed to take her statement and mull on it, thinking it over for a moment, before nodding, almost dismissively. 'I must insist on calling your parents for myself, Frankie.'

'But…why?'

He expelled slowly and his breath fanned her temple, so her blonde hair shifted a little. His eyes lifted to the motion. 'Because there is no excuse for having left you. You were pregnant. Alone. And I should have been there.'

'You didn't know—'

He pressed a finger to her lips, his eyes beseeching her for silence. 'I am not a man to run from his responsibilities.' He was so strong, so big, she felt his insistence and understood it. 'I failed you. I failed Leo. And your parents deserve to hear that from me.'

Frankie was utterly struck dumb. His admission was almost an apology, one she had never expected from him.

'You had no idea about Leo,' she said quietly in an attempt to relieve him of his burden of guilt. 'I know you would have helped me if you had.'

'We would have married,' he agreed with complete confidence, never mind what Frankie might have thought of that. 'And you would never have known a day of worry in your life.'

She silently disagreed with that. Perhaps not financial worry, but emotional? Oh, yes. This marriage was going to be fraught with stress for Frankie.

CHAPTER EIGHT

AFTER A BAKING-HOT DAY, it was bliss to sink into the cool water of the swimming pool and stare out at the glistening sea. Bliss to be alone, with her hair in a simple braid, her face wiped of make-up, her space clear of servants. Leo had thrown a tantrum in the afternoon and though Liana had remained calm and helped Frankie remember that two-year-olds threw tantrums, that there was nothing abnormal about that behaviour, especially in strong-willed little boys, Frankie was nonetheless drained. And it had less to do with Leo and more to do with Matthias than Frankie wanted to admit. Every encounter with the man who would become her husband required so much effort. So much self-control. It was becoming increasingly difficult to remember why she wanted to keep him at arm's length. Or to care.

In the face of her desire for Matthias, sex for sex's sake was a palatable option, even when she'd always believed otherwise. Her need to control this seemed futile and absurd given that they would marry. Wasn't she only fighting to delay the inevitable? Why not just succumb? Why not enjoy what he was offering?

She duck-dived beneath the water's surface and swam a lap, holding her breath until her lungs were stinging, then pushing up off the tiled bottom and resting her elbows on the sun-warmed terracotta tiles.

Frustration gnawed at her—she pushed it aside with effort, focusing on the vista before her. She couldn't imagine a better view from anywhere in the world.

A moment later, she did another lap, then another, then switched to freestyle on the water's surface. She'd been a strong swimmer through school, and she'd always enjoyed it. But nothing was as nice as this. The water in the pool was salty, the twilight sun had the perfect degree of warmth and after the trials of staying calm in the face of Leo's belligerence it was a delight to expend some energy in this way.

Three more laps, and she emerged to find that she was no longer alone. Matthias had slipped into the pool unannounced and, though he stood on the opposite side, he was watching her, and he might as well have reached out and touched her, for how her body reacted to his presence.

'Matt…' she cleared her throat '… I didn't know you were here.'

'I just arrived.'

How did he have the ability to unsettle her with a single look? Her nerves struggled to find harmony in her body.

'I spoke to your father.'

Frankie's eyes flew wide. 'Already?'

He nodded. 'I saw no point in delay.'

'No, of course not. I mean, we're getting married so soon. I just hadn't expected…' She was babbling. She clamped her lips together and made an effort to focus. 'What did he say?'

'He was pleased for us. I wondered if you might wish to ask them to remain for some time after the wedding, at least to help with Leo while we take our honeymoon.'

'Honeymoon!' The word slid over her back like warmed caramel. She almost groaned at the image it conjured of the two of them, tangled in sheets, warm, passionate, limbs entwined…

'You know, that thing that usually follows a wedding?'

Her cheeks flushed pink. 'But this marriage isn't… I mean… It's not like we need that. Surely you have too much work. Wouldn't it just be an inconvenience?'

'Do you not wish to see more of this country you are to be Queen of?'

She bit down on her lip. 'I just don't think a *honeymoon* is called for.'

'Why do you make the distinction?'

'Honestly? A honeymoon makes me think of beds strewn with rose petals and baths filled with champagne. That's not us.'

'No,' he agreed, moving through the water easily, his long legs carrying him into the deepest part without more than half his chest being submerged. 'But it does not mean we can't have fun.'

Her mouth was dry and every breath of air seemed to make her nerves quiver. 'I think we have different ideas of fun.'

He laughed. 'Do we?'

She flushed and nodded, but her heart was racing, her pulse throbbing. 'I've told you, I'm not interested in casual sex.'

'There's nothing casual about marriage,' he said logically. 'And I think you're very interested in sex with me.'

Her chest squeezed. He closed the distance between them completely and, beneath the water, his long fingers found the edge of her bikini bottoms. With his eyes holding hers, he pulled her close to him. And, damn it, she went, with no resistance whatsoever. As though she were an iron filing and he her magnetic pole.

'Matt,' she murmured as his other hand curved into the bikini bottoms. He was taunting her, his eyes daring her to say something. To tell him to stop. And, though she knew she should, the word wouldn't come out. In fact, nothing came out except a small husky sound of surrender.

'Listen to me,' he said softly, swimming through the water and pulling her with him. He eased her onto one of the steps at the corner of the pool and stood between her legs. 'I want you, and I believe you want me. This—' he gestured from her chest to his '—is like a live wire.'

Her eyes flared at the description; it was exactly how she felt.

Beneath the water, his fingers toyed with the elastic sides of her bikini bottoms, sliding down and curving around her buttocks so she held her breath at the unfamiliar but undeniably welcome contact. She was a fool, she knew—she had to stop this—but oh, it felt so good. Just another minute, she promised herself.

Using his hands to guide her, he brought her body forward a little, so she could feel the strength of his rock-hard arousal, the desire that was there for her, and she whimpered low in her throat. Memories of how he'd felt, moving inside her, made her crazy with longing.

'I am the only man who's ever made love to you. Yes?'

Her cheeks flushed and she shuttered her eyes, unable to meet the scrutiny of his gaze.

'Tell me,' he demanded, kissing her neck so her breath came fast and hard inside her. 'That your only experience of sex is with me.'

A strangled noise escaped her throat. 'Why does it matter?'

'Because if this is so, then you have so much to learn,' he said.

One of his hands moved from her rear, coming over her leg and buzzing the sensitive flesh of her inner thigh, before nudging the flimsy material of her costume aside. She held her breath, her mind no longer able to concentrate on what he'd been saying. He watched her intently as his fingers brushed over her womanhood, his eyes holding hers as he slid a finger into her moist, tight core.

'You have so much to learn about your body and its pleasures, and I want to teach you that.' He swirled his finger around and she arched her back, her eyes fixing on the sunset overhead, on the colours that were only enhanced by the sheer perfection of his touch. 'I want you.' His mouth dropped to the flesh at the base of her throat and he kissed her, slow and long, and she moaned again, wrapping her legs around his waist and surrendering to the bliss of this moment, surrendering to an inevitability she'd been fighting since he'd walked into her gallery and her body had started to feel fully alive for the first time in three years.

'I know you want to fight me—' he rolled his hips and she moaned, his words stoking her like flames in a fire '—but can you not see how good our marriage can be? Neither of us wanted this, but that doesn't mean it can't be everything we want now, Frankie.' Her name on his lips was a seduction, his promise a temptation that was almost impossible to resist. Because he was right. He was so right.

Frankie didn't believe in casual sex, but this wasn't casual. This wasn't even just sex. There was so much more between them; there always had been. At least, for Frankie. He wasn't just some man she'd rushed into bed with. She'd met him and on some level had tripped headlong into love. She'd given all of herself to Matthias that night, not just her virginity. Not just her body.

And he'd walked away with such ease.

Oh, he'd had to—duty had called him. But he'd stayed away and her heart had been breaking.

Could she really lose herself to him again? Could she really be so stupid?

'Tell me you want me,' he said, and he stood out of the

pool, removing his hand from her only so he could reach down and lift her, carrying her against his chest as though she weighed nothing.

'I…can't,' she whispered as her hands reached up and tangled in the hair at his nape, as her body stayed wet and cleaved to his. He carried her to a pool lounger, laying her down and disposing of her bikini bottoms swiftly, staring at her naked sex with eyes that were so hungry they robbed her of breath.

'You can't admit to this?' He arched, kneeling on the ground at the foot of the lounger, parting her thighs with strong, broad hands. His mouth on her was a sensual, terrifying possession and she cried out as pleasure, sharp and visceral, broke through her.

He didn't speak—he didn't need to. His actions made a mockery of her determination not to want him. His tongue ran over her, tasting her sweetness, and his fingers held her legs wide; she was all his. All of her.

She cried out as he moved faster, and then slid a finger deep into her core, tormenting her sensitive nerve-endings with his possession and absolute mastery of her body.

She was so close to breaking point, pleasure within arm's reach, and he lifted his head, his eyes staring at her, his expression impossible to decipher. 'Beg me,' he said simply.

Heat coloured Frankie's mind, cheeks and thoughts.

'Beg me,' he said again, dropping his mouth and lashing her with his tongue once more, his touch like heaven.

'I can't,' she cried, but then his name was dropping from her lips again and again and again, rent with desperate need. She called him Matthias, because here, in this kingdom, beneath the skies of Tolmirós, he was Matthias. Not Matt, who she'd fallen in love with—she could see that now, looking back through time, and knowing who she'd been then.

At twenty-one, she'd met Matt and fallen in love. But

she'd been a girl who believed in fantasies then, who thought sex and love went hand in hand. And now she saw that sex on its own could be enough.

'Beg for me and I will make you come,' he promised, lifting up and taking one of her breasts into his mouth, while his finger stayed inside her, tormenting her with memories and promises.

'Why are you doing this?' she asked, digging her nails into his shoulders as thought became impossible, as pleasure crashed over her. *Surrender*, her body begged, her heart implored. *Surrender and accept that this is enough!*

Of course it was—for some people.

But not for Frankie.

Her body was on fire, her pulse racing, her heart thumping, and she knew that satisfaction was within reach. All she had to do was beg him, to say the word *please* that she was swallowing inside her throat, and he would drive her over the edge; he would make her feel almost whole.

Almost.

But it would never be enough for the girl who'd wanted real love all her life.

'I can't,' she said, her breathing so rushed, dragged from so deep within her lungs it hurt. 'Don't make me beg.'

Surprise covered his features when he pulled up to look at her.

'Don't use what I feel to demean me,' she said, lying flat on the lounger, staring up at the evening streaked sky.

'Demean you?' he repeated, the word ragged. 'Frankie, by getting you to accept what you want, I am empowering you. Empowering you to enjoy sex, to enjoy this thing between us that is purely good. I have no interest in demeaning you. I want you to be brave, to face up to what you're feeling. Stop hiding from me.' And his eyes held hers for a long moment as his mouth dropped closer to her sex. She held her breath, propping up on elbows to watch him.

'Let us try it another way,' he said, the words deep and husky. 'Let me beg you. Let me beg you to let me do this,' and he flicked his tongue out, teasing her flesh so she made a keening sound of pleasure. 'Let me beg and you say, simply, "Yes".'

Yes.

The word was heavy in her throat, bouncing over and over, begging to be said, begging her to agree, so she could be put out of her misery.

'Just say yes,' he repeated, and his mouth moved faster and her pleasure built until her eyes were filled with a bright white light and she was no longer conscious of anything but this.

'Say yes,' he demanded, pulling her body closer so he could go deeper, his mouth possessing her in a way that was so intimate, so personal, so perfect. His hand scooped under her bottom, lifting her up, and she heard herself crying out, over and over and over, giving away a part of her soul that she had thought she would be able to keep locked up: 'Yes, Matthias, please. Please!'

He stared at the painting, his lips a grim slash on his face. *Don't use what I feel to demean me.*

Her words, issued in the heat of a sensual moment of passion, had stuck with him, chasing themselves around his head until he could barely think, until he couldn't fathom what he'd been thinking.

Don't use what I feel to demean me.

Had he been doing that?

Since she'd arrived in Tolmirós, he'd been intent on seducing her, on forcing her to stop hiding from the magnitude of their desire.

Matthias, with his experience of women and sex and attraction, knew what he shared with Frankie was rare. So rare that even three years after their first encounter he hadn't been able to put her from his mind. Three years later and he'd never met anyone who held the same appeal for him. This passion was rare and it deserved to be explored.

But at the cost of her self-esteem?

He swore under his breath, pacing to the windows that overlooked the ocean. It had all seemed so simple when first they'd arrived. Sex was a simple transaction. A conversion of lust to satiation.

Whatever his attitudes were to it, Frankie's were not the same.

And yet he'd driven his tongue over her, tasting her release, delighting in her complete surrender even when he now suspected he should have stopped. He'd thought he would feel triumph with her surrender; he'd thought he'd revel in her total acceptance of the tug of their mutual need.

He hadn't.

He'd felt only something very close to blinding panic. He'd tasted her as she'd fallen apart, and his own body had been begging him to bury his length inside her soft, welcoming core, yet he hadn't. He'd pulled away from her even when her desire had burst around them, and her willingness to succumb to pleasure had been palpable.

He'd been as beholden to passion as she, in the end, but it didn't matter. Because she'd been right. He'd been determined to get her to face what they felt for one another.

But why?

Why did he care so damned much that she should surrender to this desire?

Because he wanted her. He wanted her with the strength of a thousand stars, and he knew she felt the same. But her determination and willpower were many times stronger than his. Why? What did she want? Not just from him, but in general?

The damned fairy tale? He couldn't offer that. He didn't have it within his power to give Frankie the dream of love and happily ever after. But he could give her more than sex. He could give her enough, surely, to make her truly happy—not just in bed but as his wife?

And he wanted her to be happy, he admitted to himself now. He needed her to be happy, to smile at him as she had on those few rare occasions since coming to Tolmirós. He wanted to win her trust, to *earn* her trust, and the rest, surely, would follow.

Maybe it wouldn't. But Frankie deserved more than to have a husband who wanted only her body. She deserved as much of the dream as he could offer—surely some of her fantasy would be better than none?

'You look like a little prince,' Frankie enthused, tears sparkling on her lashes as she studied her son. He'd undergone a similar makeover to her own: a haircut, new clothes, and he looked utterly divine.

''E is so handsome. Just like his father,' Liana cooed, her eyes wrinkling at the corners as she bent down and picked Leo up. He didn't arch his back with Liana in the way he'd taken to doing with Frankie, she noticed with a wry grimace. Liana always got hugs and kisses and yeses straight away. But Frankie couldn't be cross about that— not when Liana had helped make Leo's transition to life in Tolmirós so easy.

A whisper of guilt flicked through her because there were only days to go until the wedding and though Frankie had spent her days ensuring Leo was settling well and making sure this private residence of the palace felt like home, she was distracted almost all the time.

When she'd first agreed to this, he'd told her two things. *Through the days, you'll barely know I exist. At night, you won't be able to exist without me.*

The latter was true. Since the afternoon in the pool, when she had surrendered herself to his mouth and given up her determination to resist the passion that flared between them, he'd made no effort to touch her. He'd come to bed late and lay on his side until he'd fallen asleep, and she'd lifted her head up and watched him, and flopped onto her back and wondered what he'd say if she gave into all her body's urges and straddled him, and begged him to forget what she'd said: to make love to her.

As for the days, she more than knew he existed then too.

He was everywhere she looked in this palace. He was in their son's face, Liana's pride, his servants' obedience, the kingdom's prosperity. He was in the enormous canary diamond and white gold ring he'd slid onto her finger two nights earlier, his eyes locked onto hers as he told her it reminded him of the yellow she'd painted the sunlight in the painting she'd been working on the weekend they'd met. And though it was a meaningless, throwaway comment, it had made her chest feel as if it were exploding with delirious joy, with pleasure and disbelief. With perfection.

He was everywhere, even when he'd said he wouldn't be, even when he made no effort to seduce her. Their conversations were polite, cordial, and lacking any indication that he even wanted her. Perhaps he didn't. Perhaps it was as simple as an impulse for him—she'd told him 'no' and he'd accepted that. If only Frankie had found it so easy to put him from her mind!

'Thank you for getting him ready for tonight, Liana, and for agreeing to come.'

'Of course! My place is with him at these functions— as much as you would like me to be,' she added tactfully.

'Royal parties are not much fun for children. They tire so quickly of being polite and well-behaved.' She looked at Leo with a wink and then reached into her pocket, pulling out a small round chocolate. 'And Leo knows there will be a treat at the end of the night, for his very good behaviour.'

Leo nodded sagely, and Frankie laughed. 'Is this his prince face?' she suggested, pride bursting through her.

'He has been practising.'

'Well, Leo, you've absolutely mastered it.'

Liana turned to face Frankie and, for the first time, looked at her properly. 'You are very beautiful, Frankie. Like a princess yourself, no?'

'Oh, no, but thank you,' she demurred, feeling more like someone going to a dressing up party. 'Ball gowns aren't really my caper.'

'Caper?' Liana frowned.

'Thing. They're not really my thing.' She ran her hands down the dress, a turquoise colour, it had a sweetheart neckline and was fitted to her waist, then fell into a flouncy skirt that made a beautiful swishing sound as she walked. It was a true Cinderella dress and the diamond tiara that had been styled into her hair completed the look. 'The dress is very beautiful, though.'

'It does suit you,' Liana complimented.

'Well, that's good, because I get the feeling I'm going to need to go to a few more of these things in my lifetime.' She shrugged her slender shoulders, her tan golden. She'd taken to spending time by the pool as well. Helping Leo swim, and swimming with him, lying in the sun while he napped, remembering how Matthias had felt in the water, how warm and cool had contrasted so sensually against her flesh.

Her cheeks flushed pink as the memories pushed into

her mind and then, as if she'd somehow miraculously dredged him up from fantasy to reality, Matthias strode into the room.

If she looked like a princess, then he was King Charming come to life.

The suit was jet black, his shirt whiter than white, a white tie at his neck completed the look. But he wore across his middle a burgundy sash, military style medals were pinned to his chest, and at his waist there was a gold weapon, a blade, long and sharp. He was far more handsome than any man had a right to be.

'Sword!' Leo pointed delightedly and he jumped up off his little bottom and held his hands out, so Matthias smiled at Liana and then took his son into his arms, tousling hair that had, a moment ago, been perfectly neat.

She didn't notice the way Matthias's eyes lingered on Leo's face with a hint of something other than happiness; she didn't see the way his expression flashed with regret and—oh, so briefly—fear.

'Sword,' Leo said again and Matthias relaxed, smiling as he nodded.

'Yes.'

'For me?'

Liana laughed, and Matthias pulled a face. 'Not yet. But soon.'

Leo pouted. 'I see?'

Matthias put their son down on the ground and then removed the clip from his waist. He held the sword—in its gold ceremonial sheath—so that Leo could run his fingertips over the blunted end.

'Look, Mama. Pictures.'

At this, Matthias glanced up, his eyes locking onto Frankie's, holding hers, and a look of searing heat flashed between them—a look that had the ability to blank anyone else from their presence. Her fingers fidgeted at her sides and then she smiled curtly, tightly, in a way that didn't feel natural and dragged her eyes down to the sword.

But desire stayed lodged in her chest, desperate, hungry, craving indulgence. Out of nowhere, she remembered the way his mouth had felt between her legs and her knees almost buckled with the sensual heat of her recollection.

'I see,' she murmured, moving closer.

'It's very old,' Matthias said, turning his attention back to the weapon. 'It was my great-great-great-great-great-grandfather's, said to have slain the king of a neighbouring country when war threatened at our doorstep.'

'War?' Leo was fascinated by this.

'A long time ago,' Frankie jumped in, sending a warning look to Matthias. He smiled at her and a dimple formed in his cheek that made her fingers itch to paint him. She had in her mind, so many times.

He stood, unfurling his body length and ruffling Leo's dark hair at the same time. 'You look beautiful.' The words were quietly spoken, intended purely for her ears.

'Thank you,' she said, able to take the compliment when she felt her appearance was really the result of couture and hair stylists.

'But not complete yet.'

She looked down at the dress and lifted a hand to the diamond choker she wore. 'What have I forgotten?'

His smile was enigmatic as he reached into his pocket and pulled out a rectangular velvet box.

'Would you do me the honour of wearing this tonight, Frankie?' He popped it open to reveal an award similar to those he wore—a thick piece of purple fabric to which a small gold pendant was attached. In the centre of the pendant there was a star, with an arrow striking through it.

'What is it?' she asked, watching as he pulled it from the

box. His fingers were deft and confident, and her mouth was suddenly dry.

'The Star of Aranathi,' he said. 'An award that was given to my mother—one of my country's highest.'

The meaningfulness of the gesture touched something in Frankie's stomach, and it set in place a chain reaction. Butterflies stirred to life, slowly at first, then faster, until a whole kaleidoscope was beating against her insides. She was oblivious to the watchful eyes of Liana, who'd moved Leo away and distracted him with a juice carton.

'What's it for?' she murmured. He lifted the ribbon to the top of her dress, his fingers almost clinical as they held the fabric taut enough to thread the pin through and latch it into place.

'Humanitarian efforts.'

'I don't...' Frankie frowned, studying Matthias up close. She studied him not as a woman who wanted a man, but as an artist evaluating a subject. She measured his features and imagined creating him from the nothingness of canvas and pigment. She imagined how she might mix her colours together to shade the cleft of his chin dimple and the very faint darkness beneath his eyes. It was his lashes, though, that fascinated her. They were black and curling, soft like silk and so thick, as though they were a curtain for his eyes. What of his face had been gifted by his mother, and what by his father?

When she looked at Leo, she saw so much of Matthias. But was some of the Queen there too? The Queen to whom this medal had once belonged?

'I don't know anything about her,' Frankie finished after a moment. 'But I'd like to.'

His expression shifted with pride first, and then surprise. 'Why?'

Frankie tilted her head consideringly. 'Because she was

your mother. And Leo's grandmother. And it strikes me that I should know something about your family, beyond the fact…' The sentence trailed off into nothingness as she realised what she'd been about to say.

'That they're dead,' he finished for her, his expression unchanged. She threw a scant look in Leo's direction; the boy wasn't listening. Nonetheless, Frankie's brows knitted together when she regarded Matthias. She'd prefer to handle that conversation sensitively, when it came time for Leo to learn of his father's family's deaths.

'What did your mother do to receive this award?'

'Many things.'

'War!' Frankie startled as Leo seemed to jolt out of his reverie and, from the other side of the room, whipped the straw from the juice carton and held it towards Matthias like an ancient challenge to a duel.

Matthias's face relaxed, the tension of a moment ago dissipating, his eyes crinkling at the corners as he returned, *'En garde!'*

Leo giggled and charged his father, but Matthias caught him mid-run, lifting him up easily and tickling him at the belly, so Leo's laughter pealed into the room and, before she knew it, Frankie was smiling. But it was a distracted smile, a smile that was only skin-deep.

'Excuse me, Your Majesty.' There was a knock at the door. 'It is time.'

'Of course.' Leo's smile muted itself when he addressed the servant, and Frankie saw in that moment the duality between private and public. The man and the King. The man who could smile and laugh and tease their son about long ago wars, and the King who presented a sombre and considered face to his servants at all times.

Had he been like that at fifteen? Or had he been allowed to mourn?

They were to be married in the Artheki Cathedrali, her secretary had informed her days earlier. It was five miles away, ancient, and all the Kings of Tolmirós had been married, christened and mourned within its walls for over a thousand years. That information had been inserted into the briefing and, though it was an unimportant detail, it had played on Frankie's mind.

She presumed then that Matthias's parents and brother had been buried there, that their funeral had taken place within the walls of the cathedral at which they were to marry. Had he spoken at the funeral? At fifteen years old, it wouldn't have been unusual, but her heart broke to imagine the young boy he'd been, and the pressure that must have been upon him.

She resisted the temptation to run an Internet search on the subject. Her curiosity was natural, but she would prefer her information to come from the source. Snooping around and reading articles online felt somehow wrong.

'Come, *deliciae.*' Was she imagining the way his voice caught as he addressed her? The way his eyes seemed to lock onto hers with emotion and an intent she couldn't comprehend? 'It is time for you to meet our people.'

CHAPTER NINE

'OH, MATTHIAS!' THEY were alone in a sleek dark limousine, with Liana and Leo following in the car behind. 'It's so beautiful.'

Beyond the black tinted windows of the car and the crowds that had lined the streets hoping for a real-life glimpse of the soon-to-be Queen, Frankie could see the streets of Tolmirós and they were setting her soul on fire.

'It's like something out of a beautiful story book. I had no idea!' Terracotta-roofed houses, built close together and higgledy-piggledy, one leaning this way and the next the other, were all washed in different colours of pastel paints. Little balconies had wrought-iron details and window boxes overflowing with bright purple and red plants. Many had refused to be contained to the small pots and were making joyous bids for sunshine and freedom, dancing their tendrils down the sides of the buildings, forming veins of green that shone in the late afternoon sun.

But the most remarkable thing to Frankie was the sense of history that was at every turn. These buildings were ancient. They whooshed past a church with a cupola and a bell tower, white with a shimmering blue face and enormous bronze hands. A statue of a naked man stood in front, and geraniums seemed to grow with complete abandon across a side wall. When she turned in her seat to get a better look, she saw a nun coming from the front gates, throwing something towards the ground. A moment later at least a hundred pigeons descended on the square. The nun threw her head back and laughed and then the limousine turned the corner.

Caught up in the wonderment of this picture-book streetscape, Frankie didn't realise that Matthias was watching her intently. She didn't see the way his eyes were scanning her face, reading every flicker of delight that crossed it.

'I had no idea it would be like this.'

His lips quirked. 'What did you expect?'

Frankie shrugged. 'I guess I didn't think about it. Until a week ago, Tolmirós was just some place on the edge of the Mediterranean. And since we arrived, we've been in the palace. I expected beautiful beaches and, I guess, a modern city, but this is…just…stunning.'

Pride flashed on his features and his nod was swift. 'The city of Novampoli was built in the nineteen-seventies. We needed a place that wasn't part of the port cities—much of our prosperity comes from being a safe harbour for shipping companies, but my father kick-started a technology revolution. Banking and finance are also primary industries for Tolmirós. We needed a city that would answer those requirements. The first few buildings were modest but within a decade or two high-rises began to shape the skyline. It is now a place of glass and steel, and the food there is second to none. I will take you there, when next I have occasion to go. You will like it.'

'Is it like Manhattan?' She settled back into her seat, smoothing the skirts of her dress simply for something to do with her hands.

'In some ways, but without the mix of old and new. It is more like Dubai, I think. A somewhat artificial-seeming city, in a place you wouldn't expect it. The whole island is a city, and an enormous bridge spans from the west shore to its neighbouring island, Emanakki.'

'I'd like to see it some day,' she said with a smile. 'I want to see everything.'

He laughed softly. 'And so you shall, Frankie. In fact, soon it will be your duty to see and know everything about our country.'

She angled him a look thoughtfully. 'Who were you going to marry?'

He arched a brow at her change in conversation. 'That seems irrelevant now.'

'I'm curious. Indulge me.'

'I think I told you that I hadn't yet decided…'

Feminine disapproval had her lips curling. 'Of course. You had a queen *smorgasbord* from which to select your bride. I'm just asking who it was likely to be.'

He smothered a smile at her comment and nodded. 'Lady Tianna Montavaigne was the front-runner.'

'Why?'

'She met the criteria.' He shrugged, as though it barely mattered.

But Frankie was persistent. 'In what ways?'

He compressed his lips and studied her for a long moment, his eyes tunnelling straight into her soul. 'She's royal, for one, though a distant cousin to the ruling monarch of Sweden. She's been raised to understand this lifestyle, the pressures of it, the need to be discreet, polite, dignified and private. She understands the realities of living life under a microscope.' He said the final sentence with a hint of disdain, but it was gone again almost as quickly. 'She is intelligent, beautiful, and we get on well.'

There was a pang of something in the region of Frankie's heart. 'Will she be disappointed not to marry you? Did she love you?'

He laughed and shook his head ruefully. 'It is always about love with you, no?'

Frankie's cheeks warmed as his eyes held hers thoughtfully. 'No, she doesn't *love* me.'

Frankie sighed softly. 'You act as though the very idea of marriage between two people who are in love is absurd.'

'Not absurd,' he contradicted. 'Just…romantic. Tianna knew what marriage to me would involve.'

'I just can't understand why anyone would agree to that,' she said with a shake of her head. 'A marriage without love seems so…cold. So…devastating.' She shivered.

'*You* have agreed to it,' he pointed out, watching her through half-shuttered eyes.

Her eyes flashed with pain and then she tilted her chin as though physically underscoring her determination. 'I… I know. But our circumstances are fairly unique. Were there no Leo, wild horses couldn't have dragged me into this.'

He nodded, as though her words were somehow reassuring. 'Tianna is in a relationship with her father's chauffeur. He's from Syria and came to the country as a refugee when he was a child. He's naturalised now, and she cares for him very deeply.'

Frankie blinked, her lack of comprehension apparent. 'So why in the world would she marry you?'

'Because he needs his job, because her parents would never condone the match, because she'd be disinherited and doesn't particularly fancy the idea of getting a job. There are any number of reasons to keep their relationship quiet. Marriage to me would have provided excellent cover for her to continue her relationship.'

'Oh, Matt, how can you speak so calmly about this?'

He sighed and squeezed her hand. 'I can't see there's anything wrong with making informed, intelligent choices when it comes to your future.'

The car began to slow, and the crowds outside their windows thickened. Frankie had been given a crash course in royal deportment. For hours each morning and again in the evening, she'd been drilled in the protocol that would be expected of her as the future Queen. It all jumbled in her brain now, but she tried to grab hold of it.

'Relax,' he murmured, leaning closer to look out at the view with her. 'The window will go down soon so you can wave to my people. They're excited to see you.'

Beyond the window, now that they were driving more slowly, Frankie could see signs with their official engagement portrait, taken on the balcony of the palace, her head pressed against Matthias's chest. There were handmade signs too, with her name all over them, and people wearing veils and throwing confetti.

Was Leo enjoying the spectacle? Or was he frightened by the noise? She angled herself in the seat in an attempt to look backwards but the limo was a little far away. 'Why aren't Leo and Liana in this car? There's plenty of room.'

He didn't look at her. 'In case something goes wrong.'

'Like what? He's never motion sick. He travels well…' Her voice tapered off as an alternative meaning unravelled in her brain. 'You mean in case our car crashes?'

He shrugged. 'Or theirs does. Or there's a terrorist attack.'

'So you won't ever travel with our son?'

He eyed her now, his expression implacable. 'No.'

'But you flew over here with him.'

He nodded. 'It was necessary on that one occasion. But I will not do so again. I have had this law written into our constitution.'

A shiver ran down her spine, and her chest heaved with emotion for the young man who'd felt it necessary to write in such a protection.

Surely this was a reaction to the loss of his parents and brother. She couldn't help it; she reached over and squeezed his hand, rubbing the pad of her thumb reassuringly over his skin. But he looked at her with a quizzical expression, and Frankie realised her eyes were moist. Emotions were running rampant within her.

'Surely that's a little extreme?'

His features were like ice. 'No.'

'But he's just a baby,' she murmured. 'He'd much rather travel with his mother or father.'

'He is my heir,' Matthias said through clenched teeth. 'Keeping him alive is my priority.'

She ignored the unpleasant suspicion he was speaking as a king who needed a living heir rather than a father who valued the survival of his child. Of course it was both. 'Then I'll travel with him in the future,' she said simply.

'Your place is with me,' he rebuffed gently, his eyes sweeping closed for a moment. 'And Liana is there for Leo.'

'You created this law,' she prompted softly, gently. 'So there wasn't one before this?'

His eyes fired. 'No. If there had been...' The words trailed off into nothing and now she was moving closer to him, needing him to hear her.

'If there had been,' she insisted, 'that boulder would have still been there. The car with your parents in would have crashed.'

'But Spiro would have lived.' His eyes glittered with hurt and pain and her heart twisted achingly.

'You don't know that,' she whispered softly. 'You don't know that your car wouldn't have crashed as well. You don't know that something else awful might not have happened later. There are no guarantees in life,' she said simply.

'You think I don't know that?' He turned to face her, his expression tortured, his features drawn. 'You think I don't understand how completely beholden we are to fate and sheer damned luck?'

His hurt was like a rock, pressing against her chest. 'So stop trying to control everything,' she murmured, lifting a hand to his cheek. 'I don't want our son growing up afraid of his own shadow. I don't want him being governed by protocols and edicts that overturn natural instinct. He's our son. He belongs with us.'

She pressed her head forward, so their foreheads connected, and she breathed in deeply, this connection somehow every bit as intimate as what they'd shared by the pool.

'It's my responsibility to protect you both, and I will do so with my dying breath.' The words shook with the force of his determination, and Frankie was momentarily speechless.

Then, with a surge of understanding, she cupped his cheek, holding him still. 'Is that what this is about? You think you couldn't save Spiro and now you're trying to guarantee that nothing bad will ever happen to us?' Her insight was blinding in its strength and accuracy. She knew she was right when he recoiled for a moment. But she moved with him, staying close, holding him to her. 'You were just a boy, Matthias. You couldn't do any more than you did.'

'How do you know?' he asked, uncharacteristically weary. 'You weren't there. You don't know anything about the accident…'

'I know that if you could have saved your brother or your parents, you would have. I know that if there's anyone on earth with the strength to almost make the impossible possible, it's you, Matt. You have to forgive yourself. Free yourself from this guilt.'

'Easier said than done.' He expelled a sigh and shook his head. 'I will not change my mind about Leo's safety. You'll have to respect that I know what I'm talking about.' He was himself again. Matthias Vassiliás—a king amongst men, intractable, unchangeable, determined. The emotionally charged air was gone and he sat back in his seat as if to say, *conversation closed.*

Frankie was about to argue with him, she wanted, desperately, to alleviate this guilt of his, but the windows began to move down slowly and she had only seconds to sit back in her seat and compose her features into an expression of assumed happiness, lift her hand and begin to wave slowly at the assembled crowds. The noise was deafening! People began to scream when the window went down, loud and shrill, but oh, so excited. The crowd applauded and children threw flowers at the car.

The conversation with Matthias pushed deeper into her mind, for later analysis, in the face of such a rapturous welcome. Matthias, beside her, seemed unaffected. He didn't smile nor wave, but simply watched Frankie and allowed her to have all the adoration of the people who'd come to see the woman who would be Queen.

She was so captivated by the crowds that she didn't notice the castle until they were almost on top of it but, as the car slowed to a stop, she glanced up and an involuntary rush of breath escaped her. 'Oh, Matt, look!'

His smile was just a flicker. 'I know.'

It was an ancient-looking castle, with enormous turrets that were topped with pointed roofs. As a child she'd read a book about Sir Gawain and she'd always imagined the castle to be something like this.

'It was the palace of a prominent family in the twelfth century. As civil wars gradually broke down the ranks of nobility, the palace reverted to the Crown. It serves as our parliament, and the west wing is used as a gallery for children to come and learn about the country's politics.

'I've never seen anything like it.' Windows had been

set in ancient brick, the glass rippled and uneven, showing its age.

'You should see it from the other side,' he teased but, before she could ask him what he meant, the doors were opened by a guard in a full liveried uniform and white gloves. The crowd reached a deafening pitch. Frankie moved towards the door but Matthias stilled her, holding her back in the limousine, safe from prying eyes for one more moment.

'Do you feel okay?'

She frowned. 'I feel…fine. Why?'

'This could be overwhelming. Do you need anything?'

His thoughtfulness, so unexpected, made her stomach swoop as though she'd fallen from an aeroplane. 'I'm honestly fine,' she promised. 'Really, I am.'

He nodded, a glint of admiration in his eyes as he released her hand. Remembering all that she'd been taught, she stepped from the car, concentrating on keeping her long skirt down for modesty, her head up, her eyes on the crowd, no dramatic facial movements that a camera would snap and a paper would publish for the fact it was unflattering. She also concentrated doubly hard on not falling flat on her face, which was harder than it sounded whilst wearing stiletto heels and what felt like miles of tulle and silk.

She'd been told they weren't to hold hands, nor to show any sign of affection. It was a protocol thing and, given their strange and somewhat dysfunctional relationship, she hadn't blinked at the instruction. So when he stepped from the car and put an arm around her waist, holding her to his side, she glanced up at him.

He smiled brightly, his even white teeth set in curving lips, a chiselled square jawline and every feature a standout, his dark eyes casting a spell over her, and she smiled back at him. Then he bent down and pressed a small kiss to the tip of her nose. The crowd went wild.

He lifted his head up but kept an arm wrapped around her waist in a way that she would have called protective, except the flames of desire that licked at her side were so much more dangerous than any other threat or fear she might feel.

He guided her to the crowds and she received gifts from the children who were lined up at the front. Dozens and dozens of cards, flowers, bears, and each one she admired and appreciated, before handing it to a protocol officer, hovering in the background. At the steps of the palace, Leo and Liana met them, having pulled up and made their way straight to the entrance.

Liana straightened Leo's shirt and then passed him to Matthias. With their son held in one handsome arm and the other around the waist of the woman he would marry, they stood there, smiling at the assembled crowd.

The smile on Frankie's face was dazzling, but it was a forgery.

Sadness for this man swarmed her chest, making her heart split and her mind heavy. She didn't want him to have suffered as he had. She saw now the depth of his grief—it was as much a part of him as his bones and blood. It had redefined his outlook on life. And love?

Matthias tilted his head towards her and it felt as though an elastic band was snapping inside her chest, her heart exploding out of its bracket.

He might not love her—he might not even be capable of love.

But if her sense of compassion for him taught Frankie anything it was that somewhere, somehow, without her permission, she'd done something really stupid.

She'd fallen in love with her future husband.

* * *

If the outside of the palace was mesmerising, then inside was just as much so. Enormous marble tiles lay in the entranceway, white and imposing, and a marble staircase rose from the centre. A harpist was playing as they strode inside, and more noise sounded, this time from within the palace. 'The party is on the rooftop terrace,' he said.

'Okay.' She nodded, but her mind was still exploding from the realisation she'd just had. She *couldn't* love him. No way. She was, surely, just getting lust and love mixed up, as she had back in New York. She barely knew him.

Yet somewhere along the way she'd fallen in love with a man who'd proudly proclaimed his disdain for the whole notion of love. He saw it as a useless impediment to life in general.

What a fool she was!

'You are okay?' he queried again, carrying Leo on his hip as though he'd been doing it all Leo's life.

'Uh huh.' She nodded unevenly, not daring to look at him again.

'Please, Frankie, do not be worried about Leo's safety. I will protect him, and you.'

She jolted her gaze to his, nodding. If only he knew what the real cause for her silence was!

They walked up the sweeping staircase in silence. She realised as they neared the top that Matthias had been right about something—she now barely noticed the servants that were standing on every second step, all dressed in formal military uniforms.

At the top landing, four guards stood, two on either side of enormous wide wooden doors, each carved with striking scenes that she'd have loved to have stood and studied. The doors themselves looked ancient.

As the family approached, the guards bowed low then saluted, all in perfect time with one another.

'Police!' Leo squealed, and one of the four guards lost control of his stern expression for the briefest of seconds, relaxing his lips into a spontaneous smile before focusing himself.

The tallest of the men took a large gold sceptre and banged it slowly three times against the wooden doors; they then swept inwards as if by magic.

The terrace, though filled with hundreds of people, was absolutely silent, and space had been left in the middle of the assembly—a corridor of sorts.

With his arm around her waist once more, Matthias guided Frankie forward. The group of people was silent. Frankie and Matthias were silent.

Leo was not.

'People!' he exclaimed gleefully, clapping his hand together. 'Lots and lots of people, Mama!' And everyone laughed, so Leo laughed, and then lifted his chubby little hands to cover his eyes for a moment before pulling them away and saying, 'Boo!'

More laughter, from Frankie too, who looked up helplessly at Matthias.

'And I worried he might feel nervous,' Matthias murmured from the side of his mouth.

'Apparently we have a showman on our hands,' she agreed, as Leo played peek-a-boo once more with the delighted crowd.

Conversation began to return to normal and, without the eyes of the world on them, Frankie looked around the terrace more thoroughly. It was then that she noticed something at first familiar and at second glance jarring.

'My paintings are here.' She was dumbfounded. For, hanging on the far wall of the palace, were some of her paintings. The sun was setting and it bathed them in the most beautiful natural light. She stared at the artworks with a growing sense of confusion. 'How in the world…?'

His look gave nothing away. 'You can no longer sell your paintings, Frankie. It wouldn't be appropriate. But that doesn't mean the world should be deprived of your talent.'

'I…but you…these were supposed to be showing in New York.'

He nodded. 'I bought the whole lot.'

'You bought…'

'It wouldn't have been appropriate for the show to go ahead, with news of our engagement.'

'But why buy them? If you'd said that, I would have called Charles and explained…'

'And deprived him of his commission?' He shook his head. 'He picked you to show your work; he is obviously very good at what he does. Why shouldn't he earn a reward for that?'

His perceptiveness and flattery pinballed inside her. 'I had no idea…'

'This was my intention.'

Hope flew in her chest, because the gesture was so sweet, so kind, so utterly out of left field. 'Thank you,' she said after several long seconds, as Liana approached. 'I'm truly touched.'

And, as if sensing that she might be at risk of reading too much into it, he straightened. 'It was simply the right thing to do, Frankie. Your art deserves to be seen, you cannot sell it any longer, or it would be seen that you are profiteering from your position as Queen. And this is now your country—of course the works should hang here, in Tolmirós.'

It was all so businesslike and sensible, but that didn't completely take the shine off the gesture. Because she found it almost impossible to believe that only pragmatism and common sense had motivated it. Surely, there was a thread of something else, something more?

He praised her artwork, but her artwork was *her*. Every painting was a construct of her soul, a creation of her being. To like it, to appreciate it, was to appreciate her.

'Come, *deliciae*, everybody here is eager to meet you. I hope you're not tired.'

He led her towards the Prime Minister first and for the next three hours Frankie met and spoke to more people than she could ever remember.

Matthias stayed by her side the whole time, intensely watchful, an arm around her waist at all times, shooting arrows of desire deep within her, his body warm, his eyes never leaving her.

When it came time for them to exit she was exhausted, but the fluttering of hope inside her heart refused to die down.

In a week she would marry the man she'd fallen in love with, and she refused to believe there was no hope that he would, one day, love her right back. He'd put his heart on ice, and who could blame him? He'd suffered an intense loss, a total tragedy, so he'd put his heart on ice…and Frankie was determined that she would thaw it.

CHAPTER TEN

'YOU DID WELL TONIGHT.' He watched as she strolled into their bedroom wearing a silk negligee that fell to the floor. All night he'd watched her, and he'd ignored every damned royal protocol, keeping an arm clamped vice-like around her waist because he couldn't *not* touch her. The urge had surprised the hell out of him.

At first, he'd wanted to reassure her, to protect her, just as he'd said in the car. Though she'd promised him she was fine with the event, the crowds and the attention, he'd felt she was nervous. He'd felt her energy and he'd wanted to soothe her worries. Then, when they'd stepped onto the terrace and she'd begun to charm her way around his parliament, speaking in halting Tolmirón that she'd been learning since arriving in the country, he'd felt something else. Something dark and sinister and distinctly unwelcome.

Jealousy.

He hadn't wished to share Frankie.

Every single person had wanted some of her time and attention and Frankie was so generous and giving that she would have obliged for another three hours, if he hadn't called an end to the evening with his speech. Even as he'd given the closing words he'd watched her—watched the way she stood, the way the evening wind rustled past her hair, catching it and pulling it out towards the sea, as though the wind and the ocean knew that she really did belong here in Tolmirós.

His eyes narrowed at the intensity of his thoughts, the depth of his feelings, and he suppressed them with determination.

'I had fun,' she said simply. 'It turns out I'm quite the attention-seeker.'

He lifted a brow but whatever response he'd been about to make fell out of his brain as she lifted her arms and began to style her hair. Long and waved, she lifted it onto her head into a messy bun, and the movement thrust her breasts forward, her nipples erect beneath the pale silk of the nightgown.

Oblivious to his heated inspection, she continued, 'You might have created a monster.'

He recognised that he had—but it was not the monster of which Frankie spoke. Matthias was in very real danger of becoming obsessed with Frankie.

Again.

But so much worse this time. He wanted her. All day and all night, his body craved her with a single-mindedness that he hadn't felt since he was a teenager and first learning the ways of his body's sensual needs. But tonight had shown him it was more than that. He didn't want anyone else to claim her attention. He didn't want her to talk and laugh and commiserate with *anyone*.

She'd spoken of her childhood and he'd listened, resenting the fact that she was sharing details he didn't know with a stranger.

There was danger in all those feelings and he rejected them, knowing they were not a part of his life, knowing he didn't welcome them.

'I'm kidding,' she said, and now she was looking at him, a quizzical expression on her brow. 'I just meant it wasn't as scary as I thought it would be.'

He nodded, eyes watchful. 'You're a natural.'

'Do you really think so?'

Her doubts opened vulnerability inside his chest like a chasm—a desire to shield her from ever feeling uncertain. He ignored the need to reassure her, to pepper her with praise and compliments and fill her with confidence in herself. For promises were inherent in that and he didn't want to make promises to Frankie when he had no idea of how to keep them.

'Yes.' He spoke the word like a whip cracking into the room. 'And you will have a busy week of such engagements.'

'Oh?'

'In the days before the wedding, diplomats and dignitaries will arrive to pay their respects to the woman who will be Queen. You will have many appointments.'

'I see.' She nodded thoughtfully. 'I remember.'

'You are not worried about it?'

'Well, I wish I had a better grasp on Tolmirón,' she said pragmatically, 'but, other than that, no. I'm not shy, Matthias. I have no issue talking to strangers.'

She dropped her hands to her sides and smiled brightly—Matthias's gut rolled. 'I saw that tonight.'

Her smile dropped. Damn it, the words had sounded critical, his jealousy not something he was able to disguise.

'But that's a good thing?'

His eyes narrowed. She poured herself a glass of water from the crystal decanter across the room and sipped it.

'Yes,' he said gruffly, finally, unable to take his eyes off her.

She padded across the room, so graceful and lithe. It was a warm night and the windows were open, so the hint of the ocean's fragrance was carried to them on the breeze. She climbed into bed, sitting up rather than lying down.

His fingers itched to reach out and touch her—the smooth, tanned skin of her arms drew his gaze.

'People are in awe of you,' she observed, tilting her head to look at him.

He shrugged lightly. 'I'm their King.'

'Yes, I know.' She seemed to be mulling that over. 'And tonight you seemed like it.'

'As opposed to?'

'Being King is so much a part of you. I guess I still find it hard to understand why you didn't tell me who you are. What you are. Three years ago. In New York,' she added, as if he didn't know exactly what she meant.

'It was a novelty to meet someone who didn't know,' he said truthfully. 'And I discovered I liked being treated like any other man.'

'Not like any other man,' she said, so softly the words were almost carried away towards the open window, then her ocean-green eyes latched onto his. Something pulled inside him. 'You weren't like any man I'd ever, ever met.'

He dismissed the words, refusing to let them matter to him.

'I mean it,' she said softly, her words reaching deep into his chest. 'You were so overwhelming.'

Her eyes held his, studying him in that way she had, as though she were pulling him apart piece by piece, and weighing every fragment of him in her hands. 'That's lust,' he dismissed. 'Desire.' And to prove his point he caught her hand and brought it to his lips, pressing a light kiss to her racing pulse point there. His eyes held hers as he moved his mouth to her palm and laid a kiss there, then to her thumb, which he nipped with his teeth. Her eyes fluttered shut and he felt her pulse kick up another notch beneath his fingertips.

'It was more than that,' she said throatily.

Frustration sliced through him. 'Desire is a powerful drug. Especially for someone who has no experience.'

'I'd met men I liked before,' she contradicted, dropping her gaze to the bed. He didn't want her to hide herself from him. It frustrated him. 'It wasn't like I hadn't ever been tempted by a guy. Or fantasised about what it might be like…'

Jealousy again. It was as unwelcome now as it had been earlier.

'But with you it was so different. It was as though everything I am was bound up in being with you. I felt like I needed you in the same way I need breath and water.'

'That is what it should be like,' he murmured, for it had been exactly like this for him, with Frankie.

'Like what should be like?'

'When you go to bed with someone, it should be because you want them with an intensity that almost fells you at the knees.' He regarded her with all the need he felt in that moment—and it was more than strong enough to cut his body in two.

Her cheeks flushed pink. 'So you…feel that…have felt that before? Before me?' She cleared her throat. 'With other women?'

So much was riding on that question—her hopes were so raw they hurt him. And so he lied, because it was the kindest thing for her. He lied because if he told her that he'd never felt desire like he'd known that night, like he'd known with Frankie, she would see something more in that—she would see a promise he would never give. 'Yes.' His eyes dropped to her lips and he thought about kissing her, he thought about showing her that nothing mattered more than their desire for one another. But she'd made her feelings clear and he had to respect them, even when it was practically killing him. 'That's what good sex is about.'

* * *

It was a dream he'd had hundreds of times. He was back in the car, the smell of burning hair and flesh, of smoke and smouldering metal all around him. Adrenalin raced through his veins as the limousine filled with flames. He was trapped. He knew this feeling well. He pushed at his belt; it didn't move.

His eyes were scratchy—the smoke, he knew now. His parents were dead, in the front of the car. His chest heaved as he looked towards them, saw his mother's beautiful face frozen still, horror on her features, almost as though she'd fallen asleep in the midst of a nightmare.

He turned to Spiro, bracing himself, wishing he could wake up, wishing he could reach back through time, into this dream, into the reality that had spawned it, and *do something*. But there was nothing—he was forced to relive this event again and again, the moment in which he had become truly alone.

Only Spiro wasn't there! Beside him, their faces bloodied, were Frankie and Leo.

He tasted vomit in his mouth and he stretched the belt, but it wouldn't move. His broken arm was an encumbrance he had no time for. With a curse, he called her name, but she didn't move. Leo was still, like a mannequin, so tiny, so frail.

He reached out and his fingertips curled around her fine blonde hair, clumped with blood, and blood filled his nostrils and eyes, vomit rushed through him. 'Frankie!' He called her name, urgently now, desperately, pushing at the seat belt again.

Nothing.

He was weak—powerless to help her.

Desperation tore him apart. 'Frankie!'

She lifted her head and looked at him, only her eyes

were not green now, they were dark like Spiro's had been, like Leo's were. 'You can't save us,' she murmured, rejection in her features. 'Just let us go. Let me go.'

He woke then, his forehead beaded in perspiration, his skin white. He turned towards Frankie on autopilot and almost cried out at the sight of her, fast asleep. But the dream was too real, the memory of it fractured and splintering into this time and life. 'Frankie.' He reached over and shook her arm.

She made a small noise then blinked her eyes open, looking at him.

'Matt?' In that tired, half-fogged state, she called him by the name he'd given her in New York. 'Is it Leo? What's wrong?'

Slowly, his breathing returned to normal. He looked at her for several seconds, reassuring himself that she was fine, and then he shook his head. 'Go back to sleep, Frankie. Everything's fine.'

Frankie stared at the little white bandage on her son's arm with a growing sense of rage and impotence. 'Liana—' she spoke slowly, in contrast to the way her temper was firing out of control '—what's this?'

Liana's eyes didn't quite meet Frankie's. 'From the doctor.'

'I see.' Frankie nodded, her chest heaving. She was getting married in the morning, and the last week had been both exhausting and distracting. She'd had less time for Leo than she would have liked, but she'd promised herself it would all go back to normal after the wedding. A new kind of normal, but normal nonetheless.

'Ouchie,' Leo said, looking up at his mother with big grey eyes and pointing to his arm. '*Big* ouchie.'

Frankie's heart cracked. 'Yes, I'll bet.' She bent down

and kissed her son on his cheek. He returned to his drawing. Frankie straightened and looked at Liana. 'Excuse me.'

She spun away from the older woman, striding out of the room and moving until she reached a guard. 'Where is Matthias? Where is the King?'

The guard looked somewhat surprised; she suspected her temper was showing.

'Ah, he is…occupied,' the guard apologised.

She pulled herself up to her full, not very imposing height and stared down her nose at him. 'Where. Is. My. Fiancé?'

The guard flinched and spoke into the little device at his wrist. Crackly words came back and then he nodded. 'He is in the west garden. I'll show you.'

Frankie didn't smile. She was seething. How dared Matthias take Leo's blood without so much as telling her? How dared he take her son's blood *at all*? Damn him and his DNA test!

Her anger seethed the entire way, through the palace and out of enormous glass doors, into a garden that was overgrown with oak trees and flowers. It was very beautiful. At the bottom there was a tennis court and Matthias stood down one end, hitting balls that were being served to him by a machine. As she approached, her eyes swept the surroundings—she had become adept at seeking out security guards now.

'Have us left in privacy,' she said curtly, not much caring who heard her dress down the King, but knowing on some level that the words she wanted to spit at him would be more satisfying if she could give full vent to her rage and that spectators would hold her back. Slightly.

'Ah, yes, madam.' The guard bowed and spoke into his wrist once more. Two guards stepped out of the periphery of the tennis court, moving towards their location.

Here, in the inner sanctum of the palace, security was lessened. No one could reach these parts without high-level clearance.

Frankie waited until the guards had moved back to the palace and then she closed her eyes and saw her son's little arm, imagined a needle going into his flesh, sucking blood into vials for the purpose of confirming something that any idiot with eyes in their head could easily see. And rage flooded her once more. She stormed across the lawn and slammed open the wire gate to the tennis court.

A tennis ball flew from the machine and Matthias whacked it hard, landing it with speed in the opposing side's corner.

'I need a word with you,' she snapped, crossing to the machine and staring at it. 'How do I turn this damned thing off?' She looked towards him expectantly. His eyes were watchful, his expression bland. He reached into his pocket, pulled out a small device and pressed a button. The machine went quiet.

'Yes?' he asked, still so damned calm; she wanted to shake that nonchalance from his shoulders.

'You had my son's blood taken without even telling me?'

He walked across the tennis court, his stride lithe, wearing only a pair of white shorts and a white shirt that clung to his broadly muscled chest. He was perspiring, the heat of the day intense, the tennis court in the full baking sun.

'I did tell you,' he said as he placed the racket down against the net and then came to stand in front of Frankie. His eyes skimmed her face, then dropped lower, before lifting to her eyes once more.

'When? When did you tell me you were going to get some doctor to do something so—so—invasive?'

His frown was infinitesimal. 'It is not invasive. Just a prick of a needle. The skin was numbed first and Liana was with him the whole time. She said he felt not a thing...'

'My God!' She stared at him as though he were some kind of alien. 'You didn't even go with him?'

His laugh was a short bark. 'My schedule is rather busy, *deliciae*.'

'That's your *son*!' she shouted, and rage pummelled her insides so she lifted her palms and pushed at his chest. His body was like steel, not moving, not so much as an inch. She made a guttural sound and pushed harder. Her rage grew.

'I am aware of that.' He spoke slowly. Calmly. 'I explained why the blood test was necessary.'

'But you didn't tell me *when* and I had no idea! I'm his mom! That boy has never had a single procedure in his life that I haven't been there for.' Hurt spun like a web in her chest. 'Every headache, every nose bleed, earache and injection, I have held his hand for. How dare you keep this from me?'

'Calm down, Frankie,' he said quietly. 'This is not a big deal.'

'Not a big deal?' She glared at him and hands that had been pushing him formed fists and she pummeled his chest. He watched her, his expression impossible to interpret, and then, he caught her wrists and held them still. But her anger couldn't be stemmed. She stomped her feet and her fingers formed claws and she tried to break out of his grip but he held her completely still. She charged her body at his and he caught her then, wrapping his arms around her, holding her body tight to his.

'Let me go!' she screamed. 'I can't believe you did this. I can't believe you took his blood! I can't believe you think you had any right...'

'He is my son,' he said into her ear. 'And you understood why the paternity test was necessary…'

'He's not your son!' The words had the effect of surprising Matthias sufficiently that he loosened his grip on her. She jerked out of his grip and pushed at his chest once more for good measure. Her breathing was rushed, coming in fits and spurts. 'How can he be, when you can speak of him with such callous disregard? You organised for a doctor to do something to a little boy that would have been terrifying and you didn't even go along yourself? Or tell his mother? What a heartless, unfeeling lump you are!'

A muscle jerked in his jaw. He stared at her without moving.

'You don't feel a damned thing, do you?' she demanded again, glaring at him, and emotions, feelings, needs pushed through her, surging inside her. Whatever sentimentality he lacked, she more than made up for. 'God, what an idiot I am to think you could ever change.' She stared at him with a falling heart.

He grunted something, words she didn't catch, and then he moved to her, pulling her around her waist towards his body and holding her there. He stared down at her and, before she could guess his intention, he'd dropped his mouth to hers, kissing her, punishing her, tasting her, tormenting her.

She groaned, but it was an angry groan, and then she was kissing him back, harder, punishing him right back, wanting to hurt him with the intensity of her kiss. Her hands ripped at his shirt, pushing at him impatiently. Anger seemed to have been the straw breaking the camel's back and all the feelings she had worked so hard to hold off flooded through her.

She was furious! She was so furious! But desire was

lurching inside her and she didn't want to ignore it. She wanted to use it to silence her rage!

'I hate you,' she said and in that moment she did. He stilled momentarily, then leaned down and lifted her, wrapping her legs around his waist. The power of his arousal did something to her body, weakening her, tempting her. 'I hate you,' she said again, but her mouth dropped to his shoulder, kissing his naked flesh even as her throat was raw with the ferocity of her anger.

'Good,' he said darkly, and she was so angry she didn't hear the resigned acceptance in his voice. 'So you should.'

She tasted his emotions; she felt them in every desperate lashing of his tongue, in the intensity of his grip around her waist, in the strength of his arousal. He felt—he just didn't know what to do with those feelings.

And she didn't care.

Thought had been put aside. Sense and reason were nowhere in evidence. All Frankie could do was feel and want.

She pushed at his chest and, with frustration, wriggled out of his arms; he guided her back to the ground, his eyes seeking hers for a moment. She ignored his look. She ignored everything. Her fingertips found his shorts and pushed at them; he stepped out of his shorts and shoes and then he pushed at her underpants, jerking them down her legs with impatience and desperation. She kicked them off but before her hands could find the zip of her skirt he'd lifted her once more, his eyes hunting hers with a question.

Her doubts had evaporated. She had only room for anger and need. She swore under her breath and nodded, biting down on her lower lip. 'Yes,' she groaned, as he moved her over his arousal and pushed inside her.

Her groan grew louder as pleasures so long denied moved through her body, and she remembered this. The intensity of his possession—the perfection of melding their two bodies into one.

He thrust into her, one hand on the back of her head, fingers pushing through her hair, dislodging it from the elegant style it had been put into that morning, the other hand clamped around her bottom, holding her where she was.

But it wasn't enough; she wanted so much more. With a grating cry she pushed at his chest and he stared at her for a moment, lost and confused. 'Lie down,' she commanded, and he did, pulling out of her for one devastating moment before they were one again, on the ground of the tennis court, the grass scratchy beneath her knees as she took him deep inside and rolled her hips, the power of this something she couldn't—wouldn't—ever forget. Beneath her, she saw his face grow pale and his breathing rushed, she saw desperate need fire in his veins and triumph was her companion.

Except there was no triumph in this—because she had lost. He had won. Sex was sex—there was no love in this.

She ignored the thought; the emotions it brought clawed at her throat and they were useless and unwelcome. She stared down at him, stilling slightly. 'Tell me this is meaningless,' she challenged, the gamble one she hadn't even known she was going to make. 'Tell me this means nothing.'

His eyes flared when they latched onto hers.

'Tell me while you're inside of me that this means nothing. That I mean nothing.' She felt tears slide down her cheeks, hot and fat. He caught her wrists and rolled her, flipping her onto her back and holding her still.

He moved inside her, gently at first, and then he kissed her slowly, trapping her beneath his body. Grief was equal to her desire. When would it not be?

He was skilled. Experienced. Despite the raging emotions in her chest, pleasure was inevitable. He rolled his hips and a wave began to build inside her, driving her to the edges of sanity, tipping her over it. She gripped his shoulders and he moved deeper. She cried his name out, over and over, as she fell apart.

But there was no recovery. No time to process what had happened. He kissed her lower, on her throat, and then his hands moved to the waistband of her shirt, pushing under it and finding the lace cups of her bra.

She was incandescent with pleasure. As he drove her to the edge, she kissed him harder and he kissed her right back. They tumbled off the edge of the world as they knew it, together. He exploded with the force of a thousand suns, their climax mutual and devastating.

And entirely inevitable, just as he'd always said.

CHAPTER ELEVEN

INSANITY HAD BROUGHT them together but it was dissipating quickly, leaving only confusion and regret in its wake. His body was heavy on hers and in another world, at another time, she would have lain beneath him all day, stroking his back, feeling him, wanting him anew.

But rage had been the catalyst for this and, with sensual heat evaporating, her rage surged afresh.

'I can't believe you did that.'

He pushed up on his elbows and looked at her with eyes that showed emotion—just not emotion she could make any sense of. 'You were…that was mutual.'

Her stomach plunged. 'I don't mean sex. I mean the blood test.'

Relief flashed on his features briefly and he lifted himself off her, extending a hand in an offer of assistance she ignored. She stood on her own and stared down at her outfit—it was in disarray. Shooting him a fulminating glare, she straightened her skirt and tucked her shirt back in place. Her underpants were across the tennis court; she wouldn't degrade herself by going in search of them.

He expelled a sigh. 'My parliament requires it. We've discussed that. It is done now, in any event. There is no sense arguing over an event neither of us can change.'

It was as simple as that to Matthias. Simple, pragmatic, black and white. Just like their marriage. Just like everything. 'You're unbelievable,' she muttered, looking towards the fairy tale palace with eyes that had started to see things as they really were. 'I thought this marriage made some kind of sense,' she whispered, letting her eyes close, and her heart close with them. 'I thought I could live with it. And maybe *I* can.' She could already see how addictive sleeping with Matthias would be. But it wasn't enough. Every time would destroy her a little more. 'But Leo shouldn't have to. Leo… Leo deserves so much better than this.'

There was silence. A heavy silence that throbbed with anger and disbelief. When she looked at him again he'd pulled his shorts on, but his chest was bare so she saw the way it heaved in an attempt to calm his breathing. Finally, he spoke. 'We are getting married *tomorrow.*'

'But we'll never be a family, will we?' The words were raw, thick with emotion.

The sun sliced across him, warm and bright. 'You will be my wife, and Leo is my son…'

'Sure he is,' she snapped. 'Once you have the DNA test results.'

Matthias's expression darkened. 'A DNA match will make him my legal heir; it will satisfy parliament. I do not need it to know who he is. Leo is my son. That fact has never been in dispute.' He spoke softly, perhaps attempting to soothe her, but it didn't work. She was beyond mollification.

'You'll never love me,' she said quietly. 'Will you?'

His expression flared with something like panic and her heart shattered. Yet she held her breath and she waited and she watched and, stupidly, she hoped. Finally, he shook his head. 'Love is not any part of this, as I have said all along.'

It hurt more than it should have. After what had just happened, she felt the rejection more keenly than anything else.

'And it never will be?' A glutton for punishment, apparently, she needed him to speak frankly. For him to be completely honest with her.

'No.'

So emphatic! So certain!

'So what just happened between us meant nothing to you?'

His square jaw tightened as he looked away from her. He was silent, and she took that silence as confirmation. It nearly tore her in half.

'And what about Leo?' she prompted, remembering his little bruised arm with fresh hurt. 'You do love him, don't you?'

The pause might as well have been an axe dropping. All her hopes crumbled in that moment. Reality was a pointed blade, one for which she had no shield.

'He's my son.' There was fear in Matthias's dark, swirling eyes. Fear and panic.

'For God's sake, he's not a damned possession!' she spat, forgetting her dislike for curse words and giving into the torrent of rage flowing through her like lava. 'He's not an accessory you can just put on a damned shelf! Leo is a living boy, a flesh and blood kid who doesn't give a care about your throne and your traditions and your damned cold heart! All he wants is to have a mum and a dad to play with— parents who adore him and are proud of him, who want to spend *time* with him, and delight in his achievements.'

A muscle jerked in his jaw and he spoke slowly, as though his own temper was pulling at him, begging to be indulged. 'That is not the way of royalty.'

'Says who?' she demanded. 'What was your own childhood like? I don't believe it was as cold as you are suggesting Leo's should be.'

'What do you know of my childhood?' he asked, deceptively calm.

She slammed her lips together and then her anger fired up anew. 'Nothing. But I know what mine was like. I know that my parents loved me even when they had no reason to.' Her eyes narrowed. 'I was given away, Matthias, by people who found it as easy to turn off their hearts as you apparently do, and I don't much like the idea of Leo *ever* knowing what that feels like.'

'Given away by whom?' he snapped, not understanding her implication.

'By my birth parents,' she returned, spinning away from him, her eyes caught by the hedge that grew around the tennis court.

'You're adopted?' he repeated, the words flattened of emotion.

'Yes.' There was defiance in her tone.

'Why have you never mentioned this before?'

'It didn't come up,' she said, and then bit down on her lower lip. 'And because I'm... I've lived with this shame, Matthias.' She whirled around to face him and pressed her fingertips between her breasts, as though she could score her way to her heart. 'I've lived with the knowledge that the people who should have loved me most in this world, and wanted me, didn't.'

A muscle jerked in his jaw and sympathy crossed his handsome face. 'I wish you'd told me this sooner.'

'Why?' she whispered. 'What difference does it make?'

They stared at each other in silence and then he moved closer, but she stiffened because her temper couldn't be restrained. Nor could her hurt.

'It is a part of you,' he said finally. 'A part of the woman you've become. It has been hurting you, and I would have liked... I would have liked to talk to you about it, to help you not suffer because of a decision two people made twenty-four years ago.'

'You make it sound like selling a house,' she muttered, shaking her head. 'My own parents didn't want me.' Her eyes were flinty when they lifted to his. 'Imagine what that feels like, then imagine how much I *don't* want Leo to ever know this pain.'

Her words lashed the air between them, and he stiffened visibly.

'People put their children up for adoption all the time,' he observed quietly. 'Oftentimes, because it is best for the child. Has it never occurred to you that your birth parents felt they were doing the right thing by you?'

'Of course it's occurred to me.' Her words were thick with emotion. 'I've spent my whole life trying to understand why my own mother didn't want me.' To her chagrin, the sentence burned in her throat, emotion making the words dense and acidic. 'I was determined I wouldn't repeat whatever mistake my biological parents made.' Her eyes assumed a faraway look. 'I always thought that when I had a family, it would be with a man I could spend the rest of my life with. A man I respected. A man who loved me too much to ever let me go. I thought that when I started a family, it would be with someone who would love my children like they were his purpose for living. Nothing less would be acceptable for me or whatever children I might have. I thought I'd fall in love and get married and I'd finally feel like… I'd finally feel like…' She had to suck in a deep breath to stave off a sob. 'I thought I'd feel wanted.'

The words stung the air around them, whipping through the atmosphere.

'*Deliciae—*' But what could he say? He wanted her for her son. He'd made that obvious from the moment he'd approached her.

Tears sparkled on her long lashes. 'And then I met you

and all my thoughts of saving myself for marriage went out the window. I discovered I was pregnant and had to face the reality of raising my child on my own.' She dashed at the tears that were threatening to run down her cheeks. 'It wasn't what I wanted, but I figured I could still give Leo the best of everything. And he had my parents, who loved me when they had no reason to.'

Matthias was as still as a statue, watching her with fierce concentration.

'Never would I have thought I'd be bringing my child up as a prince, the heir to a man who won't ever give him the love he deserves. A man who doesn't know how to love his own son.'

And now fresh tears ran down her cheeks, and Frankie didn't check them. She returned Matthias's gaze, her heart breaking, her soul splitting.

'I have never lied to you,' he said eventually, and she swept her eyes shut resignedly.

'I know that.' Her chest heaved. 'I knew it was unlikely you'd ever love me and, believe me, I have grappled with that fact. I have known that, in agreeing to this, I am consigning myself to the exact fate I've always sworn to avoid. You, and this marriage, are everything I didn't want for myself.' She straightened her spine, squaring her shoulders. 'But for Leo, to give him the father he deserves, I was prepared to put all that aside. What do my feelings matter when I can give him everything he should have?'

Matthias's eyes drew together, his expression not shifting. 'And what will he miss out on, living here with me? He is the Crown Prince of Tolmirós. He will want for nothing.'

'Come on, Matthias, don't be so obtuse. Children don't care about *things*. They don't care about *power*. He's just a sweet little kid, who wants to be loved. It's as easy as that.'

'I will do everything in my power to care for our son, you know that. I told you I will protect him with my dying breath...'

She shivered visibly. 'Do you think that's enough?'

His eyes glinted and slowly he nodded. 'It has to be. It is what I am offering.' He moved closer, so close they were almost touching and she could see the tiny flecks of silver in his dark eyes. 'I am what I am. I have never lied to you—I will never lie to you. I have been very careful never to make promises to you that I cannot keep.'

She bit down on her lower lip to stop it from trembling.

'I am telling you now that I will give our son a home, a future, and we will raise him as a family, just as I have always said.' His back was rigid, braced like steel. 'Our relationship is a separate concern to Leo's place here—as my son, and as my heir.'

'It's all the same thing,' she denied, shaking her head.

'No.' He lifted a hand, curling it around her cheek, stroking his thumb over her lips. 'You're offended I am not claiming to be in love with you,' he said quietly. 'And you're trying to hurt me by making that about Leo.'

'No!' she volleyed back urgently. 'I would never use our son in that way!'

He didn't relent. 'I have wondered why you are so hell-bent on idealism and commitment—why would a beautiful young woman deny herself the pleasure of sex in this day and age? And now I see. It is because you are always looking for a guarantee of security, for a promise you will not be abandoned again. You thought saving yourself for marriage would be an insurance policy of permanence.'

She drew in a harsh, raw breath at his accurate appraisal.

'You want to pick the safe option always, because you were put up for adoption and you want to make sure nothing like that will ever happen to you again.'

She opened her mouth to deny it, but the words were locked in her throat.

'How can you not see that marriage without love is a safer bet than one predicated on emotion? Emotions fade and change. How can you not see that what I am offering you is everything you want?'

Her eyes sparkled and her beautiful face fell. She shook her head slowly from side to side, but bravely held his gaze. 'If you think any of this is what I want, then you know nothing about me.'

CHAPTER TWELVE

'DO YOU THINK this marriage is what *I* wanted?'

'I know it's not,' she conceded, and the pain in her pinched expression practically tore him in two.

'I wish, more than anything, that you could have everything you've just described. I wish you could have met a man who deserves you.' He knew, as he spoke the sentence, that it was the truth. That he wasn't—and never had been—worthy of Frankie. 'I wish you hadn't met me. I wish I'd done what I knew I should have and left you alone three years ago.' He ground his teeth together. 'Hell, Frankie, do you think I haven't woken up every day regretting what I require of you? Regretting the fact that I am forced to marry you even when I know it's the last thing you want?'

'Then why are you?' she whispered.

'You know the answer to that.' His jaw was firm. 'I cannot let Leo go. He must be raised here, by you, and as my son and heir. Neither you nor I has any say in this.'

A small sound escaped her, and he thought it might have been a sob.

'I can't live here with you.' She pulled away from him, taking a step backwards.

'You must,' he said darkly, wondering at the way his stomach seemed to be swooping and tightening constantly. 'Marriage is the only option open to us.'

She nodded jerkily and she stared at him with an attempt at strength and defiance that made him feel even worse.

'I'm aware of that. I have no interest in depriving our son of a birthright he would more than likely choose for himself when he comes of age.'

Matthias tilted his head in concession, hiding the look of darkness that moved over his features.

'When you suggested this marriage, you told me I could live at another palace.'

'Mare Visum.' He remembered the conversation, and the fact he had made the promise in good faith. He hadn't cared where she might choose to live at that point. And now?

Matthias did care. He thought of her living on another island, separated from him by sea and miles, and he wanted to reject the suggestion outright.

'Leo and I will go there after the wedding,' she said, her voice almost completely steady, her eyes unflinching.

'Running away?'

She let out a small sigh and when she spoke it was with an impatience that made him feel about as big as an ant. 'I'm trying to find a way to make this work. If I was going to run away, I would have done it by now, believe me.'

Respect lifted within him, even as he warred with her words internally. To install Leo and Frankie in another palace did make perfect sense. They could spend their days happily, settling into a new lifestyle and culture, and he could continue as before. Nothing needed to change, except his country would rejoice in the knowledge of a blood heir to the throne.

It made sense. So why did he want to rail against the idea and refuse her suggestion? Why did he want to tell her he would never let his wife and child reside in a different palace to him?

The temptation to do just that terrified him, and so he nodded brusquely before he could give vent to the words that were racing through him. 'Fine.' He nodded. 'As you wish. After the wedding reception, you can be quietly moved to Mare Visum. Will this make you happy?'

For a moment her brave mask crumbled and she looked equal parts terrified and devastated. 'I'll make it work.' And then her expression hardened, like flint. 'You were right, Matthias. It turns out I'm capable of being a realist after all.' And she turned her back on him, walking slowly and calmly off the tennis court. He watched her go and told himself this would be for the best. He watched her go and told himself this odd feeling of uneasiness would disappear, just as every other feeling always had before.

Frankie was always beautiful, but dressed as a bride, her hair styled, a tiara on her head, surrounded by flowers and well-wishers, she was as stunning as he'd ever seen her.

No, that wasn't quite true. He closed his eyes for a moment and remembered the first moment he'd seen her, with no make-up, nothing special about her hair or clothes, but a smile that could power a space shuttle, and his gut pulled.

He remembered the way she'd looked when they'd made love that first time, when her face had glowed pink with rapture, her green eyes fevered with pleasure, and he had to bite back an audible groan.

He remembered the way she'd looked when he'd made love to her the day before, on the tennis court. So angry, so beautiful, so desperate with longing: the same longing that had carved him in two a long time ago.

But, while Frankie was beautiful now, there was a sadness in her features that cut through him.

He'd caused it. He'd caused it when he'd rejected her, just as she'd dreaded. He'd looked her in the eyes and told her he'd never really want *her*. He wanted their son, his heir, and she was a part of that deal.

All night it had swirled through his mind and he'd finally understood what had driven her outburst, what was at the root of all her reserve with him—she didn't want him to hurt her. She didn't want to care for him, to want him, to need him in any way, because she didn't trust him not to hurt her.

And because she wanted to be loved, and knew he'd never give her that.

Her green eyes were stormy, her lips tight, her skin pale. Standing as close as they were, at the front of the *cathedrali*, he could detect faint silver patches beneath her eyes, showing that she'd tossed and turned all night. Though she was smiling, it was unnatural and forced and there was a faint tremor in her hands as she held them clasped in front of her.

Perhaps he was the only one in the cathedral who would detect these insignificant changes but, knowing what was in her heart, hearing how she felt, knowing that this marriage was the diametric opposite of everything she'd ever wanted and that she was going through with it regardless, something pulled in the region of his heart.

He looked around the beautiful ancient building—the place he'd come to bury his parents and brother, when he'd stood in this exact spot and spoken to reassure a panicked nation, and he channelled that same ability to quell his feelings, to silence his personal needs.

Today, as on that day, he was guided by what his people needed of him, but he was also led by what Frankie deserved, by how he could go some part of the way towards fixing this for her.

Frankie would become his Queen, and then he would let her go, allow her to live as private a life as she wished. In that one small way, he could give her what she needed.

'I, Frances Preston…' she spoke loudly, as clear as a bell, just as she'd been taught '…take you, Matthias Albert Andreas Vasilliás, to be my husband.' She was glad to be saying her vows because they were generally seen to be emotional and the fact that tears danced on her eyelashes would be regarded as natural and normal. 'I promise to be true to you in good times and in bad, in sickness and in health. I promise to love you and honour you, for as long as we both shall live.'

Relieved to have said her piece, she met his eyes and flinched almost instantly. A noise sounded: Leo. She looked towards him unconsciously and her skin goosebumped at the sight of their son, the boy who would be King one day, watching on with such joy. *Please let this be okay*, she prayed, sweeping her eyes shut.

'I, Matthias Vasilliás, take you, Frances Preston, to be my wife and Queen. I promise to be true to you at all times, when you are well, and when you are not.' Frankie held her breath, knowing what was to follow, bracing herself for how it would feel to have him say the words she desperately wanted to hear and know them to be false. 'I promise to love you and cherish you, for all the days of my life.'

She couldn't help it.

She lifted her eyes to his face and saw there that he was simply performing a part, and that he was as loath to say those words as she was to hear them. Her heart didn't break. It had broken already—how could it break further?

But it disintegrated within her, being swallowed into her bloodstream, leaving only cold acceptance in its wake.

This marriage was a fraud in every way. The fact their chemistry was off the charts was just as Matthias had always said. Sex was just sex.

And finally the last vestiges of her childish hopes and naïve dreams burst about her.

Somehow, seeing the reality, made it easier for her to get through the rest of the ceremony. And, thankfully, the wedding reception was so full of dignitaries that there was always someone to talk to. Someone to dance with. Frankie took every opportunity she could to put some distance between herself and Matthias, doing whatever she could simply to pass the time, all the while knowing that she would soon be able to leave this damned palace, and her new husband, far behind.

She avoided him as best she could and she kept her heart closed off, but finally, at the end of the night, came the moment to dance with her husband. Every single guest and many of the palace servants stood at the edges of the enormous ballroom, and Frankie could fight it no longer.

For the next few minutes she had to pretend to be happy, and then they would leave and this would all be behind her.

Matthias walked to her with slow intent, his eyes holding hers in a way that made her blood gush and her chest hurt. He held a hand out and she placed hers in it, her stomach doing loops. She ignored those feelings and breathed out in an attempt to steady herself.

He led her to the middle of the dance floor and then the priest approached, a smile on his face showing they'd fooled him, at least. He held in his hands a small spool of silver thread. Once he was close enough he spoke soft words in Tolmirón, then began to loop the thread from her hand to Matthias's and back again. She remembered being told about this, but it had been so long ago she forgot the significance of it.

Some kind of tradition, though.

When their hands were bound tightly, the priest nodded and stepped away. Music began to play, soft and beautiful, and Matthias brought her closer to his chest, holding her there so she could hear the beating of his untouchable heart.

'This thread is from the Mediterranean silk crab,' he said. 'It is native to the caves of Tolmirós. Their silk grows deep beneath the ocean's surface. For as long as there are records, royal marriages have been blessed by this binding. It is said that dancing with the threads like this promises a long and happy marriage.'

Her fingers were aching beneath the beautiful silk. She inherently rejected everything he said.

'I see.'

She felt rather than heard his sigh. He didn't speak for the rest of the dance, but afterwards they stood with their hands bound, smiling at their guests.

'Is it over?' she asked quietly, her heart stammering inside her.

He tilted a glance at her, his face hiding whatever he was feeling, and then he nodded. 'We may leave.'

She kept her expression bland, her back straight, as they slipped out of the crowded ballroom to cheers and applause from all assembled. She walked beside him through the ancient corridors of the palace but as soon as they rounded the corner and were in the privacy of their residence at last, she pulled at her hand.

It wouldn't come loose. She pulled again, lifting her other hand to rip the threads free. Only they wouldn't disentangle, and it was suddenly almost impossible for Frankie to breathe.

'Please get this off,' she said, looking up at him with panic, pulling on it.

His alarm was obvious. 'Calm down, *deliciae*—'

'Don't call me that. Please. Get it off. I can't… I can't… I can't breathe.' She bit down on her lip, pulling on her hand until he held her still.

'You're only making it tighter. Just be still.'

But she couldn't. She kept pulling and he swore, reaching out and curling his fingers around her chin. 'You must be still.' He spoke loudly and firmly so that she stopped struggling and stood, her teeth chattering and her stomach in knots. Watching her the whole time, he eased a finger beneath the threads and found the loose end. He unthreaded them as quickly as he was able, but it still took longer than a minute and in that time Frankie's panic only rose, her huge eyes darkening, her face draining of colour. Finally, when he was almost done, she pulled at her hand and rubbed it in front of her.

'It's just threads,' he said in an apparent attempt to re-assure her.

Only it wasn't just threads. They were married now, bound in all the ways a man and a woman could be united: tied together for life by law and by a child and, for Frankie, by love. But her love wasn't enough. It never had been—it never would be.

She needed to get away from him as soon as possible.

He glared at the painting and, for the hundredth time in the four weeks since Leo and Frankie had left the palace, contemplated moving it. He knew he should. He knew it had no place in his life, let alone here in the place he undertook important government work.

The painting had always been a distraction, from the day it had arrived, but at least before it had been a pleasant distraction. Now it served only to plunge him into a black hole of anger, a deep place of desolate realism.

She was gone.

It had been four weeks.

He turned his attention to the documents in front of him and read them again, then, with an impatient thrust of his hand, pushed them away. It was barely afternoon, but he stood and crossed to the bar on the other side of the room and poured himself a stiff measure of whisky. He inhaled it, then threw it back, his hand slightly unsteady when he refilled the glass.

What time had he gone to bed the night before? Three? Four?

He couldn't recall.

He glared at the painting from up close, seeing the brushstrokes and imagining the way her hand would have moved as she painted it. He hated the painting in that moment with a visceral rage because it embodied so much of who Frankie was, what she was, and he'd never felt more distant from her—nor that she was more out of his reach.

A knock sounded on his door. He ignored it; the knock came again.

'What?'

His valet Niko entered, holding a brown envelope. 'Today's security memo.' Niko placed the envelope on the desk and turned to leave.

Matthias grunted by way of acknowledgement, turning his gaze to the large envelope.

They'd been gone four weeks and in that time he hadn't called her once. He'd resisted every single urge to pick up the phone and speak to her. Any time he'd thought of so much as dialling Mare Visum palace to see how she was, to speak to Leo, he'd recalled the sight of Frankie trying to pull her hand free from their ceremonial wedding bind; he'd sensed her panic and despair and he'd known that to call her would be selfish. To speak to her might improve his spirits, might reassure him that she was making sense of their new lives, but it would hurt her, he was sure of that.

And so he'd ordered security packets. Daily. It was a way to stay informed of her movements. To see her life unfurl.

He crossed to the desk now, his stride long, his fingers moving deftly as they tore the top off the envelope.

Usually the envelope included a single A4 piece of paper

with a typewritten, lacklustre report of Frankie and Leo's movements. But when he reached into the envelope for the memo, he pulled out a newspaper article as well. With a frown, his eyes ran over the words, a sense of disbelief scrambling through him.

Eggs for the Prince! the headline screamed.

Matthias read the short article, describing the delight of a local café operator who'd discovered that the beautiful blonde woman and adorable dark-haired boy who'd wandered in for breakfast the day before were, in fact, Her Majesty the Queen and the young Crown Prince.

The photos, snapped on cell phones by nearby diners, obviously, showed Frankie and Leo doing nothing more exciting than eating breakfast. Nor did it show a single security guard anywhere nearby. She wore a baseball cap low on her brow, her ponytail pulled through the back, and Leo was wearing sunglasses.

So far as disguises went, it was pretty simple.

Matthias could tell it was his wife and son.

His *wife*.

He glared at the picture and his chest ached as though it were being scraped out and emptied completely of contents.

She'd wanted to be left alone, but he'd believed she would act in their child's best interests. To take him out without any protection detail… What the hell was she playing at?

Anything could have happened! Kidnap! Murder! An accident! And she'd accused him of not caring about Leo?

He ground his teeth together and, before he could realise what he was doing, he pulled Frankie's painting off the wall and hurled it across the room, satisfied when the frame cracked upon landing. He stared at it, broken and damaged, something that had once been so beautiful and pleasing, and tried not to draw a comparison to Frankie. He told himself he was glad. The painting was nothing but a damned distraction and he was done being distracted by this.

But the longer he stared at it, the more his gut twisted, until he felt only shame.

Shame, and a deep, profound sense of grief.

He swore in his native tongue and scooped down, picking the pieces up, trying to shape it back together, almost as though a madness of sorts had descended upon him. 'Damn it,' he cursed again, when it wouldn't comply. He'd broken something beautiful. He'd broken it beyond repair.

Carefully, slowly, he placed the painting down on the desk, his powerful hands reverent with the frame where only a minute ago he'd lashed out, acting in anger.

Without thought, purely on instinct, he reached out, pressing a button on his phone; Niko answered almost immediately.

'Have the helicopter readied.'

'Yes, sir. What is your destination?'

He pressed a finger to the painting, feeling the ridges made by the layers she'd added, each with care, each with love, and his eyes closed of their own accord. He tilted his dark head back, his expression held tight.

'Mare Visum.'

The colours weren't right. She ran her brush over the top of the canvas, streaking a fine line of grey over the black, so fine it was almost translucent, giving it a pearlescent sheen. Better. But still not quite right.

She took a step back to study the painting, her frown deepening. There was a kind of magic about the moonlit nights here, on the southern tip of Tolmirós. She'd watched the moon coming over the ocean each night since coming to live in Mare Visum, and she'd tried to capture the ethereal quality on her canvas but, again and again, she'd failed.

With a grunt, she grabbed her cloth and swiped it over the bottom of the canvas, smearing the ocean she'd painted only the day before so it looked like a murky swamp, then dropping her head into her hands.

She was tired, that was all. She wasn't sleeping well.

Her stomach rolled as her mind immediately supplied the answer as to why that was.

Matthias.

Her fingers dug into her hair, pulling it loose from the braid, and she made a guttural, groaning sound of impatience. For God's sake, as if it wasn't bad enough that her dreams were tormented by memories of her husband; now he was invading her waking world?

She'd tried so hard to banish him from her thoughts.

But every time she thought she'd done it—gone an hour or two without her mind wandering to damned Matthias—he was there, his handsome face in full Technicolor in her mind's eye.

With another sound of impatience, she pulled her hands away from her face and stared at the painting, then grabbed her paintbrush, dipped it in the red oil paint and lifted it, striking a single angry line through the painting's middle.

Maybe her gift was now destroying art, rather than creating it?

She lifted her hand to mark the canvas again.

'Stop.'

His voice held her still instantly and she spun around, her eyes finding his in the doorframe. He was watching her with a stillness that made her heart do the exact opposite—it was pounding hard and fast inside her, so fast it made her knees shake. She hadn't seen him since their wedding; she had no time to prepare for seeing him now.

'Stop,' he said again, and she realised she was still holding the paintbrush in her fingertips like a sword, with blood at its tip. She dropped her gaze to it, her heart pounding, her mind racing. She sucked in a breath and looked at him once more, her expression giving little away.

'I wasn't aware you were coming to the palace,' she said, the words slightly stilted. 'I presume you've come to see Leo. He's asleep. But he'll be…'

Matthias began to walk into the room and she held her breath then, watching him as he came right in front of her and slowly took the brush from her hand.

'Stop,' he said quietly, for the third time, his eyes roaming her face, his features symmetrical, both familiar and unfamiliar to her. He stood so close she could feel warmth emanating from his powerful, broad frame, so close she could lean forward and touch him, so close she could inhale his intoxicating scent.

So close.

She shook her head slightly, taking a step backwards, and his hand shot out, steadying her before she could connect with the still-wet canvas.

His touch on her skin was like a thousand volts of electricity; it ripped through her and she clamped her mouth together to stop from letting out a groan.

Because she'd dreamed of his touch; she'd craved it to the point of insanity and despair. 'Don't,' she whispered, pulling away from him, turning her back on him and staring at the wasteland of the painting.

He was no longer touching her, but her arm felt warm where his fingers had connected with her. She swallowed in an attempt to bring moisture back to her mouth.

'Leo will be awake soon, if you want to wait in the lounge.' The words were brittle, like a porous old seashell left out in the sun.

'I came to see you.'

Her eyes swept shut at the declaration and she braced

for whatever was going to come next. She had wondered how long she would be allowed to hide out like this, before being asked to return to some kind of normality, to the royal duties that accompanied her role. Only she'd expected it would be a lowly servant who would summon her back to the palace, back to her King's side.

She hadn't expected it to be Matthias.

She wasn't prepared for this.

'Why?' A hollow whisper.

He didn't speak. He said nothing and for so long that eventually she turned to face him, and now a spark of anger was igniting inside her. 'Why?' Louder. More demanding.

Because he'd invaded her sanctuary, and without any warning; he hadn't given her any chance to raise her defences and it wasn't fair.

She held onto that anger, using it, knowing how well it served her in that moment.

He opened his mouth to say something and then appeared to change his mind.

He moved closer, but not to her, towards the painting, and he frowned as he looked at it. Self-conscious—she never liked it when people looked upon her art as it was forming on the canvas—she felt almost as if she'd been walked in on while naked. A work in progress was raw, messy, chaotic.

She tried to see it through his eyes.

It was moody and atmospheric. The destruction she'd foisted on its lower half minutes earlier only added to its brooding intensity. The red line was striking.

'I bought it, you know,' he said, and she frowned because she had no idea what he was talking about. 'The painting you were working on when we met.'

'You… It sold to a private buyer.' She shook her head, lifting her eyes from the new painting to his taut profile.

'To me.' He looked towards her abruptly, so she had no chance to flick her gaze away. 'It sold to me.'

'Why? Why did you buy it?'

His smile was dark, self-deprecating, imbued with anger and scepticism. 'Because, Frankie, I found it very hard to put you out of my mind.' He spoke darkly. 'I bought it to challenge myself—you were always there with me, and yet I knew I could never contact you. I was testing my strength and resolve by keeping that beautiful piece you'd created close to me. Taunting myself with what I couldn't ever have again.'

It made absolutely no sense.

'You got into my bloodstream, like some kind of fever, and I refused to let you weaken me.'

She bit down on her lower lip, hurt shifting inside her. 'I didn't want to weaken you.'

'I know that.' He took in a deep breath, his chest moving with the action. 'I know that.' He lifted a hand then, as if to touch her cheek, but then took a step backwards, keeping his body stiff, his expression impossible to read. He was stern. Focused. She would have said *unemotional*, except she could feel waves of emotion emanating from him.

'You were at a café with Leo.'

There was a thick undercurrent to the words. They came to her from far away, making no sense. 'This morning?'

He gave nothing away. 'It was in the papers. A photograph of the two of you.'

'Yes.' She nodded, darting her tongue out and licking her lower lip. 'I was annoyed about that. I didn't notice a photographer.'

'Anyone with a cell phone is paparazzi these days.'

That was true. She nodded.

'Did you go out without security?'

The question caught her off-guard. 'I... It was... The island is tiny and the café an easy walk. Leo and I go to the beach often, without guards. I didn't think…'

And now, as though he couldn't help himself, he put his hands on her forearms and held her still. He stared down at her and she stared back, but her heart wouldn't stop racing; blood gushed through her so fast she could hear it roaring inside her ears like an angry ocean.

'You didn't think?' he asked, haunted, and he dragged her body to his, holding her against him, and she didn't fight him; she didn't even think about fighting him.

'What if someone wanted to hurt you? Or hurt him? What if someone kidnapped Leo?'

'I was with him the whole time,' she said shakily. 'Nothing was going to happen.'

'You don't know that,' he groaned, as though he could barely speak. 'You cannot take those kinds of risks, Frankie. You can't do it. Please. Please do not take these risks.'

'It's not a risk,' she promised softly, gently, her heart turning over for him.

'How do you know this?' His jaw tightened as though he were grinding his teeth. 'You can't. You're acting on blind faith and I am not prepared to. I won't live with this kind of worry. I can't.'

Sympathy curled inside Frankie. She reached up and ran her fingers over his cheek so his breath escaped him in a single hiss. 'I understand why you feel that way,' she said softly. 'You lost your family in terrible circumstances. You couldn't save them, and now you're worried something will happen to Leo and you won't be able to save him.' His eyes flared. 'But you can't keep him in some kind of gilded cage. Not here, not in your home. I want him to have as normal a life as is possible. You have to trust that I can keep him safe. You have to trust me.'

She could see as each word hit its mark, she could see

the way his face stretched with each statement. 'I have lost everyone I ever cared for,' he said finally, the words tight as though being dragged from him against his will. 'I have no intention of losing you or Leo.'

Stupid, blind hope beat inside her, but she refused to answer it.

'Tell me why,' she said, her whole body attuned to every movement of his.

'Tell you what?' He was guarded again, cautious. 'What do you want from me?'

She blinked thoughtfully. 'Tell me why you're so furious about this.'

'You are my wife—he is my son...'

She shook her head. It wasn't good enough. 'You were prepared to marry someone else two months ago,' she reminded him with steady determination. 'If something happened to us, you could simply remarry. Have another child.'

'Don't,' he ground out, and hope in her chest flared larger, brighter.

'What? You're a realist, remember? You can marry whomever you want and have as many children as you need. Why do you care about me and Leo?'

'He is my son!' The words were torn from him, and then he was dragging a hand through his hair, pulling at it, his eyes tortured, haunted, and she hated having to push him, but deep down she knew how essential it was.

'Yes, and you can't bear the thought of something happening to him, can you? It would kill you if he was hurt in any way?'

'Of course!' he roared. 'Damn it, Frankie, I'm done losing people I—'

'Say it,' she demanded, crossing her arms over her chest.

'I'm done losing people,' he finished, stepping back from

her, putting physical space between them as though that would defuse this.

Frankie wasn't going to back down though. 'I never expected you to take a coward's response, Matthias.'

'How dare you call me a coward?' He laughed, but it was a sound of desperation—a dying man trying to grab a life raft.

'I dare because I faced every single one of my fears when I married you. I married a man I love with all my heart, who claimed he'd never love me. I married you knowing I was relegating myself to a life of loneliness. I married you with only the smallest seed of hope that you might ever care for me how I needed you to. And now you won't even admit that you love our son? When it's the most natural thing in the world?'

He glared at her and her heart raced. 'I love him, okay? I love him so much I am terrified of how I'll live if anything ever happens to our child. I look at him and I see my brother—my brother as he was in the accident when I couldn't even reach him, I couldn't save him. I couldn't save them, Frankie. My whole family died and I couldn't do a damned thing. What if something happens to Leo?' He waved a hand over his eyes, then blinked at her with despair. 'What if something happens to you?'

She hated seeing him like this. She moved to him and put a hand on his shoulder but he stayed firm, unreceptive.

'Don't. I cannot ask you to reassure me, and I don't want to lie to you. I made a choice that first night I met you that I wouldn't love you, Frankie. I have made that choice all along, even when, yes—okay, fine—when every single cell in my body aches to say what you need to hear. Even when I know I probably fell in love with you the second we met.'

Frankie drew in a shaking breath.

'But I *chose* not to act on that. I chose not to let that control my actions.'

He stood before her, a king of men, and she saw only the fifteen-year-old he'd been.

She shook her head, lifting up on tiptoe and brushing her lips to his. He stood rock-still.

'I can't do this,' he said, but his hands lifted into her hair and held her where she was. He pressed his forehead to hers and she made a small sound, deep in her throat.

'You can't keep yourself shut off from life because of an accident,' she said simply when his pain was complex and ran so deep. 'Just like I can't live in fear of rejection all my life because my birth parents chose not to raise me. We neither of us need to be defined by our past, Matt.'

'When my family died—' he spoke quietly but their faces were so close she heard his words as though they were being breathed into her soul '—I wanted to turn my back on the kingdom. I wished I'd died too, Frankie. I wanted to die.'

'But you didn't. You became the leader they needed you to be…'

'Once. I did that once.' He pressed a kiss to her cheek and she turned her head, capturing his lips with hers. 'If anything ever happened to you and Leo, if I lost either of you, I don't think I could do this again.'

Her heart, so broken, so splintered, began to pull together and she knew then that she had to be strong—not just for herself, but for Leo and Matt as well. 'I can't promise nothing will ever happen to me. Or Leo. Life comes with so few guarantees. But Matt, you can't keep pushing us away. Not when we're right here, your wife and your son, so in love with you. You can't keep pushing us away just because something *might* happen, one day. You can't throw our family away because you're afraid. Not when, by being brave, there's a good chance we'll all get everything we ever wanted in life…'

He shook his head against hers, his hand moving to curl around her cheek, his other fastening around her back.

'I ruined it,' he said, the words husky.

She looked up at him, frowning.

'The painting. I was so… I do not know. Angry. Afraid. No, I was terrified. When I saw that newspaper article, I took the painting from the wall and threw it to the ground, and I stared at the broken frame, the once beautiful object I had destroyed because I was afraid, and I felt… I ruined the painting,' he said gruffly. 'And I cannot bear that I have ruined our marriage too. I cannot bear the idea that fear has made me hurt you and push you away, that I have put you through the kind of pain I have felt this last month…'

'You say fear, but I look at you and I see a man who is so brave. What you've been through and turned your life into? I don't know anyone else who could have done that.'

'Don't. Do not speak so highly of me when I have been a coward, pushing you away rather than admitting how I feel for you…'

'You came here today,' she said softly. 'You're here because you love me, aren't you?'

His eyes glistened black in his handsome face. 'Yes,' he said on a whoosh of relief, a smile crossing his face. 'I am.'

'Then you are brave,' she promised. 'And I love you.'

'How is it possible?' he asked, wonderment and weight in the question.

'Because you are good and kind and because I believe in fairy tales and for ever.' She pressed a kiss against his nose and his eyes fell closed. 'Because I'm an optimist, and because my heart is as much yours as it ever was.'

'Your heart is a fool,' he groaned huskily. 'To love a man so unworthy of you.'

'You are more worthy of me than you give yourself credit for.'

'I doubt that,' he said with a shake of his head. 'But I will spend the rest of my life trying to deserve you.'

He scooped down and lifted her up, cradling her against his chest, and she laughed at the sudden movement. 'What are you doing?'

'I have missed you, Frankie, in every single way. This last month has been an agony. I have longed to talk to you. To show you my kingdom—*our* kingdom. I have wanted to see your wonder as you discover what is so special about Tolmirós, and I have missed Leo with an intensity that is impossible to describe. I have missed you in every way, and right now I want to make love to you as I should have all along—hold you close and tell you that I love you, tell you that everything you have wanted all your life is right here. I want this day to be the first day of your fairy tale, Frankie.'

'I thought you didn't believe in fairy tales,' she couldn't help teasing.

'I didn't.' He was serious. 'Until I met you—and I found myself living in one regardless.'

He kissed her then, a kiss of longing and love, and it inflated her soul. 'You have given me everything I ever wanted—my wife, my son, a family, a future. And I almost lost you because I couldn't admit that. I've been such a *vlakás*.'

She had no idea what the word meant. 'Yes.' Her agreement was sanguine as she wrapped her arms around his neck. 'But I forgive you.'

'You were right about my upbringing,' he said throatily. 'I don't often think about my childhood. I try not to, anyway.' He furrowed his brow. 'But that day, when you were so angry with me, you said my childhood wasn't cold. That it was full of love. And you were right. My mother adored

Spiro and me. She would have fought like a wildcat, as you did, to protect her children.'

Frankie's stomach churned with sadness for this woman, this poor woman. 'I'd like to know more about her,' she said honestly, and lifted her hand to his chest. 'I'd like to hear about your family.'

She could feel his resistance; she could see that it was something he was fighting, but then he nodded tightly. 'I think I'd like to talk to you about them. In time.'

It was enough. She lifted up and pressed a kiss to his cheek. 'We have all the time in the world, Matthias. I'm not going anywhere.'

EPILOGUE

NINE MONTHS LATER to the day, baby Emilia Vasilliás was born—a beautiful little sister for Tolmirós's thriving Crown Prince Leo.

Matthias had been by his wife's side the entire time—from the moment they'd discovered she was pregnant, only a week after her return to the palace, all the way to the delivery.

As he'd promised, in his office he was King, but he was also a man. A husband and a father, and as he watched her deliver him of another beautiful child he was mainly a bundle of nerves.

He hated seeing her in pain; he longed to be able to carry that pain, to experience it for her, so that she didn't need to feel the agony she was enduring. But she was so strong, so brave, and after hours of labour a baby's cry broke through the hospital and they looked upon their princess for the first time.

'She is beautiful, like you,' he said, the words thick as he placed the bundled-up child on his wife's chest.

Exhausted but delirious, Frankie stared at her daughter, emotions welling inside her. 'She's so like Leo was,' Frankie murmured, a smile on her lips, tears on her lashes. 'The same little nose and look, your dimple,' she said, looking up at Matthias. Her heart exploded at the sight of the big, strong King with suspiciously moist eyes of his own.

'She is divine,' he agreed, the words thick with feeling. 'A princess for our people.'

'A sister for Leo.' Frankie grinned, stroking their baby's dark pelt of hair. She pressed a kiss to Emilia's forehead and then relaxed back against the bed. 'How perfect she is.'

'How perfect you are,' Matthias corrected, kissing Frankie's cheek. 'A true warrior queen.'

Their marriage was blessed with three more children— a family of seven—and each birth was rejoiced at and celebrated by the people of Tolmirós, just as the country cheered when Leo, a young man of twenty-eight, announced his engagement to an Australian doctor. His parents were beside him when he married, and by the time Leo welcomed his first child onto this earth, Matthias's life was so rich and full, his family so extensive, that he loathed to think of a time when he had almost turned his back on what could have been. He remembered, of course, the instinct to push Frankie away, to close himself off to love because he had lost so much once before.

But brave warrior Queen Frankie had seen through that and she'd fought for what they were, regardless of her own fears and insecurities. And for that he loved her almost more than anything.

Fairy tales generally ended with the idea of people living happily ever after, but Matthias no longer thought about endings—he thought about each day as it came, and he lived with gratitude and peace. Come what may, he had been blessed, and blessed again—more than all the fairy tales in all the land.

* * * * *

UNTAMED
BILLIONAIRE'S
INNOCENT BRIDE

CAITLIN CREWS

I can't believe that this is my 50th book for Mills & Boon! What a delightful ride it's been so far!

I want to thank Jane Porter, whose novels inspired me to try to write my first Modern Romance and whose friendship, mentorship and stalwart sisterhood have changed my life in a million glorious ways.

I want to thank my two marvelous editors, Megan Haslam and Flo Nicoll, who I simply couldn't do without. What would these stories be without your guidance, encouragement, excitement, fantastic editing and endless help? I shudder to think! And I want to thank the wonderful Jo Grant as well, for always being such a shining light for category romance and those of us who write it.

But most of all I want to thank you, my readers, for letting me tell you my stories.

Here's to fifty more!

xoxox

CHAPTER ONE

LAUREN ISADORA CLARKE was a Londoner, born and bred.

She did not care for the bucolic British countryside, all that monotonous green with hedges this way and that, making it impossible to *get* anywhere. She preferred the city, with all its transportation options endlessly available—and if all else failed, the ability to walk briskly from one point to the next. Lauren prized punctuality. And she could do without stiff, uncomfortable footwear with soles outfitted to look like tire tread.

She was not a hiker or a rambler or whatever those alarmingly red-cheeked, jolly hockey-sticks sorts called themselves as they brayed about in fleece and clunky, sensible shoes. She found nothing at all entertaining in huffing up inclines only to slide right back down them, usually covered in the mud that accompanied all the rain that made England's greenest hills that color in the first place. Miles and miles of tramping about for the dubious pleasure of "taking in air" did not appeal to her and never had.

Lauren liked concrete, bricks, the glorious Tube and abundant takeaways on every corner, thank you. The very notion of *the deep, dark woods* made her break out in hives.

Yet, here she was, marching along what the local innkeeper had optimistically called a road—it was little better than a footpath, if that—in the middle of the resolutely thick forests of Hungary.

Hive-free thus far, should she wish to count her blessings.

But Lauren was rather more focused on her grievances today.

First and foremost, her shoes were not now and never had been sensible. Lauren did not believe in the cult of *sensible shoes.* Her life was eminently sensible. She kept her finances in order, paid her bills on time, if not early, and dedicated herself to performing her duties as personal assistant to the very wealthy and powerful president and CEO of Combe Industries at a level of consistent excellence she liked to think made her indispensable.

Her shoes were impractical, fanciful creations that reminded her that she was a woman—which came in handy on the days her boss treated her as rather more of an uppity appliance. One that he liked to have function all on its own, apparently, and without any oversight or aid.

"My mother gave away a child before she married my father," Matteo Combe, her boss, had told her one fine day several weeks back in his usual grave tone.

Lauren, like everyone else who had been in the vicinity of a tabloid in a checkout line over the past forty years, knew all about her boss's parents. And she knew more than most, having spent the bulk of her career working for Matteo. Beautiful, beloved Alexandrina

San Giacomo, aristocratic and indulged, had defied reason and her snooty Venetian heritage when she'd married rich but decidedly unpolished Eddie Combe, whose ancestors had carved their way out of the mills of Northern England—often with their fists. Their love story had caused scandals, their turbulent marriage had been the subject of endless speculation and their deaths within weeks of each other had caused even more commotion.

But there had never been the faintest whisper of an illegitimate son.

Lauren had not needed to be told that once this came out—and it would, because things like this always came out eventually—it wouldn't be whispers they'd have to be worried about. It would be the all-out baying of the tabloid wolves.

"I want you to find him," Matteo had told her, as if he was asking her to fetch him a coffee. "I cannot begin to imagine what his situation is, but I need him media-ready and, if at all possible, compliant."

"Your long-lost brother. Whom you have never met. Who may, for all you know, loathe you and your mother and all other things San Giacomo on principle alone. This is who you think might decide to comply with your wishes."

"I have faith in you," Matteo had replied.

And Lauren had excused that insanity almost in that same instant, because the man had so much on his plate. His parents had died, one after the next. His fluffy-headed younger sister had gone and gotten herself pregnant, a state of affairs that had caused Matteo to take a swing at the father of her baby. A perfectly reasonable reaction, to Lauren's mind—but unfortunately, Matteo had taken said swing at his father's funeral.

The punch he'd landed on Prince Ares of Atilia had been endlessly photographed and videoed by the assorted paparazzi and not a few of the guests, and the company's board of directors had taken it as an opportunity to move against him. Matteo had been forced to subject himself to an anger management specialist who was no ally, and it was entirely possible the board would succeed in removing him should the specialist's report be unflattering.

Of course, Lauren excused him.

"Do you ever *not* excuse him?" her flatmate Mary had asked idly without looking up from her mobile while Lauren had dashed about on her way out the morning she'd left London.

"He's an important and very busy man, Mary."

"As you are always on hand to remind us."

The only reason Lauren hadn't leaped into *that* fray, she told herself now as she stormed along the dirt path toward God knew where, was because good flatmates were hard to find, and Mary's obsession with keeping in touch with her thirty thousand best friends in all corners of the globe on all forms of social media at all times meant she spent most of her time locked in her room obsessing over photo filters and silly voices. Which left the flat to Lauren on the odd occasions she was actually there to enjoy it.

Besides, a small voice inside her that she would have listed as a grievance if she allowed herself to acknowledge it, *she wasn't wrong, was she?*

But Lauren was here to carry out Matteo's wishes, not question her allegiance to him.

Today her pair of typically frothy heels—with studs and spikes and a dash of whimsy because she didn't own a pair of sensible shoes appropriate for mud and woods and never would—were making this unplanned trek through the Hungarian woods even more unpleasant than she'd imagined it would be, and Lauren's imagination was quite vivid. She glared down at her feet, pulled her red wrap tighter around her, thought a few unkind thoughts about her boss she would never utter out loud and kept to the path.

The correct Dominik James had not been easy to find.

There had been almost no information to go on aside from what few details Matteo's mother had provided in her will. Lauren had started with the solicitor who had put Alexandrina's last will and testament together, a canny old man better used to handling the affairs of aristocrats than entertaining the questions of staff. He had peered at her over glasses she wasn't entirely convinced he needed, straight down his nose as he'd assured her that had there been any more pertinent information, he would have included it.

Lauren somehow doubted it.

While Matteo was off tending to his anger management sessions with the future of Combe Industries hanging in the balance, Lauren had launched herself into a research frenzy. The facts were distressingly simple. Alexandrina, heiress to the great San Giacomo fortune, known throughout the world as yet another poor little rich girl, had become pregnant when she was barely fifteen, thanks to a decidedly unsuitable older boy she shouldn't have met in the first place. The family had discovered her pregnancy when she'd been unable to keep hiding it and had transferred her from the convent school she had been attending to one significantly more draconian.

The baby had been born in the summer when Alexandrina was sixteen, spirited away by the church, and Alexandrina had returned to her society life come fall as if nothing had happened. As far as Lauren could tell, she had never mentioned her first son again until she'd made provisions for him in her will.

To my firstborn son, Dominik James, taken from me when I was little more than a child myself, I leave one third of my fortune and worldly goods.

The name itself was a clue. James, it turned out, was an Anglicized version of Giacomo. Lauren tracked all the Dominik Jameses of a certain age she could find, eventually settling on two possibilities. The first she'd dismissed after she found his notably non–San Giacomo DNA profile on one of those ancestry websites. Which left only the other.

The remaining Dominik James had been raised in a series of Catholic orphanages in Italy before running off to Spain. There he'd spent his adolescence, moving from village to village in a manner Lauren could only describe as itinerant. He had joined the Italian Army in his twenties, then disappeared after his discharge. He'd emerged recently to do a stint at university, but had thereafter receded from public view once more.

It had taken some doing, but Lauren had laboriously tracked him down into this gnarled, remote stretch of Hungarian forest—which Matteo had informed her, after all her work, was the single notation made in the paper version of Alexandrina's will found among Matteo's father's possessions.

"That was what my father wrote on his copy of my mother's will," Matteo had said cheerfully. *Cheerfully*, as if it didn't occur to him that knowing the correct Dominik James was in Hungary might have been information Lauren could have used earlier.

She didn't say that, of course. She'd thanked him.

Matteo's father might have made notes on Alexandrina's will, but he'd clearly had no intention of finding the illegitimate child his wife had given away long before he'd met her. Which meant it was left to Lauren to not only make this trek to locate Dominik James in the first place, but also potentially to break the news of his parentage to him. Here.

In these woods that loomed all about her, foreign and imposing, and more properly belonged in a fairy tale.

Good thing Lauren didn't believe in fairy tales.

She adjusted her red wrap again, pulling it tighter around her to ward off the chill.

It was spring, though there was no way of telling down here on the forest floor. The trees were thick and tall and blocked out the daylight. The shadows were intense, creeping this way and that and making her feel…restless.

Or possibly it wasn't shadows cast by tree branches that were making her feel one way or another, she told herself tartly as she willed her ankles not to roll or her sharp heels to snap off. Perhaps it was the fact that she was here in the first place. Or the fact that when she'd told the innkeeper in this remote mountain town that she was looking for Dominik James, he'd laughed.

"Good luck with that," he had told her, which she

had found remarkably unhelpful. "Some men do not want to be found, miss, and nothing good comes of ignoring their issues."

Out here in these woods, where there were nothing but trees all around and the uneasy sensation that she was both entirely alone and not alone at all, that unhelpful statement felt significantly more ominous.

On and on she walked. She had left the village behind a solid thirty minutes ago, and that was the last she'd seen of anything resembling civilization. She tried to tell herself it was lucky this path didn't go directly up the side of the brooding mountains, but it was hard to think in terms of luck when there was nothing around but dirt. Thick trees. Birds causing commotions in the branches over her head. And the kind of crackling sounds that assured her that just because she couldn't see any wildlife, it didn't mean it wasn't there.

Watching. Waiting.

Lauren shuddered. Then told herself she was being ridiculous as she rounded another curve in her path, and that was when she saw it.

At first, she wasn't sure if this was the wooded, leafy version of a desert mirage—not that she'd experienced such a thing, as there were no deserts in London. But the closer she got, the more she could see that her eyes were not deceiving her, after all. There was a rustic sort of structure peeking through the trees, tucked away in a clearing.

Lauren drew closer, slowing her steps as the path led her directly toward the edge of the clearing. All she'd wanted this whole walk was a break from the encroaching forest, but now that there was a clearing, she found it made her nervous.

But Lauren didn't believe in nerves, so she ignored the sensation and frowned at the structure before her. It was a cottage. Hewn from wood, logs interlocking and tidy. There was smoke curling up from its chimney, and there was absolutely no reason that a dedicated city dweller like Lauren should feel something clutch inside her at the sight. As if she'd spent her entire life wandering around without knowing it, half-lost in forests of wood and concrete alike, looking for a cozy little home exactly like this one.

That was ridiculous, of course. Lauren rubbed at her chest without entirely meaning to, as if she could do something about the ache there. She didn't believe in fairy tales, but she'd read them. And if any good had ever come from seemingly perfect cottages slapped down in the middle of dangerous forests, well. She couldn't remember that story. Usually, an enchanted cottage led straight to witches and curses and wolves baring their teeth—

But that was when she noticed that the porch in front of the cottage wasn't empty as she'd thought at first glance. That one of the shadows there was a man.

And he was staring straight at her.

Her heart did something acrobatic and astonishing inside her chest, and she had the strangest notion that if she surrendered to it, it could topple her straight to the ground. Right there on that edge where the forest fought to take back the clearing.

But Lauren had no intention of crumpling.

No matter who was lurking about, staring at her.

"Mr. Dominik James?" she asked briskly, making her voice as crisp and clear as possible and projecting it across the clearing as if she wasn't the slightest bit unnerved, because she shouldn't have been.

Though she was standing stock-still, she couldn't help but notice. As if her legs were not necessarily as convinced as she was that she could continue to remain upright. Especially while her heart kept up its racket and ache.

The man moved, stepping out from the shadow of the porch into the sunlight that filled the clearing but somehow did nothing to push back the inky darkness of the forest.

It only made her heart carry on even worse.

He was tall. Much too tall, with the kind of broad shoulders that made her palms itch to…do things she refused to let herself imagine. His hair was dark and thick, worn carelessly and much too long for her tastes, but it seemed to make his strong, bold jaw more prominent somehow. His mouth was flat and unsmiling, yet was lush enough to make her stomach flip around inside her. He was dressed simply, in a long-sleeved shirt that clung to the hard planes of his chest, dark trousers that made her far too aware of his powerful thighs, and boots that looked as if they'd been chosen for their utility rather than their aesthetics.

But it was his eyes that made everything inside Lauren ring with alarm. Or maybe it was awareness.

Because they were gray. Gray like storms, just like Matteo's.

San Giacomo gray, Lauren thought, just like Alexandrina's had been. Famously.

She didn't need him to identify himself. She had no doubt whatsoever that she was looking at the lost San Giacomo heir. And she couldn't have said why all the tiny hairs on the back of her neck stood up straight as if in foreboding.

She willed herself to forge on.

"My name is Lauren Clarke," she informed him, trying to remember that she was meant to be efficient. Not…whatever she was right now, with all these strange sensations swishing around inside her. "I work for Matteo Combe, president and CEO of Combe Industries. If you are somehow unfamiliar with Mr. Combe, he is, among other things, the eldest son of the late Alexandrina San Giacomo Combe. I have reason to believe that Alexandrina was also your mother."

She had practiced that. She had turned the words over and over in her head, then gone so far as to practice them in the mirror this morning in her little room at the inn. Because there was no point hemming and hawing and beating around the bush. Best to rip the plaster off and dive straight in, so they could get to the point as quickly as possible.

She'd expected any number of responses to her little speech. Maybe he would deny the claim. Maybe he would launch into bluster, or order her away. She'd worked out contingency plans for all possible scenarios—

But the man in front of her didn't say a word.

He roamed toward her, forcing her to notice the way he moved. It was more liquid than it ought to have been. A kind of lethal grace, given how big he was, and she found herself holding her breath.

The closer he came, the more she could see the expression on his face, in his eyes, that struck her as a kind of sardonic amusement.

She hadn't made any contingency plan for that.

"When Mrs. Combe passed recently, she made provisions for you in her will," Lauren forced herself to continue. "My employer intends to honor his mother's wishes, Mr. James. He has sent me here to start that process."

The man still didn't speak. He slowed when he was face-to-face with Lauren, but all he did was study her. His gaze moved all over her in a way that struck her as almost unbearably intimate, and she could feel the flush that overtook her in reaction.

As if he had his hands all over her body. As if he was testing the smoothness of the hair she'd swept back into a low ponytail. Or the thickness of the bright red wool wrap she wore to ward off the chill of flights and Hungarian forests alike. Down her legs to her pretty, impractical shoes, then back up again.

"Mr. Combe is a man of wealth and consequence." Lauren found it was difficult to maintain her preferred crisp, authoritative tone when this man was so…close. And when he was looking at her as if she were a meal, not a messenger. "I mention this not to suggest that he doesn't wish to honor his commitments to you, because he does. But his stature requires that we proceed with a certain sensitivity. You understand."

She was aware of too many things, all at once. The man—Dominik, she snapped at herself, because it had to be him—had recently showered. She could see the suggestion of dampness in his hair as it went this way and that, indicating it had a mind of its own. Worse still, she could smell him. The combination of soap and warm, clean, decidedly healthy male.

It made her feel the slightest bit dizzy, and she was

sure that was why her heart was careening about inside her chest like a manic drum.

All around them, the forest waited. Not precisely silent, but there was no comforting noise of city life—conversations and traffic and the inevitable sounds of so many humans going about their lives, pretending they were alone—to distract her from this man's curious, penetrating, unequivocally gray glare.

If she believed in nerves, she'd have said hers were going haywire.

"I beg your pardon," Lauren said when it was that or leap away from him and run for it, so unsettled and unsteady did she feel. "Do you speak English? I didn't think to ask."

His stern mouth curled the faintest bit in one corner. As Lauren watched, stricken and frozen for reasons she couldn't begin to explain to herself, he reached across the scant few inches between them.

She thought he was going to put his hand on her—touch her face, or smooth it over her hair, or run one of those bluntly elegant fingers along the length of her neck the way she'd seen in a fanciful romantic movie she refused to admit she'd watched—but he didn't. And she felt the sharpest sense of disappointment in that same instant he found one edge of her wrap, and held it between his fingers.

As if he was testing the wool.

"What are you doing?" Lauren asked, and any hope she'd had of maintaining her businesslike demeanor fled. Her knees were traitorously weak. And her voice didn't sound like her at all. It was much too breathy. Embarrassingly insubstantial.

He was closer than he ought to have been, because

she was sure there was no possible way *she* had moved. And there was something about the way he angled his head that made everything inside her shift.

Then go dangerously still.

"A beautiful blonde girl walks into the woods, dressed in little more than a bright, red cloak." His voice was an insinuation. A spell. It made her think of fairy tales again, giving no quarter to her disbelief. It was too smoky, too deep and much too rich, and faintly accented in ways that kicked up terrible wildfires in her blood. And everywhere else. "What did you think would happen?"

Then he dropped his shockingly masculine head to hers, and kissed her.

CHAPTER TWO

HE WAS KISSING HER.

Kissing her, for the love of all that was holy.

Lauren understood it on an intellectual level, but it didn't make sense.

Mostly because what he did with his mouth bore no resemblance to any kiss she had ever heard of or let herself imagine.

He licked his way along her lips, a temptation and a seduction in one, encouraging her to open. To him.

Which of course she wasn't going to do.

Until she did, with a small sound in the back of her throat that made her shudder everywhere else.

And then that wicked temptation of a tongue was inside her mouth—*inside* her—and everything went a little mad.

It was the angle, maybe. His taste, rich and wild. It was the impossible, lazy mastery of the way he kissed her, deepening it, changing it.

When he pulled away, his mouth was still curved.

And Lauren was the one who was shaking.

She assured herself it was temper. Outrage. "You can't just…go about *kissing* people!"

That curve in his mouth deepened. "I will keep that

in mind, should any more storybook creatures emerge from my woods."

Lauren was flustered. Her cheeks were too hot and that same heat seemed to slide and melt its way all over her body, making her nipples pinch while between her legs, a kind of slippery need bloomed.

And shamed her. Deeply.

"I am not a storybook creature." The moment she said it, she regretted it. Why was she participating in whatever bizarre delusion this was? But she couldn't seem to stop herself. "Fairy tales aren't real, and even if they were, I would want nothing to do with them."

"That is a terrible shame. What are fairy tales if not a shorthand for all of mankind's temptations? Fantasies. Dark imaginings."

There was no reason that her throat should feel so tight. She didn't need to swallow like that, and she certainly didn't need to be so *aware* of it.

"I'm sure that some people's jobs—or lack thereof— allow them to spend time considering the merit of children's stories," she said in a tone she was well aware was a touch too prissy. But that was the least of her concerns just then, with the brand of his mouth on hers. "But I'm afraid my job is rather more adult."

"Because nothing is more grown-up than doing the bidding of another, of course."

Lauren felt off-kilter, when she never did. Her lips felt swollen, but she refused to lift her fingers to test them. She was afraid it would give him far too much advantage. It would show him her vulnerability, and that was unconscionable.

The fact she had any vulnerability to show in the first place was an outrage.

"Not everyone can live by their wits in a forest hut," she said. Perhaps a bit acerbically.

But if she expected him to glower at that, she was disappointed. Because all he did was stare back at her, that curve in the corner of his mouth, and his eyes gleaming a shade of silver that she felt in all those melting places inside her.

"Your innkeeper told me you were coming." He shifted back only slightly, and she was hyperaware of him in ways that humiliated her further. There was something about the way his body moved. There was something about him. He made her want to lean in closer. He made her want to reach out her hands and—

But of course she didn't do that. She folded her arms across her chest, to hold him off and hold herself together at the same time, and trained her fiercest glare upon him as if that could make all the uncomfortable feelings go away.

"You could have saved yourself the trouble and the walk," he was saying. "I don't want your rich boss and yes, I know who he is. You can rest easy. I'm not interested in him. Or his mother. Or whatever 'provisions' appeared in the wills of overly wealthy people I would likely hate if I'd known them personally."

That felt like a betrayal when it shouldn't have felt like anything. It wasn't personal. She had nothing to do with the Combe and San Giacomo families. She had never been anything but staff, for which she often felt grateful, as there was nothing like exposure to the very wealthy and known to make a person grateful for the things she had—all of which came without the scrutiny and weight of all those legacies.

But the fact this man didn't want his own birthright…rankled. Lauren's lips tingled. They felt burned, almost, and she could remember the way his mouth had moved on hers so vividly that she could taste him all over again. Bold and unapologetic. Ruthlessly male.

And somehow that all wrapped around itself, became a knot and pulled tight inside her.

"My rich boss is your brother," she pointed out, her voice sharper than it should have been. "This isn't about money. It's about family."

"A very rich family," Dominik agreed. And his gaze was more steel than silver then. "Who didn't want me in the first place. I will pass, I think, on a tender re-union brought about by the caprice of a dead woman."

Her heart lurched when he reached out and took her chin in his hand. She should have slapped him away. She meant to, surely.

But everything was syrupy, thick and slow. And all she could feel was the way he gripped her. The way he held her chin with a kind of certainty that made every-thing inside her quiver in direct contrast to that firm hold. She'd gone soft straight through. Melting hot. Im-possibly…changed.

"I appreciate the taste," he rumbled at her, sardonic and lethal and more than she could bear—but she still didn't pull away from him. "I had no idea such a sharp blonde could taste so sweet."

And he had already turned and started back toward his cabin by the time those words fully penetrated all that odd, internal shaking.

Lauren thought she would hate herself forever for the moisture she could feel in her own eyes, when she hadn't permitted herself furious tears in as long as she could remember.

"Let me make certain I'm getting this straight," she threw at his back, and she certainly *did not* notice how muscled he was, everywhere, or how easy it was to imagine her own hands running down the length of his spine, purely to marvel in the way he was put together. *Certainly not.* "The innkeeper called ahead, which means you knew I was coming. Did he tell you what I was wearing, too? So you could prepare this Red Riding Hood story to tell yourself?"

"If the cloak fits," he said over his shoulder.

"That would make you the Big Bad Wolf, would it not?"

She found herself following him, which couldn't possibly be wise. Marching across that clearing as if he hadn't made her feel so adrift. So shaky.

As if he hadn't kissed her within an inch of her life, but she wasn't thinking about that.

Because she couldn't think about that, or she would think of nothing else.

"There are all kinds of wolves in the forests of Europe." And his voice seemed darker then. Especially when he turned, training that gray gaze of his on her all over again. It had the same effect as before. Looking at him was like staring into a storm. "Big and bad is as good a description as any."

She noticed he didn't answer the question.

"Why?"

Lauren stopped a foot or so in front of him. She found her hands on her hips, the wrap falling open. And she hated the part of her that thrilled at the way his gaze tracked over the delicate gold chain at her throat. The silk blouse beneath.

Her breasts that felt heavy and achy, and the nipples

that were surely responding to the sudden exposure to colder air. Not him.

She had spent years wearing gloriously girly shoes to remind herself she was a woman, desperately hoping that each day was the day that Matteo would see her as one for a change. He never had. He never would.

And this man made her feel outrageously feminine without even trying.

She told herself what she felt about that was sheer, undiluted outrage, but it was a little too giddy, skidding around and around inside her, for her to believe it.

"Why did I kiss you?" She saw the flash of his teeth, like a smile he thought better of at the last moment, and that didn't make anything happening inside her better. "Because I wanted to, little red. What other reason could there be?"

"Perhaps you kissed me because you're a pig," she replied coolly. "A common affliction in men who feel out of control, I think you'll find."

A kind of dark delight moved over his face.

"I believe you have your fairy tales confused. And in any case, where there are pigs, there is usually also huffing and puffing and, if I am not mistaken, blowing." He tilted that head of his to one side, reminding her in an instant how untamed he was. How outside her experience. "Are you propositioning me?"

She felt a kind of red bonfire ignite inside her, all over her, but she didn't give in to it. She didn't distract herself with images of exactly what he might mean by *blowing*. And how best she could accommodate him like the fairy tale of his choice, right here in this clearing, sinking down on her knees and—

"Very droll," she said instead, before she shamed

herself even further. "I'm not at all surprised that a man who lives in a shack in the woods has ample time to sit around, perverting fairy tales to his own ends. But I'm not here for you, Mr. James."

"Call me Dominik." He smiled at her then, but she didn't make the mistake of believing him the least bit affable. Not when that smile made her think of a knife, sharp and deadly. "I would say that Mr. James was my father, but I've never met the man."

"I appreciate this power play of yours," Lauren said, trying a new tactic before she could get off track again, thinking of *knives* and *blowing* and *that kiss*. "I feel very much put in my place, thank you. I would love nothing more than to turn tail and run back to my employer, with tales of the uncivilized hermit in the woods that he'd be better off never recognizing as his long-lost brother. But I'm afraid I can't do that."

"Why not?"

"Because it doesn't matter why you're here in the woods. Whether you're a hermit, a barbarian, an uncivilized lout unfit for human company." She waved one hand, airily, as if she couldn't possibly choose among those things. "If I could track you down, that means others will, as well, and they won't be nearly as pleasant as I am. They will be reporters. Paparazzi. And once they start coming, they will always come. They will surround this cabin and make your life a living hell. That's what they do." She smiled. Sunnily. "It's only a matter of time."

"I spent my entire childhood waiting for people to come," he said softly, after a moment that stretched out between them and made her...edgy. "They never did. You will forgive me if I somehow find it difficult to believe that now, suddenly, I will become of interest to anyone."

"When you were a child you were an illegitimate mistake," Lauren said, making her voice cold to hide that odd yearning inside her that made her wish she could go back in time and save the little boy he'd been from his fate. "That's what Alexandrina San Giacomo's father wrote about you. That's not my description." She hurried to say that last part, something in the still way he watched her making her stomach clench. "Now you are the San Giacomo heir you always should have been. You are a very wealthy man, Mr. James. More than that, you are part of a long and illustrious family line, stretching back generations."

"You could not be more mistaken," he said in the same soft way that Lauren didn't dare mistake for any kind of weakness. Not when she could see that expression on his face, ruthless and lethal in turn. "I am an orphan. An ex-soldier. And a man who prefers his own company. If I were you, I would hurry back to the man who keeps you on his leash and tell him so." There was a dangerous gleam in his eyes then. "Now, like a good pet. Before I forget how you taste and indulge my temper instead."

Lauren wanted nothing more. If being a pet on Matteo's leash could keep her safe from this man, she wanted it. But that wasn't the task that had been set before her. "I'm afraid I can't do that."

"There is no alternative, little red. I have given you my answer."

Lauren could see he meant that. He had every intention of walking back into this ridiculous cottage in the middle of nowhere, washing his hands of his birthright and pretending no one had found him. She felt a surge of a different kind of emotion at that, and it wasn't one that spoke well of her.

Because *she* wouldn't turn up her nose at the San Giacomo fortune and everything that went along with it. She wouldn't scoff at the notion that maybe she'd been a long-lost heiress all this time. Far better that than the boring reality, which was that both her mother and father had remarried and had sparkly new families they'd always seemed to like a whole lot more than her, the emblem of the bad decisions they'd made together.

They'd tossed her back and forth between them with bad grace and precious little affection, until she'd finally come of age and announced it could stop. The sad truth was that Lauren had expected one of them to argue. Or at least pretend to argue. But neither one of them had bothered.

And she doubted she would mind that *quite* so much if she had aristocratic blood and a sudden fortune to ease the blow.

"Most people would be overjoyed to this news," she managed to say without tripping over her own emotions. "It's a bit like winning the lottery, isn't it? You go along living your life only to discover that all of a sudden, you're a completely different person than the one you thought you were."

"I am exactly who I think I am." And there was something infinitely dangerous beneath his light tone. She could see it in his gaze. "I worked hard to become him. I have no intention of casting him aside because of some dead woman's guilt."

"But I don't—"

"I know who the San Giacomos are," Dominik said

shortly. "How could I not? I grew up in Italy in their shadow and I want no part of it. Or them. You can tell your boss that."

"He will only send me back here. Eventually, if you keep refusing me, he will come himself. Is that what you want? The opportunity to tell him to his face how little you want the gift he is giving you?"

Dominik studied her. "Is it a gift? Or is it what I was owed from my birth, yet prevented from claiming?"

"Either way, it's nothing if you lock yourself up in your wood cabin and pretend it isn't happening."

He laughed at that. He didn't fling back his head and let out a belly laugh. He only smiled. A quick sort of smile on an exhale, which only seemed to whet Lauren's appetite for real laughter.

What on earth was happening to her?

"What I don't understand is your zeal," he said, his voice like a dark lick down the length of her spine. And it did her no favors to imagine him doing exactly that, that tongue of his against her flesh, following the flare of her hips with his hands while he… She had to shake herself slightly, hopefully imperceptibly, and frown to focus on him. "I know you have been searching for me. It has taken you weeks, but you have been dogged in your pursuit. If it occurred to you at any point that I did not wish to be found, you did not let that give you the slightest bit of pause. And now you have come here. Uninvited."

"If you knew I was searching for you—" and she would have to think about what that meant, because that suggested a level of sophistication the wood cabin far out in these trees did not "—why didn't you reach out yourself?"

"Nobody sets himself apart from the world in a tiny cottage in a forest in Hungary if they wish to have visitors. Much less unannounced visitors." His smile was that knife again, a sharp, dangerous blade. "But here you are."

"I'm very good at my job." Lauren lifted her chin. "Remarkably good, in fact. When I'm given a task to complete, I complete it."

"He says jump and you aim for the moon," Dominik said softly. And she could hear the insult in it. It sent another flush of something like shame, splashing all over her, and she didn't understand it. She didn't understand any of this.

"I'm a personal assistant, Mr. James. That means I assist my employer in whatever it is he needs. It is the nature of the position. Not a character flaw."

"Let me tell you what I know of your employer," Dominik said, and his voice went lazy as if he was playing. But she couldn't quite believe he was. Or that he ever did, come to that. "He is a disgrace, is he not? A man so enamored of this family you have come all this way to make me a part of that he punched his sister's lover in the face at their father's funeral. What a paragon! I cannot imagine why I have no interest involving myself with such people."

Lauren really was good at her job. She had to remind herself of that at the moment, but it didn't make it any less true. She pulled in a breath, then let it out slowly, trying to understand what was actually happening here.

That this man had a grudge against the people who had given him to an orphanage was clear. Understandable, even. She supposed it was possible that he wasn't turning his nose up at what Matteo was offering so much as the very idea that an offer was being made at all, all these years too late to matter. She could understand that, too, having spent far more hours than she cared to admit imagining scenarios in which her parents begged for her time—so she could refuse them and sweep off somewhere.

And if she had been a man sent to find him, she supposed Dominik would have found a different way to get under her skin the same way he would any emissary sent from those who had abandoned him. All his talk of kissing and fairy tales was just more misdirection. Game-playing. Like all the scenarios she'd played out in her head about her parents.

She had to assume that his refusal to involve himself with the San Giacomos was motivated by hurt feelings. But if she knew one thing about men—no matter how powerful, wealthy or seemingly impervious—it was that all of them responded to hurt feelings as if the feelings themselves were an attack. And anyone in the vicinity was a collaborator.

"I appreciate your position, Dominik," she said, trying to sound conciliatory. Sweet, even, since he was the first person alive who'd ever called her that. "I really do. But I still want to restore you to your family. What do I have to do to make that happen?"

"First, you go wandering around the forbidding woods in a red cloak." Dominik shook his head, making a faint *tsk*-ing sound. "Then you let the Big Bad Wolf find out how you taste. Now an open-ended offer? My, my. What big eyes you have, little red."

There was no reason she should shiver at that, as if he was making predictions instead of taking part in this same extended game that she had already given too much of her time and attention.

But the woods were all around them. The breeze whispered through the trees, and the village with all its people was far, far away from here.

And he'd already kissed her.

What, exactly, are you offering him? she asked herself.

But she had no answer.

Looking at Dominik James made Lauren feel as if she didn't know herself at all. It made her feel like her body belonged to someone else, shivery and nervous. It made her tongue feel as if it no longer worked the way it should. She didn't like it at all. She didn't like *him*, she told herself.

But she didn't turn on her heel and leave, either.

"There must be something that could convince you to come back to London and take your rightful place as a member of the San Giacomo family," she said, trying to sound reasonable. Calmly rational. "It's clearly not money, or you would have jumped at the chance to access your own fortune."

He shrugged. "You cannot tempt me with that kind of power."

"Because, of course, you prefer to play power games like this. Where you pretend you have no interest in power, all the while using what power you do have to do the exact opposite of anything asked of you."

It was possible she shouldn't have said that, she reflected in some panic as his gaze narrowed on her in a way that made her...shake, deep inside.

But if she expected him to shout or issue threats, he

didn't. He only studied her in that way for another moment, then grinned. Slowly.

A sharp blade of a grin that made her stop breathing, even as it boded ill.

For her. For the heart careening around and battering her ribs.

For all the things she wanted to pretend she didn't feel, like a thick, consuming heat inside her.

"By all means, little red," he said, his voice low. "Come inside. Sit by my fire. Convince me, if you can."

CHAPTER THREE

DOMINIK JAMES HAD spent his entire life looking for his place in the world.

They had told him his parents were dead. That he was an orphan in truth, and he had believed that. At first. It certainly explained his circumstances in life, and as a child, he'd liked explanations that made sense of the orphanage he called home.

But when he was ten, the meanest of the nuns had dropped a different truth on him when she'd caught him in some or other mischief.

Your mother didn't want you, she had told him. *And who could blame her with you such a dirty, nasty sneak of a boy. Who could want you?*

Who indeed? Dominik had spent the next ten years proving to everyone's satisfaction that his mother, whoever she was, had been perfectly justified in ridding herself of him. He had lived down to any and all expectations. He'd run away from the orphanage and found himself in Spain, roaming where he pleased and stealing what he needed to live. He'd considered that happiness compared to the nuns' version of corporal punishment mixed in with vicious piety.

He had eventually gone back to Italy and joined the

army, more to punish himself than as any display of latent patriotism. He'd hoped that he would be sent off to some terrible war where he could die in service to Italy rather than from his own nihilistic urges. He certainly hadn't expected to find discipline instead. Respect. A place in the world, and the tools to make himself the kind of man who deserved that place.

He had given Italy his twenties. After he left the service, he'd spent years doing what the army had taught him on a private civilian level until he'd gotten restless. He'd then sold the security company he'd built for a tidy fortune.

Left to his own devices as a grown man with means, he had bettered himself significantly. He had gotten a degree to expand his thinking. His mind. And, not inconsiderably, to make sure he could manage his newfound fortune the way he wanted to do.

He didn't need his long-lost family's money. He had his own. The computer security company he had built up almost by accident had made him a very wealthy man. Selling it had made him a billionaire. And he'd enjoyed building on that foundation ever since, expanding his financial reach as he pleased.

He just happened to enjoy pretending he was a hermit in the Hungarian woods, because he could. And because, in truth, he liked to keep a wall or a forest between him and whatever else was out there. He liked to stay arm's length, at the very least, from the world that had always treated him with such indifference. The world that had made him nothing but bright with rage and sharp with fury, even when he was making it his.

Dominik preferred cool shadows and quiet trees these days. The comfort of his own company. Nothing brighter than the sun as it filtered down through the trees, and no fury at all.

Sharp-edged blondes with eyes like caramel who tasted like magic made him...greedy and hot. It made him feel like a long-lost version of himself that he had never meant to see resurrected.

He should have sent her away at once.

Instead, he'd invited her in.

She walked in front of him, those absurd and absurdly loud shoes of hers making it clear that she was not the sort of woman who ever expected to sneak up on a person, especially when they hit the wood of his porch. And he regretted letting her precede him almost at once, because while the cloak she wore—so bright and red it was almost as if she was having a joke at his expense—hid most of that lush and lean body from his view, it couldn't conceal the way her hips swung back and forth like a metronome.

Dominik had never been so interested in keeping the beat before in his life. He couldn't look away. Then again, he didn't try that hard.

When she got to his front door, a heavy wood that he'd fashioned himself with iron accents because perhaps he really had always thought of himself as the Big Bad Wolf, he reached past her. He pushed the door open with the flat of one hand, inviting her in.

But that was a mistake, too.

Because he had already tasted her, and leaning in close made him...needy. He wanted his mouth right there on the nape of her neck. He wanted his hands on the full breasts he'd glimpsed beneath that sheer blouse she wore. He wanted to bury his face between her legs, then lose himself completely in all her sweet heat.

Instead, all he did was hold the door for her. Meekly, as if he was some other man. Someone tamed. Civilized.

A hermit in a hut, just as he pretended to be.

He watched her walk inside, noting how stiff and straight she held herself as if she was terrified that something might leap out at her. But this cabin had been made to Dominik's precise specifications. It existed to be cozy. Homey.

It was the retreat he had never had as a boy, and he had absolutely no idea why he had allowed this particular woman to come inside. When no one else ever had.

He wasn't sure he wanted to think about that too closely.

"This is a bit of a shock," she said into the silence that stretched taut between them, her gaze moving from the thick rugs on the floor to the deep leather chairs before the fire. "I expected something more like a hovel, if I'm honest."

"A hovel."

"I mean no disrespect," she said, which he thought was a lie. She did that thing with her hand again, waving at him in a manner he could only call dismissive. It was...new, at least. "No one really expects a long-haired hermit to live in any kind of splendor, do they?"

"I am already regretting my hospitality," Dominik murmured.

He looked around at the cabin, trying to see it through the eyes of someone like Lauren, all urban chic and London snootiness. He knew the type, of course, though he'd gone to some lengths to distance himself from such people. The shoes were a dead giveaway. Expensive and pointless, because they were a statement. She wanted everyone who saw them to wonder how she walked in them, or wonder how much they cost, or drift away in a sea of their own jealousy.

Dominik merely wondered what it said about her that her primary form of expression was her shoes.

He also wondered what she was gleaning about him from this cabin that was his only real home. He didn't know what she saw, only what he'd intended. The soaring high ceilings, because he had long since grown tired of stooping and making himself fit into spaces not meant for him. The warm rugs, because he was tired of being cold and uncomfortable. The sense of airiness that made the cottage feel as if it was twice its actual size, because he had done his time in huts and hovels and he wasn't going back. The main room boasted a stone fireplace on one end and his efficient kitchen on the other, and he'd fashioned a bedchamber that matched it in size, outfitted with a bed that could fit two of him—because he never forgot those tiny cots he'd had to pretend to be grateful for in the orphanage.

"It's actually quite lovely," she said after a moment, a note of reluctant surprise in her voice. "Very…comfortable, yet male."

Dominik jerked his chin toward one of the heavy chairs that sat before his fire. Why there were two, he would never know, since he never had guests. But when he'd imagined the perfect cabin and the fireplace that would dominate it, he had always envisioned two cozy leather chairs, just like these. So here they were.

And he had the strangest sensation, as Lauren went and settled herself into one of them, that he had anticipated this moment. It was almost as if the chair had been waiting for her all this time.

He shook that off, not sure where such a fanciful notion had come from. But very sure that he didn't like it. At all.

He dropped into the chair opposite hers, and lounged there, doing absolutely nothing at all to accommodate her when he let his long legs take over the space between them. He watched her swallow, as if her throat was dry, and he could have offered her a drink.

But he didn't.

"I thought you intended to convince me to do your bidding," he said after a moment, when the air between them seemed to get thick. Fraught. Filled with premonition and meaning, when he wanted neither. "Perhaps things are different where you're from, but I would not begin an attempt at persuasion by insulting the very person I most wanted to come around to my way of thinking. Your mileage may vary, of course."

She blinked at him, and it was almost as if she'd forgotten why they were there. She shrugged out of that wrap at last, then folded her hands in her lap, and Dominik let his gaze fall all over her. Greedily. As if he'd never seen a woman before in all his days.

She was sweet and stacked, curvy in all the right places. Her hair gleamed like gold in the firelight, the sleek ponytail at her nape pulled forward over one shoulder. There was a hint of real gold at her throat, precisely where he wanted to use his teeth—gently, so gently, until she shuddered. Her breasts begged for a man's hands and his face between them, and it would take so little. He could shift forward, onto his knees, and take her in hand that easily.

He entertained a few delicious images of himself doing just that.

And she didn't exactly help matters when she pulled

that plump lower lip of hers between her teeth, the way he'd like to do.

But Dominik merely sank deeper into his chair, propped his head up with his fist, and ignored the demands of the hardest, greediest part of him as he gazed at her.

"I would be delighted to persuade you," she said, and did he imagine a certain huskiness in her voice? He didn't think he did. "I expected to walk in here and find you living on a pallet on the floor. But you clearly like your creature comforts. That tells me that while you might like your solitude, you aren't exactly hiding from the world. Or not completely. So what would it take to convince you to step back into it?"

"You have yet to explain to me why that is something I should want, much less consider doing."

"You could buy a hundred cabins and litter them about all the forests of Europe, for a start."

He lifted one shoulder, then let it fall. "I already have a cabin."

And properties across the globe, but he didn't mention that.

"You could outfit this cabin in style," she suggested brightly. "Make it modern and accessible. Imagine the opportunities!"

"I never claimed to live off the grid, did I? I believe you are the one who seems to think this cabin belongs in the Stone Age. I assure you, I have as much access to the modern world as I require."

Not to mention his other little shack that wasn't a shack at all, set farther up the mountainside and outfitted with the very latest in satellite technology. But that was yet another thing that could remain his little secret.

"You could buy yourself anything you wanted."

"All you have to offer me is money," he said after a moment. "I already told you, I have my own. But the fact that you continue to focus on it tells me a great deal about you, I think. Does this brother of mine not pay you well?"

She stiffened at that, and a crease appeared between her brows. "Mr. Combe has always been remarkably generous to me."

He found the color on her cheeks…interesting. "I cannot tell if that means he does or does not pay you what you deserve. What's the going rate for the kind of loyalty that would lead a woman clearly uncomfortable with the outdoors to march off into the forest primeval, deep into the very lair of a dangerous stranger?"

Her chin tipped up at that, which he should not have found as fascinating as he did. "I fail to see how my salary is your business."

"You have made anything and everything my business by delivering yourself to my door." And if he was overly intrigued by her, to the point his fingers itched with the need to touch her all over that curvy body until she sounded significantly less cool, that was his burden to carry. "Why don't you tell me why you're really here?"

The color on her cheeks darkened. The crease between her brows deepened. And it shouldn't have been possible to sit any straighter in that chair, but she managed it.

"I have already told you why I'm here, Mr. James."

"I'm sure they told you in the village that I come in at least once a week for supplies. You could have waited for me there, surrounded by creature comforts and room service. There was no need at all to walk through the woods to find me, particularly not in those shoes."

She looked almost smug then. As if he'd failed some kind of test.

"You don't need to concern yourself with my shoes," she said, and crossed her legs, which had the immediate effect of drawing his attention to the shoes in question. Just as she'd intended, he assumed. "I find them remarkably comfortable, actually."

"That you find them comfortable, or want me to think you do, doesn't mean they are. And it certainly doesn't make them practical for a brisk hike on a dirt path."

That gaze of hers was the color of a sweet, sticky dessert, and he wanted to indulge. Oh, how he wanted to indulge. Especially when her eyes flashed at him, once again letting him know that she felt superior to him.

Little did she know, he found that entertaining.

Even as it made him harder.

"In my experience, anyone who is concerned with the practicality of my footwear is casting about in desperation for some way to discount what I have to say," she told him. "Focus on my shoes and we can make sweeping generalizations about what sort of person I am, correct? Here's a little secret. I like pretty shoes. They don't say anything about me except that."

Dominik grinned, taking his time with it and enjoying it when she swallowed. Hard.

"Let me hasten to assure you that I'm in no way desperate. And I would love nothing more than to discount what you say, but you have said very little." He held her gaze. "Make your case, if you can. Explain to me why I should leave the comfort of my home to embrace this family who have ignored me for a lifetime already. I'm assuming it would be convenient for them in some way. But you'll understand that's not a compelling argument for me."

"I already told you. The paparazzi—"

He shook his head. "I think we both know that it is not I who would dislike it if your reporters found me here. I am perfectly content to deal with trespassers in my own way." He could see by the way her lips pressed together that she was imagining exactly how he might handle trespassers, and grinned wider. "But this rich boss of yours would not care for the exposure, I imagine. Is that not why you have made your way here, after searching for me so diligently? To convince me that his sudden, surpassing concern for my privacy is a genuine display of heretofore unknown brotherly love rather than his own self-interest?"

"Mr. Combe was unaware that he had a brother until recently," she replied, but her voice had gone cool. Careful, perhaps. "If anything should convince you about his intentions, it should be the fact that he reached out to find you as soon as he knew you existed."

"I must remember to applaud."

She didn't sigh or roll her eyes at that, though the tightness of her smile suggested both nonetheless. "Mr. Combe—"

"Little red. Please. What did you imagine I meant when I asked you to convince me? I've already had my mouth on you. Do you really think I invited you in here for a lecture?"

He didn't know what he expected. Outrage, perhaps. Righteous indignation, then a huffy flounce out of the cabin and out of his life. That was what he wanted, he assured himself.

Because her being here was an intrusion. He'd invited her in to make certain she'd never come back.

Of course you did, a sardonic voice inside him chimed in.

But Lauren wasn't flouncing away in high dudgeon. Instead, she stared back at him with a dumbfounded expression on her face. Not as if she was offended by his suggestion. But more as if…such a thing had never occurred to her.

"I beg your pardon. Is this some kind of cultural divide I'm unfamiliar with? Or do you simply inject sex into conversations whenever you get bored?"

"Whenever possible."

She laughed, and what surprised him was that it sounded real. Not part of this game at all.

"You're wasting your time with me." Her smile was bland. But there was a challenge in her gaze, he thought. "I regret to tell you, as I have told every man before you who imagined they could get to my boss through me, that I have no sexual impulses."

If she had pulled a grenade out of her pocket and lobbed it onto the floor between them, Dominik could not have been more surprised.

He could not possibly have heard her correctly. "What did you just say?"

There before him, his very own Little Red Riding Hood…relaxed back against the leather of her armchair. Something he also would have thought impossible moments before. And when she smiled, she looked like nothing so much as an oversatisfied cat.

"I'm not a sexual person," she told him, and Dominik

was sure he wasn't mistaking the relish in her voice. It was at odds with the sheen of something a whole lot like vulnerability in her gaze, reminding him of how she'd melted into his kiss. "It's a spectrum, isn't it? Some people's whole lives are completely taken over by the endless drive for sex, but not me. I've never understood all the fuss, to be honest."

He was half convinced he'd gone slack-jawed in astonishment, but he couldn't seem to snap out of it long enough to check. Not when she was sitting there talking such absolute nonsense with an expression that suggested to him that she, at least, believed every word she was saying.

Or, if he looked closer, *wanted* to believe it, anyway.

"You are aware that a kiss is a sexual act, are you not?"

"I've kissed before," Lauren said, and even shook her head at him, wrinkling up her nose as if he was… silly. Him. *Silly.* "I experimented with kissing when I was at university. As you do. That's how I know that it isn't for me."

"You experimented," he repeated as if that would make sense of what she was saying with such astonishing confidence—though, again, when he looked closer he was almost sure it was an act. Did he merely want it to be? "With kissing."

"As I said, there are all sorts. Not everyone is consumed with the urge to flail about naked. Not that there's anything wrong with that, but some of us have other things to think about." Her expression turned virtuous and Dominik was sure, then, that while she might believe what she was saying, he'd…rocked her foundations. She was overselling it. "More important things."

"And what, dare I ask, is it that consumes your thoughts if not…flailing?"

"You've made quite a few references to my being at Mr. Combe's bidding, but I take my job very seriously. It requires dedication. Focus and energy. I couldn't possibly siphon all of that off into all that trawling about from pub to pub every night, all to…"

"Flail. Naked."

"Exactly."

Dominik knew two things then as surely as he knew himself, his own capabilities and the fact she was lying about her own sexuality. One, if he wasn't misunderstanding what she was telling him, his sharp, majestically shoed and caramel-eyed blonde was a virgin. And two, that possibility made him hard.

Very nearly desperately so.

Because he already knew how she tasted. He'd heard the noises she'd made when he kissed her, and no matter what she told herself and was trying to tell him now, he did not believe that she had been unaffected.

He knew otherwise, in fact, as surely as he knew his own name.

"I can see how you're looking at me," Lauren said. She was still entirely too relaxed, to his way of thinking, leaning back in the leather chair as if she owned it. Clearly certain that she was in total control of this conversation. And him. "I don't understand why men take this as such a challenge."

Dominik's mouth curved. "Do you not?"

It was her turn to shrug. "I'm perfectly comfortable with who I am."

"Obviously." He settled back against his chair until he mirrored her. And for a long moment, every second of which he could feel in the place where he was hardest, he simply…studied her. Until her smile faded and she looked a whole lot less *certain.* "For reference, little red, people who are perfectly comfortable with themselves rarely mentioned their sexuality at all, much less bludgeon others over the head with it."

"Oh, I see." Her smile was bland again, and this time, distinctly pitying besides, though he could see the uncertainty she tried to hide. "You're upset because you think I'm saying this because I didn't like your kiss. Don't worry, Mr. James. I don't like any kissing. Not just yours."

"Of the two of us sitting here, Lauren," he said, enjoying the taste of her name in his mouth and the faint tremor in her sweet lower lip that told him the truths she couldn't, "I am the one who is actually comfortable with himself. Not to mention fully aware. I know exactly how much you liked my kiss without you needing to tell me all these stories."

"I'm glad to hear it." Her chin tipped up again, her eyes flashing as if that could hide the glint of doubt there. "I've seen this a thousand times before, you know. First, you will proposition me. Then you'll throw a temper tantrum when I decline your kind offer to see what I'm missing, with you as selfless guide. It's always the same old story."

"Is it? Why don't you tell it to me?"

She waved that hand of hers again. "You will want to kiss me, certain that a mere touch of your lips will awaken me to the joys of the flesh. It won't work, it's already failed to awaken me to anything, but you won't believe me. I can see you already don't believe me." She had the gall to try to look bored. "And if it's all the same to you, I'd rather fast-forward straight through that same old song and dance. It's tedious."

"If you insist." He found himself stroking his jaw with his fingers, because he knew that if he reached over to put them on her, she would take it as evidence of this theory of hers. This *song and dance.* No matter how much she liked it. "And what is on the other side? Once we're finished with all this fast-forwarding?"

"Why, business, of course. What else?"

"But in this case, little red, your business and mine are the same. Aren't you here to tempt me out of my humble cabin and into the great, wide world?"

"I am. All you need to do is name your price."

And Dominik was not an impulsive man. Not anymore. He had learned his lesson, time and again, in his misspent youth.

But there was something about this woman that got to him. She was still smiling at him in that pitying way when he'd already tasted her. When he knew better. He couldn't tell if she was lying to herself as well as him, but try as he might, he couldn't think of a single good reason to deny himself.

Not when Lauren Clarke was the most entertainment he'd had in ages.

And Dominik was no longer in the army. He no longer ran his security company. If he wanted to live his life in pursuit of his own amusement, he could now.

Even if it meant involving himself with the blood relations he had located when he was still in the army, but had never seen any reason to contact.

Because like hell would he go begging for scraps.

"You must let me kiss you whenever I wish," he said, keeping his voice mild so she wouldn't see that driving need for her inside him, greedy and focused. "That's it. That is my price. Agree and I will go wherever you wish for me to go and do whatever you wish me to do."

"Don't be ridiculous."

He could tell she thought he was kidding, because she didn't bother to sit up straight. Her cheeks didn't flush, and she was still smiling at him as if he was a fool. He felt like one. But that didn't make him want to take back what he'd said.

Especially when he could see the truth all over her, where she couldn't smile it away.

"This fairy tale obsession of yours has gone too far, I think. Let's return to the real world, which I understand is hard out here in an enchanted cottage in the deep, dark woods."

"The first thing you will learn about me is that I'm never ridiculous," Dominik told her, his voice low. "And when I make a promise, I keep it. Will you? You must let me kiss you whenever I like. However I like. This is a simple request, surely. Particularly for a person such as you who doesn't care one way or the other about kissing."

"I already told you, I know how this goes." She'd lost that smile, and was frowning at him then. "You say *kissing*, but that's not what you mean. It always goes further. There's always a hand."

"I do have a hand, yes. Two, in fact. You've caught me."

"One way or another it always leads back to the same discussion. When we can just have it now." She shook her head. "I'm just not sexual. That's the beginning and the end of it."

"Marvelous. Neither am I, by your definition."

Dominik gazed at her, and hoped he didn't look as wolfish as he felt. "Let's be nonsexual together."

She blinked at him, then frowned all the more. "I don't think…"

"We can make rules, if you like." It was his turn to smile, and so he did, all the better to beguile her with. "Rule number one, as discussed, you must allow me to kiss you at my whim. Rule number two, when you no longer wish me to kiss you, you will tell me to stop. That's it. That's all I want."

"But…" Her voice was faint. He counted that as a victory.

"And in return for this, little red, I will trot back to England on your boss's leash and perform the role of long-lost brother to his satisfaction. What will that entail, do you think? Will it be acts of fealty in public view? Or will it simply be an appropriate haircut, the better to blend with the stodgy aristocracy?"

She looked bewildered for a moment, and if Dominik had ever had the slightest inkling to imagine himself a good man—which he hadn't—he knew better then. Because he liked it. He liked her off balance, those soft lips parting and her eyes dazed as if she hardly knew what to do with herself.

Oh, yes, he liked it a great deal.

"I don't understand why, when you could have anything in the world, you would ask for…a kiss."

He could feel the edge in his own smile then. "You cannot buy me, Lauren. But you can kiss me."

She looked dubious, but then, after a moment or two, she appeared to be considering it.

Which Dominik felt like her hands all over his body, skin to skin.

"How long do you imagine this arrangement will go on?" she asked.

He shrugged. "As long as your Mr. Combe requires I remain in his spotlight, I suppose."

"And you give me your word that you will stop when I tell you to."

"I would not be much of a man if I did not," he said, evenly. "There are words to describe those who disregard such clear instructions, but *man* is not among them."

"All you want from the news that you're one of the richest men alive is a kiss," she said after another moment, as if she was selecting each word with care. "And I suppose you can't get much kissing out here in the middle of nowhere, so fair enough, if that's what you like. But why would you choose me?"

Dominik restrained himself—barely—from allowing his very healthy male ego to tell her that he had no trouble finding women, thank you very much. That this cabin was a voluntary retreat, not an involuntary sentence handed down from on high. But he didn't say that.

"What can I say? I've always had a weakness for Little Red Riding Hood."

She sighed, and at the end, it turned into a little laugh. "Very well. If that's what you want, I'll kiss you. But we leave for England as soon as possible."

"As you wish," Dominik murmured, everything in him hot and ready, laced through with triumph and something far darker and more intense he didn't want to name. Not when he could indulge it instead. "But first, that kiss. As promised."

CHAPTER FOUR

LAUREN WAS BAFFLED.

Why would anyone want a kiss—or, she supposed, a number of kisses—when there were so many other things he could have asked for? When the world was at his feet with the combined Combe and San Giacomo fortunes at his service?

She had met a great many men in her time, most of them through work, so she considered herself something of an expert in the behavior of males who considered themselves powerful. But she'd never met anyone like Dominik James. He had no power at all that she could see, but acted like he was the king of the world. It didn't make sense.

But it didn't matter. She wasn't here to understand the man. All she had to do was bring him back to London, and no matter that she felt a good deal less steady than she was pretending.

"Now?" she asked. She looked around the cabin as if sense was another rug tossed over the wood floor that could rise up and assert itself if she could only locate it. "You want me to kiss you *now*?"

Dominik lounged there before her, something glittering in the depths of his gray eyes, though the rest of his face was perfectly serious. He patted his knee with his free hand while what she thought was a smile *almost* changed the stern line of his mouth.

She pushed herself to her feet, still feeling that odd, liquid sensation all throughout her body. It was the way she felt when she slipped on a new pair of the shoes she loved. It made her feel…dangerous, almost. She'd always loved the feeling, because surely that was what a woman was meant to feel.

She'd long thought that if Matteo ever looked at her the way she looked at her shoes, she'd feel it. But he never had.

Lauren didn't understand why she felt it now, in a cabin in the middle of the woods. Or why Dominik was so determined to ruin it with more kissing.

Because the way he'd kissed her out there in the clearing had been different from her halfhearted youthful experiments, true. But Lauren knew it wouldn't last, because it never did. She knew that sooner or later he would grow ever more keen while she became less and less interested.

That was how it had always gone. She had discovered, time and again, that *thinking* about kissing was far preferable to the unfortunate reality of kissing.

She preferred this moment, right now. The moment when a man looked at her and imagined she was a desirable woman. Feminine straight through and capable of feeling all those things that real women did.

Capable of wanting and being wanted in return, when the truth was, *want* wasn't something that Lauren was capable of.

But he had already kissed her, and she told herself that was a good thing. She already knew what she'd agreed to. And it wasn't as if kissing Dominik had been as unpleasant as it always had been in the past.

Quite the opposite, a sly voice deep inside her very nearly purred.

She brushed that aside. It was the unexpected hike, no doubt, that had made her feel so flushed. So undone. She was unaccustomed to feeling those sorts of sensations in her body—all over her body—that was all.

"Perhaps you do not realize this, since you dislike kissing so much, but it is generally not done while standing across the room," Dominik said with that thread of dark amusement woven into his voice that she couldn't quite track. She could feel it, though. Deep inside all those places where the hike through the woods had made her sensitive.

She didn't understand that, either.

"Do you expect me to perch on your knee?" she asked without trying all that hard to keep the bafflement out of her voice.

"When and where I want," he said softly, gray eyes alight. "How I want."

And Lauren was nothing if not efficient. She had never been wanted, it was true, and was lacking whatever that thing was that could make her want someone else the way others did so readily. So she had learned how to be needed instead.

She had chosen to pursue a career as a personal assistant because there was no better way to be needed—constantly—than to take over the running of someone's life. She liked the high stakes of the corporate world, but what she loved was that Matteo truly *needed* her. If she didn't do her job he couldn't do his.

He needed her to do this, too, she assured herself. He wanted his brother in the fold, media-ready and compliant, and she could make it happen.

And if there was something inside her, some prickle of foreboding or something much sweeter and more dangerous, she ignored it.

The fire crackling beside them seemed hotter all of a sudden. It seemed to lick all over the side of her body, and wash across her face. She had never sat on a man's lap before, or had the slightest desire to do such a thing, and Dominik did nothing to help her along. He only watched her, no longer even the hint of a smile anywhere on his face, save the suggestion of one like silver in the endless gray of his gaze.

She stepped between his legs, thrust out before him in a way that encouraged her to marvel at both their length and strength, and then she eased herself down, putting out a hand to awkwardly prop herself against him as she sat.

"Do you plan to kiss me from this position?" She could swear he was laughing at her, though his face remained stern. "You are aware that kissing requires that lips meet, are you not?"

He had kissed her so smoothly out there at the edge of the woods. So easily. And now that Lauren thought about it, she had never been the one to initiate a kiss. She had always been a recipient. But there was something deep inside her that refused to tell him that.

It was the same something that bloomed with shame—because it had to be shame, surely—there between her legs.

She shouldn't have thought about that just then. Because she was sitting there on his hard, muscled thighs, so disastrously and intriguingly hot beneath her, and she couldn't seem to help herself from squirming against him.

And as she did she could feel something tense and electric hum to life in the space between them.

The fire was so hot. The air seemed to thicken with it as if there were flames dancing up and down the length of her arms, and the strangest part was that it didn't hurt. Burning should hurt, surely, but in this case it only seemed to make her breathless.

She eased closer to the wall of his chest, twisting herself so she was level with his face, and close enough to kiss him. Or she thought it was the correct distance, having never experimented with this position before.

He moved, but only a little, sliding his hands to grip her lightly at her waist.

Lauren couldn't think of a single reason why that should make her shudder.

Everywhere.

She gulped in a breath, aware of too many things at once. Those broad, blunt fingers of his like brands through the thin shell of her blouse. The iron forge of him beneath her, making her pulse and melt in places she'd never felt much of anything before.

This close, and knowing that a kiss was about to happen, she noticed things she hadn't before. The astonishing lines of his face, from his high cheekbones to the blade of his nose. The supremely male jut of his chin. And that thick, careless hair of his, that for some reason, she longed to sink her fingers into.

Her heartbeat slowed, but got louder. And harder, somehow, as if it was trying to escape from her chest.

She searched that implacable gray gaze of his, though

she couldn't have said what she was looking for. She burned still, inside and out, and the fire seemed to come at her from all sides, not just from the fireplace.

Slowly, carefully, she lowered her mouth.

Then she pressed her lips against his.

For one long beat, there was only that. The trembling inside her, the feel of his firm lips beneath hers.

There, she thought, with a burst of satisfaction. *This is even easier than I expected—*

But that was when he angled his head.

And he didn't kiss the way she had, halting and unsure.

He smiled against her mouth, then licked his way inside, and Lauren…ignited.

It was as if the cabin caught fire and she was lost in the blaze.

She couldn't seem to get close enough. Dominik's big hands moved from her waist, snaking around her back to hold her even more fiercely. And she moved closer to him, letting her own hands go where they liked. His wide, hard shoulders. His deliciously scratchy jaw. And all that gloriously dark hair of his, thick and wild, like rough silk against her palms.

And still he kissed her, lazy and thorough at once, until she found herself meeting each thrust of his wicked tongue. Until she was the one angling her head, seeking that deliriously sweet fit.

As if they were interlocking parts, made of flame, intoxicating and dangerous at once.

Lauren was the one meant to be kissing him, and this was nothing but a bargain—but she forgot that. She forgot everything but the taste of him. His strength and all that fire, burning in her and around her until she thought she might have become her own blaze.

And she felt a different kind of need swell in her then, poignant and pointed all at once. It swept her from head to toe, then pooled in the place between her legs where she felt that fire most keenly and pulsed with a need too sharp to be shame—

She wrenched her lips from his, startled and shamed and something else that keened inside her, like grief.

For a moment there was nothing but that near-unbearable fire hanging in the air between them. His eyes were silver and bright, and locked to hers. That mouth of his was a temptation and a terror, and she didn't understand how any of this was happening.

She didn't understand much of anything, least of all herself.

"You promised," Lauren managed to say.

And would likely spend the rest of her life reliving how lost and small she sounded, and how little she thought she had it in her to fix it. Or fight her way back to her efficient and capable self.

"I did," he agreed.

His voice was a dark rasp that made her quiver all over again, deep inside.

"You promised and you've already broken that promise. It didn't even take you—"

Her voice cut off abruptly when he ran his palm down the length of her ponytail and tugged it. Gently enough, so there was no reason she felt…scalded straight through.

"What promise did I break?" he asked mildly. So mildly she found herself frowning at him, because she didn't believe it.

"One kiss," she said severely.

And the way his mouth curved then, there below the knowing silver of his gaze, made her shiver.

"You're the one who has to say stop, little red. I don't remember you saying anything of the kind. Do you?"

And for another beat she was...stupefied.

Unable to breathe, much less react. Unable to do anything but gape at him.

Because he was quite right. She hadn't said anything at all.

In the next second she launched herself off him, leaping back in a way that she might have found comical, had she not been so desperate to put space between her and this man she'd made a devil's bargain with.

"This was our agreement, was it not?" Dominik asked, in that same mild voice. He only watched her—looking amused, she couldn't help but notice—as she scrambled around to the back of the chair facing him. "I hope you do not plan to tell me that you are already regretting the deal we made."

And Lauren did not believe in fairy tales. But it occurred to her, as she stared back at this man who had taken her over, made her a stranger to herself, and made her imagine that she could control something she very much feared was far more likely to burn her alive—she realized that she'd been thinking about the wrong kind of fairy tale.

Because there were the pretty ones, sweeping gowns and singing mice. Everything was princesses and musical numbers, neat and sweet and happy-ever-afters all around.

But those weren't the original fairy tales. There were darker ones. Older versions of the same stories, rich with the undercurrent of blood and sacrifice and grim consequences.

There were woods that swallowed you whole. Thorn bushes that stole a hundred years from your life. There were steep prices paid to devious witches, locked rooms that should have stayed closed, and children sent off to pay their fathers' debts in a variety of upsetting ways.

And there were men like Dominik, whose eyes gleamed with knowledge and certainty, and made her remember that there were some residents of hidden cottages who a wise girl never tried to find in the first place.

But Lauren hadn't heeded all the warnings. The man so difficult to find. The innkeeper's surprise that anyone would seek him out. That damned uninviting path through the woods.

She'd been so determined to prove her loyalty and capabilities to Matteo during this tough period in his life. If he wanted his long-lost older brother, she, by God, would deliver said older brother—once again making it clear that she alone could always, always give her boss what he needed.

Because she did so like to be needed.

She understood that then, with a lurch deep inside her, that once Matteo had mentioned Dominik this had always been where she would end up. This had always been her destination, which she had raced headlong toward with no sense of self-preservation at all.

This deal she'd made. And what it would do to her.

And she knew, with that same lurch and a kind of spinning sensation that threatened to take her knees out from under her, that it was already much too late to save herself from this thing she'd set in motion.

"I don't regret anything," she lied through lips that no longer felt like hers. And though it was hard to meet that too-bright, too-knowing gray gaze of his, she forced herself to do it. And to hold it. "But we need to head back to England now. As agreed."

His lips didn't move, but she could see that smile of his, anyway. All wolf. All fangs.

As if he'd already taken his first bite.

"But of course," he said quietly. "I keep my promises, Lauren. Always. You would do well to remember that."

CHAPTER FIVE

BY THE TIME they made it down out of the mountains in the hardy SUV Dominik kept back behind the cabin, then onto the private plane Lauren had waiting for them at the nearest airfield, she'd convinced herself that she'd simply…gotten carried away.

Once out of the woods, the idea that she'd let *trees* get into her head and so deep beneath her skin struck her as the very height of foolishness.

She was a practical person, after all. She wasn't excitable. It was simply the combination of hiking around in heels and a man who considered kissing currency.

It was the oddness that had gotten to her, she told herself stoutly. And repeatedly.

By the time they boarded the plane, she had regained her composure. She was comfortable on the Combe Industries jet. In her element. She bustled into her usual seat, responded to her email and informed Matteo that she had not only found his brother, but would also shortly be delivering him to England. As requested.

It was amazing how completing a few basic tasks made her feel like herself again.

As if that strange creature who had lost herself on a strange man's lap had never existed at all.

She threw herself into the work that waited for her, delighted that it gave her the opportunity to continue pretending she had no idea who that girl could have been, wild with abandon on Dominik's knee. The farther they got from those woods, the farther she felt from all those bizarre sensations that had been stirred up in her.

Fairy tales, for God's sake. What had she been thinking?

Lauren resolved that she would do whatever she could to make sure she never succumbed to that kind of nonsense again, no matter what bargains she might have made to get Dominik on this plane.

But all through the short flight, no matter how ferociously she tried to concentrate on her computer screen and all the piled-up emails that required her immediate attention, she was aware of Dominik. Of that considering gray gaze of his, following her every move.

And worse, the heat it kicked up in its wake, winding around and around inside her until she was terribly afraid it would make her burst wide open.

Fairy tale nonsense, she told herself sharply. People didn't *burst*, no matter what they felt.

That was what came of tramping about in the wilderness. Too much clean air obviously made her take leave of her senses.

Back in London she felt even more like herself. Calm. Competent. In control and happily surrounded by tarmac. Concrete. Brick buildings. All the solid reminders of the world she knew. And preferred to inhabit, thank you very much.

"England's greenest hills appeared to be rather more gray puddles and a procession of dingy, squat holdings,"

Dominik said from beside her in the backseat of the car that picked them up from the private airfield outside the city. "What a disappointment."

Lauren congratulated herself on her total lack of reaction to him. He was nothing more than a business associate, sharing a ride.

"Surely, you must know that it rains in England," she said, and even laughed. "A great deal, in fact."

She would have said nothing could possibly divert her attention from her mobile, but every cell in her body went on high alert when Dominik turned. And then faced her, making it impossible for her to pretend she didn't notice the way his big body took up more than his fair share of room in the car. His legs were too long, and those boots of his fascinated her. They seemed so utilitarian. So ruthlessly masculine.

And she couldn't even bring herself to think about the rest of him. All those long, smoothly muscled limbs. All that strength that simmered in him, that she was dimly surprised he managed to contain.

He didn't sit like a San Giacomo. He might look like one of them, or a feral version, anyway, but he was far more...elemental. Matteo and his sister, Pia, shared those same gray eyes, and they had both looked stormy at one time or another.

But Lauren couldn't help thinking that Dominik *was* a storm.

And her body reacted appropriately, prickling with unease—or maybe it was electricity.

Lightning, something in her whispered.

"What happens now?" Dominik asked, but his voice was lazy. Too lazy. She didn't believe he cared what happened now. Or ever. This was all a game to him.

Just as she was.

That thought flustered her, and she didn't make it any better by instantly berating herself for feeling anything at all. She tried to settle her nerves—the ones she didn't believe in—as she stared at him sternly.

"What would you like to happen?" she asked, and told herself she didn't know why she felt as if she were made of glass.

"I assume you are even now in the process of delivering me safely into the bosom of my warm, welcoming family." His smile was as sharp as she felt inside. Jagged. "Will there be a fatted calf?"

"I'm currently delivering you to the London headquarters of Combe Industries," Lauren replied as crisply as she could manage. Especially when all she could seem to concentrate on was his sardonic mouth. "Once there, you and I will wait for further instructions from Mr. Combe."

"Instructions." Dominik looked amused, if darkly. "I can hardly wait."

Lauren gripped her mobile in her hand and made herself stop when she realized she was making her palm ache.

"Mr. Combe is actually not in England at present," she said, and she didn't know why she was telling him this now. It could have waited until they were out of this car. Until they were safely in the office, the place where she felt most at home. Most capable. "He is currently in Perth, Australia. He's personally visiting each and every Combe Industries office."

If Lauren had expected Matteo to greet the news that she'd found his brother by leaping onto a plane and heading straight home to meet him, she kept that to herself. Because Matteo showed no sign of doing anything of the kind.

And it felt disloyal to find that frustrating, but she did.

"The great saint is not in England?" Dominik asked in mock outrage. "But however will we know how best to serve him if he isn't here to lay out his wishes?"

"He is perfectly able to communicate his wishes at all times," she assured him. "It's actually my job to make certain he can, no matter where he is. Don't worry. You'll know exactly what he expects of you."

That was the wrong thing to say, but she only realized that once the words were out there between them. And Dominik's eyes gleamed like silver as he gazed at her.

"Between you and me, little red, I have never done well with expectations." His voice was much too low for her peace of mind. It was too intimate. Too…insinuating. "I prefer to blaze my own trail."

"There is no blazing of trails in the San Giacomo family," she retorted with far more fervor than she'd intended. But she tried to keep her expression impassive when his dark brows rose. "The San Giacomos have existed in some form or another for centuries. They were once a major economic force in the Venetian Empire. While their economic force might have faded over time, their social capital has not."

"They sound marvelous," Dominik murmured. "And wholly without the blood of innocents on their hands, I am sure."

"I couldn't say what the San Giacomo family did in the eighth century, of course. But I think you'll find that Matteo Combe is a good and decent man."

"And you his greatest defender," Dominik said, and there was something less lazy about his voice then. "He must pay you very well indeed."

Her breath caught, but Lauren pushed on. "Whether you like expectations or do not, I'm afraid that the blood in your veins means you must meet them, anyway."

That dark amusement in Dominik's eyes made them bright against the rain outside. "Must I?"

"There are more eyes on the San Giacomos now than usual," Lauren said, and wasn't nervous. Why would she be nervous?

"It would seem to me that those eyes are more focused on the Combe side of the family," Dominik said after a moment. "Less Venetian economic might and more Yorkshire brawler, if I remember correctly."

Lauren didn't instantly bristle at that, which struck her as evidence of more disloyalty on her part.

"I'm not sure that there's any particular model of behavior for how a man is expected to act at his father's funeral," she said quietly. "Especially when his mother died only weeks before."

"I wouldn't know," Dominik replied, and that voice of his wasn't the least bit lazy any longer. "Having never met anyone who would claim me as a son in the first place."

Lauren felt as if he'd slapped her. Worse, she felt a flush of shame as if she deserved the slap he hadn't actually given her.

"Why don't we wait to have this argument—"

Dominik laughed. "Is this an argument? You have a thin skin indeed, little red. I would have called this a discussion. And a friendly one, at that."

"—until we are in the office, and can bring Mr.

Combe in on a call. Then he can answer all these questions instead of me, which seems more appropriate all around."

"Wonderful," Dominik said, and then his mouth curved in a manner she could only call challenging. "Kiss me."

And she had truly convinced herself that the bargain they'd struck had been some kind of hiking-inspired dream. A Hungarian-woods-inspired nightmare, made of altitude and too much wildlife. She had been sure it had all been some kind of hallucination. She'd been *sure*.

You're such a liar, a voice deep inside her told her.

"You can't mean now. Here."

"Will you make me say it every time?" Dominik's voice was soft, but the look on his face was intense. Intent. "When, where and how I want. Come now, Lauren. Are you a woman of your word or not?"

And it was worse, here. In the back of a town car like so many other town cars she'd ridden in, on this very same stretch of motorway. Here in England, on the outskirts of London, where she had always prided herself on her professionalism. Her competence and efficiency. Where she had built a life made entirely of needs she could meet, and did.

She still hadn't figured out who the Lauren Isadora Clarke was who had kissed this man with such abandon and hunger. But the intrusion of the fairy tale story she refused to accept was real into her life—her real life—was a shock. A jolt.

Her stomach went into free fall.

And Dominik shook his head sadly, making that *tsk*-ing sound as if he could read her every thought right there on her face. "You agreed to this bargain, Lauren. There's no use pretending you suddenly find the notion disgusting." His eyes were much too bright. "It is almost as if kissing makes you feel things, after all."

That shook her out of the grip of her horror—because that was what she told herself it had to be, that wild, spinning sensation that made her feel drunk from the inside out. It spurred her into action, and she didn't stop to question why it was she was so determined that this man never know that his kiss was the only one that had ever gotten to her at all.

It was information he never, ever needed to know.

She hardly wanted to admit it to herself.

And she threw herself across the backseat, determined that whatever else happened, she would do what she'd promised she would. That way, he would never know that she didn't want to do it *because* she wasn't bored by him the way she wanted to be.

Dominik caught her as she catapulted herself against his chest, then shifted her around so that she was sitting draped over his lap, which didn't help anything at all.

He was much too hard. There was the thick, enticing steel of his thighs, and that hard ridge that rose between them. And Lauren felt...soft and silly, and molten straight through.

And she was sitting on him again, caught in the way he gazed at her, silver in his eyes and his hands at her waist again.

"I know you know how to do this, little red," he said, his voice a soft taunt. "Or are you trying to play games with me?"

"I don't play games," she said stiffly.

As if, should she maintain proper posture and a chilly

tone, she might turn this impossible situation to her advantage. Or at least not drown in it.

"So many things you don't do," Dominik murmured, dark and sardonic. "Until you do."

She wanted him to stop talking. And she wanted to get this over with, as quickly as possible, and somehow those two things fused together and made it seem a terrific idea to lift her hands and use them to frame his face.

He stopped talking.

But the trouble with that was, her brain also stopped working.

She was entranced, suddenly and completely, with that strong jaw of his. She marveled at the feel of him, the rasp of his unshaven jaw beneath her palms.

A giant, hot fist she hadn't known lurked there inside her opened then. Slowly, surely, each finger of pure sensation unfurled, sending ribbons of heat to every last part of her.

She studied the sweep of his cheekbones, the lush shape of his mouth, and felt the shiver of it, so deep inside her it made parts she hadn't known she had bloom into life.

And she had the craziest urge to just…rub herself against him.

But instead, she kissed him.

She had some half-baked notion that she would deliver a peck, then retreat, but the moment she tasted him again she forgot about that. His mouth was a temptation and sin at once, and she was giddy with it. With his taste and heat.

With him, full stop.

So she angled her head and took the kiss deeper.

Just the way he'd taught her.

And for a little while, there was nothing at all but the slide of her tongue against his. The tangle of their breath, there in the close confines of the back of the car as it moved through the London streets.

Nothing but that humming thing that kicked up between them, encircling them both, then shuddering through Lauren until she worried, in some distant part of her head, that she would never be the same.

That she was already forever changed.

She kissed him and kissed him, and when she pulled her mouth away from his she fully expected him to follow her.

But he didn't.

She couldn't begin to describe the expression on his face then, or the steady sort of gleam in his gaze as he reached over and traced the shape of her mouth.

"Good girl," he said, and she knew without having to ask that he was deliberately trying to be provocative. "It's nice to know that you can keep your promise even after you get what you want."

"I am a woman of my word, Mr. James," she said crisply, remembering herself as she did.

And suddenly the fact that she was sitting on him, aware of all those parts of him pressed so intimately against her, was unbearable.

She scrambled off him and had the sinking suspicion that he let her go. And then watched her as if he could see straight through her.

And that was the thing. She believed he could.

It was unacceptable.

"The only thing you need to concern yourself about is the fact that you will soon be meeting your family for the first time," she said, frowning at him. "It wouldn't be surprising if you had some feelings around that."

"I have no feelings at all about that."

"I understand you may wish—"

"You do not understand." His voice was not harsh, but that somehow made the steel in it more apparent. "I was raised in an orphanage, Lauren. As an orphan. That means I was told my parents were dead. When I was older, I learned that they might very well be alive, but they didn't want me, which I believed, given no one ever came to find me. I don't know what tearful, emotional reunion you anticipate I'm about to have with these people."

Lauren was horrified by the part of her that wanted to reach over to him again. This time, just to touch him. It was one more thing that didn't make sense.

"You're right, I can't understand. But I do know that Mr. Combe will do everything in his power to make sure this transition is easy for you."

"You are remarkably sure of your Mr. Combe. And his every thought."

"I've worked for him for a long time."

"With such devotion. And what exactly has he done to deserve your undying support?"

She flexed her toes in her shoes, and she couldn't have said why that made her feel so obvious, suddenly. Silly straight through, because he was looking at her. As if he could see every last thing about her, laid out on a plate before him.

Lauren didn't want to be known like that. The very notion was something like terrifying.

"I see," Dominik said, and there was a different sort of darkness in his voice then. "You are not sexual, you tell me with great confidence, but you are in love with your boss. How does that work, exactly?"

"I'm not in…" She couldn't finish the sentence, so horrified was she. "And I would never…" She wanted to roll down the window, let the cool air in and find her breath again, but she couldn't seem to move. Her limbs weren't obeying her commands. "Matteo Combe is one of the finest men I have ever known. I enjoy working for him, that's all."

She would never have said that she was in love with him. And she would certainly never have thought about him in any kind of sexual way. That seemed like a violation of all the years they'd worked together.

All she wanted—all she'd ever wanted—was for him to appreciate her. As a woman. To see her as something more than his walking, talking calendar.

"And this paragon of a man cannot stir himself to return home to meet the brother you claim he is so dedicated to? Perhaps, Lauren, you do not know the man you love so much as well as you think."

"I know him as well as I need to."

"And I know he's never tasted you," Dominik said with all his dark ruthlessness. It made her want to cry. It made her want to…*do something* with all that restlessness inside her. "Has he?"

Lauren could barely breathe. Her cheeks were so red she was sure they could light up the whole of the city on their own.

"Not answering the question is an answer all its own, little red," Dominik murmured, his face alight with what she very much feared was satisfaction.

And she was delighted—relieved beyond measure— that the car pulled up in front of the Combe Industries building before she was forced to come up with some kind of reply.

But she didn't pretend it was anything but a reprieve, and likely a temporary one, when she pushed open the door and threw herself out into the blessedly cool British evening.

Where she tried—and failed, again and again—to catch her breath and recover from the storm that was Dominik James.

CHAPTER SIX

THERE WAS NO doubt at all that the man on the video screen was Dominik's brother. It was obvious from the shape of his jaw to the gray of his eyes. His hair was shorter, and every detail about him proclaimed his wealth and high opinion of himself. The watch he wore that he wasn't even bothering to try to flash. The cut of his suit. The way he sat as if the mere presence of his posterior made wherever he rested it a throne.

This was the first blood relative Dominik had ever met, assuming a screen counted as a meeting. This... aristocrat.

He couldn't think of a creature more diametrically opposed to him. He, who had suffered and fought for every scrap he'd ever had, and a man who looked as if he'd never blinked without the full support of a trained staff.

They stared at each other for what seemed like another lifetime or two.

Dominik stood in Lauren's office, which was sprawling and modern and furnished in such a way to make certain everyone who entered it knew that she was very important in her own right—and even more so, presumably, as the gatekeeper to the even more massive and dramatically appointed office beyond.

Matteo Combe's office, Dominik did not have to be told.

His only brother, so far as he knew. The man who had received all the benefit of the blood they shared, while Dominik had been accorded all the shame.

Matteo Combe, the man whose bidding Lauren did without question.

Dominik decided he disliked the man on the screen before him. Intensely.

"I would have known you anywhere," Matteo said after they'd eyed each other a good long while.

It would have pained Dominik to admit that he would have known Matteo, too—it was the eyes they shared, first and foremost, and a certain similarity in the way they held themselves—so he chose not to admit it.

"Brother," Dominik replied instead, practically drawling out the word. Making it something closer to an insult. "What a pleasure to almost meet you."

And when Lauren showed him out of the office shortly after that tender reunion, Dominik took a seat in the waiting area that was done up like the nicest and most expensive doctor's office he'd ever seen, and reflected on how little he'd thought about this part. The actually having family, suddenly, part.

Because all he'd thought about since she'd walked into his clearing was Lauren.

When he'd searched for his parents, he'd quickly discovered that the young man who'd had the temerity to impregnate an heiress so far above his own station had died in an offshore oil rig accident when he was barely twenty. An oil rig he'd gone to work on because he couldn't remain in Europe, pursuing his studies, after his relationship with Alexandrina had been discovered.

And when Dominik had found all the Combes and San Giacomos with precious little effort—which, of course, meant they could have done the same—he'd had wanted nothing to do with them. Because he wanted nothing from them—look what they'd done to the boy who'd fathered him. They had gotten rid of both of them, in one way or another, and Dominik had risen from the trash heap where they'd discarded him despite that abandonment. His mother's new boy and girl, who had been pampered and coddled and cooed over all this time in his stead, were nothing to him. What was the point of meeting with them to discuss Alexandrina's sins?

He'd been perfectly content to excel on his own terms, without any connection to the great families who could have helped him out of the gutter, but hadn't. Likely because they'd been the ones to put him there.

But it hadn't occurred to him to prepare himself to look into another man's face and see...his own.

It was disconcerting, to put it mildly.

That they had different fathers was evident, but there was no getting around the fact that he and Matteo Combe shared blood. Dominik scowled at the notion, because it sat heavily. Too heavily.

And then he transferred that scowl back to the screen inside Lauren's office, where Matteo was still larger than life and Lauren stood before him, arguing.

He didn't have to be able to hear a word she said to know she was arguing. He knew some of her secrets now. He knew the different shapes she made with that mouth of hers and the crease between her brows that broadcast her irritation. He certainly knew what she looked like when she was agitated.

And he found he didn't much care for the notion that whatever she called it or didn't call it, she had a thing for her boss.

Her boss. His brother.

"Is he one of the ones you've experimented with?" he asked her when she came out of the office, the screen finally blank behind her.

She was frowning even more fiercely than before, which he really shouldn't have found entertaining, especially when he hadn't had the pleasure of causing it. He lounged back in his seat as if it had been crafted specifically for him and regarded her steadily until she blinked. In what looked like incomprehension.

"I already declined to dignify that question with a response."

"Because dignity is the foremost concern here. With your boss." He refused to call the man *Mr. Combe* the way she did. And calling him by his Christian name seemed to suggest that they had more of a personal relationship—or any personal relationship, for that matter—than Dominik was comfortable having with anyone who shared his blood. "I want to know if he was one of your kissing experiments."

Lauren maintained her blank expression for a moment.

But then, to his eternal delight, she went pink and he couldn't seem to keep from wondering about all the other, more exciting ways he could make her flush like that.

"Certainly not." Her voice was frigid, but he'd tasted her. He knew the ice she tried to hide behind was a lie. "I told you, I admire him. I enjoy the work we do together. I have never *kissed*—"

She cut herself off, then pulled herself up straight. It only made Dominik wonder what she might have said if she hadn't stopped herself. "You and I have far more serious things to talk about than kissing experiments, Mr. James."

"I have always found kissing very serious business indeed. Would you like me to demonstrate?"

That pink flush deepened and he wanted to know where it went. If it changed as it lowered to her breasts, and what color her nipples were. If it made it to her hips, her thighs. And all that sweetness in between. He wanted to peel off that soft silk blouse she wore and conduct his own experiments, at length.

And the fact that thinking about Lauren Clarke's naked body was far preferable to him than considering the fact he'd met his brother, more or less, did not escape him. Dominik rarely hid from himself.

But he had no need, and less desire, to tear himself open and seek out the lonely orphan inside.

"Mr. Combe thinks it best that we head to Combe Manor. It is the estate in Yorkshire where his father's family rose to prominence. He understands you are not a Combe. But he thinks it would cause more comment to bring you directly to any of the San Giacomo holdings in Italy at this point."

Dominik understood that *at this point* was the most important part of Lauren's little speech. That and the way she delivered it, still standing in her own doorway too stiffly, her voice a little too close to nervous. He studied her and watched her grow even more agitated—and then try to hide it.

It was the fact that she wanted to hide her reactions from him that made him happiest of all, he thought.

"I don't know who you think is paying such close attention to me," Dominik said after a moment. "No one has noticed that I bear more than a passing resemblance to a member of the San Giacomo family in my entire lifetime so far. I cannot imagine that will change all of a sudden."

"It will change in an instant should you be found in a San Giacomo residence, looking as you do, as the very ghost of San Giacomos past."

He inclined his head. Slightly. "I am very good at living my life away from prying eyes, little red. You may have noticed."

"Those days are over now." She stood even straighter, and he had the distinct impression she was working herself up to say something else. "You may not feel any sense of urgency, but I can tell you that the clock is ticking. It's only a matter of time before Alexandrina's will is leaked, because these things are always leaked. Once it is, the paparazzi will tear apart the earth to find you. We need to be prepared for when that happens."

"I feel more than prepared already. In the sense of not caring."

"There are a number of things it would make more sense for us to do now, before the world gets its teeth into you."

"How kinky," he murmured, just to please himself.

And better still, to make her caramel eyes flash with that temper he suspected was the most honest thing about her.

"First, we must make your exterior match the San Giacomo blood that runs in your veins."

He found his mouth curving. "Are you suggesting a makeover? Have I strayed into a fairy tale, after all?"

"I certainly wouldn't call it that. A bit of tailoring and a new wardrobe, that's all. Perhaps a lesson or two in minor comportment issues that might arise. And a haircut, definitely."

Dominik's grin was sharp and hot. "Why, Lauren. Be still my heart. Am I the Cinderella in this scenario? I believe that makes you my Princess Charming."

"There's no such thing as a Princess Charming." She sniffed. "And anyway, I believe my role here is really as more of a Fairy Godmother."

"I do not recall Cinderella and her Fairy Godmother ever being attached at the lips," he said silkily. "But perhaps your fairy tales are more exciting than mine ever were."

"I hate fairy tales," she threw at him. "They're strange little stories designed to make children meek and biddable and responsible for the things that happen to them when they're not. And also, we need to get married."

That sat there between them, loud and not a little mad.

Dominik's gaze was fused to hers and, sure enough, that flush was deepening. Darkening.

"I beg your pardon." He lingered over each word, almost as if he really was begging. Not that he had any experience with such things. And there was so much to focus on, but he had to choose. "All this urban commotion must be getting to me." He made a show of looking all around the empty office, then, because he had never been without a flair for the dramatic when it suited him—and this woman brought it out in him in spades. "Did you just ask me to marry you?"

"I'm not *asking* you, personally. I'm telling you that

Mr. Combe thinks it's the best course of action. First, it will stop the inevitable flood of fortune hunters who will come out of the woodwork once they know you exist before they think to start. Second, it will instantly make you seem more approachable and civilized, because the world thinks married men are less dangerous, somehow, than unattached ones. Third, and most important, it needn't be real in any sense but the boring legalities. And we will divorce as soon as the furor settles."

Dominik only gazed back at her, still and watchful.

"Come now, Lauren. A man likes a little romance, not a bullet-pointed list. The very least you could do is bend a knee and mouth a sweet nothing or two."

"I'm not *proposing* to you!" Her veneer slipped at that, and her face reddened. "Mr. Combe thinks—"

"Will I be marrying my own brother?" He lay his hand over his heart in mock astonishment. "What sort of family *is* this?"

He thought her head might explode. He watched her hands curl into fists at her sides as if that alone could keep her together.

"You agreed to do whatever was asked of you," she reminded him, fiercely. "Don't tell me that you're the one who's going to break our deal. Now. After—"

After kissing him repeatedly, he knew she meant to say, but she stopped herself.

The more he stared back at her without saying a word, the more agitated she became. And the more he enjoyed himself, though perhaps that made him a worse man than even he'd imagined. And he'd spent a great quantity of time facing his less savory attributes head-on, thanks in part to the ministrations of the nuns who had taught him shame and how best to hate himself for existing. The army had taken care of the rest.

These days Dominik was merrily conversant on all his weaknesses, but Lauren made him…something else again.

But that was one more thing he didn't want to focus on.

"What would be the point of a marriage that wasn't real?" he asked idly. "The public will need to have reason to believe it's real for it to be worth bothering, no?"

The truth was that Dominik had never thought much about marriage one way or the other. Traditional family relationships weren't something he had ever seen modeled in the orphanage or on the streets in Spain. He had no particular feelings about the state of marriage in any personal sense, except that he found it a mystifying custom, this strange notion that two people should share their lives. Worse, themselves.

And odder still, call it love—of all things—while they did it.

What Dominik knew of love was what the nuns had doled out in such a miserly way, always shot through with disappointment, too many novenas and demands for better behavior. Love was indistinguishable from its unpleasant consequences and character assassinations, and Dominik had been much happier when he'd left all that mess and failure behind him.

He had grown used to thinking of himself as a solitary being, alone by choice rather than circumstance. He liked his own company. He was content to avoid others. And he enjoyed the peace and quiet that conducting his affairs to his own specifications, with no outside opinion and according to his own wishes and whims, afforded him. He was answerable to no one and chained to nothing.

The very notion of marrying anyone, for any reason, should have appalled him.

But it didn't.

Not while he gazed at this woman before him—

That pricked at him, certainly. But not enough to stop. Or leave, the way he should have already.

He told himself it was because this was a game, that was all. An amusement. What did he care about the San Giacomo reputation or public opinion? He didn't.

But he did like the way Lauren Clarke tasted when she melted against him. And it appeared he liked toying with her in between those meltings, too.

"What we're talking about is a publicity stunt, nothing more," she told him, frowning all the while. "You understand what that means, don't you? There's nothing real about it. It's entirely temporary. And when it ends, we will go our separate ways and pretend it never happened."

"You look distressed, little red," he murmured, because all she seemed to do as she stood there before him was grow redder and stiffer, and far more nervous, if the way she wrung her hands together was any indication.

He didn't think she had the slightest idea what she was doing. Which was fair enough, as neither did he. Evidently. Since he was still sitting here, lounging about in the sort of stuffy corporate office he'd sworn off when he'd sold his company, as if he was obedient. When he was not. Actually subjecting himself to this charade.

Participating in it wholeheartedly, in point of fact, or he never would have invited her into his cabin. Much less left it in her company—then flown off to rainy, miserable England.

"I wouldn't call myself distressed." But her voice told him otherwise. "I don't generally find business concerns *distressing*. Occasionally challenging, certainly."

"And yet I am somehow unconvinced." He studied the way she stood. The way she bit at her lower lip. Those hands that telegraphed the feelings she claimed not to have. "Could it be that your Mr. Combe, that paragon of virtue and all that is wise and true in an employer by your reckoning, has finally pushed you too far?"

"Of course not." She seemed to notice what she was doing with her hands then, because she dropped them back to her sides. Then she drew herself up in that way she did, lifted her chin and met his gaze. With squared shoulders and full-on challenge in her caramel-colored eyes—which, really, he shouldn't have found quite as entertaining as he did. What was it about this woman? Why did he find her so difficult to resist? He, who had made a life out of resisting everything? "Perhaps you've already forgotten, but you promised that you would do whatever was asked of you."

He stopped trying to control his grin. "I recall my promises perfectly, thank you. I am shocked and appalled that you think so little of the institution of marriage that you would suggest wedding me in some kind of cold-blooded attempt to fool the general populace, all of whom you appear to imagine will be hanging on our every move."

He shook his head at her as if disappointed unto his very soul at what she had revealed here, and had the distinct pleasure of watching her grit her teeth.

"I find it difficult to believe that you care one way

or the other," she said after a moment. "About fooling anyone for any reason. And, for that matter, about marriage."

"I don't." He tilted his head to one side. "But I suspect you do."

He thought he'd scored a hit. She stiffened further, then relaxed again in the next instant as if determined not to let him see it. And then her cheeks flamed with that telltale color, which assured him that yes, she cared.

But a better question was, why did he?

"I don't have any feelings about marriage at all," she declared in ringing tones he couldn't quite bring himself to believe. "It was never something I aspired to, personally, but I'm not opposed to it. I rarely think about it at all, to be honest. Are you telling me that you lie awake at night, consumed with fantasies about your own wedding, Mr. James?"

"Naturally," he replied. And would have to examine, at some point, why he enjoyed pretending to be someone completely other than who he was where this woman was concerned. Purely for the pleasure of getting under her skin. He smiled blandly. "Who among us has not dreamed of swanning down an expensive aisle, festooned in tulle and lace, for the entertainment of vague acquaintances?"

"Me," she retorted at once. And with something like triumph in her voice.

"Of course not, because you are devoid of feelings entirely, as you have taken such pains to remind me."

"I'm not sentimental." Except she looked so deeply pleased with herself just then it looked a whole lot like an emotion, whether she wanted to admit such things or not. "I apologize if you find that difficult to accept."

"You have no feelings about marriage. Sex. Even kissing, no matter how you react while doing it. You're an empty void, capable only of doing the bidding of your chosen master. I understand completely, Lauren."

That she didn't like that description was obvious by the way she narrowed her eyes, and the way she flattened her lips. Dominik smiled wider. Blander.

"How lucky your Mr. Combe is to have found such devotion, divorced of any inconvenient sentiment on your part. You might as well be a robot, cobbled together from spare parts for the singular purpose of serving his needs."

If her glare could have actually reached across the space between them and struck him then, Dominik was sure he would have sustained mortal blows. What he was less certain of was why everything in him objected to thinking of her as another man's. In any capacity.

"What I remember of my parents' marriage is best not discussed in polite company," she said, her voice tight. He wondered if she knew how the sound betrayed her. How it broadcast the very feelings she pretended not to possess. "They divorced when I was seven. And they were both remarried within the year, which I didn't understand until later meant that they had already moved on long before the ink was dry on their divorce decree. The truth is that they only stayed as long as they did because neither one wanted to take responsibility for me." She shook her head, but more as if she was shaking something off than negating it. "Believe me, I know better than anyone that most marriages are nothing but a sham. No matter how much tulle and expense there might be. That doesn't make me a robot. It makes me realistic."

Something in the way she said that clawed at him, though he couldn't have said why. Or didn't want to know why, more accurately, and accordingly shoved it aside.

"Wonderful," he said instead. "Then you will enjoy our sham of a marriage all the more, in all its shabby realism."

"Does that mean you'll do it, then?"

And he didn't understand why he wanted so badly to erase that brittleness in her tone. Why he wanted to reach out and touch her in ways that had nothing to do with the fire in him, but everything to do with that hint of vulnerability he doubted she knew was so visible. In the stark softness of her mouth. In the shadows in her eyes.

"I will do it," he heard himself say. "For you."

And every alarm he'd ever wired there inside him screeched an alert then, at full volume.

Because Dominik did not do things for other people. No one was close enough to him to ask for or expect that kind of favor. No one got close to him. And in return for what he'd always considered peace, he kept himself at a distance from everyone else. No obligations. No expectations.

But there was something about Lauren, and how hard she was clearly fighting to look unfazed in the face of her boss's latest outrageous suggestion. As if an order to marry the man's unknown half brother was at all reasonable.

You just agreed to it, a voice in him pointed out. *So does it matter if it's reasonable?*

One moment dragged on into another, and then it was too late to take the words back. To qualify his acceptance. To make it clear that no matter what he might have said, he hadn't meant it to stand as any form of obligation to this woman he barely knew.

Much less that boss of hers who shared his blood.

"For me?" she asked, and it was as if she, too, had suddenly tumbled into this strange, hushed space Dominik couldn't seem to snap out of.

He didn't want to call it sacred. But he wasn't sure what other word there was for it, when her caramel eyes gleamed like gold and his chest felt tight.

"For you," he said, and he had the sense that he was digging his own grave, shovelful by shovelful, whether he wanted it or not. But even that didn't stop him. He settled farther back against his chair, thrust his legs out another lazy inch and let one corner of his mouth crook. "But if you want me to marry you, little red, I'm afraid I will require a full, romantic proposal."

She blinked. Then swallowed.

"You can't be serious."

"I don't intend to make a habit of marrying. This will have to be perfect, the better to live on all my days." He nodded toward the polished wood at his feet. "Go on, then. On your knees, please."

And he was only a man. Not a very good one, as he'd acknowledged earlier. There was no possibility of issuing such an order without imagining all the other things she could do once she was there.

So he did. And had to shift slightly where he sat to accommodate the hungriest part of him.

"You agreed that any marriage between us will be a sham," she was saying, her voice a touch too husky for someone so dedicated to appearing unmoved. "You used that very word. It will be a publicity stunt, and only a publicity stunt, as I said."

"Whatever the marriage is or isn't, it begins right here." He ignored the demands that clamored inside him, greedy and still drunk on his last taste of her. "Where there is no public. No paparazzi. No overbearing employer who cannot stir himself to greet his long-lost brother in person."

She started to argue that but subsided when he shook his head.

"There are only two people who ever need to know how this marriage began, Lauren. And we are both right here, all alone, tucked away on an abandoned office floor where no one need ever be the wiser."

She rolled her eyes. "We can tell them there was kneeling all around, if that's really what you need."

"We can tell them anything you like, but I want to see a little effort. A little care, here between the two of us. A pretty, heartfelt proposal. Come now, Lauren." And he smiled at her then, daring her. "A man likes to be seduced."

Her cheeks had gone pale while he spoke, and as he watched, they flooded with bright new color.

"You don't want to be seduced. You want to humiliate me."

"Six of one, half dozen of another." He jutted his chin toward the floor again. "You need to demonstrate your commitment. Or how else will I know that my heart is safe in your hands?"

The color on her cheeks darkened, and her eyes flashed with temper. And he liked that a hell of a lot more than her robot impression.

"No one is talking about hearts, Mr. James," she snapped at him. "We're talking about damage control. Optics. PR."

"You and your Mr. Combe may be talking about all of those things," he said and shrugged. "But I am merely a hermit from a Hungarian hovel, too long-haired to make sense of your complicated corporate world. What do I know of such things? I'm a simple man, with simple needs." He reached up and dramatically clasped his chest, never shifting his gaze from hers. "If you want me, you must convince me. On your knees, little red."

She made a noise of sheer, undiluted frustration that nearly made him laugh. Especially when it seemed to make her face that much brighter.

He watched as she forced her knees to unlock. She took a breath in, then let it out. Slowly, as if it hurt, she took a step toward him. Then another.

And by the time she moved past his feet, then insinuated herself right where he wanted her, there between his outstretched legs, he didn't have the slightest urge to laugh any longer. Much less when she sank down on her knees before him, just as he'd imagined in all that glorious detail.

She knelt as prettily as she did everything else, and she filled his head as surely as his favorite Hungarian *palinka*. He couldn't seem to look away from her, gold and pink and that wide caramel gaze, peering up at him from between his own legs.

The sight of her very nearly unmanned him.

And he would never know, later, how he managed to keep his hands to himself.

"Dominik James," she said softly, looking up at

him with eyes wide, filled with all those emotions she claimed she didn't feel—but he did, as if she was tossing them straight into the deepest part of him, "will you do me the honor of becoming my husband? For a while?"

He didn't understand why something in him kicked against that qualification. But he ignored it.

He indulged himself by reaching forward and fitting his palm to the curve of her cheek. He waited until her lips parted because he knew she felt it, too, that same heat that roared in him. That wildfire that was eating him alive.

"But of course," he said, and he had meant to sound sardonic. Darkly amused. But that wasn't how it came out, and he couldn't think of a way to stop it. "I can think of nothing I would like to do more than marry a woman I hardly know to serve the needs of a brother I have never met in the flesh, to save the reputation of a family that tossed me aside like so much trash."

There was a sheen in her gaze that he wanted to believe was connected to that strangely serious thing in him, not laughing at all. And the way her lips trembled, just slightly.

Just enough to make the taste of her haunt him all over again.

"I… I can't tell if that's a yes or no."

"It's a yes, little red," he said, though there was no earthly reason that he should agree to any of this.

There was no reason that he should even be here, so far away from the life he'd carved out to his specifications. The life he had fought so hard to win for himself.

But Lauren had walked into his cabin, fit too neatly into the chair that shouldn't have been sitting there, waiting for her, and now he couldn't seem to keep himself from finding out if she fit everywhere else, too.

A thought that was so antithetical to everything he was and everything he believed to be true about himself that Dominik wasn't sure why he didn't trust her away from him and leave. Right now.

But he didn't.

Worse, he didn't want to.

"It's a yes," he said, his voice grave as he betrayed himself, and for no reason, "but I'm afraid, as in most things, there will be a price. And you will be the one to pay it."

CHAPTER SEVEN

LAUREN DIDN'T UNDERSTAND anything that was happening.

She had been astounded when Matteo had suggested marriage, so offhandedly as if it was perfectly normal to run around marrying strangers on a whim because he thought that would look better in some theoretical tabloid.

"Marry him," he'd said, so casually, from the far side of the world. "You are a decent, hardworking sort and you've been connected to the family without incident for years."

"I think you mean employed by the family and therefore professional."

"You can take him in hand. Make sure he's up to the task. And by the time the shock fades over my mother's scandalous past, you'll have made him everything he needs to be to take his place as a San Giacomo."

"Will this new role come with combat pay?" she'd asked, with more heat than she normally used with her boss, no matter what was going on. But then, she wasn't normally dispatched into the hinterland, made to *hike*, and then kissed thoroughly and repeatedly. She was... not herself. "Or do you expect me to give up my actual life for the foreseeable future for my existing salary, no questions asked?"

She never spoke to Matteo that way. But he didn't normally react the way he had then, either, with nothing but silence and what looked very much like sadness on his face. It made Lauren wish she hadn't said anything.

Not for the first time, she wondered exactly what had gone on between Matteo and the anger management consultant the Combe Industries board of directors had hired in a transparent attempt to take Matteo down. He'd gone off with her to Yorkshire, been unusually unreachable and then had set off on a round-the-world tour of all the Combe Industries holdings.

A less charitable person might wonder if he was attempting to take the geographic tour.

"You can name your price, Lauren," he said after what felt like a very long while, fraught with all the evidence she'd ever needed that though they might work very closely together, they had no personal relationship. Not like that. "All I ask is that you tame this brother of mine before we unleash him on the world. The board will not be pleased to have more scandal attached to the Combe name. And the least we can do is placate them a little."

And she'd agreed to ask Dominik, because what else could she do? For all Dominik's snide commentary, the truth was that she admired Matteo. He was not his father, who had always been willing to take the low road—and usually had. Matteo had integrity, something she knew because no matter how she might have longed for him to *see* her, he never had. He treated her as his personal assistant, not as a woman. It was why she felt safe while she wore her outrageously feminine heels. It was why she felt perfectly happy dedicating herself to him.

If he had looked at her the way Dominik did, even once, she would never have been able to work for him at all. She would never have been able to sort out what was an appropriate request and what wasn't, and would have lost herself somewhere in the process.

She'd been reeling from that revelation when she'd walked out to pitch the marriage idea, fully expecting that Dominik would laugh at the very notion.

But he hadn't.

And she'd meant to present the whole thing as a very dry and dusty sort of business proposition, anyway. Just a different manner of merger, that was all. But instead of a board meeting of sorts, she was knelt down between his legs, gazing up at him from a position that made her whole body quiver.

And unless she was very much mistaken, he had actually agreed to marry her.

For a price.

Because with this man, there was always a price.

How lucky you want so badly to pay it, an insinuating, treacherous voice from deep inside her whispered. *Whatever it is.*

"What kind of price?" Lauren frowned at him as if that could make them both forget that she was kneeling before him like a supplicant. Or a lover. And that he was touching her as if at least one of those things was a foregone conclusion. "I have already promised to kiss you whenever you like. What more could you want?"

His palm was so hard and hot against the side of her face. She felt it everywhere, and she knew that seemingly easy touch was responsible for the flames she could feel licking at her. All over her skin, then deeper still, sweet and hot in her core.

Until she *throbbed* with it. With him.

"Do you think there are limits to what a man might want?" he asked quietly, and his voice was so low it set her to shattering, like a seismic event. Deep inside, where she was already molten and more than a little afraid that she might shake herself apart.

"You're talking about sex again," she said, and thought she sounded something like solemn. Or despairing. And neither helped with all that unbearable *heat*. "I don't know how many ways I can tell you—"

"That you are not sexual, yes, I am aware." He moved his thumb, dragging it gently across her lower lip, and his mouth crooked when she hissed in a breath. His eyes blazed when goose bumps rose along her neck and ran down her arms, and his voice was little more than a growl when he spoke again. "Not sexual at all."

Something in the way he said that made her frown harder, though she already knew it was futile. And it only seemed to make that terrible, knowing blaze in his gray eyes more pronounced.

And much, much hotter. Inside her, where she still couldn't tell if she hated it—or loved it.

"What do you want from me?" she asked, her voice barely above a whisper.

And she thought that whatever happened, she would always remember the way he smiled at her then, half wolf and all man. That it was tattooed inside her, branded into her flesh, forever a part of her. Whether she liked it or not.

"What I want from you, little red, is a wedding night."

That was another brand, another scar. And far more dangerous than before.

Lauren's throat was almost too dry to work. She wasn't sure it would. "You mean…?"

"I mean in the traditional sense, yes. With all that entails."

He shifted, and she had never felt smaller. In the sense of being delicate. *Precious*, something in her whispered, though she knew that was fanciful. And worse, foolish.

Dominik smoothed his free hand over her hair, and let it rest at the nape of her neck. And the way he held her face made something in her do more than melt.

She thought maybe it sobbed.

Or she did.

"Find a threshold, and I will carry you over it," he told her, his voice low and intent. And the look in his gray eyes so male, very nearly *possessive*, it made her ache. "I will lay you down on a bed and I will kiss you awhile, to see where it goes. And all I need from you is a promise that you will not tell me what you do and do not like until you try it. That's all, Lauren. What do you have to lose?"

And she couldn't have named the things she had to lose, because they were all the one thing—they were all *her*—and she was sure he would take them, anyway.

He would take everything.

Maybe she'd known that from the moment she'd seen the shadows become a man, there in that clearing so far from the rest of the world. There in those woods that had taunted her from the first, whispering of darkness and mystery in a thousand ways she hadn't wanted to hear.

Maybe it had always been leading straight here.

But between the heat of his hands and that shivering deep inside her, she couldn't seem to mind it as much as she should have.

As much as she suspected she would, once she survived this. *If* she survived this.

She should get up right this minute. She should move herself out of danger—out of arm's reach. She should tell Dominik she didn't care what he did with his new-found name and fortune, just as she should ring Matteo back and tell him she had no intention of marrying a stranger on command.

She knew she should do all those things. She *wanted* to do all those things.

But instead, she shivered. And in that moment, there at his feet with all his focus and intent settled on her, she surrendered.

If surrender was a cliff, Lauren leaped straight off it, out into nothing. She hadn't done anything so profoundly foolish since she was nine years old and had thought she could convince her parents to pay more attention to her by acting out. She'd earned herself instead an unpleasant summer in boarding school.

But surrendering here, to Dominik, didn't feel like that. It didn't feel like plummeting down into sharp rocks.

It felt far more like flying.

"I will give you a wedding night," she heard herself agree, her voice very stern and matter-of-fact, as if that could mask the fact that she was capitulating. As if she could divert his attention from the great cliff she'd just flung herself over. "But that's all."

"Perhaps we will leave these intimate negotiations until after the night in question," Dominik said, that undercurrent of laughter in his voice. "You may find you very much want a honeymoon, little red. Who knows? Perhaps even an extended one. This may come as a surprise to you, but there are some women who would clamor for the opportunity to while away some time in my bed."

Wedding nights. Honeymoons. *Time in bed.* This was all a farce. It had to be.

But Lauren was on her knees in the offices of Combe Industries, and she had just proposed marriage to a man she'd only met this morning.

So perhaps *farce* wasn't quite the right word to describe what was happening.

Something traitorous inside her wanted to lean in closer, and that terrified her, so she took it as an opportunity to pull away. Cliff or no cliff.

Except he didn't let her.

That hand at her nape held her fast, and something about that…lit her up. It was as if she didn't know what she was doing any longer. Or at all. But maybe he did.

And suddenly she was kneeling up higher, her hands flat on his thighs, her face tilted toward his in a manner she could have called all kinds of names.

All of them not the least bit her. Not the person she was or had ever been.

But maybe she was tired of Lauren Isadora Clarke. And everything she'd made herself become while she was so busy not feeling things.

Like this. Like him.

"It's not a real proposal until there's a kiss, Lauren," Dominik told her. Gruffly, she thought. "Even you must know this."

"Isn't it enough that I promised you a wedding

night?" she asked, and she might have been horrified at the way her voice cracked at that, but there were so many horrors to sift through. Too many.

And all of them seemed to catch fire and burn brighter as she knelt there between his legs, not sure if she felt helpless or far more alarming, *alive*.

Alive straight through, which only made it clear that she never had been before. Not really.

"Kiss me, little red," he ordered her, almost idly. But there was no mistaking the command in his voice all the same. "Keep your promise."

His voice might have been soft, but it was ruthless. And his gray eyes were pitiless.

And he didn't seem to mind in the least when she scowled at him, because it was the only thing she knew how to do.

"Now, please," he murmured in that same demanding way. "Before you hurt my feelings."

She doubted very much that his feelings had anything to do with this, but she didn't say that. She didn't want to give him more opportunity to comment on hers. Or call her a robot again.

"I don't understand why you would want to kiss someone who doesn't wish to kiss you," she threw at him in desperation.

"I wouldn't." Those gray eyes laughed at her. "But that description doesn't apply to either one of us, does it?"

"One of us is under duress."

"One of us, Lauren, is a liar."

She could feel the heat that told her that her cheeks were red, and she had the terrible notion that meant he was right. And worse, that he could see it all over her face.

She had no idea.

In a panic, she mimicked him, hooking one hand around the hard column of his neck and pulling his mouth to hers.

This man who had agreed to marry her. To pretend, anyway, and there was no reason that should work in her the way it did, like a powder keg on the verge of exploding. Like need and loss and yearning, tangled all together in an angry knot inside her.

And she was almost used to this now. The delirious slide, the glorious fire, of their mouths together.

He let her kiss him, let her control the angle and the depth, and she made herself shiver as she licked her way into his mouth. All the while telling herself that she didn't like this. That she didn't want this.

And knowing with every drugging slide of his tongue against hers that he'd been right all along.

She was a liar.

Maybe that was why, when his hands moved to trace their way down her back, she moaned at the sensation instead of fighting it. And when he pulled her blouse from the waistband of her formal trousers, she only made a deeper noise, consumed with the glory of his mouth.

And the way he kissed her and kissed her, endless and intoxicating.

But then his bare hand was on her skin, moving around to the front of her and then finally—finally, as if she'd never wanted anything more when she'd never wanted it in the first place, when it had never occurred to her to imagine such a thing—closing over the swell of one breast.

And everything went white around the edges.

Her breast seemed to swell, filling his palm, with her nipple high and hard.

And every time he moved his palm, she felt it like another deep lick—

But this time in the hottest, wildest, most molten place of all between her legs.

She could feel his other hand in her hair, cradling the back of her head and holding her mouth where he wanted it, making absolutely no bones about the fact that he was in charge.

And it was thrilling.

Lauren arched her back, giving him more of her, and it still wasn't enough.

The kiss was wild and maddening at the same time, and she strained to get closer to him, desperate for something she couldn't name. Something just out of reach—

And when he set her away from him, with a dark little laugh, she thought she might die.

Then thought that death would be an excellent escape when reality hit her.

Because she was a disheveled mess on the floor of her office, staring up at the man who'd made her this way.

Perilously close to begging for things she couldn't even put into words.

She expected him to taunt her. To tell her she was a liar again, and remind her of all the ways he just proved it.

But Dominik stayed where he was, those gray eyes of his shuttered as he gazed back at her.

And she knew it was as good as admitting a weakness out loud, but she lifted her fingers and pressed them to her lips, not sure how she'd spent so many years on this earth without recognizing the way her own flesh could be used against her. And then tingle in the aftermath, like it wasn't enough.

As if she was sexual, after all.

"The company maintains a small number of corporate flats in this building," she managed to tell him when she'd composed herself a little, and she didn't sound like herself. She sounded like a prerecorded version of the woman she'd been when she'd left these offices to fly to Hungary. She wasn't sure she had access to that woman anymore. She wasn't sure she knew what had become of her.

But she was very sure that the creature she was now, right there at his feet, would be the undoing of her.

Assuming it wasn't already too late.

She climbed off the floor with as much dignity as she could muster. For the first time in her life, she cursed the fact that she wore such ridiculous shoes, with such high heels, that it was impossible to feel steady even when she was standing.

Right, a little voice inside her murmured archly. *Blame the shoes. It's definitely the* shoes.

"Corporate flats," he repeated after another long moment, that dark gaze all over her. "How…antiseptic."

But when she called down to the security desk to have one of the guards come and escort him there, he didn't argue.

Lauren told herself that she liked the space he left behind him. That it wasn't any kind of emptiness, but room for her to breathe.

And once she was alone, there was no one to see her when she sank down into her chair behind her desk, where she had always felt the most competent. There was no one to watch as she buried her face in her hands—still too hot, and no doubt too revealing—and let all those emotions she refused to look at and couldn't name spill down her cheeks at last.

CHAPTER EIGHT

By MORNING SHE'D pulled herself together. The tears of the night before seemed to have happened to someone else. Someone far more fragile than Lauren had ever been, particularly in the crisp light of day. She showered in the bathroom off the executive suite, rinsing away any leftover emotion as well as the very long previous day, and changed into one of the complete outfits she kept at the office precisely for mornings like this.

Well. Perhaps not *precisely* like this. She didn't often plan and execute her own wedding. She'd worn her highest, most impractical pair of heels as a kind of tribute. And she was absolutely not thinking—much less overthinking—about the many questionable bargains she'd made with the strange man she'd found in the forest.

She knocked briskly on the door to the corporate flat at half nine on the dot, aware as she did that she didn't expect him to answer. A man as feral as Dominik was as likely to have disappeared in the night as a stray cat, surely—

But the door swung open. And Dominik stood there, dressed in nothing but a pair of casual trousers slung low on his hips, showing off acres and acres of…*him*.

For a moment—or possibly an hour—Lauren couldn't seem to do anything but gape at him.

"Did you imagine I would run off in the night?" he asked, reading her mind yet again. And not the most embarrassing part, for a change. She tried to swallow past the dryness in her throat. She tried to stop staring at all those ridges and planes and astonishing displays of honed male flesh. "I might have, of course, but there were restrictions in place."

She followed him inside the flat, down the small hall to the efficient kitchen, bright in the morning's summer sunlight. "You mean the security guards?"

He rounded the small counter and then regarded her over his coffee, strong enough that she could smell the rich aroma and blacker than sin. "I mean, Lauren, the fact I gave you my word."

Lauren had allowed sensation and emotion and all that nonsense to get the best of her last night, but that was over now. It had to be, no matter how steady that gray gaze of his was. Or the brushfires it kicked up inside her, from the knot in her belly to the heat in her cheeks. So she cleared her throat and waved the tablet she carried in his direction, completely ignoring the tiny little hint of something bright like shame that wiggled around in all the knots she seemed to be made of today.

"I've sorted everything out," she told him, aware that she sounded as pinched and knotted as she felt. "We will marry in an hour."

Dominik didn't change expression and still, she felt as if he was laughing at her.

"And me without my pretty dress," he drawled.

"The vicar is a friend of the Combe family," she said as if she hadn't heard him. And she had to order herself not to fuss with her own dress, a simple little shift that was perfect for the office. And would do for a fake wedding, as well. "I took the liberty of claiming that ours is a deep and abiding love that requires a special license and speed, so it would be best all round if you do not dispute that."

"I had no intention of disputing it," Dominik said in that dark, sardonic voice of his that made her feel singed. "After all, I am nothing but a simple, lonely hermit, good for nothing but following the orders of wealthy aristocrats who cannot be bothered to attend the fake weddings they insisted occur in the first place. I am beside myself with joy and anticipation that I, too, can serve your master from afar in whatever way he sees fit. Truly, this is the family I dreamed of when I was a child in the orphanage."

He displayed his joy and anticipation by letting that impossible mouth of his crook, very slightly, in one corner, and Lauren hated that it felt like a punch. Directly into her gut.

"It is the romance of it all that makes my heart beat faster, little red," Dominik continued, sounding very nearly merry. If she overlooked that hard gleam in his eyes. "If you listen, I am certain you can hear it."

Lauren placed her tablet down on the marble countertop in a manner that could only be described as pointed. Or perhaps aggressive. But she kept her eyes on Dominik as if he really was some kind of wolf. As if looking away—for even an instant—could be the death of her.

And it wasn't his heart that she could hear, pounding loud enough to take down the nearest wall. It was hers.

"Could you take this seriously?" she demanded. "Could you at least try?"

He studied her for another moment as he lifted his coffee to his mouth and took a deep pull. "I didn't run off in the night as I assure you I could have done if I wished, regardless of what laughable corporate security you think was in place. The vicar bears down on us even as we speak. How much more seriously do you imagine I can take this?"

"You agreed to do this, repeatedly. I'm not sure that *I* agreed to submit myself to your…commentary."

She didn't expect that smile of his, bright and fierce. "Believe me, Lauren, there are all manner of things you might find yourself submitting to over the course of this day. Do not sell yourself short."

And she hated when he did that. When he said things in that voice of his, and they swirled around inside her—heat and madness and something like hope— making it clear that he was referring to all those dark and thorny things that she didn't understand.

That she didn't *want* to understand, she told herself stoutly.

"I've already agreed," she reminded him, with more ferocity than was strictly required. But she couldn't seem to bite it back. She had always been in such control of herself that she'd never learned how to *take* control of herself. If there were steps toward becoming composed, she didn't know them, and she could blame that on Dominik, too. "There's no need for all these insinuations."

"You've agreed? I thought it was I who agreed. To everything. Like a house pet on a chain."

His voice was mild but his gaze was…not.

"You asked me for a wedding night," she reminded him, her heart still pounding like it wanted to knock her flat. "And you know that I keep my promises. Every time you've asked to kiss me, I've allowed it."

"Surrendered to it, one might even say, with notable enthusiasm. Once you get started."

"My point," she said through her teeth, not certain why she was suddenly so angry, only that she couldn't seem to keep it inside her, where she was shaky and too hot and not the least bit *composed*, "is that you don't have to continue with all the veiled references. Or even the euphemisms. You demanded sex in return for marrying me, and I agreed to give it to you. The end."

It was a simple statement of fact, she thought. There was no reason at all that he should stare at her that way as if he was stripping all the air from the flat. From the world.

"If it is so distasteful to you, Lauren, don't."

But his voice was too smooth. Too silky. And all she could hear was the undercurrent beneath it, which roared through her like an impenetrable wall of flame.

"Don't?" she managed to echo. "Is that an option?"

"While you are busy marinating in the injustice of it all, remind yourself that it is not I who tracked you down in the middle of a forest, then dragged you back to England. If I wish to go through with a sham marriage for the sheer pleasure of the wedding night you will provide me as lure, that is my business." Dominik tilted his head slightly to one side. "Perhaps you should ask yourself what you are willing to do for a paycheck. And why."

"It's a little more complicated than that."

"Is it? Maybe it is time you ask yourself what you

wouldn't do if your Mr. Combe asked it. You may find the answers illuminating."

"You obviously enjoy keeping to yourself." Lauren wasn't sure why all that breathless fury wound around and around inside her, or why she wanted nothing more than to throw it at him. She only wished she could be sure of her aim. "But some people prefer to be on a team."

"The team that is currently enjoying a holiday in scenic Australia? Or the one left here with a list of instructions and a heretofore unknown half brother to civilize through the glorious institution of marriage?" He smirked. "Go team."

Her jaw ached and she realized, belatedly, that she was clenching her teeth. *"You agreed."*

"So I did." And all he was doing was standing there across a block of marble, so there was no reason he should make her feel so…dizzy. "But then again, so did you. Is that what this is about, little red? Are you so terrified of the things you promised me?"

That took the wind out of her as surely as if she'd fallen hard and landed worse.

"What does it matter if I'm terrified or not?" She only realized after she'd said it that it was as good as an admission. "Would it change your mind?"

"It might change my approach," he said, that gleaming, dark thing in his gaze again, and she didn't understand how or why it connected to all that breathlessness inside her. Almost as if it wasn't *fury* at all. "Then again, it might not."

"In any case, congratulations are in order," she managed to say, feeling battered for no good reason at all. "In short order you will have a wife. And shortly after that, a wedding night sacrifice, like something out of the history books."

He laughed, rich and deep, and deeper when she scowled at him. "Do you think to shame me, Lauren? There are any number of men who might stand before you and thunder this way and that about how they dislike the taste of martyrdom in their beds, but not me."

"I am somehow unsurprised."

Dominik didn't move and yet, again, Lauren felt as if he surrounded her. As if those hands of his might as well have been all over her. She felt as if they were.

"You're not terrified of me," he said with a quiet certainty that made her shake. "You're terrified of yourself. And all those things you told yourself you don't know how to feel." That laughter was still all over his face, but his gray gaze made her feel pinned to the floor where she stood. "You're terrified that you'll wake up tomorrow so alive with feeling you won't know who you are."

"Either that or even more bored than I am right now," she said, though her throat felt scraped raw with all the things she didn't say. Or scream.

"Yes, so deeply bored," he said, and laughed again. Then he leaned forward until he rested his elbows on the countertop between them, making it impossible to pretend she didn't see the play of his muscles beneath the acres and acres of smooth male skin that he'd clearly shared with the sun in that Hungarian clearing. "But tell me this, Lauren. Does your boredom make you wet?"

For a moment she couldn't process the question. She couldn't understand it.

Then she did, and a tide of red washed over her, igniting her from the very top of her head to the tender spaces between her toes. No one had ever asked her a question like that. She hadn't known, until right now, that people really discussed such things in the course of an otherwise more or less regular day. She told herself she was horrified. Disgusted. She told herself she didn't even know what he meant, only that it was vile. That *he* was.

But she did know what he meant.

And she was molten straight through, red hot and flush with it, and decidedly not bored.

"You have twenty minutes," she told him when she could be sure her voice was clipped and cold again. "I trust you will be ready?"

"I will take that as a yes," he rumbled at her, entirely too male and much too sure of himself. "You are so wet you can hardly stand still. Don't worry, little red. You might not know what to do about that. But I do."

He straightened, then rounded the counter. Lauren pulled herself taut and rigid as if he was launching an attack—then told herself it was sheer relief that wound its way through her when he made no move toward her at all. He headed toward the flat's bedroom instead.

"You're welcome to join me in the shower," he said over his shoulder, and she didn't have to see his face to know he was laughing at her. "If you dare."

And she was still standing right where he'd left her when she heard the water go on. Frozen solid at the edge of the counter with her hands in fists, curled up so tight her nails were digging into her palms.

She made herself uncurl her fingers, one at a time. She made herself breathe, shoving back the temper and the fury until she could see what was beneath it.

And see that once again, he was right. It was fear.

Not of him. But of herself.

And how very much she wanted to see, at last, what it was she'd been missing all this time.

That was the thought that had kept sneaking into her head over the course of the long night.

She'd hardly slept, there on that couch in her office where she spent more time than she ever had in the flat she shared with Mary. And Lauren had always prided herself on not feeling the things that others did. She'd congratulated herself on not being dragged into the same emotional quagmires they always were. It made her better at doing her job. It made it easier to navigate the corporate world.

But Dominik had forced her to face the fact that she *could* feel all kinds of things, she just…hadn't.

Lauren had spent so long assuring herself she didn't want the things she couldn't feel. Or couldn't have. Her parents' love, the happy families they made without her, the sorts of romantic and sexual relationships all her friends and colleagues were forever falling in and out of with such abandon. She'd told anyone who asked that she wasn't built for those sorts of entanglements.

Secretly, she'd always believed she was above them. That she was better than all that mess and regret.

But one day of kissing Dominik James on demand and she was forced to wonder—if it wasn't about better or worse, but about meeting someone who made her feel things she hadn't thought she could, where did that leave her except woefully inexperienced? And frozen in amber on a shelf of her own making?

Lauren didn't like that thought at all. She ran her hands over her sensible shift dress, her usual office wear, and tried to pretend that she wasn't shaking.

But what if you melted? whispered a voice deep inside her that she'd never heard before, layered with insinuation and something she was terribly afraid might be grief. *What if you let Dominik melt you as he pleased?*

She let out a breath she hadn't known she was holding. And she swayed on her feet, yet knew full well it wasn't because of the skyscraper height of her shoes.

And she entertained a revolutionary thought. If she had to do this, anyway—if she was going to marry this man, and stay married to him for as long as it took to ride out the public's interest in yet another family scandal—shouldn't she take it as an opportunity?

She already knew that Dominik could make her feel things that she never had before. And yes, that was overwhelming. A mad, wild whirl that she hardly knew how to process. Especially when she'd been certain, all her life, that she wasn't capable of such things.

Maybe she didn't know how to want. But it had never occurred to her before now that she hadn't been born that way. That maybe, just maybe, that was because no one had ever wanted her—especially the people who should have wanted her the most.

She didn't know why Dominik wanted to play these games with her, but he did. He clearly did, or he wouldn't be here. Lauren was persuasive, but she knew full well she couldn't have forced that man to do a single thing he didn't want to do.

So why shouldn't she benefit, too?

She had spent a lot of time and energy telling herself that she didn't care that she was so clearly different from everyone else she met. That she was somehow set apart from the rest of the human race, unmoved by their passions and their baser needs. But what if she wasn't?

What if she wasn't an alien, after all?

That was what one of her kissing experiments had called her when she had declined his offer to take their experiment in a more horizontal direction. Among other, less savory names and accusations.

Just as Dominik had called her a robot.

What if she…wasn't?

What if she melted, after all?

Lauren waited until he reemerged from his bedchamber, dressed in a crisp, dark suit that confused her, it was so well-made. His hair was tamed, pushed back from his face, and he'd even shaved, showing off the cut line of his ruthlessly masculine jaw. He looked like what he was—the eldest son of the current generation of San Giacomos. But she couldn't concentrate on any of the surprisingly sophisticated male beauty he threw around him like light, because she knew that if she didn't say what she wanted right here and now, she never would.

"I will give you a wedding night," she told him.

"So we have already agreed," he said in that silky way of his that made her whole body turn to jelly. And her stomach doing flips inside her didn't exactly help. "Is this a renegotiation of terms?"

"If it takes more than one night, that's all right," she forced herself to tell him, though it made her feel queasy. And light-headed. Especially when he stopped tugging at his shirt cuffs and transferred all his considerable attention to her. "I want to learn."

"Learn what?"

And maybe his voice wasn't particularly, dangerously quiet. Maybe it just sounded like that in her head, next to all that roaring.

"Everyone has all this sex," she said, the words

crashing through her and out of her. She couldn't control them. She couldn't do anything but throw them across the room like bombs. "People walk around *consumed* by it, and I want to know why. I don't just mean I want you to take my virginity, though you will. And that's fine."

"I'm delighted to hear you're on board," he said drily, though it was the arrested sort of gleam in his eyes that she couldn't seem to look away from. Because it made her feel as if a great wind was blowing, directly at her, and there was nothing she could do to stop it. "No one likes an unenthusiastic deflowering. Gardening metaphors aside, it's really not all that much fun. Anyone who tells you otherwise has never had the pleasure. Or any pleasure, I can only assume."

"I have no idea what you're on about." He looked even more taken aback by that, and she moved toward him—then thought better of it, as putting herself in arm's reach of this man had yet to end well for her. Even if that was her current goal. "I want to understand why people *yearn*. I want to understand what all the fuss is about. Why people—you among them—look at me like something's wrong with me if I say I'm not interested in it. Can you do that, Dominik?"

Maybe it was the first time she'd called him by his name. She wasn't sure, but she felt as if it was. And he looked at her as if she'd struck him.

"I've spent my whole life never quite understanding the people around me." And Lauren knew she would be horrified—later—that her voice broke then, showing her hand. Telling him even more than she'd wanted. "Never really getting the joke. Or the small, underlying assumptions that people make about the world because of these feelings they cart about with them wherever they go. I never got those, either. Just once I want to know what the big secret is. I want to know what all the songs are about. I want to know what so many parents feel they need to protect their children from. I want to *know*."

"Lauren…"

And she didn't recognize that look on his face then. Gone was the mocking, sardonic gleam in his eyes. The theatrics, the danger. The challenge.

She was terribly afraid that what she was seeing was pity, and she thought that might kill her.

"I know this is all a game to you," she said hurriedly, before he could crush her, and had that out-of-body feeling again. As if she was watching herself from far away, and couldn't do a single thing to stop the words that kept pouring out of her mouth. "Maybe you have your own dark reasons for wanting to do what Mr. Combe wants, and I don't blame you. Family dynamics are difficult enough when you've known the players all your life. But you said that there could be certain things that were between the two of us. That are only ours. And I want this to be one of them." Her heart was in her throat and she couldn't swallow it down. She could only hope she didn't choke on it. "I want to know *why*."

He straightened then, and she couldn't read the expression he wore. Arrested, still. But there was a different light in those near-silver eyes of his. He held out his hand, that gray gaze steady on hers, as if that alone could hold her up.

She believed it.

Lauren was tempted to call the way he was looking at her *kind*. And she had absolutely no idea why that should make her want to cry. Or how she managed to keep from doing just that when her sight blurred.

"Come," Dominik said, his voice gruff and sure as if he was already reciting his vows before the vicar. And more shocking by far, as if those vows meant something to him. "Marry me, little red, and I will teach you."

CHAPTER NINE

WHEN HE LOOKED back on this episode and cataloged his mistakes—something Dominik knew he would get to as surely as night followed day—he would trace it all back to the fatal decision to step outside his cabin and wait for the Englishwoman the innkeeper had called from town to tell him was headed his way.

It had seemed so innocuous at the time. No one ever visited his cabin, with or without an invitation, and he hadn't known what would come of entertaining the whims of the one woman who had dared come find him. He'd been curious. Especially when he'd seen her, gold hair gleaming and that red cloak flowing around her like a premonition.

How could he have known?

And now Dominik found himself in exactly the sort of stuffy, sprawling, stately home he most despised, with no one to blame but himself. Combe Manor sat high on a ridge overlooking the Yorkshire village that had once housed the mills that had provided the men who'd lived in this house a one-way ticket out of their humble beginnings.

They had built Combe Manor and started Combe Industries. Dominik had also fought his way out of a rocky, unpleasant start…but he'd chosen to hoard his wealth and live off by himself in the middle of the woods.

Dominik felt like an imposter. Because he was an imposter.

He might have shared blood with the distant aristocrat he'd seen on the screen in a London office, but he didn't share…this. Ancient houses filled with the kind of art and antiques that spoke of wealth that went far beyond the bank. It was nearly two centuries of having more. Of having everything, for that matter. It was generations of men who had stood where he did now, staring out the windows in a library filled with books only exquisitely educated men read, staring down at the village where, once upon a time, other men scurried about adding to the Combe coffers.

And he knew that the Combe family was brand-spanking-new in terms of wealth when stood next to the might and historic reach of the San Giacomos.

Dominik might share that blood, but he was an orphan. A street kid who'd lived rough for years and had done what was necessary to feed himself, keep himself clothed and find shelter. A soldier who had done his duty and followed his orders, and had found himself in situations he never mentioned when civilians were near.

Blood was nothing next to the life he'd lived. And he was surprised this fancy, up-itself house didn't fall down around his ears.

But when he heard the soft click of much too high heels against the floor behind him, he turned.

Almost as if he couldn't help himself.

Because the house still stood despite the fact he was here, polluting it. And more astonishing still, the woman who walked toward him, her blond hair shining and a wary look on her pretty face, was his wife.

His wife.

The ceremony, such as it was, had gone smoothly. The vicar had arrived right on time, and they had recited their vows in a pretty sort of boardroom high on top of the London building that housed his half brother's multinational business. Lauren had produced rings, proving that she did indeed think of everything, they had exchanged them and that was that.

Dominik was not an impulsive man. Yet, he had gone ahead and married a woman for the hell of it.

And he was having trouble remembering what *the hell of it* was, because all he could seem to think about was Lauren. And more specific, helping Lauren out of those impossible heels she wore. Peeling that sweet little dress off her curves, and then finally—*finally*—doing something about this intense, unreasonable hunger for her that had been dogging him since the moment he'd laid eyes on her.

The moment he'd stepped out of the shadows of his own porch and had put all of this into motion.

There had been no reception. Lauren had taken a detour to her office that had turned into several hours of work. Afterward she had herded him into another sleek, black car, then back to the same plane, which they'd flown for a brief little hop to the north of England. Another car ride from the airfield and here they were in an echoing old mausoleum that had been erected to celebrate and flatter the kinds of men Dominik had always hated.

It had never crossed his mind that he was one of them. He'd never wanted to be one of them.

And the fact he'd found out he was the very thing he loathed didn't change a thing. He couldn't erase the life he'd led up to this point. He couldn't pretend he'd had a different life now that he was being offered his rich mother's guilt in the form of an identity that meant nothing to him.

But it was difficult to remember the hard line he planned to take when this woman—his *wife*, to add another impossibility to the pile—stood before him.

"I have just spoken to Mr. Combe," she began, because, of course, she'd been off the moment they'd set foot in this house. Dominik had welcomed the opportunity to ask himself what on earth he was doing here while she'd busied herself with more calls and emails and tasks that apparently needed doing *at once*.

And Dominik had made any number of mistakes already. There was the speaking to her in the first place that he would have to unpack at some later date, when all of this was behind him. Besides, he'd compounded that error, time and again. He should never have touched her. He should certainly never have kissed her. He should have let her fly off back to London on her own, and he certainly, without any doubt, should never have married her.

The situation would almost be funny if it wasn't so… preposterous.

But one thing Dominik knew beyond a shadow of any doubt. He did not want to hear about his damned brother again. Not tonight.

"Do me this one favor, please," he said in a voice that came out as more of a growl than he'd intended. Or maybe it was exactly the growl that was called for, he thought, when her eyes widened. "This is our wedding night. We have a great many things to accomplish, you and I. Why don't we leave your Mr. Combe where he belongs—across the planet, doing whatever it is he does that requires you to do five times as much in support."

He expected her to argue. He was sure he could see the start of it kicking up all over her lovely face and in the way she held her shoulders so tight and high.

But she surprised him.

She held his gaze, folded her hands in front of her and inclined her head.

Giving him what he wanted.

And the same demon that had spurred him on from the start—pushing him to walk out onto that porch and start all of this in the first place—sat up inside him, clearly not as intimidated by a stately library and a grand old house the way he was.

"What's this?" he asked quietly. "Is that all it took to tame you, little red? A ring on your finger and a few vows in front of the vicar? That's all that was required to make you soft? Yielding? Obedient?"

She made a sound that could as easily have been a cough as a laugh. "I am not certain I would call myself any of those things, no matter what jewelry I wear on my fingers. But I agreed to the wedding night. And…whatever else. I have every intention of going through with it."

"You make it sound so appealing." He eyed her, not sure if he was looking for her weaknesses or better yet, the places she was likely to be most sensitive. "You could do worse than a little softness. Yielding will make it sweeter for the both of us. And obedience, well…"

He grinned at that, as one image after the next chased through his head.

"I've never been much good at that, either, I'm

afraid." She said it with such confidence, tipping her chin up to go with it. And more than that, pride. "If you're looking for obedience, I'm afraid you're in for some disappointment."

"You cannot truly believe you are not obedient." He moved toward her, leaving the window—and its view of the ruins of the mills that had built this place—behind him. "You obey one man because he pays you. What will it take, I wonder, for you to obey your husband with even a portion of that dedication?"

And he had the distinct pleasure of watching her shiver, goose bumps telling him her secrets as they rippled to life on her skin.

He was so hard he thought it might hurt him.

Dominik crossed the vast expanse of the library floor until he was in front of her, and then he kept moving, wandering in a lazy circle around her as if she was on an auction block and he was the buyer.

Another image that pulsed in him like need.

"I asked you to teach me." And he could hear all the nerves crackling in her voice. As obvious as the goose bumps down the length of her arms. "Does that come with extra doses of humiliation or is that merely an add-on extra?"

"It's my lesson to teach, Lauren. Why don't you stop trying to top from the bottom?"

He'd made a full circle around her then, and faced her once more. And he reveled in the look on her face. Wariness and expectation. That sweet pink flush.

And a certain hectic awareness in her caramel-colored eyes.

She was without doubt the most beautiful woman he had ever seen. And she was his.

She had made herself his.

"What do you want me to do?" Lauren asked, her voice the softest he'd ever heard it.

He reached out to smooth his hand over all her gleaming blond hair, still pulled back in that sleek, professional ponytail. He considered that tidy ponytail part of her armor.

And he wanted none of that armor between them. Not tonight.

"It's time to play Rapunzel," he told her. When she only stared back at him, he tugged on the ponytail, just sharp enough to make her hitch in a breath. "Let down your hair, little red."

He watched the pulse in her throat kick into high gear. Her flush deepened, and he was fairly certain she'd moved into holding her breath.

But she obeyed him all the same, reaching back to tug the elastic out of her hair. When it was loose she ran her free hand through the mass of it, letting it fall where it would, thick and gold and smelling of apples.

She kept saying she didn't believe in fairy tales, but Dominik was sure he'd ended up in the midst of one all the same. And he knew the price of taking a bite out of a sweet morsel like Lauren, a golden-haired princess as innocent as she was sweet to look upon, but he didn't care. Bake him into a pie, turn him into stone—he meant to have this woman.

He made a low, rumbling sound of approval, because with her hair down she looked different. Less sharp. Less sleek. More accessible. The hair tumbled over her shoulders and made her seem…very nearly romantic.

Dominik remembered the things he'd promised her, and that ache in him grew sharper and more insistent by the second, so he simply bent and scooped her up into his arms.

She let out the breath she'd been holding in a kind of gasp, but he was already moving. He held her high against his chest, a soft, sweet weight in his arms, and after a startled moment she snuck her arms around his neck.

And that very nearly undid him.

The sort of massive, theatrical staircase that had never made sense to him dominated the front hall, and he took the left side, heading upstairs.

"Oh, the guest suites are actually—" she began, shifting in his arms and showing him that frown of hers he liked far too much.

"Is anyone else here?"

He already knew the answer. She had told him the house was empty when they'd landed in Yorkshire. She'd told him a lot of information about the house, the grounds, the village, the distant moors and mountains—as if she'd believed what he truly wanted today was a travelogue and a lecture on the Combe family.

"You know that Mr. Combe is in Australia, and his sister, Pia—" She cut herself off, her gaze locking to his. "Well. She's your sister, too, of course. And she is currently in the kingdom of Atilia."

"The island."

"Yes, it's actually several islands in the Ionian Sea—"

"I don't care." He didn't. Not about Matteo Combe or Pia Combe or anything at all but the woman in his arms. "How many beds are there in a house like this?"

"Fifteen," she replied, her gaze searching his. Then widening as he smiled.

"Never fear, Lauren. I intend to christen them all."

He took the first door he found, carrying her into a sprawling sitting room that led, eventually, into an actual bedroom. The bed itself was a massive thing, as if they'd chopped down trees that could have been the masts of ships to make all four posters, but Dominik found his normal disgust about class issues faded in the face of all the lovely possibilities.

There were just so many things an imaginative man could do with bedposts and a willing woman.

He set her down at the side of the bed and smiled wider when she had to reach out to steady herself. "Those shoes may well be the death of you. It is the shoes, is it not? And not something else entirely that leaves you so...unbalanced?"

She shot him a look, but she didn't say anything. She reached down, fiddled with the buckle around one delicate ankle, then kicked her shoe off. She repeated it on the other side, and when she was done she was nearly a foot shorter.

And then she smiled up at him, her gaze as full of challenge as it was of wariness.

"I didn't realize all the witty banter came as part of the package. I thought it would just be, you know, straight to it. No discussion."

"You could have gotten that in any pub you've ever set foot in with precious little effort on your part."

He shrugged out of the formal suit jacket he'd been wearing all day, like the trained monkey he'd allowed himself to become. And he was well aware of the convulsive way she swallowed, her gaze following his shoulders as if she couldn't bring herself to look away from him.

Dominik liked that a little too much. "Why didn't you?"

He started on his buttons then, one after the next, unable to keep his lips from quirking as she followed his fingers as they moved down his chest. And took much too long to raise her gaze back to his.

"Pardon?"

"If you were curious about experimenting with your nonsexual nature, Lauren, why not get off with a stranger after a few drinks? I think you'll find it's a tried and true method employed by people everywhere."

"As appealing as that sounds, I was never curious before. I was never curious before—"

She looked stricken the moment the words were out. And the word she'd been about to say hung between them as surely as if she'd shouted it. *You.*

I was never curious before you.

And Dominik felt...hushed. Something like humbled.

"Don't worry," he found himself saying, though his voice was gruff and he'd planned to be so much more smooth, more in control, hadn't he? "I promise you will enjoy this far more than a drunken fumble in the toilets after too much liquid courage and a pair of beer goggles."

She blinked as if she was imagining that, and Dominik didn't want a single thing in her head but him.

He tossed his shirt aside, then nodded at her. "Your dress, wife. Take it off."

Her breath shuddered out of her, and her hands trembled when she reached down to grip the hem of the shift dress she wore. She had to wiggle as she lifted it, peeling it up and off and displaying herself to him as she went.

Inch by luscious inch.

At last, he thought as she tossed the dress aside and stood there before him wearing nothing but a delicate lace bra that cupped her perfect breasts, and a pair of pale pink panties that gleamed a bit in the last of the light of the waning summer afternoon.

She made his mouth water.

And God, how she made him ache.

He reached over and put his hands on her, finally. He drew her hair over her shoulders, then followed the line of each arm. Down to find her fingers, particularly the one that wore his ring, then back up again. He found the throat where her pulse pounded out a rhythm he could feel in the hardest part of him, and each soft swell of her breast above the fabric that covered them and held them aloft.

She was like poured cream, sweet and rich, and so soft to the touch he had to bite back a groan. He traced his way over the tempting curve of her belly, her hips made for his hands, and then behind to her pert bottom.

She was warm already, but she became hot beneath his palms.

And he was delighted to find that when she flushed, she turned bright red all the way down to her navel. Better by far than he'd imagined.

He dropped to his knees, wrapped his arms around her and dropped his mouth to a spot just below her navel, smiling when she jolted against him.

Because touching her wasn't enough. He wanted to taste her.

First, he retraced his steps, putting his mouth everywhere he could reach, relishing each shocked and greedy little noise she made. The way she widened her stance, then sagged back against the high bed as if her knees could no longer hold her. She buried her hands in his hair, but either she didn't know how to guide him, or didn't want to, so he made his own path.

And when her eyes looked blind with need, he reached up and unhooked her bra, carefully removing it so he could expose her breasts to his view.

Perfect. She was perfect, and he leaned in close so he could take his fill of her. He pulled one nipple deep into his mouth, sucking until she cried out.

And Dominik thought it was the most glorious sound he had ever heard.

When he was finished with both nipples, they stood harder and more proud. And she was gripping the bed sheets behind her, her head tipped back so all of her golden hair spread around her like a halo.

He shifted forward, lifting her up and setting her back on the bed so he could peel the panties from her hips.

As he pulled them down her satiny legs, she panted. And was making the slightest high-pitched sounds in the back of her throat, if he wasn't mistaken.

She only got louder when he lifted up her legs and set them on his shoulders so they dangled down his back, and then he lost himself in the fact he had full, unfettered access to all that molten sweetness between her legs.

The scent of her arousal roared in him, making him crazy.

Making him as close to desperate as he'd ever been.

He looked up and let his lips curve when he found her gazing back at him, a look of wonder on her face.

And something like disbelief in her eyes.

"You… My legs…" She hardly sounded like herself.

"All the better to eat you with, my dear," he said, dark and greedy.

And then he set his mouth to the core of her, and showed her exactly how real the fairy tales were, after all.

CHAPTER TEN

It hit her like a punch, thick and deep, setting Lauren alight from the inside out.

It made her go rigid, then shake.

But that didn't stop Dominik.

Her husband.

He was licking into her as if he planned to go on forever. He was using the edge of his teeth, his wicked tongue and the scrape of his jaw. His shoulders kept her thighs apart, and he didn't seem to care that her hands were buried in his hair. And tugging.

And after the first punch, there was a different, deeper fire. A kind of dancing flame she hardly knew how to name, and then there was more.

A shattering.

As if there were new ways to burn, and Dominik was intent on showing her each and every one of them.

The third time she exploded, he pulled his mouth away from her, pressing his lips against her inner thigh so she could feel him smile.

He stood, hauling her with him as he went, and then somehow they were both in the middle of a giant bed in one of the family's suites she had never dared enter on her previous trips to Combe Manor.

He rolled over her, and Lauren realized she must have lost time somewhere, because he was naked, too. She had no memory of him stripping off his trousers.

Not that she cared.

Because she could feel him everywhere, muscled legs between her, and the heat of his skin. All that lean weight of his. The crispness of the hair that dusted his decidedly male body. His eyes were like silver, hot and indulgent at once, and he braced himself over her as she ran her hands down all the planes and ridges of his beautiful chest, the way she'd wanted to since he'd opened the door this morning.

It was finally her turn to touch him. And she was determined to touch *all* of him, with all the fascination she hadn't know she held inside her. But there was no denying it as she followed her fingers wherever they wanted to go. There was no pretending it didn't swell and dance inside her.

"I don't understand how a man can be so beautiful," she whispered, and if that was betraying herself the way she feared it was, she couldn't bring herself to care about that.

Because he took her mouth then, a hard, mad claiming, and it thrilled her.

She surged against him, unable to get close enough. Unable to process each and every sensation that rolled over her, spiraled around inside her and made her want nothing more than to press every part of her against every part of him.

And she could feel it then. The hardest part of him, there between them. Velvet and steel, insistent against the soft skin of her belly.

It made her shudder all over again.

He slanted his mouth over hers, and then his hands were working magic between them. She heard the faint sound of foil, and then he settled himself between her legs as if all this time, her whole life, she had been made to hold him just like this.

Dominik had asked her if she was wet before. And now she knew what he meant in an entirely different way.

But he growled his approval as his fingers found the neediest part of her, playing with her until she bucked against him, her head thrashing back against the mattress.

He lifted her knees, then settled himself even more completely between them, so he was flush against her.

"Tell me if you don't feel anything," he said, his voice nearly unrecognizable, there at her ear.

"If I don't…" she began.

But then she could feel him, there at her center.

He pressed against the resistance he found; her body protested enough to make her wince, and then it was over.

Or just beginning, really.

Because he kept pressing. In and in, and there was too much. She couldn't name the things she felt; she could barely experience them as they happened—

"Remember," and his voice was a growl again. "You are nonsexual, little red. You do not feel what others do. Is that how this feels?"

But she couldn't answer him.

She couldn't do anything but dig her fingers into his shoulders as he opened her, pressed deeper and stretched her farther still.

Then finally, and yet too soon, he stopped.

And for a moment he only gazed down at her, propped up on his elbows with nothing but silver in his gaze and that very nearly stern set to his mouth.

While he was buried completely within her body.

And the knowledge of that, mixed with the exquisite sensation, so full and so deep, made her break apart all over again.

Less like a fist this time, and more like a wave. Over and over, until it wore itself out against the shore.

And when she opened her eyes again, she could see Dominik's jaw clenched tight and something harder in his gaze. Determination, perhaps.

"You're killing me," he gritted out.

She tried to catch her breath. "Am I doing it wrong?"

And he let out a kind of sigh, or maybe it was a groan, and he dropped down to gather her even more firmly beneath him.

"No, little red, you're not doing it wrong."

But she thought he sounded tortured as he said it.

Then Lauren couldn't care about that, either, because he began to move.

And it was everything she'd never known she wanted. She had never known she could want at all. It was the difference between a dark, cloudy sky, and a canopy of stars.

And she couldn't breathe. She couldn't *think*. She could only feel.

She was all sensation. All greed and passion, longing and desire, and all of it focused on the man who moved within her, teaching her with every thrust.

About need. About want.

About everything she had been missing, all these lonely years.

He taught her about hope, and he taught her about wonder, and still he kept on.

Lesson after lesson, as each thrust made it worse. Better.

As he made her undeniably human, flesh and passion made real, as surely as any kiss in a fairy tale story.

Until there was nothing between them but fire.

The glory of flames that danced and consumed them, made them one, and changed everything.

And when she exploded that time, he went with her.

He shouldn't have gone out on that porch, Dominik thought grimly a long while later as the sky outside darkened to a mysterious deep blue, and Lauren lay sprawled against his chest, her breathing even and her eyes closed.

He should have stayed in Hungary. He should have laughed off the notion that he was an heir to anything.

And he never, ever should have suggested that they make this marriage real.

He felt…wrecked.

And yet he couldn't seem to bring himself to shift her off him. It would be easy enough to do. A little roll, and he could leave her here. He could leave behind this great house and all its obnoxious history. He could pretend he truly didn't care about the woman who'd rid herself of him, then later chosen this.

But he had promised to take part in this whole charade, hadn't he? He'd promised not only to marry Lauren, but to subject himself to the rest of it, too. Hadn't she mentioned comportment? The press?

It was his own fault that he'd ended up here. He accepted that.

But he could honestly say that it had never occurred to him that sex with Lauren could possibly be this… ruinous.

Devastating, something in him whispered.

He hadn't imagined that anything could get to him. Nothing had in years. And no woman had ever come close.

Dominik had never experienced the overwhelming sensation that he wasn't only naked in the sense of having no clothes on—he was naked in every sense. Transparent with it, so anyone who happened by could see all the things in him he'd learned to pack away, out of view. First, as an orphan who had to try his best to act perfect for prospective parents. Then as a kid on the street who had to act tough enough to be left alone. Then as a soldier who had to act as if nothing he was ordered to do stayed with him.

And he couldn't say he much cared for the sensation now.

He needed to get up and leave this bed. He needed to go for a long, punishing run to clear his head. He needed to do something physical until he took the edge off all the odd things swirling around inside him, showing too much as if she'd knocked down every last boundary he had, and Dominik certainly couldn't allow that—

But she stirred then, shifting all that smooth, soft heat against him, and a new wave of intense heat washed over him.

She let out a sigh that sounded like his name, and what was he supposed to do with that?

Despite himself, he held on to her.

Especially when she lifted her head, piled her hands beneath her chin and blinked up at him.

And the things he wanted to say appalled him.

He cleared his throat. "Do you feel sufficiently in-doctrinated into the sport?"

He hardly recognized his own voice. Or that note in it that he was fairly certain was...playfulness? And his hands were on her curves as if he needed to assure himself that they were real. That she was.

"Is it a sport? I thought of it more as a pastime. A habit, perhaps." She considered it, and what was wrong with him that he enjoyed watching a woman *think*? "Or for some, I suppose, an addiction."

"There are always hobbyists and amateurs, little red," he found himself saying, a certain...*warmth* in his voice that he wanted to rip out with his own fingers. But he didn't know where to start. "But I have never counted myself among them."

He meant to leave, and yet his hands were on her, smoothing their way down her back, then cupping her bottom. He knew he needed to let her go and make sure this never happened again, but she was smiling.

And he hardly knew her. Gone was all that sharp-ness, and in its place was a kind of soft, almost dreamy expression that made his chest hurt.

As if she was the one teaching him a lesson here.

"I beg your pardon. I didn't realize I was addressing such a renowned star of the bedroom," she said, and her lovely eyes danced with laughter.

It only served to remind him that she didn't laugh nearly enough.

"I will excuse it," he told her. "Once."

He needed to put distance between them. Now. Dominik knew that the way he knew every other fact of his existence. He knew it like every single memory he had of the nuns. The streets. The missions he'd been sent on.

He wasn't a man built for connection. He didn't want to be the kind of man who could connect with people, because people were what was wrong with the world. People had built this house. A person had given him away. He wanted nothing to do with *people*, or he never would have taken himself off into the woods in the first place.

But this pretty, impossible person was looking at him as if he was the whole world, her cheeks heating into red blazes he couldn't keep from touching. He ran his knuckles over one, then the other, silky smooth and wildly hot.

"It is still our wedding night," she pointed out.

"So it is."

Lauren lowered her lashes, then traced a small pattern against his chest with one fingertip.

"I don't know how this works. Or if you can. Physically, I mean. But I wondered… I mean, I hoped…" She blew out a breath. "Was that the whole of the lesson?"

And Dominik was only a man, after all, no matter how he'd tried to make himself into a monster, out there in his forest. And the part of him that had been greedy for her since the moment he'd seen her could never be happy with so small a taste.

Will you ever be satisfied? a voice in him asked. *Or will you always want more?*

That should have sent him racing for the door. He needed to leave, right now, but he found himself lifting her against him instead. He drew her up on her knees so she straddled him, and watched as she looked down between them, blinked and then smiled.

Wickedly, God help him.

"By all means," he encouraged her, his hands on her hips. "Allow me to teach you something else I feel certain you won't feel, as shut off and uninterested in these things as you are."

She found him then, wrapping her hands around the hardest expression of his need and guiding him to the center of her heat.

As if she'd been born for this. For him.

"No," she murmured breathlessly. And then smiled as she took him inside her as if he'd been made to fit her so perfectly, just like that. "I don't expect I'll feel anything at all."

And there was nothing for it. There was no holding back.

Dominik gave himself over to his doom.

CHAPTER ELEVEN

THE SITUATION DID not improve as the days slid by and turned inevitably into weeks.

Dominik needed to put a stop to the madness. There was no debate on that topic. The pressing need to leave the mess he'd made here, get the hell out of England, and away from the woman he never should have married, beat in him like a drum. It was the first thing he thought of when he woke. It dogged him through the long summer days. It even wormed its way into his dreams.

But one day led into the next, and he went nowhere. He didn't even try to leave as if he was the one who'd wandered into the wrong forest and found himself under some kind of spell he couldn't break.

Meanwhile, they traded lesson for lesson.

"I know how to use utensils, little red," he told her darkly one morning after he'd come back from a punishing run—yet not punishing enough, clearly, as he'd returned to Combe Manor—and had showered and changed only to find the formal dining room set with acres of silver on either side of each plate. There was a mess of glasses and extra plates everywhere he looked.

And Lauren sat there with her hair pulled back into

the smooth ponytail he took personally and that prissy look on her face.

The very same prissy look that made him hard and greedy for her, instantly.

"This won't be a lesson about basic competence with a fork, which I'll go ahead and assume you mastered some time ago," she told him tartly. Her gaze swept over him, making him feel as if he was still that grubby-faced orphan, never quite good enough. He gritted his teeth against it, because that was the last thing he needed. The present was complicated enough without dragging in the past. "This will be about formal manners for formal dinners."

"Alternatively, I could cook for myself, eat with own my fingers if I so desire and continue to have the exact same blood in my veins that I've always had with no one the least bit interested either way. None of this matters."

He expected her to come back at him, sharp and amusing, but she didn't. She studied him for a moment instead, and he still didn't know how to handle the way she looked at him these days. It was softer. Warmer.

It was too dangerous. It scraped at him until he felt raw and he could never get enough of it, all the same.

"It depends on your perspective, I suppose," she said. "It's not rocket science, of course. The fate of the world doesn't hang in the balance. History books won't be written about what fork you use at a banquet. But the funny thing about manners is that they can often stand in for the things you lack."

"And what is it I lack, exactly? Be specific, please. I dare you."

"I'm talking about me, Dominik. Not you."

And when she smiled, the world stopped.

He told himself it was one more sign he needed to get away from her. Instead, he took the seat opposite her at the table as if he really was under her spell.

Why couldn't he break it?

"When I was nine my parents had been divorced for two years, which means each of them was married again. My stepmother was pregnant. I didn't know it at the time, but my mother was, too. I still thought that they should all be spending a great deal more time with me. So one day I decided I'd run away, thereby forcing them to worry about me, and then act like parents."

She smiled as if at the memory, but it wasn't a happy smile. And later Dominik would have to reflect on how and why he knew the difference between her *smiles*, God help him. As if he'd made a study against his will, when he wasn't entirely paying attention.

"I rode the buses around and around, well into the evening," she said with that same smile. "And they came together, just as I'd hoped, but only so they could blame each other for what a disaster I was. Within an hour of my return they'd agreed to send me off to boarding school for the summer, so others could deal with me and they wouldn't have to do it themselves."

"I understand that not all parents are good ones," Dominik said, his voice low. "But I would caution you against complaining about your disengaged, yet present, parents while in the presence of a man who had none. Ever. Disengaged or otherwise."

"I'm not complaining about them," Lauren replied quietly. "They are who they are. I'm telling you how I came to be at a very posh school for summer. It was entirely filled with children nobody wanted."

"Pampered children, then. I can assure you no orphanage is *posh*."

"Yes. Someone, somewhere, paid handsomely to send us all to that school. But it would have been hard to tell a lonely nine-year-old, who knew she was at that school because her parents didn't want anything to do with her, that she was *pampered*. Mostly, I'm afraid, I was just scared."

Dominik stared back at her, telling himself he felt nothing. Because he ought to have felt nothing. He had taught her that sensation was real and that she could feel it, but he wanted none of it himself. No sensation. No emotion.

None of this scraping, aching thing that lived in him now that he worried might crack his ribs open from the inside. Any minute now.

"They taught us manners," Lauren told him in the same soft, insistent tone. "Comportment. Dancing. And it all seemed as stupid to me as I'm sure it does to you right now, but I will tell you this. I have spent many an evening since that summer feeling out of place. Unlike everyone else my age at university, for example, with all their romantic intrigue. These days I'm often trotted off to a formal affair where I am expected to both act as an emblem for Combe Industries as well as blend into the background. All at once. And do you know what allows me to do that? The knowledge that no matter what, I can handle myself in any social situation. People agonize over which fork to choose and which plate is theirs while I sit there, listening to conversations I shouldn't be hearing, ready and able to do my job."

"Heaven forbid anything prevent you from doing your job."

"I like my job."

"Do you? Or do you like imagining that your Mr. Combe cannot make it through a day without you?" He shrugged when she glared at him. "We are all of us dark creatures in our hearts, little red. Think of the story from the wolf's point of view next time. Our Red Riding Hood doesn't come off well, does she?"

He thought she had quite a few things to say to that, but she nodded toward the silverware before them instead. "We'll work from the outside in, and as we go we'll work on appropriate dinner conversation at formal occasions, which does not include obsessive references to fairy tales."

Dominik couldn't quite bring himself to tell her that he already knew how to handle a formal dinner, thank you. Not when she thought she was giving him a tool he could use to *save himself*, no less.

Just as he couldn't bring himself—allow himself— to tell her all those messy things that sloshed around inside him at the thought of her as a scared nine-year-old, abandoned by her parents and left to make *manners* her sword and shield.

He showed her instead, pulling her onto his lap before one of the interminable courses and imparting his own lesson. Until they were both breathing too heavily to care that much whether they used the correct fork— especially when his fingers were so talented.

He meant to leave the following day, but there was dancing, which meant he got to hold Lauren in his arms and then sweep her away upstairs to teach her what those bed posts were for. He meant to leave the day after that, but she'd had videos made of all the San Giacomo holdings.

There was something every day. Presentations on all manner of topics. Lessons of every description, from comportment to conversation and back again. Meetings with the unctuous, overly solicitous tailors, who he wanted to hate until they returned with beautiful clothes even he could tell made him look like the aristocrat he wasn't.

Which he should have hated—but couldn't, not when Lauren looked at him as if he was some kind of king.

He needed to get out of there, but he had spent an entire childhood making up stories about his imaginary family in his head. And he didn't have it in him to walk away from the first person he'd ever met who could tell him new stories. Real stories, this time.

Because Lauren also spent a significant part of every day teaching him the history of the San Giacomos, making sure he knew everything there was to know about their rise to power centuries ago. Their wealth and consequence across the ages.

And how it had likely come to pass that a sixteen-year-old heiress had been forced to give up her illegitimate baby, whether she wanted to or not.

He found that part the hardest to get his head around—likely because he so badly wanted to believe it.

"You must have known her," he said one day as summer rain danced against the windows where he stood.

They were back in the library, surrounded by all those gleaming, gold-spined books that had never been put on their self-important shelves for a man like him, no matter what blood ran in his veins. Lauren sat with her tablet before her, stacks of photo albums arrayed on the table, and binders filled with articles on the San Giacomo family. All of them stories that were now his, she told him time and time again. And all those stories about a family that was now his, too.

Dominik couldn't quite believe in any of it.

He'd spent his childhood thirsty for even a hint of a real story to tell about his family. About himself. Then he'd spent his adulthood resolved not to care about any of it, because he was making his own damned story.

He couldn't help thinking that this was all…too late. That the very thing that might have saved him as a child was little more than a bedtime story to him now, with about as much impact on his life.

"Alexandrina," he elaborated when Lauren frowned at him. "You must have known my mother while she was still alive."

And he didn't know how to tell her how strange those words felt in his mouth. *My mother.* Bitter and sweet. Awkward. Unreal. *My mother* was a dream he'd tortured himself with as a boy. Not a real person. Not a real woman with a life, hopes and dreams and possibly even *reasons.*

It had never occurred to him that his anger was a gift. Take that away and he had nothing but the urge to find compassion in him somewhere…and how was a man meant to build his life on that?

"I did know her," Lauren said. "A little."

"Was she…?"

But he didn't know what to ask. And he wasn't sure he wanted to know the answers.

"I couldn't possibly be a good judge." Lauren was choosing her words carefully. And Dominik didn't know when he'd become so delicate that she might imagine he needed special handling. "I worked for her son, so we were never more than distantly polite the few times we met. I don't know that any impression I gleaned of her would be the least bit worthwhile."

"It is better than no impressions, which is what I have."

Lauren nodded at that. "She was very beautiful."

"That tells me very little about her character, as I think you know."

"She could be impatient. She could be funny." Lauren thought a moment. "I think she was very conscious of her position."

"Meaning she was a terrible snob."

"No, I don't think so. Not the way you mean it. I never saw her treat anyone badly. But she had certain standards that she expected to have met." She smiled. "If she was a man, people would say she knew her own mind, that's all."

"I've read about her." And he had, though he had found it impossible to see anything of him in the impossibly glamorous creature who'd laughed and pouted for the cameras, and inspired so many articles about her *style*, which Dominik suspected was a way to talk about a high-class woman's looks without causing offense. "She seemed entirely defined by her love affairs and scandals."

"My abiding impression of her was that she had learned how to be pretty. And how to use that prettiness to live up to the promise of both the grand families she was a part of. But I don't think it ever occurred to her that she could be happy."

"Could she?" Dominik asked, sardonic straight through. "I didn't realize that was on offer."

"It should always be on offer," Lauren replied with a certain quiet conviction that Dominik refused to admit got to him. Because it shouldn't have. "Isn't that the point?"

"The point of what, exactly?"

"Everything, Dominik."

"You sound like an American advertisement," Dominik said after a moment, from between his teeth. "No one is owed happiness. And certainly, precious few find it."

He hadn't meant to move from the windows, but he had. And he was suddenly standing in front of that sofa, looking down at Lauren.

Who gazed straight back at him, that same softness on her face. It connected directly to that knot inside him he'd been carrying for weeks now. That ache. That infernal clamoring on the inside of his ribs that demanded he leave, yet wouldn't let him go.

"Maybe if we anticipated happiness we might find a little along the way." Her voice was like honey, and he knew it boded ill. He knew it was bad for him. Because he had no defenses against that kind of sweetness. Caramel eyes and honey voice—and he was a goner. "Why not try?"

"I had no idea that our shabby little marriage of convenience would turn so swiftly into an encounter group," he heard himself growl. When she didn't blanch at that the way he'd expected she would, he pushed on. "So-called happiness is the last refuge and resort of the dim-witted. And those who don't know any better, which I suppose is redundant. I think you'll find the real world is a little too complicated for platitudes and whistling as you work."

Lauren lifted one shoulder, then dropped it. "I don't believe that."

And it was the way she said it that seemed to punch holes straight through Dominik's chest. There was no defiant tilt to her chin. There was no angry flash of temper in her lovely eyes. It was a simple statement, more powerful somehow for its softness than for any attempt at a show of strength.

And there was no reason he should feel it shake in him like a storm.

"You don't believe that the world is a terrible place, as complicated as it is harsh, desperate people careening about from greed to self-interest and back again? Ignoring their children or abandoning them in orphanages as they see fit?"

"The fact that people can be awful and scared only means that when we happen upon it, we should cling to what happiness we can."

"Let me guess. You think I should be more grateful that after all this time, the woman who clearly knew where I was all along told others where to find me. But only after her death, so they could tell me sad stories about how she *might* have given me away against her will. You want me to conclude that I ended up here all the same, so why dwell on what was lost in the interim? You will have to forgive me if I do not see all this as the gift you do."

"The world won't end if you allow the faintest little gleam of optimism into your life," Lauren said with that same soft conviction that got to him in ways he couldn't explain. And didn't particularly want to analyze. "And who knows? You could even allow yourself to hope for something. Anything. It's not dim-witted and it's not because a person doesn't see the world as it is." Her gaze was locked to his. "Hope takes strength, Dominik. Happiness takes work. And I choose to believe it's worth it."

"What do you know of either?" he demanded. "You, who locked yourself away from the world and convinced yourself you disliked basic human needs. You are the poster child for happiness?"

"I know because of you."

The words were so simple.

And they might as well have been a tornado, tearing him up.

"Me." He shook his head as if he didn't understand the word. As if she'd used it to bludgeon him. "If I bring you *happiness*, little red, I fear you've gone and lost yourself in a deep, dark woods from which you will never return."

She stood up then, and he was seized with the need to stop her somehow. As if he knew what she was going to say when of course, he couldn't know. He refused to know.

He should have left before this happened.

He should have left.

His gaze moved over her, and it struck him that while he'd certainly paid close attention to her, he hadn't truly *looked* at her since they'd arrived here weeks ago. Not while she was dressed. She wasn't wearing the same sharp, pointedly professional clothing any longer—and he couldn't recall the last time she had. Today she wore a pair of trousers he knew were soft like butter, and as sweetly easy to remove. She wore a flowing sort of top that drooped down over one shoulder, which he liked primarily because it gave him access to the lushness beneath.

Both of those things were clues, but he ignored them.

It was the hair that was impossible to pretend hadn't changed.

Gone was the sleek ponytail, all that blond silk ruthlessly tamed and controlled. She wore it loose now, tumbling around her shoulders, because he liked his hands in it.

Had he not been paying attention? Or had he not wanted to see?

"Yes, you," she said, answering the question he'd asked, and all the ones he hadn't. "You make me happy, Dominik. And hopeful. I'm sorry if that's not what you want to hear."

She kept her gaze trained on his, and he didn't know what astounded him more. That she kept saying these terrible, impossible things. Or that she looked so fearless as she did it, despite the color in her cheeks.

He wanted to tell her to stop, but he couldn't seem to move.

And she kept right on going. "I thought I knew myself, but I didn't. I thought I knew what I needed, but I had no idea. I asked you to teach me and I meant very specifically about sex. And you did that, but you taught me so much more. You taught me everything." She smiled then, a smile he'd never seen before, so tremulous and full of hope—and it actually hurt him. "I think you made me whole, Dominik, and I had no idea I wasn't already."

If she had thrust a sword into the center of his chest, then slammed it home, he could not have felt more betrayed.

"I did none of those things," he managed to grit out. "Sex is not happiness. It is not hope. And it is certainly no way to go looking for yourself, Lauren."

"And yet that's who I found." And she was still aiming that smile at him, clearly unaware that she was killing him. "Follow the bread crumbs long enough, even into a terrible forest teeming with scary creatures and wolves like men, and there's no telling what you'll find at the other end."

"I know exactly what you'll find on the other end. Nothing. Because there's no witch in a gingerbread house. There's no Big Bad Wolf. You were sent to find me by a man who was executing a duty, nothing more. And I came along with you because—"

"Because why, exactly?" Again, it was the very softness and certainty in her voice that hit him like a gut punch. "You certainly didn't have to invite me into your cabin. But you did."

"Something I will be questioning for some time to come, I imagine." Dominik slashed a hand through the air, but he didn't know if it was aimed at her—or him. "But this is over, Lauren. You had your experiment and now it's done."

"Because I like it too much?" She had the audacity to laugh. "Surely, you've done this before, Dominik. Surely, you knew the risks. If you open someone up, chances are, they're going to like it. Isn't that what you wanted? Me to fall head over heels in love with you like every virgin cliché ever? Why else would you have dedicated yourself to *my experiment* the way you did?"

He actually backed away from her then. As if the word she'd used was poison. Worse than that. A toxic bomb that could block out the sun.

It felt as if she'd blinded him already.

"There is no risk whatsoever of anyone falling in love with me," he told her harshly.

"I think you know that isn't true." She studied him as if he'd disappointed her, as if he was *currently* letting her down, right there in full view of all the smug volumes of fancy books he'd never read and never would. "I assumed that was why you stayed all this time."

"I stayed all this time because that was the deal we made."

"The deal we made was for a wedding night, Dominik. Maybe a day or so after. It's been nearly two months."

"It doesn't matter how long it's been. It doesn't matter why. I'm glad that you decided you can feel all these emotions." But he wasn't glad. He was something far, far away from *glad*. "But I don't. I won't."

"But you do." And that was the worst yet. Another betrayal, another weapon. Because it was so matter-of-fact. Because she stared right back at him as if she knew things about him he didn't, and that was unbearable. Dominik had never been *known*. He wanted nothing to do with it. "I think you do."

And Dominik never knew what he might have said to that—how he might have raged or, more terrifying, how he might not have—because the doors to the library were pushed open then, and one of Combe Manor's quietly competent staff members stood there, frowning.

"I'm sorry to interrupt," she said, looking back and forth between them. "But something's happened, I'm afraid." She gestured in the direction of the long drive out front. "There are reporters. Everywhere. Cameras, microphones and shouting."

The maid's eyes moved to Dominik, and he thought she looked apologetic. When all he could feel was that emptiness inside him that had always been there and always would. Even if now, thanks to Lauren, it ached.

The maid cleared her throat. "They're calling for you, sir. By name."

CHAPTER TWELVE

IN THE END, Lauren was forced to call the Yorkshire Police to encourage the paparazzi to move off the property, down to the bottom of the long drive that led to Combe Manor from the village proper and away from the front of the house itself.

But the damage was done. The will had been leaked, as Lauren had known it would be eventually, and Dominik had been identified. That he had quietly married his half brother's longtime personal assistant had made the twenty-four-hour news cycle.

She quickly discovered that she was nothing but a shameless gold digger. There was arch speculation that Matteo had dispatched her to corral Dominik, marry him under false pretenses and then…work him to Matteo's advantage somehow.

It was both close to the truth and nothing like the truth at all, but any impulse she might have had to laugh at it dissipated in the face of Dominik's response.

Which was to disappear.

First, he disappeared without actually going anywhere. It was like looking into a void. One moment she'd been having a conversation—admittedly, not the most pleasant conversation—with him. The next, it was as if the Dominik she'd come to know was gone and a stranger had taken his place.

A dark, brooding stranger, who looked at her with icy disinterest. And as far as she could tell, viewed the paparazzi outside the same. He didn't call her *little red* again, and she would have said she didn't even like the nickname.

But she liked it even less when he stopped using it.

Her mobile rang and rang, but she ignored the calls. From unknown numbers she assumed meant more reporters. From Pia, who had likely discovered that she had another brother from the news, which made Lauren feel guilty for not insisting Matteo tell her earlier. And from the various members of the Combe Industries Board of Directors, which she was more than happy to send straight to voice mail.

"It's Mr. Combe," she said when it rang another time. "At last."

"You must take that, of course," Dominik said, standing at the windows again, glaring off into the distance. "Heaven forfend you do not leap to attention the moment your master summons you."

And Lauren couldn't say she liked the way he said that. But she didn't know what to do about it, either.

"We always knew this day would come," she told him, briskly, when she'd finished having a quick damage control conversation with Matteo. "It's actually surprising that didn't happen sooner."

"We have been gilding this lily for weeks now," Dominik replied, his voice that dark growl that made everything in her shiver—and not entirely from delight. "We have played every possible Pygmalion game there is. There is nothing more to be accomplished here."

"Where would you like to go instead?" She had opened up the cabinet and turned on the television earlier, so they could watch the breathless news reports and the endless scroll of accusation and speculation at the bottom of the screen. Now she turned the volume up again so she could hear what they were saying. About her. "I suppose we should plan some kind of function to introduce you to—"

"No."

"No? No, you don't want to be introduced to society? Or no, you don't want—"

"You fulfilled your role perfectly, Lauren." But the way he said it was no compliment. It was...dangerous. "Your Mr. Combe will be so proud, I am sure. You have acted as my jailer. My babysitter. And you have kept me out of public view for very nearly two months, which must be longer than any of you thought possible. You have my congratulations. I very nearly forgot your purpose in this."

His voice didn't change when he said that. And he didn't actually reach out and strike her.

But it felt as if he did.

"I thought this would happen sooner, as a matter of fact," Lauren managed to say, her heart beating much too wildly in her chest. Her head spinning a little from the hit that hadn't happened. "And my brief was to give you a little polish and a whole lot of history, Dominik. That's all. I found a hermit in a hut. All Mr. Combe asked me to do was make you a San Giacomo."

"And now I am as useless as any one of them. You've done your job well. You are clearly worth every penny he pays you."

It was harder to keep her cool than it should have

been. Because she knew too much now. He was acting like a stranger, but her body still wanted him the way it always did. He had woken her this morning by surging deep inside her, catapulting her from dreams tinged with the things he did to her straight into the delirious reality.

She didn't know how to handle this. The distance between them. The fury in his dark gaze. The harsh undercurrent to everything he said, and the way he looked at her as if she had been the enemy all along.

She should have known that the price of tasting happiness—of imagining she could—meant that the lack of it would hurt her.

More than hurt her. Looking at him and seeing a stranger made her feel a whole lot closer to broken.

She should have known better than to let herself *feel*.

"I know this feels like a personal attack," she said, carefully, though she rather thought she'd been the one personally attacked. "But this is about how the San Giacomo and Combe families are perceived. And more, how Matteo and his sister have been portrayed in the press in the wake of their father's death. No one wanted you to be caught up in that."

"And yet here I am."

"Dominik. Please. This is just damage control. That's the only reason Mr. Combe didn't proclaim your existence far and wide the moment he knew of you."

That gaze of his swung to her and held. Hard, like another blow. It made her want to cry—but she knew, somehow, that would only make it worse.

"You cannot control damage, Lauren. I would think you, of all people, would know this. You can only do your best to survive it."

And she had no time to recover from that.

Because that was when the self-satisfied newscaster on the television screen started talking about who Dominik James really was.

"We've just been made aware that Dominik James is not merely the long-lost heir to two of Europe's most prominent families," the man said. "Our sources tell us he is also a self-made billionaire who ran his own security company until he sold it recently for what is believed to be a small fortune in its own right. Dominik himself has been widely sought after by celebrities and kings alike, and a number of governments besides."

Then they flashed pictures of him, in case Lauren had somehow missed the implications. There were shots of Dominik in three-piece suits, his hair cropped close to his head, shaking hands with powerful, recognizable men. In and out of formal balls, charity events and boardrooms.

Nothing like a feral hermit at all.

"Oh, dear," Dominik said when the newscast cut to some inane commercial, too much darkness in his voice. "Your table settings will not save you now, Lauren. It has all been a lie. I am not at all who you thought I was. Why don't you tell me more about how happy you are?"

And Lauren remembered exactly why she'd decided emotion wasn't for her. She had been nine years old and sent off to a terrifying stone building filled with strangers. She'd stayed awake the whole of that first night, sobbing into her pillow so her roommate didn't hear her.

Since then, she'd forgotten that these terrible emotions could sit on a person like this. Crushing her with their weight. Suffocating her, yet never quite killing her.

Making her own heartbeat feel like an attack.

"You didn't need me at all," she managed to say, parts of her breaking apart on the inside like so many earthquakes, stitched together into a single catastrophe she wasn't sure she would survive. No matter what he'd said about damage.

But she didn't want to let him see it.

"No," Dominik said, and there was something terrible there in his gray eyes that made her want to reach out to him. Soothe him somehow. But his voice was so cold. Something like cruel, and she didn't dare. "I never needed you."

"This was a game, then." She didn't know how she was speaking when she couldn't feel her own face. Her outsides had gone numb, but that paralysis did not extend inside, where she was desperately trying to figure out what to do with all that raw upheaval before it broke her into actual pieces. "You were just playing a game. I can understand that you wanted to find out who your family really was. But you were playing the game with me."

And maybe later she would think about how he stood there, so straight and tall and bruised somehow, that it made her ache. With that look on his face that made her want to cry.

But all she could do at the moment was fight to stay on her feet, without showing him how much he was hurting her. It was crucial that she swallow that down, hide it away, even as it threatened to cut her down.

"Life is damage, Lauren," he said in that same dark, cold way. "Not hope. Not happiness. Those are stories fools tell to trick themselves into imagining otherwise. The true opiate of the masses. The reality is that people lie. They deceive you. They abandon you whenever possible, and may use you to serve their own ends. I never needed you to polish me. But you're welcome all the same. Someday you'll thank me for disabusing you of all these damaging notions."

Her mobile rang again, Matteo's name flashing on her screen.

And for the first time in as long as she could remember, Lauren didn't want to answer. She wanted to fling her mobile across the room and watch it shatter against the wall. Part of her wanted very much to throw it at Dominik, and see if it would shatter that wall.

But she did neither.

She looked down at the mobile, let her thoughts turn violent, and when she looked up again Dominik was gone.

And she sat where she was for a very long time, there on a Combe family sofa before a television screen that repeated lie after lie about who she was until she was tempted to believe it herself.

Her mobile rang. It rang and rang, and she let it.

Outside, the endless summer day edged into night, and still Lauren sat where she was.

She felt hollowed out. And yet swollen somehow. As if all those unwieldy, overwhelming emotions she'd successfully locked away since she was a child had swept back into her, all at once, until she thought they might break her wide open.

It was the first time in almost as long that she didn't have the slightest idea what to do. How to fix this. Or even if she wanted to.

All she knew was that even now, even though Dominik had looked at her the way he had, and said those things to her, he was still the one she wanted to go to. It was his arms she longed for. His heat, his strength.

How could she want him to comfort her when he was the one who had hurt her?

But she wasn't going to get an answer to that question.

Because when she went looking for him, determined to figure at least some part of this out, she discovered that Dominik hadn't simply disappeared while he'd stood there before her.

He'd actually gone.

He'd packed up his things, clearly, as there was nothing to suggest he'd been here at all. And then he must have let himself out while she'd been sitting there in the library where he'd left her, trying her best not to fall apart.

And she didn't have to chase after him to know he had no intention of coming back.

Because she had fallen for him, head over heels. But he had only ever been playing a game.

And Lauren would have to learn to live with that, too.

Lauren launched herself back into her life.

Her real life, which did not include mysterious men with hidden fortunes who lived off in the Hungarian woods. The life she had built all by herself, with no support from anyone.

The life that she was sure she remembered loving, or at least finding only a few months ago.

"You still love it," she snapped at herself one morning, bustling around her flat on her way to work. "You love every last part of it."

"You know when you start talking to yourself," Mary

said serenely, splashing the last of the milk into her tea, "that's when the stress has really won."

Lauren eyed her roommate and the empty jug of milk. "Is that your mobile ringing?"

And as Mary hurried out of the room, she told herself that she was fine. Good.

Happy and hopeful, as a matter of fact, because neither one of those things had anything to do with the surly, angry man who'd done exactly what she'd asked him to do and then left after staying much longer than she'd expected he would.

She had what she wanted. She knew what other people felt. She understood why they went to such great lengths to have sex whenever possible. And she was now free to go out on the pull whenever she pleased. She could do as Dominik had once suggested and take herself off to a local pub, where she could continue conducting the glorious experiment in her own sexual awakening. On her own.

He didn't need her. And she certainly didn't need him.

Lauren decided she'd get stuck into it, no pun intended, that very night.

She thought about it all day long. She made her usual assenting, supportive sounds during the video conference from wherever Matteo was in the world today, but what she was really thinking about was the debauchery that awaited her. Because Dominik had been no more than a means to an end, she told herself. Merely a stepping-stone to a glorious sensual feast.

She left work early—which was to say, on time for once—and charged into the first pub she saw.

Where she remained for the five minutes it took to

look around, see all the men who weren't Dominik and want to cry.

Because it turned out that the only kind of awakening she wanted was with him.

Only and ever with him, something in her said with a kind of finality that she felt knit itself inside her like bone.

And maybe that was why, some six weeks after the tabloids had discovered Dominik—when all that bone had grown and gotten strong—she reacted to what ought to have been a perfectly simple request from Matteo the way she did.

"I'll be landing in San Francisco shortly," he told her from his jet.

"And then headed home, presumably," she interjected. "To attend to your empire."

"Yes, yes," he said in a way that she knew meant, *or perhaps not*. "But what I need you to do is work on that marriage."

Lauren had him on the computer monitor at her desk so she could work more easily on her laptop as he fired his usual instructions at her.

But she stopped what she was doing at that and swiveled in her chair, so she could gaze at him directly.

"Which marriage would that be?" she asked. Tartly, she could admit. "Your sister's? You must know that she and her prince are playing a very specific cat and mouse game—"

Matteo was rifling through papers, frowning at something off screen, and she knew that his sister's romantic life was a sore point for him. Was that why she'd brought it up? When she knew that wasn't the marriage he meant?

"I mean your marriage, Lauren," he said in that distracted way of his. She knew what that meant, too. That her boss had other, more important things on his mind. Something she had always accepted as his assistant, because that was her job—to fade into his background and make certain he could focus on anything he wished. But he was talking about *her*. And the marriage he'd suggested, and she'd actually gone ahead and done on his command. "There's a gala in Rome next week. Do you think your husband is sufficiently tamed? Can he handle a public appearance?"

"Well, he's not actually a trained bear," she found herself replying with more snap in her voice than necessary. "And he was handling public appearances just fine before he condescended to come to Combe Manor. So no need to fear he might snap his chain and devour the guests, I think."

"You can field the inevitable questions from paparazzi," Matteo said, frowning down at the phone in his hand. The way he often did—so there was no reason for it to prick at Lauren the way it did. *Maybe it is time you ask yourself what you* wouldn't *do if your Mr. Combe asked it*, Dominik had said. *You may find the answers illuminating.* But what about what Matteo wouldn't do for her? Like pay attention to the fact she was an actual person, not a bit of machinery? "You know the drill."

"Indeed I do. I know all the drills."

She'd created the drills, for that matter. And she wasn't sure why she wanted to remind Matteo of that.

"Just make sure it looks good," Matteo said, and he looked at her then. "You know what I mean. I want a quiet, calm appearance that makes it clear to all that the

San Giacomo scandal is fully handled. I want to keep the board happy."

"And whether the brother you have yet to meet is happy with all these revelations about the family he never knew is of secondary interest, of course. Or perhaps of no interest at all."

She was sure she'd meant to say that. But there it was, out there between them as surely as if she'd hauled off and slapped her boss in the face.

Matteo blinked, and it seemed to Lauren as if it took a thousand years for him to focus on her.

"Is my brother unhappy?" he asked. Eventually.

"You will have to ask him yourself," she replied. And then, because she couldn't seem to stop herself, "He's your brother, not mine."

"He is your husband, Lauren."

"Do you think it is the role of a wife to report on her husband to her boss? One begins to understand why you remain unmarried."

Something flashed over his face then, and she didn't understand why she wasn't already apologizing. Why she wasn't hurrying to set things right.

"You knew the role when you took it." Matteo frowned. "Forgive me, but am I missing something?"

And just like that, something in Lauren snapped.

"I am your personal assistant, Mr. Combe," she shot at him. "That can and has included such things as sorting out your wardrobe. Making your travel arrangements. Involving myself more than I'd like in your personal life. But it should never have included you asking me to marry someone on your behalf."

"If you had objections you should have raised them

before you went ahead and married him, then. It's a bit late now, don't you think?"

"When have I ever been permitted to have objections in this job?" She shook her head, that cold look on Dominik's face flashing through her head. And the way he'd said *your master*. "When have I ever said no to you?"

Matteo's frown deepened, but not because he was having any kind of emotional response. She knew that. She could see that he was baffled.

"I value you, Lauren, if that's what this is about. You know that."

But Lauren wasn't the same person she had been. It wasn't the value Matteo assigned to her ability to do her job that mattered to her. Not anymore.

She could look back and see how all of this had happened. How she, who had never been wanted by anyone, threw herself into being needed instead. She'd known she was doing it. She'd given it her all. And she'd been hired by Matteo straight out of university, so it had felt like some kind of cure of all the things that ailed her to make sure she not only met his needs, but anticipated them, too.

She had thought they were a team. They had been, all these years. While he'd had to work around his father and now he was in charge.

But Dominik had taught her something vastly different than how to make herself indispensable to the person who paid her.

He had taught her how to value herself.

He'd taught her how to want. How to *be wanted*.

And in return, he'd taught her how to want *more*.

Because that was the trouble with allowing herself

to want anything at all when she'd done without for so long. She wasn't satisfied with half measures, or a life spent giving everything she had to a man who not only couldn't return it, but whom she didn't want anything from.

She didn't want to sacrifice herself. It turned out that despite her choice of profession, she wasn't a martyr. Or she didn't want to be one.

Not anymore.

She knew what she wanted. Because she knew what it felt like now to be wanted desperately in return—no matter that Dominik might not have admitted that. She still knew.

He had stayed so long at Combe Manor. He had showed her things that she'd never dared dream about before. And he had taken her, over and over again, like a man possessed.

Like a man who feared losing her the same way she'd feared losing him.

If he hadn't cared, he wouldn't have snuck away. She knew that, too.

Lauren looked around the office that was more her home than her flat had ever been. The couch where she'd slept so many nights—including the night before her wedding. The windows that looked out over the city she'd loved so desperately not because she required its concrete and buildings, she understood now, but because it had been her constant. The one kind of parent that wouldn't turn its back on her.

But she didn't need any of these things any longer.

Lauren already had everything she needed. Maybe she always had, but she knew it now. And it was time instead to focus on what she *wanted*.

"And I have valued these years, Mr. Combe," she said now, lifting her head and looking Matteo in the eye. "More than you know. But it's time for me to move on." She smiled when he started to protest. "Please consider this my notice. I will train my replacement. I'll find her myself and make certain she is up to your standards. Never fear."

"Lauren." His voice was kind then.

But it wasn't his kindness she wanted.

"I'm sorry," she said quietly. "But I can't do this anymore."

And that night she lay in her bed in the flat she paid for but hardly knew. She stared at her ceiling, and when that grew old, she moved to look out the window instead.

There was concrete everywhere. London rooftops, telephone wires and the sound of traffic in the distance. The home she'd made. The parent she'd needed. London had been all things to her, but in the end, it was only a city. Her favorite city, true. But if it was any more than that, she'd made it that way.

And she didn't want that any longer. She didn't need it. She craved…something else. Something different.

Something wild, a voice in her whispered.

Lauren thought about want. About need. About the crucial distinction between the two, and why it had taken her so long to see it.

And the next morning she set off for Hungary again.

By the time she made it to the mountain village nestled there at the edge of the forest it was well into the afternoon.

But she didn't let that stop her. She left the hired car near the inn she'd stayed in on the last night of her life before she'd met Dominik and everything changed, and she began to walk.

She didn't mind the growing dark, down there on the forest floor. The temperature dropped as she walked, but she had her red wrap and she pulled it closer around her.

The path was just as she remembered it, clear and easy to follow, if hard going against the high, delicate heels she wore. Because of course she wore them.

Lauren might have felt like a new woman. But that didn't mean she intended to betray herself with sensible shoes.

On she walked.

And she thought about fairy tales. About girls who found their way into forests and thought they were lost, but found their way out no matter what rose up to stop them. Especially if what tried to stop them was themselves.

It was only a deep, dark forest if she didn't know where she was going, she told herself. But she did. And all around her were pretty trees, fresh air and a path to walk upon.

No bread crumbs. No sharp teeth and wolves. No witches masquerading as friends, tucked up in enchanted cottages with monstrous roses and questionable pies.

No foreboding, no wicked spells.

There was only Lauren.

And she knew exactly what she wanted.

When she reached the clearing this time, she marched straight through it. There was no one lurking in the shadows on the front porch, but she hadn't really expected there would be. She walked up, anyway, went straight to the front door and let herself in.

The cabin was just as she remembered it. Shockingly cozy and inviting, and entirely too nice. It was a clue, had she bothered to pay attention to it, that the man she'd come to find—her husband—wasn't the mountain man she'd expected he would be.

Best of all, that same man sat before the fire now, watching her with eyes like rain.

"Turn around, Lauren," he said, his voice like gravel. "If you leave now, you'll make it back to the village before full dark. I wouldn't want to be wandering around the woods at night. Not in those shoes. You have no idea what you might encounter."

"I know exactly what I'll find in these woods," she replied. And she let her gaze go where it liked, from that too-long inky-black hair he'd never gotten around to cutting to her specifications to that stern mouth of his she'd felt on every inch of her body. "And look. There you are."

He shook his head. "You shouldn't have come here."

"And yet I did. Without your permission. Much as you ran off from Combe Manor without so much as a hastily penned note."

"I'm sure whatever mission you're on now is just as important as the last one that brought you here to storm about in my forest," he said, and something like temper flashed over his face—though it was darker. Much, much darker. "But I don't care what your Mr. Combe—"

"He didn't send me. I don't work for him anymore, as a matter of fact." She held his gaze and let the storm in it wash over her, too. "This is between you and me, Dominik."

The air between them shifted. Tightened, somehow.

"There is no you and me."

"You may have married me as a joke," she said softly, "but you did marry me. That makes me your wife."

"I need a wife about as much as I need a brother. I don't do family, Lauren. Or jokes. I want nothing to do with any of it."

"That is a shame." She crossed her arms over her chest and she stared him down as if he didn't intimidate her at all. "But I didn't ask you if you needed a wife. I reminded you that you already have one."

"You're wasting your time."

She smiled at him, and enjoyed it when he blinked at that as if it was a weapon she'd had tucked away in her arsenal all this time.

God, she hoped it was a weapon. Because she needed all of those she could find.

And she had no qualms about using each and every one she put her hands on.

"Here's the thing, Dominik," she said, and she wanted to touch him. She wanted to bury her face in the crook of his neck. She wanted to wake up with him tangled all around her. She wanted him, however she could get him. She wanted whatever a life with him looked like. "You taught me how to want. And don't you see? What I want is you."

CHAPTER THIRTEEN

"YOU CAN'T HAVE ME," Dominik growled at her, because that was what he'd decided. It was what made sense. "I never was a toy for you to pick up and put down at will, Lauren. I assumed that was finally clear."

And yet all he wanted to do was get his hands on her.

He knew he couldn't allow that. Even if he was having trouble remembering the *why* of that at the moment, now that she was here. Right here, in front of him, where he'd imagined her no less than a thousand times a night since he'd left England.

But he didn't. Because touching her—losing himself in all that pink and gold sweetness of hers—was where all of this had gone wrong from the start.

"I introduced you to sex, that's all," he said through gritted teeth, because he didn't want to think about that introduction. The way she'd yielded completely, innocent and eager and so hot he could still feel it. As if he carried her inside him. "This is the way of things. You think it means more than it does. But I don't."

"I tested that theory," she told him, and it landed on him like a punch, directly into his gut. "You told me I could walk into any pub in England and have whatever sex I wanted."

"Lauren." And he was surprised he didn't snap a few teeth off, his jaw was so tight. "I would strongly advise you not to stand here in my cabin and brag to me about your sexual exploits."

"Why would you care? If you don't want me?" She smiled at him again, self-possessed and entirely too calm. "But no need to issue warnings or threats. I walked in, took a look around and left. I don't want sexual exploits, Dominik. I told you. I want you."

"No," he growled, despite the way that ache in his chest intensified. "You don't."

"I assure you, I know my own mind."

"Perhaps, but you don't know me."

And he didn't wait for her to take that on board. He surged to his feet, prowling toward her, because she had to understand. She had to understand, and she had to leave, and he had to get on with spending the rest of his life trying to fit the pieces back together.

After she'd torn him up, crumpled him and left him in this mess in the first place.

Because you let her, the voice in him he'd tried to ignore since he'd met her—and certainly since he'd left her—chimed in.

"I thought at first it was the media attention that got to you, but you obviously don't mind that. You've had it before. Why should this be any different?"

And she didn't remind him of his lies of omission. They rose there between them like so much heat and smoke, and still, the only thing he could see was her.

"I don't care about attention." He wanted things he couldn't have. He wanted to *do* something, but when he reached out his hand, all he did was fit it to her soft, warm cheek.

Just to remind himself.

And then he dropped his hand to his side, but that didn't make it better, because she felt even better than he remembered.

"Dominik. I know that you feel—"

"You don't know what I feel." His voice was harsh, but his palm was on fire. As if touching her had branded him, and he was disfigured with it. And maybe it was the fact she couldn't seem to see it that spurred him on. "You don't have great parents, so you think you know, but you don't. There's no doubt that it's your parents who are the problem, not you. You must know this."

"They are limited people," she said, looking taken aback. But she rallied. "I can't deny that I still find it hurtful, but I'm not a little girl anymore. And to be honest, I think they're the ones who are missing out."

"That sounds very adult. Very mature. I commend you. But I'm not you. This is what I'm trying to tell you." And then he said the thing he had always known, since he was a tiny child. The thing he'd never said out loud before. The thing he had never imagined he even needed to put into words, it was so obvious. "There's something wrong with me, Lauren."

Her eyes grew bright. And he saw her hands curl into fists at her sides.

"Oh, Dominik." And he would remember the way she said his name. Long after she was gone, he would replay it again and again, something to warm him when the weather turned cold. It lodged inside him, hot and shining where his heart should have been. "There's nothing wrong with you. Nothing."

"This is not opinion. This is fact." He shook his head, harshly, when she made to reach for him. "I was six days old when I arrived in the orphanage. And brand-new babies never stay long in orphanages, because there are always those who want them. A clean slate. A new start. A child they can pretend they birthed themselves, if they want. But no one wanted me. Ever."

She was still shaking her head, so fiercely it threatened the hair she'd put in that damned ponytail as if it was her mission to poke at him.

"Maybe the nuns are the ones who wanted you, Dominik. Did you ever think of that? Maybe they couldn't bear to give you up."

He laughed at that, though it was a hollow sound, and not only because her words had dislodged old memories he hadn't looked at in years. The smiling face of the nun they'd called Sister Maria Ana, who had treated him kindly when he was little, until cancer stole her away when he was five. How had he forgotten that?

But he didn't want to think about that now. The possibility that someone had been kind to him didn't change the course of his life.

"Nobody wanted me. Ever. With one or two people in your life, even if they are your parents, this could be coincidence. Happenstance. But when I tell you that there is not one person on this earth who has ever truly wanted me, I am not exaggerating." He shoved those strange old memories aside. "There's something wrong with me inside, Lauren. And it doesn't go anywhere. If you can't see it, you will. In time. I see no point in putting us both through that."

Because he knew that if he let her stay, if he let her do this, he would never, ever let her go. He knew it.

"Dominik," she began.

"You showed me binders full of San Giacomos,"

he growled at her. "Century upon century of people obsessed with themselves and their bloodlines. They cataloged every last San Giacomo ever born. But they threw me away. *She* threw me away."

"She was sixteen," Lauren said fiercely, her red cloak all around her and emotion he didn't want to see wetting her cheeks. But he couldn't look away. "She was a scared girl who did what her overbearing father ordered her to do, by all accounts. I'm not excusing her for not doing something later, when she could have. But you know that whatever else happened, she never forgot you. She knew your name and possibly even where you lived. I can't speak for a dead woman, Dominik, but I think that proves she cared."

"You cannot care for something you throw away like trash," he threw at her.

And her face changed. It…crumpled, and he thought it broke his heart.

"You mean the way you did to me?" she asked.

"I left you before it was made perfectly obvious to you and the rest of the world that I don't belong in a place like that. I'm an orphan. I was a street kid. I joined the army because I wanted to die for a purpose, Lauren. I never meant for it to save me."

"All of that is who you were, perhaps," she said with more of that same ferocity that worked in him like a shudder. "But now you are a San Giacomo. You are a self-made man of no little power in your own right. And you are my husband."

And he didn't understand why he moved closer to her when he wanted to step away. When he wanted— needed—to put distance between them.

Instead, his hands found their way to her upper arms and held her there.

He noticed the way she fit him, in those absurd shoes she wore just as well as when she was barefoot. The way her caramel-colored eyes locked to his, seeing far too much.

"I don't have the slightest idea how to be a husband."

"Whereas my experience with being a wife is so extensive?" she shot right back.

"I don't—"

"Dominik." And she seemed to flow against him until she was there against his chest, her head tipped back so there was nothing else in the whole of the world but this. Her. "You either love me or you don't."

He knew what he should say. If he could spit out the words he could break her heart, and his, and free her from this.

He could go back to his quiet life, here in the forest where no one could disappoint him and he couldn't prove, yet again, how little he was wanted.

Dominik knew exactly what he should say.

But he didn't say it.

Because she was so warm, and he had never understood how cold he was before she'd found him here. She was like light and sunshine, even here in the darkest part of the forest.

And he hadn't gone with her to England because she was an emissary from his past. He certainly hadn't married her because she could tell him things he could have found out on his own about the family that wanted to claim him all of a sudden.

The last time Dominik had done something he didn't

want to do, simply because someone else told him to do it, he'd been in the army.

He could tell himself any lie at all, if he liked—and Lord knew he was better at that by the day—but he hadn't married this woman for any reason at all save one.

He'd wanted to.

"What if I do?" he demanded, his fingers gripping her—but whether to hold her close or keep her that crucial few inches away, he didn't know. "What do either one of us know about love, of all things?"

"You don't have to know a thing about love." And she was right there before him, wrapping her arms around his neck as if she belonged there. And fitting into place as if they'd been puzzle pieces, all this time, meant to interlock just like this. "Think about fairy tales. Happy-ever-after is guaranteed by one thing and one thing only."

"Magic?" he supplied. But his hands were moving. He tugged the elastic from her gleaming blond hair and tossed it aside. "Terrible spells, angry witches and monsters beneath the bed?"

"What big worries you have," she murmured, and she was smiling again. And he found he was, too.

"All the better to save you with, little red," he said. "If you'll let me."

"I won't." She brushed his mouth with hers. "Why don't we save each other?"

"I don't know how."

"You do." And when he frowned at her, she held him even closer, until that ache in his chest shifted over to something sweeter. Hotter. And felt a lot like forever.

"Happy-ever-after is saving each other, Dominik. All it takes is a kiss."

And this was what she'd been talking about in that sprawling house in Yorkshire.

Hope. The possibility of happiness.

Things he'd never believed in before. But it was different, with her.

Everything was different with her.

So he gathered her in his arms, and he swept her back into the grandest kiss he could give her, right there in their enchanted cottage in the deep, dark woods.

And sure enough, they lived happily ever after.

Just like a fairy tale.

Twelve years later Dominik stood on a balcony that overlooked the Grand Canal in Venice as night fell on a late summer evening. The San Giacomo villa was quiet behind him, though he knew it was a peace that wouldn't last.

His mouth curved as he imagined the chaos his ten-year-old son could unleash at any moment, wholly unconcerned about the disapproving glares of the ancient San Giacomos who lurked in every dour portrait that graced the walls of this place.

To say nothing of his five-year-old baby girls, a set of the twins that apparently ran in the family, that neither he nor Lauren had anticipated when she'd fallen pregnant the second time.

But now he couldn't imagine living without them. All of them—and well did he remember that he was the man who had planned to live out his days as a hermit, all alone in his forest.

The truth was, he had liked his own company. But he exulted in the family he and Lauren had made together.

The chaos and the glory. The mad rush of family life, mixed in with that enduring fairy tale he hadn't believed in at first—but he'd wanted to. Oh, how he'd wanted to. And so he'd jumped into, feet first, willing to do anything as long as she was with him.

Because she was the only one who had ever wanted him, and she wanted him still.

And he wanted her right back.

Every damned day.

They had built their happy-ever-after, brick by brick and stone by stone, with their own hands.

He had met his sister shortly after Lauren had come and found him in the forest. Pia had burst into that hotel suite in Athens, greeted him as if she'd imagined him into being herself—or had known of him, somehow, in her heart of hearts all this time—until he very nearly believed it himself.

And he'd finally met his brother—in the flesh— sometime after that.

After a perfectly pleasant dinner in one of the Combe family residences—this one in New York City—he and Matteo had stood out on one of the wraparound terraces that offered a sweeping view of all that Manhattan sparkle and shine.

"I don't know how to be a brother," Dominik had told him.

"My sister would tell you that I don't, either," Matteo had replied.

And they'd smiled at each other, and that was when Dominik had started to believe that it might work. This strange new family he would have said he didn't want. But that he had, anyway.

His feelings about Matteo had been complicated, but he'd realized quickly that most of that had to do with the fact Lauren had admired him so much and for so long. Something Matteo put to rest quickly, first by marrying the psychiatrist who had been tasked with his anger management counseling, who also happened to be pregnant with his twin boys. But then he'd redeemed himself entirely in Dominik's eyes by telling Lauren that Combe Industries couldn't function without her.

And then hiring her back, not as his assistant, but as a vice president.

Dominik couldn't have been prouder. And as Lauren grew into her new role in the company she'd given so much of her time and energy, he entertained himself by taking on the duties of the eldest San Giacomo. He found that his brother and sister welcomed the opportunity to allow him to be the face of their ancient family. A role he hadn't realized anyone needed to play, but one it shocked him to realize he was…actually very good at.

He heard the click of very high heels on the marble behind him, and felt his mouth curve.

Moments later his beautiful wife appeared. She'd taken some or other call in the room set aside in the villa for office purposes, and she was already tugging her hair out of the sleek ponytail she always wore when she had her professional hat on. She smiled back at him as the faint breeze from the water caught her hair, still gleaming gold and bright.

"You look very pleased with yourself," she said. "I can only hope that means you've somehow encouraged the children to sleep. For a thousand hours, give or take."

"That will be my next trick." He shifted so he could pull her into his arms, and both of them let out a small sigh. Because they still fit. Because their puzzle pieces connected even better as time passed. "I was thinking about the banquet last night. And how it was clearly my confident use of the correct spoon midway through that won the assembled patrons of the arts over to my side."

Lauren laughed at that and shook her head at him. "I think what you meant to say was thank you. And you're very welcome. No one knows how difficult it was to civilize you."

He kissed her then, because every kiss was another pretty end with the happy-ever-after that went with it. And better yet, another beginning, stretching new, sweeter stories out before them.

And he wanted nothing more than to lift her into his arms and carry her off to the bed they shared here—another four-poster affair that he deeply enjoyed indulging himself in—but he couldn't. Not yet, anyway.

Because it wasn't only the two of them anymore. And he knew his daughters liked it best when their mama read them stories before bed.

He held her hand in his as they walked through the halls of this ancient place, amazed to realize that he felt as if he belonged here. And he imagined what it might have been like to be raised like this. With two parents who loved him and cared for him and set aside whatever it was they might have been doing to do something like read him a bedtime story.

He couldn't imagine himself in that kind of family.

But he'd imagined it for his own kids, and then created it, and he had to think that was better. It was the future.

It was his belief made real, every time his children smiled.

"I love you," Lauren said softly when they reached the girls' room as if she could read every bittersweet line in his heart.

And he knew she could. She always had.

"I love you, too, little red," he told her.

More than he had back then, he thought. More all the time.

And then he stood in the doorway as she swept into the room where her daughters waited. He watched, aware by now that his heart wouldn't actually burst—it would only feel like it might—as his two perfect little girls settled themselves on either side of their gorgeous mother. One with her thumb stuck deep in her mouth. The other with her mother's beautiful smile.

And when his son came up beside him, a disdainful look on his face because he was ten years old and considered himself quite a man of the world, Dominik tossed an arm over the boy's narrow shoulders.

"I'm going to read you a fairy tale," Lauren told the girls.

"Fairy tales aren't real," their son replied. He shrugged when his sisters protested. "Well, they're not."

Lauren lifted her gaze to meet Dominik's, her caramel-colored eyes dancing.

And every time Dominik thought he'd hit his limit, that he couldn't possibly love her more—that it was a physical and emotional impossibility—she raised the bar.

He felt certain that she would keep right on doing it until the day they both died.

And he thought that was what happy-ever-after was all about, in the end.

Not a single kiss, but all the kisses. Down through the years. One after the next, linking this glorious little life of theirs together. Knitting them into one, over and over and over again.

Hope. Happiness. And the inevitable splashes of darkness in between, because life was life, that made him appreciate the light all the more.

And no light shined brighter than his beautiful wife. His own little red.

The love of his life.

"Of course fairy tales are real," he told his son. And his two wide-eyed little girls. Because he was living proof, wasn't he? "Haven't I told you the story of how your mother and I met?"

He ruffled his son's hair. And he kept his eyes on the best thing that had ever wandered into the deep, dark woods, and then straight into his heart.

"Once upon a time, in a land far, far away, a beautiful blonde in a bright red cloak walked into a forest," he said.

"And it turned out," Lauren chimed in, "that the big bad wolf she'd been expecting wasn't so bad, after all."

And that was how they told their favorite story, trading one line for the next and laughing as they went, for the rest of their lives.

* * * * *

COMING SOON!

We really hope you enjoyed reading this book. If you're looking for more romance, be sure to head to the shops when new books are available on

Thursday 27th June

To see which titles are coming soon, please visit

millsandboon.co.uk/nextmonth

MILLS & BOON

Coming next month

DEMANDING HIS HIDDEN HEIR
Jackie Ashenden

'*Buono notte,* Mrs St George,' Enzo said in that deep voice she knew so well, the one that had once been full of heat and yet now was so cold. 'I think you and I need to have a little chat.'

'A chat?' she said huskily, her chin firming, the shock and fear in her gaze quickly masked. 'A chat about what?'

With an effort, Enzo dragged his gaze from her throat.

So, she was going to pretend she didn't know what he was talking about, was she? Well, unfortunately for her, he wasn't having it.

'I'm not here to play games with you, Summer,' he said coldly. 'Or should I say *Matilda.* I'm here to talk about my son.'

Another burst of quicksilver emotion flashed in her eyes, then it was gone, nothing but a cool wall of grey in its place. 'Yes, that's my name. You don't have to say it like a pantomime villain. And as to a son…Well.' Her chin came up. 'I don't know what you're talking about.'

'Is that how you're going to play this?' He didn't bother to temper the acid in his tone. 'You're going to pretend you don't know anything about that child you just rescued downstairs? The child with eyes the same colour as mine?' He took a step towards her. 'Perhaps you're going to pretend that you don't know who I am either.'

She held her ground, even though she didn't have anywhere to go, not when there was a wall behind her. 'No, of course not.' Her gaze didn't flicker. 'I know who you are, Enzo Cardinali.'

The sound of his name in her soft, husky voice made a bolt of lightning shoot straight down his spine, helplessly reminding him of other times when she'd said it.

'Good.' He kept his voice hard, trying not to let the heat creep into it. 'Then if you know who I am you can explain to me why you didn't tell me that I have a son.'

She was already pale; now she went the colour of ashes. But

that defiant slant to her chin remained, the expression in her eyes guarded. 'Like I said, I don't know what you're talking about.'

Enzo's rage, already inflamed by his body's betrayal, curdled into something very close to incandescence and it burned like fire in his blood, thick and hot.

He'd never been so angry in all his life, some distant part of him vaguely appalled at the intensity of his emotions—a reminder that he needed to lock it down, since his iron control was the only thing that set him apart from his power-hungry father.

But in this moment he didn't care.

This woman, this beautiful, sexy, infuriating woman, hadn't told him he had a son and, more, she'd kept it from him for four years.

Four. Years.

He took another step towards her, unable to help himself, the heat in his veins so hot it felt as if it was going to ignite him where he stood. 'I see. So you *are* going to pretend you know nothing. How depressingly predictable of you.'

'Simon is *my* son.' Her hands had gone into fists at her sides and she didn't move, not an inch. 'And H-Henry's.' Her gaze was as cool as winter rain, but that slight stutter gave her away.

'No.' Enzo kept his voice honed as a steel blade. 'He is not. Those eyes are singular to the Cardinali line. Which makes him mine.'

'But I—'

'How long have you known, *Matilda*? A year? Two?' He took another step, forcing her back against the wall.

Enzo put a hand on the wall at one side of her silky red head and leaned in close so she had no choice but to stare straight at him. 'Look at me, *cara*. Look at me and tell me that you don't see your son staring back.'

Continue reading
DEMANDING HIS HIDDEN HEIR
Jackie Ashenden

Available next month
www.millsandboon.co.uk